Seek If You Dare

andrew argyle

This book is a work of fiction. Names, characters, incidents and places are a product of the author's imagination or are used fictitiously. Locales and public places are sometimes used for atmospheric purposes. Any resemblance to actual people, living or dead, or to businesses, companies, events, institutions or locales is completely coincidental.

Published by andrew argyle publishing

ISBN: 978-0-9954665-1-7

Initial editing: Amy Butcher Content, Montreal, Canada (www.amybcontent.com)

Later editing and copywriting: Rebecca Parsley, Dolphin International Communications Ltd (www.dolphin-international.com)

Cover design: 'Rob Whitney Design', Lincoln UK

Author's website: **www.andrewargyle.com**

For Sir Guy Sterling –
Thanks for letting me into your life; it's been fun getting to know you.

The Guy Sterling thriller series:

(1) *Seek If You Dare*
(2) *What Lies Within*
(3) *They Died Tomorrow*

Also by andrew argyle, the crime novel:

The Dreams that Make Us

Seek If You Dare

"You do not know that region,
the dangerous place where you
might find the polluted creature:
seek it if you dare!"

Beowulf, old English poem.

ONE

Cities can be uncaring places, somewhere an individual can often find himself completely and utterly ignored. For some people, this is an essential advantage.

And so it was that nobody heeded the elderly tramp, all grey beard and grubby clothing, as he shuffled his way up the litter-strewn, open stairway of a seven-storey block of neglected council flats. One step at a time. Familiar graffiti marked his route all the way to the disused front door of an apartment shoehorned into the sixth floor. Here he stopped and carefully placed his long, weathered holdall on the dirty concrete floor, before turning the scratched metal knob with his gloved right hand. He paused but didn't look round, then leaned firmly and purposefully on the door with surprising strength until, with a slow, wooden crack, it surrendered under the concentrated pressure. Stooping arthritically, the tramp picked up his old bag and entered. He was pleased to be out of the afternoon summer sunshine, which, whilst warming the access balcony on the front of the building, made him feel conspicuous.

With the sudden agility of a much younger man, he pushed the feeble door behind him with his left foot. The remains of the shattered lock hung uselessly down from the rotten wood; the door knocked into its scarred frame, shook and came to rest slightly ajar. Through the gap, sunshine penetrated the musty flat, picking out particles of dust that danced and swirled like midges in the disturbed air. The man stepped back calmly and squeezed the door closed, forcing the torn lock to hold it tightly in place. Dipping his hand into a pocket of his long coat he withdrew two white rubber wedges which he rammed firmly under the door a half-metre or so apart. He didn't know how long his task would take and it would be more than inconvenient – fatal, in fact – if he were disturbed at any time.

The tramp removed his brown gloves and slipped them into his coat pocket, leaving in place the yellowish, transparent surgical gloves he wore underneath. He turned and walked swiftly into the empty flat. It had a concrete stillness, bereft for several months now of the noises and smells of occupancy. A short hallway led him to a small rear room where peeling and faded cartoon wallpaper still clung stubbornly to the mouldy walls. It was very warm, almost hot, and a musty, decaying odour assaulted his nose, crying out for a window to be flung open so the relatively fresh urban air could relieve it. The man was aware his shirt was damp; he could feel the familiar sensation of fabric starting to stick to his back.

He stepped towards the undersized window opposite the door, hanging back slightly from the casement. He was close enough, he knew, as he wiped his brow with the sleeve of his tatty brown coat. The view was nothing special, but perfect for him. Through the cracked and grimy glass, the density of the Birmingham suburb stretched out below him, close and claustrophobic. A random collection of blocks of flats and terraced housing fought for air, space and identity. From behind him, the bright sun lit up the scene – just as he'd known it would. The man smiled to himself – his judgment had once more been reliable and precise. Research, always research. It was essential. He took a closer look at the immediate vicinity, confirming he wasn't immediately overlooked. He'd calculated that, too - and a low profile would assist him further. Again, research – and experience, of course.

He placed his swinging holdall on the dusty lino floor and tossed his dirty coat into a corner. Athletically he knelt, unzipped the bag and pulled out an MK13 Mod 5 sniper rifle, all black and silver metal and light wood. It felt good in his hands as he unfolded the stock into position and fitted the long black silencer to the thin silver barrel. He primed his gun with a hard magazine of .300 Winchester Magnums before tapping its side three times with his fingers – a superstitious tradition that had never, not once, let him down.

Raising himself up carefully, he kept low as he edged towards the window. With steady and gentle care he pushed it slightly open, allowing the general hum of the basking city to enter. He could smell the urban air, tired and heavy with petrol fumes – so different to the heady scents of his home city an entire continent away.

He knelt on the floor, his side pressed firmly against the wall and his elbow resting on the inside ledge. He threaded the rifle carefully and slowly through the narrow gap he'd created, level with the window's base and pointing to the distant horizon. With swift and darting movements of his fingers and eyes, he set the black telescopic sight to his complete satisfaction.

He smiled to himself, enjoying the routine of the moment.

He shifted his position until the chosen rear garden, some six hundred and twenty metres away and a couple of streets over, was well in view. Easing the rifle round slowly, he used the optic to examine the scene. A simple, concrete-slab patio led to a worn patch of tired-looking lawn that was surrounded by unkempt borders and a run-down wooden fence. In leisurely fashion, he switched his view to the back windows. Nothing, save reflections on glass. Moving the optic left, he let the open back door take centre stage. Keeping a constant eye on his target, the man recalled the telephone conversation that morning when he had answered his mobile to the expected call, and heard the deep voice give its command.

If necessary he'd wait for hours, doing nothing but look through his scope, but he knew she was there. He was sure that on this warm, sunny Tuesday afternoon, the garden would prove an irresistible haven. Sure enough, some fifteen minutes later, a woman came out of the open kitchen door. Picking up the end of a washing line that lay coiled on the dry grass, she stretched it across the width of the small plot before hooking it tightly onto a wooden post. Returning to the kitchen she narrowly avoided colliding with two small children who came running into the garden. The man could all but hear their shouts of delight. He recognised them from photographs – the nine-year-old boy and the seven-year-old girl. He'd seen the brief. And he knew now he would only have to wait a few more moments. Then he'd be gone, as anonymously as he had arrived.

As anticipated, the woman returned carrying a laundry basket filled with wet clothes. She placed it on a white plastic garden chair and, whilst the children ran around her in a frantic and energetic game of tag, she laughed at their antics as she started to hang out the washing.

The tramp re-positioned the rifle, the end of the body resting in his left hand which in turn was supported by the lower window frame. He could feel the hard, cold edge of the metal pressing firmly and securely into the side of his knuckles. He screwed up his face in concentration as his right eye picked out the detail of the scene through the narrow telescopic sight. It came to rest on the rear of the woman's head, her silky brown hair filling his vision, right in the centre of his cross-haired reticle. She hung up more clothes. He held his aim steady. She dipped into the washing basket. He waited patiently for her to straighten. She turned ever-so-slightly towards her children. He eased his aim indiscernibly to his left. He did not allow himself to be distracted by the playing children, as an amateur might have been; instead he eased the trigger with all his experience, instincts and skill. The noise was imperceptible; the impact wasn't. She was dead before she hit the ground. The tramp watched through the scope as the children froze and then ran to their prostrate mother. There were screams and yells and tears. Panic and shock. The tramp raised his head, staring at the children in the distant garden. *Get over it, kids. Bambi did.*

With swift efficiency, he hastily packed away the rifle into his holdall and tossed the empty cartridge in after it. He threw on his coat, pulled on his gloves, picked up his bag and hurried to the door, where he stowed the rubber wedges in his coat pocket before tugging it open, to the anguish of the broken lock. He paused and took a deep breath before shuffling out of the flat. Then he ambled slowly down the stairs in the same way he'd arrived. One step at a time. Completely and utterly ignored in a large city.

TWO

In the Birmingham suburb of Aston, the emergency services were busy. Three police cars were parked outside a formerly insignificant terrace house, just one of the line of dwellings that ran the length of the narrow street, each with their front door a step up from the cracked pavement. Their only view was an almost identical row of houses opposite and an array of parked cars. Blue and white tape, accompanied by stationary police officers, restricted access to sporadic groups of rubbernecking residents and a single reporter from the *Birmingham Herald*. The early evening sun was losing its strength but could still cause dark shadows to lengthen.

Detective Superintendent Grant stepped out of the white plastic tent that had been erected in the scrubland of the house's diminutive rear garden and surveyed the scene around her. The neglected plot was just one of a series of uninterrupted oblongs which ran between the backs of the two rows of terraced housing. The rough and disorderly patchwork reflected the varying degrees of interest and financial resources devoted to the Victorian properties by their respective owners or tenants. The occasional window still hosted the odd spectator, but most of the on-lookers had left. Their curiosity at seeing a scene from a television detective series played out for real in the precincts of their own homes was satiated. The spectacle was over, and an immobile white tent could only command attention for so long, no matter what drama had happened earlier.

Grant found the environment beguilingly peaceful now that the body, the children and the initial experts had gone. All necessary photographs had been taken; all hand-searches carried out. Somewhere inside a variety of bureaucratic buildings around England's second city files were being opened, new numbers and references created, and data loaded and processed. It was an orderly and predictable system that had been part of Grant's life for rather more years than she cared to remember.

She tucked some lengths of her fading, slightly greying, auburn hair behind her ear and turned towards the rear of the modest terrace house and its open kitchen door. The brickwork was worn, in need of some re-pointing in places. She noticed the deterioration was generally in the high and more inaccessible places – in accordance, no doubt, with some minor sub-clause of Sod's Law. Twisting her head round, she shielded her hazel eyes against the low sun and looked at the blocks of council flats in the mid-distance. Even now enquiries were ongoing there. However, she knew from a distant, confidential briefing by the chief constable that her conscientious team would inevitably return with no helpful information. If she were a betting woman, she thought, she'd put a decent wager on it. But betting was a mug's game.

These were the circumstances under which she'd been instructed to make the call. There was no doubt about it. She reached for her mobile, which was clipped to the belt of her blue skirt – or should have been. She looked down and cursed – the leather holder was empty. More hassle. With an audible, frustrated sigh, she re-entered the back door and strode briskly through the untidy, claustrophobic house to the road at the front. *How can people live like this?*

She left the door ajar for the short walk to her unwashed red Honda, which was long overdue for replacement. As she neared where it had been parked erratically in the centre of the road, she recognised the *Birmingham Herald* reporter in his torn jeans and garish t-shirt standing on his own behind the tape. Toby, Tom? Something like that. A young hack for sure, no matter what his name was.

She opened the car door, and he called out to her from nine or ten metres away.

"Any identification, Superintendent?" His enthusiastic voice told her he was experiencing the thrill of the chase as he pushed his voice recorder towards her, his face expectant.

She raised her hand towards him as if stopping traffic. "I've no comment to make at this stage," she said flatly. Why was the media so relentless, so desperate to glean news? And the grizzlier it was, the better they liked it. They were irritating, like wasps; they got in the way of the task in hand.

"Go on – give us something, Super. Who was she?"

How she hated that abbreviated title. Grant glanced into the car. "No comment," she called out clearly.

"It wasn't her house, was it?"

She forcefully tossed the packaging from her hurried lunch into the footwell. *Why can't anything be simple*? "No comment," she called again over her shoulder, her tone louder and firmer than before.

"I've heard she's been shot."

"Is that the gossip?" Grant said, almost to herself, as she leant further inside the car to snatch up her wayward mobile from the side of the driver's seat.

"It's true then?"

She straightened up and ran her hand through her hair before slamming the car door. She turned and stared at the hack. "I said I've no comment to make. Can you spell that? The family needs to be informed and a full statement will be made when it's time – probably at a press conference if your luck's in. Standard stuff, right? Now, I've got a job to do."

She gripped her phone tightly and walked back towards the house.

"Go on, who was she?" the reporter called after her.

Grant ignored him and re-entered the property, closing the door behind her.

It was, however, a good question. The victim had been a thirty-five-year-old married mother of two. Grant related to that, except she herself was now five years older and divorced. The dead mother had been staying at a friend's house, very different to her own place, very different indeed. But although who she'd been was a good question, it wasn't the most interesting question. The most interesting question related to her connection. That, and the manner of her death, had prompted Grant's call. She was aware from the briefing that this death may not be the last and wondered what was to follow. She looked at her mobile to see yet more waiting messages. *Would they ever stop?*

She moved inside, away from the closed front door, and selected a contact. She raised the phone to her ear.

She recognised the chief constable's patient, measured tones as he answered his phone after a couple of rings. That was pretty prompt for him. She leant back against the painted hallway wall and stared at the blonde head of a large, naked doll that stuck out randomly between the chipped banister rails opposite. She drummed her fingers impatiently on the wall behind her.

"Have you heard, sir?" she said, hoping she wouldn't have to waste time retelling the whole story.

"Aston?"

"Yes," she replied. *What else?*

"Of course – that's why you're there."

"We need to meet. It's classic – all the hallmarks, and I mean all."

"She was connected?"

"Yes, for sure - that's what I mean. Sounds like you're occupied, sir," she said crisply and drummed her fingers a little quicker. *Let's have some focus.* She stepped forward and plucked the sleeping doll off the staircase.

"I'll be back at Lloyd House in two hours," he said. "We'll meet then. I want a full brief." He rang off.

Grant turned the cheap doll round and its bright blue eyes popped open to greet her. She stared into the dirty plastic face – another girl who'd lost her carer that afternoon. Here one second, gone the next. A frequently-buried maternal emotion forced its way to the surface and slapped her hard, reminding her that life can change in an instant. No warning. No logic. No fairness. How was her twins' birthday party going at home? She carefully laid the abandoned doll back down on the staircase and, as its eyes gently closed, she forcefully repressed her emotions and returned to the garden to take a call from forensics.

THREE

Sir Guy Sterling strode confidently into the busy hotel bar and glanced at his Seamaster watch. Seven fifteen. The timing was perfect. That suited him; he was always on time, helped on this occasion by light Saturday traffic.

He surveyed the busy scene around him and accepted a gin and tonic from a passing waiter bearing a selection of drinks on a tray. At six feet four inches with a military-straight back, he was well placed to take in the crowd. It was all black bow ties and dinner suits, groups of three or four with occasional pairings, all talking in varying degrees of joviality and earnestness as they enjoyed pre-dinner drinks. There were no women. This was the first time he'd attended a dinner of the Bull Club, Birmingham's oldest charity, but when its chairman had invited him as a last-minute guest, he could hardly decline. Not when said chairman was David Richardson, the chief constable of the West Midlands police.

He suddenly spotted David across the packed room. He was standing a little apart from the crowded bar, talking to a short, overweight man who was wearing an expensive dinner suit and flamboyant red bow tie. As Guy started to move towards them, David spotted his approach and beckoned him over.

"Guy. Good to see you. Thanks again for stepping in at the last moment."

"My pleasure, David. Pleased to be invited, even as a last-minute substitute."

"Have you met Mike Burns?" David said,

presenting his elderly companion and introducing Guy.

They shook hands, and the overweight man smiled and looked hard at Guy, who said, "I hadn't appreciated this was an all-male club."

David nodded slightly. "It's been a male preserve for generations, thanks to the adroitness of our lawyer members. I like female company of course, but sometimes it's good to be just boys together, huh? This is my last monthly meeting as chairman, Guy – at fifty-eight I've reached my sell-by date, I guess – and no doubt things will change. They always do."

Guy nodded. He was slightly taller than David, whom he'd first met when Guy must have been about seventeen, some twenty years ago. David's well-groomed black hair was now greying imperceptibly at the temples, but otherwise he was the same, slim-built, charismatic gentleman of yesteryear.

"Your first visit to our club then?" Mike questioned with a strong Birmingham accent. "You're not local?"

"Shropshire, so no."

"Guy's family has owned a chunk of that county for generations, Mike," David explained. "He's the seventh baronet, so mind your manners," he added with a broad smile, taking a sip from his glass.

Guy raised his eyebrows in humorous dismissal of David's comment. "I've followed David's career," he said. "We got to know each other when he was deputy chief constable over my way. You?"

"Local – Tamworth direction."

David said, "Mike's one of my guests tonight, Guy. You can get to know each other over dinner."

Turning to Mike, he added, "Guy's not long out of the army."

"Really? What were you doing?"

Guy ran his hand through his thick blond hair. "Oh, helped out here and there. It was a good career, but the estate beckoned when my father died."

"He's being modest," David said. "*Major* Sterling was in the SAS and all kinds of secret stuff besides. You won't get anything out of him, mind – he knows all the secrets of interrogation."

"I'll try my best," Mike said, and winked at Guy. Guy smiled. "Seems a long time since I resigned my commission."

"I wouldn't say three years is a long time," David said. "Being in the police force for some thirty-seven years, now that's a long time."

"Time to hand over to your deputy, right? That'll be some change," Mike said, before excusing himself.

After Mike left them, David leaned closer to Guy and said in a lowered voice, "Bit of a hidden agenda tonight, Guy."

Guy paused as he raised his glass to his mouth. "Meaning?"

"Meaning I want to talk to you after dinner," David replied, and took a sip of his orange juice. "We'll be going through to eat shortly, but there are some people I want you to meet later. I'd like your help, your views. We have a situation in the city that could spiral out of control."

FOUR

Guy loosened his black tie slightly and leant back in his dining chair, a glass of 1955 Fonseca Vintage Port in his right hand. He studied the people around him, his fingers absent-mindedly twirling the glass. The dinner was winding down, and some members of the club were gradually making their way to the hotel door and home. Guy recalled that in the days before the smoking ban a room like this would have been heavy with lazy cigar smoke. Although he didn't smoke himself, he'd always enjoyed the reassuring atmosphere it created after formal dinners such as this.

"Interesting chat with Mike, Guy? You seemed to be well away there," David said as he approached the table.

"Quite the entrepreneur, isn't he?" Guy replied. "Seems to have done it all from quite a humble background. Don't blame him for retiring – indeed, I admire the chap. Not quite had it handed to him on a plate like me."

"You don't make major as young as you did without effort and ability."

"The cookie crumbled well for me, David. Right time, right place and all that. Guess it happens like that sometimes."

"True, but you usually have to make it happen. Results require action, always have." David paused for a beat then said, "You must miss it. The action. Who wouldn't? Not many insurgents to sort out in rural Shropshire. Just the odd wayward partridge or trespassing pheasant, huh?"

Guy shrugged and crossed his legs. “No, I don’t miss it at all,” he said. “I love running the Hofton estate and my foundation – always something to do, and very worthwhile.”

David leaned forward in an almost conspiratorial way. “Did you hear about Tuesday’s shooting in Aston on the news?” he asked, looking closely at Guy.

Guy nodded. “Sure, caught something about it,” he said. “Some woman, they didn’t say who. It was a very bland, brief, matter-of-fact report. In fact, come to think about it, I’ve not heard anything more. Why do you ask?”

David leaned back in his chair, and Guy noticed him look furtively around. “There’s a bigger picture, Guy. A good three or four-years’ worth of bigger picture, maybe more. Not just here either – national, possibly wider still.”

Guy felt a stirring of interest. “Sounds like something your boss would know about.”

David nodded and pulled his chair in even closer. “The Home Secretary is fully up to date for sure. There are pressures, Guy. It’s big within certain circles, and I *mean* big.” He wiped his hand across his face. “Don’t believe any bullshit that who you are doesn’t matter, that we’re all entitled to the same attention. Your public profile or your wealth matters to those who have the power at their fingertips, to the major decision makers, believe me. And what’s important to those guys is what’s always pushed right up the ‘to do’ lists of everyone else further down the food chain. Last Tuesday brought this phenomenon onto my patch, into my back yard, and I want to be the one who’s seen to sort it out before I retire and take the miserly pension."

"Right, the blaze of glory thing. The legacy."

David nodded and took another sip of his drink. "Something like that. You see, Guy, standard stuff isn't working. That's evident. Everyone's still at the beginning, even after all this time and even after all that's happened. I've got one of my best on it, a detective called Grant, and I need to win this."

Guy watched David's face and read a hint of desperation in his eyes. "You've been a good friend to my family, David. But how can I help you now? I don't wear any uniform anymore, let alone one of yours."

"That's why I'm speaking in confidence to you now. Man to man, officer to officer, friend to friend. There's something you can do – a task."

"What sort of task?" Guy asked.

"Adventurous, risky, moral. Helpful to many people."

"Legal?"

David looked at him without blinking. "Adventurous, risky, moral, helpful to many people. You were known as 'The Maverick' in the army, weren't you? I can give you some discreet support, but essentially you'll be acting alone. I need your talents, Guy."

"I'm not sure," Guy said, slowly and deliberately, clutching his glass of port as he studied the other man's face and reactions. "It sounds like something that'll need a lot of thought. What sort of task? I get the adventurous, risky thing, but doing what, exactly?"

David finished his drink and placed the empty

glass on the table. "The answer to that comes later, Guy. The next step is to come with me now. As I said earlier, there are some people I want you to meet."

Guy, intrigued, allowed his curiosity to overcome his concerns. He finished his own drink and stood up. "I trust you enough to meet them, but no commitment yet, okay?" he said. "I'll walk away if it's not for me as a civilian, even if it would've been of interest to me as Major Sterling. With that understanding, David, lead on. Let's see what you're up to, and what's causing such grief at the top of the food chain."

FIVE

Guy and David left through the hotel's revolving front door and paused on the pavement. They were one of the last to leave. Guy glanced up at the clear night sky and the canopy of stars that fought to break through the city's light pollution. In front of him, a night-time flurry of cars and taxis moved around the oval forecourt. With a steady thump of metallic doors and determined hum of revving engines, vehicles collected their black-tied passengers and moved away. Assorted headlights revolved around the driveway, illuminating vehicles, pedestrians and the road that led to home.

"My driver's waiting for me in the executive car park," David said. "It's just a few minutes stroll – okay?"

"Sure," Guy replied, buttoning his jacket as he followed.

After the meal and drinks he'd enjoyed, Guy welcomed the exercise. Despite it being late August, the night air had a distinct autumnal chill, although it wasn't unpleasant. The two men turned down a well-lit, three-metre wide crushed-gravel path. On either side was close-boarded fencing, some two metres high and strung between solid wooden posts.

"So, what's happened in Aston, David?"

As he asked the question, Guy noticed a youth in jeans, trainers and a hoodie ambling up the alleyway towards them. About thirty metres away, his hands were thrust deep in his pockets so that his shoulders were pulled forward into a stoop. A cigarette hung casually from his mouth.

"It's a worrying development," David said, only just keeping pace with Guy. "I've had a number of updates from my team – my deputy is heavily involved and has pushed the detective superintendent forward onto the case, although I didn't know her that well…"

Guy's attention drifted back to the approaching youth. In his early twenties, casual yet purposeful. Why was he coming from the executive car park, and at this time of night? Instinct clicked in. He glanced behind him. No one. The youth was now about ten metres away. Guy watched as the youth took his right hand out of his pocket, completed a long, glowing drag on his cigarette, and then threw it like a dart on to the ground. He suddenly stopped walking and looked up at Guy and David as they moved nearer. He stood in their path some three metres ahead.

"'Scuse me, gents,' he said with a strong Birmingham accent. "You got any spare change for my bus home?"

Guy and David paused. A short streetlight to their right looped over the fence and cast strong shadows. Guy was always empathetic towards those in need of financial help, but he never gave money to street beggars – who knew what habit he could be feeding? He looked down at the smoking cigarette butt. Someone who could spend money on cigarettes above a 'bus home' was, however, well down the empathetic pecking order. On this occasion, Guy also sensed trouble.

David started to decline the request when the youth suddenly produced a knife. It flashed in his right hand, held level, threatening and obvious. Guy couldn't help his attention being drawn to it – he knew knives.

This was a Boker pocket-knife, German-made in the city of Solingen. Its stainless steel, black blade, some seven centimetres long, was already sprung and locked securely with a liner-lock mechanism. Olive wood handle. A quality product. Lethal in a professional hand, dangerous in an amateur's. And this youth was an amateur, Guy had no doubt. Try talking first.

"Look, mate, there's no need for that," he appealed. "Someone's going to get hurt. And it won't be us."

He placed his left hand on David's right arm and guided him backwards, noting the look of shock on his friend's face. The youth took half a step towards Guy, greasy, lank hair drifting from under the hood. Medium build, no more than five feet ten, Guy reckoned, his eyes scouring the boy's face while remaining ever-conscious of the poised right arm. Was he high? Desperate? Was he logical? The face, half lit and half in shadow, gave no clear indications. Guy noticed unshaven stubble and a six-centimetre scar on the youth's left cheek picked out by the neon light.

"Hurt?" Scarface scoffed. "That'll be your problem." He twisted the knife round slowly in his hand. "Give me your wallets. Now. Quick, I'm serious." He held out his left hand as he spoke, his fingers beckoning rapidly.

Guy continued to ease David behind him and moved closer to the youth. Two metres.

"Sorry, mate," Guy said calmly, "but you've picked on the wrong guys. Now give it a rest."

"Shut it!" the youth said sharply, still waving the knife erratically. "Just do as I say. I'll use this, believe me…" He started to look agitated as the fingers of his left hand moved together rhythmically and rapidly into a series of tight fists. He rocked slightly on the balls of his feet.

"Nothing doing."

The youth paused as if he was trying to assess his adversary. Guy could almost read the thought process. The blond man was taller and stronger than he was, and this was going nowhere unless he started the action. It would be embarrassing to back off now. He'd lose face. But he had the knife, and that was a valuable advantage.

"Last chance," Scarface said, "before I fucking hurt you, and hurt you bad. Give me your sodding wallets."

Guy said, "Look, you're not going to get anything from us, okay? Now back off, turn around, and scarper. We'll forget all about it. It never happened, okay? We won't chase you. We'll just stand here peacefully and watch you go. Might even wave."

"Piss off. I've got the knife, right? I give the orders, so shut it. Now, last chance – let's have your fucking wallets."

"Look," Guy said firmly. "We've had a long day and we want to get home. You're in the way. So, for the final time, scram or I'm going to take your toy and break your fragile arm. So – is it home to bed like a good boy, or a ride in an ambulance to A&E? Your call. I'll give you five seconds to get your head round it."

Scarface snapped. He took a step forward towards Guy, drew back his arm and then lunged it rapidly forward towards Guy's stomach. Guy shoved

David hard with his left hand, conscious of the chief constable stumbling backwards under the force of the push. He stepped nimbly to his right as the blade flashed towards him, his training kicking in. *Never be a standing target*. The knife missed, moving past him at waist level. In that fleeting moment, the outstretched arm became an easier and essential target. Guy rapidly brought his own arm over the youth's vulnerable limb, clasping his elbow around Scarface's in a vice-like lock. He pulled the youth's right arm, hand and knife tightly into his body, aware he could just feel the line of the knife pressing lengthways into the edge of his back. But the tightness of the grip and the knife's close proximity to his jacket prevented the youth from getting any angle or leverage to stab further.

Scarface attempted to pull away and, as his shoulders pulled back, Guy summoned all his strength and released his right fist in a vicious upward punch. It connected with the left side of the youth's face in a more than solid blow; the lad's head was jerked backwards under the force. The youth was now off balance, a fall prevented only by the tight grip in which Guy clasped his right arm. When he reached the end of his follow through, Guy retracted his arm and seized the youth's right shoulder, spinning him round with the momentum. A sharp crack resonated around the alley as Scarface's arm snapped like a dry branch. At the same time, Guy hurled him headfirst into one of the sturdy wooden fenceposts. The knife fell at Guy's feet and Scarface, screaming in agony, twisted round and slid down the post until he sat on the ground, leaning against the fence and clutching his damaged arm.

Guy picked up the knife and closed it with a flick before slipping it into his jacket pocket. He took out his mobile and looked down at Scarface, who whimpered without looking up.

"Right," Guy said, heart pounding but keeping his breath steady. "That was the A&E option, then. I'll call the ambulance as the task may be beyond you. Now, I strongly suggest you keep your butt sitting right there or else they won't be able to find you. And that would give them a wasted trip, which would be a shame, wouldn't it? I'll leave you to explain things to anyone who may be interested, and I'll toss your toy somewhere safe so you can forget all about it. Okay?"

He turned to David who was standing three or four metres back down the path, a shaken expression on his face. "Come on then, David. Not much more we can do here. Let's go."

David moved forward down the path, giving the broken youth a wide berth as if there might still be some fight left in him.

Guy glanced across and could easily see that wasn't the case. "He's out of it, David. You're okay. He's facing several weeks in plaster while he reflects on who he picks fights with. I'll call an ambulance."

SIX

Lloyd House is an eleven-storey, concrete and glass building dating back to the 1960s. Situated prominently on Colmore Circus in the core of Birmingham city centre, it has served as force headquarters of West Midlands Police for decades. The chief constable's driver dropped them off in the secure area at the rear of the building at a little after 10.45pm, and Guy followed the officer to an upper floor.

The place had a night-time stillness, populated only by the late shift. David's office was large with a light, modern desk and, to one side, a low table surrounded by easy chairs with wooden arms. Guy noticed on the wall near one of the windows a slightly-faded photograph of David being presented with the Queen's Police Medal.

"Grab a seat," David said casually. He walked over to a wall-mounted cupboard and took out a bottle of malt and a couple of glass tumblers. He turned to face Guy and held up his find as if it was an exhibit. "Whiskey?" he asked.

"No, thanks."

Guy watched David pour himself a large glass and take an immediate swig. His hands trembled slightly as he replaced the stopper and returned the bottle to its home. He turned to face Guy.

"Thanks again for what you did back there, Guy. Personally I'd have given him my wallet, but then I've not had self-defence training like you. Well, not for years anyway." He finished the whiskey in a single gulp and placed the glass on a side table. With a shake of his head, he strode round to his desk, picked up the phone and pressed three numbers.

"I'm in now, Caroline…yes…running late? Okay...thanks, that's perfect." He replaced the receiver.

"The detective you mentioned? Running late?" Guy asked.

"No, she's on her way up. Apparently, my deputy, Peter Wright, is running late – I wanted him to join us. He will as soon as he gets here."

"Tell me about Caroline, then."

"Detective Superintendent Caroline Grant. An astute detective, I understand from Peter. Comes with an attitude though, from what I've witnessed. Wants to succeed and doesn't suffer fools. It's still a man's world at her level, but not many men will take her on, I gather. They've learnt that – and so has she."

"She sounds a challenge."

"She's also a huge asset, I gather. On Peter's advice, I've put her on the Aston case."

David walked back across the room and sat down in a chair to Guy's left. Guy formed the view he was carrying, if not the weight of the world on his shoulders, something not far short of it. The position of chief constable had to be a pretty lonely one.

Guy was about to throw in a further comment when there was a sudden, sharp knock on the door. It opened simultaneously, Grant entering at a determined pace without waiting for any acknowledgement from David. She pushed the door firmly shut behind her, almost slamming it. Guy watched her, noting the choleric entrance: *I'm here, notice me and listen up.*

She walked briskly towards them and the two

men rose promptly to meet her. Guy noticed her hazel eyes flicking over him as if she was assessing a suspect, weighing him up.

"I feel a little underdressed," she said. "Obviously no memo was sent – I didn't appreciate the dress code for this meeting was black tie." No smile. Guy noticed her white blouse and knee-length, navy, classic-cut business skirt.

"Caroline, this is Sir Guy Sterling. He was my guest at the club dinner."

Grant offered her hand and looked Guy straight in the eyes. "Sir Guy."

"Call me Guy, please, Superintendent."

"Then I'm Caroline."

Guy nodded and studied her discreetly as she settled down in a seat opposite him, noting the slim frame and freckled face. Attractive, he mused, with a liveliness that merged with a supreme air of confidence and determination. The kind of characteristics that must have propelled her up the ranks, and the kind of characteristics to which Guy himself related.

She turned to David. "Sir, I thought you wanted to discuss the events of Tuesday again. I was just wondering –"

"Why Guy's here?"

"Frankly, yes."

David placed his elbow on the arm of the chair, disclosing a heavy gold cufflink on his starched, white cuff. Looking hard at Grant he said, "Guy's family and I go back a long way. I knew them when I was in Shropshire, knew them well. I trust him implicitly. Guy was in the army, a major in the SAS and latterly deployed with HUMINT until about three years ago…"

"HUMINT?" Grant asked, flicking a couple of glances at Guy. Still assessing.

"Part of the British Army's Intelligence Corps, Caroline," David explained. "They glean information from prisoners of war, refugees or possible terrorists – anything that might help us understand an enemy's intentions."

"You mean interrogation? Waterboarding and so forth?" she said disdainfully.

"That'll do, Caroline," David said. "A little more respect, please."

Guy continued to take in the exchange and Grant herself, intrigued by her. He noted there were no rings on her left hand.

She paused for a beat as if calculating a different approach, then said, "Okay, so you're good at asking difficult questions of difficult people, Guy," before turning to David and adding: "But trust him to do what?"

David said, "Assist you."

Grant eyeballed her superior. "How *exactly* can he do that?" she asked, as her grip tightened on the arms of the chair. "I've got a trained and experienced team already, so why on earth would I need assistance from a civilian – albeit one with a military background? We have our own way of doing things as well you know, sir."

David didn't seem willing to shift his position. Guy watched, his eyes taking in the early combat, his mind weighing it up.

Grant turned a harsh glare on him. "Nothing to say, Guy? Quiet, aren't you?"

"Caroline!" David interjected forcefully.

Guy raised his hand gently. "It's okay, David. Caroline has concerns, I can see that. Fools rush in, Caroline. I was always taught to observe and assess before showing my hand. 'Get the measure of the fight, boy, before you step in,' my father used to say. It's served me well."

"How sweet," Grant said with strong sarcasm.

David said, "Enough, Caroline. We are all professionals here. I understand where you're coming from, but I am however interested in Guy's take on this."

She looked at Guy. He'd seen friendlier looks on the faces of professional boxers at their pre-fight weigh-ins. "His take? So, what *police* experience have you actually had then, Guy, to enable you to give us your 'take'?" The boxer was drilling into him.

"None. Is that an issue?" Guy held her look.

"*None?*" Grant leaned back in her chair and crossed her arms firmly. If she'd been a teenager she would have pouted, Guy could picture it. He smiled inwardly at the thought – an external smile however would have set off a Vesuvius-scale reaction, no doubt.

"Caroline, I'd suggest you hear this out," David said firmly. Guy could see he was getting irritated by his junior officer's reaction. He seemed to be taking the blatant rejection of his idea very badly. "I know it's late and it's been a long day, but there's a time and a place."

Grant said nothing, just tweaked a piece of non-existent lint off the sleeve of her white blouse and flicked it away. Guy's eyes didn't leave her. Her body language spoke to him: *I'm not playing anymore*.

David stood up and took the couple of steps to

the window. He looked out into the blackness. Without turning he said, "Guy doesn't know anything about what's happening here. He's heard about the Aston shooting on the news, that's all. I want to put him fully in the picture, take him into our confidence. He was one of the youngest majors in the SAS and was a highly regarded sniper. This whole matter is too important to turn away views from another perspective. We may well be dealing with an ex-military in Aston. Guy's got the experience to assist."

Guy was looking at David's back, but he could feel Grant's eyes boring into him again. This was not the evening he'd planned.

David turned around to face him. "We believe this was a contract killing, Guy. A professional sniper from a well-selected position. No witnesses, nothing. We're scouring local CCTV, but nothing yet..." He glanced at Grant, who nodded. "As I mentioned to you earlier, there seems to be a pattern. One that's been happening for at least three if not four years. There are two key factors that link this to other such incidents."

"Incidents like this?" Guy said. "You mean there have been more sniper attacks like this? I don't remember anything like this before."

"They do say you shouldn't believe everything you read in the papers," Grant drawled in a slow, patronising voice. She uncrossed her arms. "It's also true to say you shouldn't believe everything you *don't* read in the papers. Not everything makes it in and that's not just because of idleness or super-injunctions. Sometimes, faceless government also plays the old boy network. Deals are done and promises made. Things happen that aren't reported, Guy – there's more news than newsprint. As an ex-army man, I thought you'd have worked that out."

David glared at her then looked at Guy. "They've not all been sniper attacks, Guy, but they've all been professional killings. That's the first key factor. They're slickly done. No trace and certainly no helpful clues. Shootings, hit-and-runs, knife attacks – stuff like that. They've occurred all over this country and, we believe, there have been several on the continent. Gratefully, none have happened here in the West Midlands before though –"

"Until now," Guy said.

David nodded. "Exactly, until now."

Guy absentmindedly ran his hand through his hair and said, "I'm still a bit lost. If there've been a disparate collection of killings both here and abroad, how can you say they're connected?"

Grant stared at him. "Because," she said, "there are *two* principal factors as David mentioned just now – if you heard him. The killings being of a consistent, professional standard being the first of them."

"And the second?"

"The second factor," Grant continued, "is that all the victims are connected."

"Connected? To each other?" Guy asked.

Grant shot him a withering glance. "No, of course not. To someone else."

"Someone else?"

"Look," Grant said, moving to the edge of her chair and remonstrating with her right hand. "If you're going to keep repeating everything I say, we're going to be here all bloody night…"

"Detective Superintendent, that's enough," David said firmly.

"Well –"

"Enough," David repeated sharply.

Guy was tempted to react, but he restrained himself. Let David sort out his subordinate – this was, after all, his patch and his fight.

Grant pushed herself firmly back into her seat and crossed her arms again.

David continued, "Guy's not here to receive the third degree from you, nor from anyone. He's a friend, not some suspect and I've simply asked him here to see if he can assist as a favour, okay? I know this situation is understandably getting to us, but let's keep it calm and professional, right? *Right?*"

Grant nodded slowly and looked at the floor.

"Now, where were we?" David asked.

"The second factor," Guy prompted. *Get the measure of the fight, boy.*

"Right, connections. All the victims, at least the ones we surmise fall into this group, are well connected. They're relatives of well-known people from industrialists to celebrities. It would be easy to rush to conclusions – money and so on – but we're keeping an open mind."

"What do these wealthy relatives say about it? There must be a common theme."

"There is," David said. "Silence. Total silence. None of them have come up with any persuasive stories as to why their brother, niece, son or whoever has been the victim of what on all accounts appears to be a professional hit."

Guy said, "Scared?" Either that, he surmised, or lack of knowledge. Someone who was ignorant was likely to say they were ignorant rather than remain silent. Being scared was a very different game, a very different reaction.

David shrugged. "Possibly."

"So who was she, David?" Guy asked.

"Who?"

"Tuesday's victim."

"Her name was Julie Reid, a married mother of two. Husband plays a bit of football locally; you'll know of him –"

"Jonny Reid?"

"Spot on," David acknowledged. "Jonny Reid – Birmingham United, and England every now and then. One of the Premier League's over-paid multi-millionaires."

Grant joined in. "I informed him about Julie that evening. Thrashed by Chelsea and then told he was a widower – not sure which he took worse, to be honest. Never seen such little reaction before. Usually it's genuine grief and self-pity. But our Jonny just launched into nannies and boarding school – unbelievable."

"Has he said anything helpful?" David asked.

"Not a lot. I've arranged to see him again in the morning before he goes to training in the afternoon – maybe I'll get some sense out of him then."

"I'd like Guy to visit too."

"What, with me? In what capacity, sir?"

"No, after you've been. I'd like Guy to work alongside us, in tandem so to speak. Initially to observe and hopefully to win trust."

Grant sat forward, slightly redder in the face. "I really don't see how that's going to help – or how it's going to work."

Guy could see a situation spiralling out of control. "Hang on," he said, "I've not committed to anything yet, David. I just said I'd come along to meet some people this evening, as you'll recall. You said you wanted me to do a task, I appreciate that, but I'm not rushing in until there's an agreed plan. I need to think about this – and maybe you two should discuss it further. And I haven't even met Peter Wright yet."

David sat forward and scowled. "The decision is mine, Guy, not Caroline's. If you'll help, she'll co-operate – won't you, Caroline?"

"The decision is also mine, David," Guy said, firmly but calmly.

David nodded gently.

Grant promptly stood up. "With respect, sir, I think this meeting's through. It's very late, I've had a long day and perhaps in the morning more rational views can be taken."

She spun round and strode to the door. She paused with her hand on the knob and looked back at the men, who had both raised themselves to their feet. Guy had done so out of natural politeness; he suspected for David it was out of anger.

"Detective Superintendent, the meeting closes when I say so."

"Then unless there's AOB, I suggest you close it now to keep it all nice and tidy…sir." She tugged the door open and strode out, slamming it behind her.

SEVEN

At that moment, an eighteen-year-old girl was leaning against the closed rear door in the back of a silver Maserati Quattroporte GLS. The distinctive scent of Chanel No 5 filled the car, and her boyfriend's taciturn driver eased the car forward and up the street. She self-consciously tugged down the hem of her short dress, but it stubbornly refused to move.

Was that a record change for her? Pretty close. She hadn't expected the call from her boyfriend, or his unique invitation. He usually came to her modest flat or took her somewhere discreet, away from watching eyes. She was aware of all the risks and complications their relationship held – as well as their age gap – but it was exciting, novel, and financially rewarding.

She glanced out of the window and watched the orange-lit city streets run to their natural end, allowing the rural roads to take over. She knew it wouldn't be long.

After the brief summons she'd rushed into her small bedroom and thrown some clothes into a bag. She stripped off her t-shirt and jeans, knickers and pink, girly socks, pausing briefly to admire her toned, petite frame in the full-length mirror. She grabbed a scanty, expensive black dress out of her wardrobe – a 'hello present' her boyfriend had called it when they had gone out on yet another careful date. Now she stood before the mirror and held it up in front of her, noting how it barely covered her narrow, girlish hips. She smiled and swayed slightly, hugging it to her slim waist before pulling it tightly over her naked body.

The sharp turn off the road took the car down a long, tree-lined drive to a set of ornate, electric gates. After a pause they swung open. The Maserati hummed forward as if knowing it was home, before coming to a stop with a soothing crunch on the gravel circle set in front of a substantial brick house. Her boyfriend had told her it was over two hundred and fifty years old, and her own research had confirmed it was a classic Georgian mansion.

She stepped out of the car and smoothed down her dress, while the driver took her bag round the side of the house. As she tottered up to the door in her highest heels, it opened ahead of her and her boyfriend appeared under the outside light. She reached out and they embraced.

She pulled back to look at him. Hell, he was so good looking. Better in the flesh than on those television interviews, without a doubt.

"Hi," she said. "I'm here as requested, with a bag and everything. Can we go get a drink then, Jonny Reid?"

EIGHT

Guy watched David pace up and down his office. The police officer exuded an air of combined anger and frustration, possibly tinged with a hint of embarrassment. He remained silent to allow David time to work the situation through. Guy had seen such run-ins before when he was in the regiment. Admittedly Caroline's reaction had been extreme, almost truculent, and it could certainly have undermined David's standing in Guy's eyes if he hadn't fully appreciated the issues at stake, or if he hadn't known David for so long. He'd seen junior officers debate and question suggested tactics at briefings or strategy meetings when details of an SAS operation were at the early planning stage. But there had always been a level of respect for the higher authority, even from the most egocentric and ambitious of officers.

There was a sudden knock on the door and for a fleeting second Guy thought Caroline had returned, but it sprang open and a uniformed policeman of evident rank entered. Aged about fifty, Peter Wright carried some unhealthy weight which clung to his stomach and jowls. He had a jovial face and thick grey hair, neatly cut.

David stopped pacing and greeted his visitor. "Peter. Glad you could make it."

The deputy chief constable was introduced to Guy and the three of them took a seat, Peter taking the chair recently vacated by Grant.

"Sorry for the late arrival, David," Peter said. "Out on an official do – I don't usually wear my work clothes on a Saturday evening, Guy. So, why the late meeting? Aston, I presume?"

"Of course," David said. "I've asked Guy for his assistance." He summed up Guy's background for Peter, who appeared impressed.

"Up for some police work, then?" Peter asked Guy.

Guy was concerned he was being pulled not of his own choosing in a direction that was new to him. He had no knowledge of police work and, if he was honest, it was a mystery to him. Interrogation and the extraction of essential information was a far cry from pure detection. He said, "We're still discussing it, Peter. No decision yet. And I rather suspect I would be an unwanted member of the team for Caroline Grant."

"Really? That would surprise me."

David painted a picture of the earlier meeting and of Grant's stormy exit.

Peter looked thoughtful. "Right, I see. I guess the challenge now is that if you don't take it up, Guy, then this would have repercussions, like ripples on a pond from a dropped stone. Caroline's opinion of herself will skyrocket as she'll presume she's frightened you off."

"But she hasn't," Guy said firmly.

"Still," Peter continued, "I wouldn't blame you if you didn't volunteer for the challenge. You sound a busy man."

"I don't run from challenges, Peter."

David shifted forward in his chair. "So you'll help?"

"I will," Guy said, turning to him. "I can't allow

her to think that she's beaten me into submission. I'm not wired like that. You could say I was too competitive, always have been. In addition, your authority, David, would be shot through as either she would see it that I'd changed my mind in the face of her reaction, or you'd been premature in stating I was going to help when I hadn't actually agreed to it."

David said, "So what are you going to do?"

"Well, the only way out is for me to save your face and take up the gauntlet thrown down stubbornly by an outranked superintendent." Guy paused, then added, "I owe you a lot, David, especially for all the support you gave me after my parents' deaths. I feel drawn to help you as much as I can – you know, pay back some of that debt. I'd be lying if I said the return to some adventure had no attractions. However…" His voice trailed away.

Peter was looking carefully at Guy, seemingly taking in every word.

David pulled off his black bow tie and tossed it over onto his desk. It slid off and fell to the floor. He turned to Guy. "I'm close to going down the bloody disciplinary route with her, Guy." He paused and drummed the fingers of his right hand rhythmically on the wooden arm of the chair.

"But we need her on the case, David," Peter said.

Guy said, "I guess my apparent involvement must have come as somewhat of a surprise to her – and to me, come to that. At the end of the day, no decision has been taken and indeed can't be until I've thought it through a little more. Although I'm not a policeman, I have skills that could be brought to bear. But Caroline will take it as a criticism, that you haven't the confidence she can solve this on her own with her usual team. It's a slap in the face, you might say. And the support she sees you giving her is from someone without the experience *she* considers necessary." He paused and watched David carefully. "Tell me, how *do* you see it working?"

David appeared lost in thought as he subconsciously rubbed his chin slowly with his right hand. He said, "I see you operating alongside Caroline, feeding off her information and, in turn, passing on to her anything you find of interest. People are clamming up and we need to open them up or work round them. We're dealing with professionals here, Guy. I can't promise you'll be safe; indeed, I can promise you it'll be dangerous – but you're trained for that, aren't you?"

"You said I'd be on my own."

"Yes and no. Clearly, we can't be seen to be supporting you – you'll understand that – but in the background, Peter and I will do what we can – won't we, Peter? This is too serious for us not to take every angle, huh?"

Peter nodded.

"I'm going out on a limb here, Guy," David continued. "I'm risking the pension and probably more besides." He paused and stared across the room in front of him. "But you're right, I want to leave in a blaze of glory, and I can't think of anyone better than you to assist. Sounds frightfully selfish, but hey – why can't an old bugger like me be selfish every now and then?"

Peter and Guy smiled.

Guy said, "Obviously I want to help you, but I'd

be risking more than a pension."

"I appreciate that – but weren't you doing that in Afghanistan, Iraq and indeed in Libya long before the Arab Spring and Gaddafi's fall? You proved to me earlier this evening that you can look after yourself." He met Peter's quizzical look. "I'll tell you later."

"Sure," Guy said. "But remember I was part of a trained team – limited rules of engagement as well as proper gear and back up. Now I've got responsibilities, a charity and an estate to run. People rely on me, David, plus of course there's my fiancée, Sophie, and the bland fact that I have no heir, either. The accident changed all my life plans."

"Accident?" Peter asked.

"Both my parents and my younger sister were killed in a car accident about three years ago, Peter. It's why I left the army – I inherited the baronetcy and the estate."

David looked pensive and then leaned forward. "Guy, there's something I haven't told you about the accident. Now might be the time. It didn't seem relevant, but something's been niggling at me, lurking in the background persistently, especially this week."

Guy felt a surge of adrenalin and sat forward. Peter also turned to listen.

"What do you mean?" Guy asked.

"Two days before the accident your father rang me. He said he wanted to get together. He didn't say why, just that he wanted to meet; it was as simple as that. He sounded – how can I put it? – worried, concerned. Not in a panic, else I'd have arranged to meet up with him earlier, but there was some urgency. I can feel that now. I've always kicked myself for not going sooner, but my diary was busy – I was up in London at the time – so we agreed I'd pop over when I was back in Shrewsbury. Two days later your parents and poor Ruth were dead by the side of the road."

"Why didn't you mention this before – and why now?"

"Not sure. Didn't seem relevant, I guess."

"Is it relevant now?"

David stared straight ahead before turning to look at him. "I just don't know, Guy. Maybe. Maybe not. Something or nothing. There may be no connection at all between the call and the accident as it was, after all, an accident."

"Yet Dad never had a single bump in his life – not even a scratch in a car park. He never had a speeding ticket, nor even a parking ticket come to that. So his actions that afternoon were out of character – totally, completely out of character."

"To be overtaking where he was? I agree. Sir William was always a cautious man, certainly when it came to driving. Laws were important to him; you'll remember he was a right stickler for them. But the coroner found him at fault."

"Based on the lorry driver's evidence," Guy said. "The red car was never traced, remember? Whoever was in that car must have been aware of what was happening – they were at the heart of it."

"Many people don't stop at accidents for a hundred different reasons. I guess we'll never know why things happened as they did, but to take good lives like that…I'm so sorry, Guy."

Guy reflected, re-living the moment when his colonel had told him about the tragedy. He'd been very close to his parents, and especially to his younger sister. She was aged just twenty-two when she died in that car; a young nurse with her whole career ahead of her. He fought back his emotions and looked at David. "Are you thinking there's some kind of connection between my father and what's going on here? Wealth and death, I grant you, but it seems a long shot."

"You may be right," David said. "But what if there is a connection? What if Sir William wanted advice because he was under some sort of threat? You know, he wanted to speak to me as an influential friend, in a way no one else in this long, sorry saga has done since then."

Guy said, "So you think I could play the same role, the confidante, because I'm not police but have a title and some credibility? You think it could lead to some family answers?"

David said nothing. Peter continued to take in the exchange.

"You're manipulating me, David," Guy said.

Still, David stayed silent.

"Give me a straight answer, David. Are you giving me false motivation or is there a connection between the death of my family and the death of that woman in Aston?"

David looked up slowly. "Guy, I honestly don't know. I've told you all I can. I don't know why I keep thinking about your dad's call and the accident. An old policeman's instinct, maybe? It's probably nothing, nothing at all."

Guy looked at him. David seemed as perplexed

about any such connection as he was. Perplexed. What kind of state was that? When had he ever needed time for thought? Then it struck him. Indecision. What the hell was all this about? Throughout his army career he'd been decisive, a talent that had not only saved the lives of others but also his own on several occasions – just like in the alleyway earlier. Maybe since his retirement from the regiment he'd slipped slowly and imperceptibly into a comfort zone where time was never an issue. Quandaries, such as there were any, could be thought over for days and days, and tackled as required with a bag of money from someone born not so much with a silver spoon in his mouth, but a silver ladle. This wasn't the Guy he'd been – 'The Maverick'. Here he was being presented with an opportunity to find his old self and he was *thinking* about it – that summed up the change. And, furthermore, if David was right, if there *was* a connection between his father's telephone call and current events, then he might, just might, get a better understanding of why his life had turned upside down on that dreadful day.

"Look, David. Let's take it a step at a time. You wanted me to speak to Jonny Reid after Caroline's further chat with him in the morning. I'll do that, but that's all for now, right? Let me review it all after that, okay?"

David sat up. He looked enthused. "Excellent. That's a start. Now, you've got my mobile number so use it whenever you want, twenty-four seven. You'll need a weapon – what would you choose?"

"I'm sorted on that front."

David looked surprised. "Oh, okay then." He

turned to Peter. “Anything to add?”

Guy thought Peter looked very pensive.

Peter said, “No, I don’t think so. Good luck with Caroline, David.” He glanced at his watch. “I need to get going. You stopping in Birmingham, Guy?”

“Sure – at the Hyatt. I guess for a couple of nights now. My fiancée’s joining me soon.”

“Is that wise in the circumstances?” David asked, raising himself from his chair.

It had never occurred to Guy that it wouldn’t be. This was his adventure after all, not hers. He noted the concern in David’s tone but dismissed it. Sophie would be fine – wouldn’t she?

NINE

Guy walked into St Philip's Place in the heart of Birmingham city centre and identified the black-painted iron bench described by the caller in the voicemail message. It was one of a row located at the eastern end of Birmingham's baroque cathedral, in the churchyard that had been re-born as a public urban square. It was criss-crossed with asphalt paths which now took city workers to offices and coffee houses rather than Christians to the Anglican place of worship.

Guy was dressed in chino jeans, a blue open-necked shirt and a light linen jacket which was just cool enough as the midday sun broke sporadically through the scattering of white clouds and gradually turned up the heat on an already-warm Sunday morning.

He put on his sunglasses and glanced around him. He'd never liked cities. "You were born to be a country boy," his father had said, putting his arm round his son's ten-year-old shoulders as they'd stood together in the Hofton estate parkland, looking down at the red-bricked Elizabethan manor.

A steady flow of well-dressed people started to ebb out of the far end of the cathedral, collecting in pools and trickling away home – no doubt for a traditional roast dinner. Religion to Guy was a formal affair he'd endured when he was young. His memory, probably false, registered long services at the stone church of St Chad's in West Hofton, or occasional family gatherings on high days and holy days in the cold, private chapel on the Hofton estate. His mother would lean over him as his boyish legs swung rapidly below the pew. "Stop fidgeting, Guy," she would whisper before taking his hand in a reassuring embrace. His upbringing had encouraged him to feel the presence of a Christian God but, save for times when life had been emotional or dramatic, he'd left God alone and hadn't troubled Him.

"Hello, Guy."

He turned to see Grant, dressed in an elegant business suit, walking up to him.

"Good morning, Caroline." He made to rise politely, but she sat down firmly next to him without offering a handshake. Not a good omen. As she made herself comfortable, he studied her for signs of mood. Her sunglasses didn't help him.

She placed her arm on the back of the bench and looked at him. "So, you're on board, then? David can be very persuasive."

"It was my decision, not David's."

"Of course it was," she said with less-than-subtle sarcasm. "You sound defensive…"

He paused long enough to stop an unhelpful response, then said, "I gather you spoke to David before you rang me this morning?"

Grant looked nonchalant and straightened her skirt. "We had a brief word. I'm not impressed by his decision. In fact, I think it's bloody stupid. However, the bottom line is he's the chief constable, so there we are. I've made my views very plain."

Guy didn't doubt that she had. "And you'll cooperate?"

"Do I have a choice?"

"Of course. Follow the order or walk the plank –

not recommended if you can't swim."

"Believe me, I can swim."

Guy recalled her voicemail. "You said in your message you wanted to meet."

Grant crossed her legs at the ankles. "No, I said we *ought* to meet. I've a boss to keep happy and a high-profile investigation to run. Why would I *want* to meet with you?"

Guy kept his composure, although it was becoming increasingly difficult. "Your horse is pretty high, Caroline. Have you not thought that I may, just may, be able to give you the extra support and insight you need?"

Grant frowned and stared at him. "How on earth can you do that, Guy? This isn't the army, you know, or some sort of Sandhurst exercise. This is real life, real crime, real murder. You're just going to be in the way and waste my time – witness what's happening now. I could be back at Lloyd House doing proper police work rather than sitting on some park bench with a blue-blooded stranger."

Despite rising anger, Guy maintained his control. "My blood is as red as everyone else's. I know because I saw it several times when I was in action, playing soldiers," he said, slowly and deliberately. He looked at the people walking by and took a mental deep breath. "Look, Caroline, I'm on board now whether you like it or not –"

"I don't like it."

"I'd never have guessed. But that's life, isn't it? You don't always get what you want – Julie Reid certainly didn't. And that's what matters, doesn't it?

Catching the guy behind her murder – and the murders of all these apparent others. That's the goal, that's the aim, okay?" He paused and took a second inward deep breath in as many minutes. "So, you saw Reid?" he asked.

Grant gave a sarcastic smile and seemed to relax slightly as if the introduction of a fresh adversary meant the skirmish was over – for now, at any rate. "Yeah, and a fat lot of good that was. He displayed all the attitude of 'not my problem'. Claims he knew nothing about why someone had shot his wife, the mother of his children. Claims he had no idea why she took off with their children to a friend's in Aston. A lot of claims, but no logic."

"You're joking," Guy said in disbelief.

"I don't joke."

That, Guy could believe.

Grant stretched, drew her legs up and leant squarely back on the bench with her arms crossed, staring into the middle distance as if surveying the city's architecture. She said, "His main concern seemed to be the press – you know, what the papers are reporting."

"And what are they reporting? Couldn't see anything in even the Sundays this morning."

"You won't," Grant replied with a satisfied and slightly smug look. "We've asked for a temporary news blackout after the initial soundbites went out. It's actually being respected. Can't trust the internet though, and there's bugger all we can do about that. There's stuff on the usual social media sites, but it's pretty harmless."

Guy looked at her. More freckles on her face than he'd noticed last night. "So, how does he explain

Julie's presence in Aston? He must have known she'd gone there."

Grant turned her head to look at him and adjusted her sunglasses slightly. "He says she just packed a bag last Monday and that was that."

"Marital issues?"

"They weren't exactly Romeo and Juliet, we all know that from the press – well, some of us do. I guess you don't often read the gossip pages beyond looking at the scantily-clad girls on page three of *The Sun*."

Guy let it go.

She continued, seemingly unfazed by her own rudeness. "They've had their challenges, but he said they were making a go of it. Having said that, some teenage girl walked in on us. Pretty and about half his age – didn't look as if she'd just arrived, either. Our Jonny said she was just a friend – just a one-night stand in my view, which rather sums him up, doesn't it? Wife murdered and the girlfriend's over in the marital bed before it's even cooled. I can't get my head round it."

"She may have been just a friend," Guy said.

"Yeah, right," Grant said with an exaggerated sneer. "And Elvis is working nightclubs. Have you always been gullible?"

"You're very quick to judge and condemn."

"I was there, Guy. I know what I saw."

Guy paused and then asked, "Did Jonny say whether he'd communicated with Julie at all while she was staying in Aston?"

"He said they'd spoken a couple of times. It apparently wasn't unusual for her to stay with friends in Birmingham."

"But what about the kids and school?"

"There are cars."

"So he declined to give more information?"

Grant stood up. "Looks like we're back into repetition."

Guy rose too. He was feeling increasingly frustrated with her. "I'm trying to get the picture from you, Caroline. You're not being overly helpful."

Guy watched her face redden again. This time he knew what was coming.

"Look," she said, her hands rising to her hips. "I've told you what I know, right? I've done what I was ordered by David – and that *was* because he ordered me to, not because it makes any sense. I'm livid about all this, okay? It's not personal…" She paused, and then looked Guy straight in the eyes. "No, actually it *is* personal. Who am I kidding? You've been dumped on me under the chauvinistic Old Pal's Act, probably because David believes you can help us solve this so he can ride off into the sunset with enough plaudits to carry him through to his sodding dotage. I'm not impressed, I'm really not, and he should know better. It's not how the police operate and if you had anything about you, anything at all, you'd have buggered off back home to your bloody mansion in Shropshire. So yes, it is pretty personal."

Guy was conscious of people witnessing the outburst as they ambled by, but he was beyond caring. "Okay, fine, so before you go back to your office and play top policewoman –"

"Officer. Police *officer* – we don't do police*women* anymore."

"Why ever not? You're not ashamed of your gender, are you?"

Grant glared at him. "The reason –"

"Frankly, I'm not interested in the reason," he interrupted her. "No doubt greater minds than mine – indeed, actual police minds – discussed the issue long and hard in meeting after meeting, committee after committee, and found it was for the best. I'm really not that bothered, Caroline. Just be aware that I'll also go and talk to Reid, this afternoon if I can."

Grant looked superior and said, "He won't talk to you."

"Who says?"

"He does. No more police questions, he said. Said he'd told us all he could."

"Just as well I'm not the police then, hmm?"

Grant said nothing, just stared at him and made to walk off.

"I've done my bit," she said at last. "I've reported progress, and now I'm going to get on with some proper police work. You're meant to report any of your progress to me, but I'll not hold my breath. Goodbye."

She walked away.

Guy called after her. "I'll keep my side of the bargain, Caroline. I'll speak to you in due course and tell you what he says."

She dropped her arm dismissively as she walked away. "Whatever," she called, without turning.

Guy sat back down on the bench and stared at his outstretched legs. Just how was he going to speak to the multi-millionaire footballer, let alone extract something that would justify a call to Grant? Maybe he should have buggered off back to Shropshire after all.

TEN

The silver Morgan AeroMax cruised effortlessly down the A38 dual carriageway, heading north from Birmingham and around Sutton Coldfield towards the village of Shenstone. Hand-crafted and with flowing lines, the hard-top sports car was an interesting mix of traditional and hi-tech. Guy loved that. Every time he drove this car, the favourite in his collection, he revelled in its appearance and handling. A boy's toy. When he'd taken possession of this limited-edition vehicle, he'd left others to fight over the remaining ninety-nine. Although English-manufactured, it boasted a powerful 4.8-litre BMW V8 engine; he could forgive the German intrusion as the performance justified it.

He adjusted the neat sun visor slightly with his left hand, taking in the deep blue, late-summer sky with its wispy banks of elegant white cloud. It was still very warm, but the air-conditioning kept him comfortable. The roads were typically quiet for a Sunday afternoon although that would change with the next morning's rush hour.

The signpost at the side of the road advised him that Shenstone was left. He crossed over the near-empty M6 toll road and followed the signs into the village. A right turn took him into a narrow lane and through some trees until a large development of playing fields and low, modern buildings appeared, partially hidden to his left behind a lengthy screen of thick Leyland cypress. A wide asphalt entrance appeared in which stood a security barrier and a large grey kiosk. An elderly security guard carrying a clipboard stepped out of the kiosk and partially obscured the sign, which declared this to be Birmingham United's training facility.

As the guard approached his idling car, Guy lowered his window, and smiled at him.

The guard's face remained impassive. His neatly cut grey hair showed beneath his cap, and he stooped slightly. "Can I help you, sir?"

Guy put him in his mid to late sixties. This could be a useful age in these circumstances and Guy was ready. "I hope so. I've an appointment with Jonny Reid."

The guard raised his clipboard and studied it with squinting eyes. "And you are…?"

"Julian Adams, from his agents."

The guard's eyes ran up and down the paper. He pulled the sheet up with his left hand, checked the one underneath and then let it fall. "I'm sorry, Mr Adams, you're not on the list."

Guy frowned and leaned his head forward as if wanting to look at the clipboard. "My secretary made the appointment last week. Don't tell me it hasn't made the clipboard. I've not exactly travelled a hundred yards to get here."

The guard checked his board again, and then rubbed his cheek with his free hand. "I'm sorry about that, sir. Matter of security." He drew himself up to his full height before he relaxed back into his stoop and stared at Guy.

"Looks like I've had a wasted journey?"

"It would seem so, sir."

"What's your name?"

The guard paused slightly, as if assessing the situation. "Alan, sir."

"Well, Alan, couldn't you at least get a message to Jonny for me? If he knew I was here, things might be different. I presume he's here…"

"Of course, he is, sir. All the squad's here. You'll know the manager wasn't too happy about yesterday's game; three losses in a row now – there's some work to be done."

An evident United fan as well as a loyal employee.

Guy nodded. "Can you get a message to him?"

"Not allowed, sir," Alan said with a stoical look. "You'll have to re-arrange everything and make sure it's all fixed up properly."

"What time will they finish?"

Alan scratched the top of his head, his cap lifting slightly and shaking under the movement. "Who knows?" he said. "Could be half an hour, could be a couple of hours."

The gatekeeper was not to be shifted by the normal course of persuasion.

Guy assumed an earnest expression. "Look, Alan, this is really quite frustrating. I'm sure you can understand that. I appreciate where you're coming from but, as you can see from these papers, it's quite urgent."

Guy picked up a large, white envelope from the passenger seat and handed it to Alan, who glanced into the envelope and slid his hand inside. He looked back at Guy.

"Well," he said, "I can see there is some urgency. I guess oversights can happen and you have come a long way. Perhaps if we can keep this little confusion and misunderstanding between us, sir, I could let you in."

Guy smiled politely. "That would be kind."

Alan walked back to his kiosk clutching the clipboard and his new envelope and raised the barrier. Guy drove the Morgan through the gateway. He imagined Alan hastily transferring the money to his pocket and wondered if the man had ever seen so many £20 notes before in his life; the money would not be unwelcome as he headed for retirement.

ELEVEN

Guy followed the signs to the virtually empty visitors' car park. He locked his car and looked around. On the opposite side of the pristine drive, football pitches stretched as far as he could see. A vast, green space lined and regularly interspersed with white goalposts, their nets waiting patiently. Other than a small group of jogging sportsmen, there was no visible activity in the place.

He walked towards the flat-roofed, two-storey building with its cedar-clad walls and entered the main door, the silver metal and clear glass opening automatically before him. The air-conditioned reception area was spacious, furnished with soft-leather sofas and low glass tables. It was well lit by the sunlight that streamed in through the large windows and doorway, and there was a respectful, hushed atmosphere.

A young woman sat behind a curved wooden reception desk and spoke in low tones on a telephone headset. The club's crest, ostentatiously large, was mounted high on the wall behind her. To the sound of his own footfall, Guy crossed the polished tiled floor and stood nearby. She glanced at him, acknowledged his presence and finished her call by pressing a button on her switchboard with a flourish. She looked up at him with a receptionist's smile.

"Welcome to Birmingham United. Can I assist you, sir?"

"I'm here to see Jonny Reid, please. The name's Sterling, Guy Sterling."

"Is he expecting you, Mr Sterling?"

"I'd like to think so. Is he available now?"

"They're all in the seminar room at the moment, but they shouldn't be long," she said. "Why not take a seat, Mr Sterling, as they'll be leaving through here?" She motioned towards one of the sofas.

Guy thanked her and sat down. He picked up a new copy of *Country Life* and flicked idly through page after glossy page. Each was filled with photographs of stately, classical houses, shown to best advantage by aerial shots and artistic foregrounds of yew and cedar branches, all seeking a willing – and wealthy – buyer.

Guy smiled to himself, realising how fortunate he'd been in never having to think about buying a house. As the seventh baronet of the Sterling baronetcy, he'd inherited the family-owned Hofton Manor, its Shropshire estate and London properties, which had been theirs since the early 1600s. The family seemed to have handled politics, religion and even the English Civil War pretty well, managing to remain Royalists and true supporters of the deposed King Charles in even the darkest of times. It was an inheritance Guy didn't take lightly, and he was always grateful for his good fortune. The houses he saw now in the magazine would undoubtedly go to new money: entrepreneurs, celebrities and wealthy footballers, rather than the children of nobility or those favoured by the monarch. How times had changed.

The seminar-suite door opened and three men in casual clothes walked through chatting earnestly, heading for the exit. The door had hardly closed when a tall, dark-haired man entered, pausing slightly to hold the door for someone following him. Guy recognised him as Phil White, the reasonably regular England goalkeeper. The man following him was Jonny Reid. A familiar face to Guy – short, cropped, slightly thinning brown hair, dark eyes and a chiselled chin alive with his trademark stubble. He was dressed in jeans with a plain white t-shirt and expensive, black leather jacket.

Guy dropped the magazine on the low table in front of him and rose from the sofa. "Jonny, may I have a brief word with you, please?"

Jonny paused mid-sentence and shot Guy a glance. Phil White turned to observe. "And who are you?" Jonny asked as his eyes flicked over Guy, scrambling for recognition.

"We haven't met…yet. But we need to speak. The name's Guy and I think I may have something of interest to you."

Jonny looked tempted, but not convinced. "Guy who?" He turned to Phil White. "You get on, Whitesie. I'll sort this."

"Sure?" White asked.

"Sure. Off you go."

White moved to the main door as others started to filter out from behind Jonny. The footballer took a couple of steps over to where Guy was standing.

"Right, Guy who?" No smile, just an intense stare.

"Guy Sterling. I need to talk to you about Tuesday. I was sorry –"

"How did you get in here? You from the papers?" Jonny asked with a negative glance.

"No. I've no time for those parasites. I'm just interested in helping you."

Jonny stared at him as if weighing matters up. "I'll give you three minutes, and it had better be good, Sterling, else I'll have you thrown out. Come in here."

He led Guy into a small meeting room and closed the door behind them. A large window looked out onto the front of the building, giving plenty of light to the modern wood furniture. An outsized photograph of jubilant United players holding aloft the FA Cup at Wembley dominated the side wall, more than two years old now.

Jonny perched on the edge of the table with one foot off the floor and his arms crossed. He looked quizzically at Guy. "Well?"

Guy moved to the window, watched the players crossing to a car park filled with Porsches, Aston Martins and Mercedes, and then turned slowly to Jonny. Guy had spent the lunchtime working on this crucial pitch.

"I'm from an organisation called International Investigations –"

"Never heard of it." Jonny looked unimpressed.

"Not many have, so don't be hard on yourself. We help the wealthy sort out issues that can otherwise be…shall we say, difficult?"

A thought appeared to flash across Jonny's face. "Is this a sting? Are you recording this?"

"Smart, but no. You can look me up if you want." Guy reached into his jacket pocket and passed a business card to Jonny. It was his standard card, no reference to the newly invented International Investigations, but Jonny didn't seem to notice that omission. He glanced at it and tossed it onto the table before leaning over to pour himself a glass of mineral water from a bottle there. He looked at Guy over the rim as he took a long drink.

"Okay, so you're some sort of nobility from Shropshire. Doesn't tell me much save that you're interfering in my life. I've already had some stuck-up policewoman grilling me all morning, I don't want some bloody aristocrat repeating the exercise all afternoon." He stood up from the table.

Guy realised he was about to lose his chance. The thought he'd have nothing for Grant resurrected itself, motivating him to go on. "Look," he said. "I know the police can be somewhat heavy-handed. I understand that. I'm not police – just someone who wants to help you, and others."

"Others?"

Progress.

"Yes. Julie wasn't alone. The police believe others have been murdered in a similar way – others also connected to wealthy individuals." Guy felt he could give a bit. The more he looked at Jonny, the more he realised how totally unfazed this man was. Here was someone who a few days earlier had become a widower, whose children had suddenly lost their mother, and who'd been questioned twice about his wife's death by the police. And yet here he was at work, chatting to his mates as if none of that horror had happened.

"I presume you're representing some celebrity or other?" Jonny asked.

"You may think that." Guy looked him straight in the eyes and held his stare. "Jonny, the reality is that this is going to happen again. Not to you, but to someone like you – Whitesie, for example."

Jonny bristled. "You can leave him out of it."

"Why? He's just as likely to be a victim as you've been. Don't you want to help him?"

"Well –"

"Pretty harsh if you didn't want to, I guess." Guy sat back so he was propped on the window ledge. "Be frank with me, Jonny. What do you know about all this?"

"No more than I told that bloody policewoman."

"Have you been threatened?"

Jonny looked as though Guy had just kicked him, hard. "You what? No one threatens me. No one." He was starting to look annoyed. He stood up and paced up and down.

"Why was Julie at her friend's house?"

Jonny stopped and turned to face Guy. He said, sarcastically, "Because she was visiting, why the fuck do you think?"

"Hiding from someone?"

"Look, if she was going to hide, she'd be far better hiding at home."

Guy guessed it would be a large house with a big estate – easy to disappear, but she'd have been a prisoner in her own home. And for how long?

"Maybe. Maybe not," Guy said. "Are you being blackmailed?"

"This is crazy." Jonny swung his arm angrily and slid the glass fast down the table. It flew off the end and broke on the painted wall. "I've nothing more to say to you."

Guy was concerned the noise would summon

someone. There wasn't much time, he realised. "One more thing. Except for that outburst just then, I have to say you seem pretty cool that your wife and the mother of your children was suddenly killed just last Tuesday. How come? I'd be in pieces – certainly wouldn't be back at work."

Jonny raised his voice. "I rather think that's my business, don't you? My wife's dead, okay? No threats, no warnings, no explanations. That's how it is. I'll handle it how I want to, right? There's nothing I can add, so why don't you just go screw yourself and leave me alone? I don't expect to hear from you again – got it?"

Guy held the other man's stare. "Then when you read about the sudden death of some celebrity's wife or son, don't let it weigh on your mind that there was something you could have done."

Jonny took several quick steps towards Guy and stood centimetres from him, as though playing the tough man to some rival in a showdown on the pitch. With Guy perched on the windowsill, Jonny had some height advantage. His face was red, his eyes narrow and he hissed at Guy. "How many times must I say it, you fucking idiot? I'm not being threatened, and I don't know what happened or why it has. Go ask that weird brother of hers, huh, and stop pestering me. There's nothing I can add. Nothing. Okay? Now piss off."

With that he turned, pulled the door open and left the room. Guy watched him go and, although it didn't make any sense, his experience told him that Jonny had been telling the truth.

TWELVE

Once outside United's training facility, Guy turned the Morgan back towards Birmingham. As he drove, he told himself he'd fulfilled his promise to David – and part of him acknowledged that he'd rather enjoyed the different experience and the challenge it had presented.

He also knew he should report back to Caroline Grant – but what would he say? That he'd met up with Jonny Reid? That he believed him? He could hear Caroline's withering response. He could handle that, of course. But what now? Back off or carry on? He glanced at his mobile. No calls or messages from Caroline, so she clearly didn't see any need to update him every five minutes. There was, however, a loving one from Sophie to say she was heading to the Birmingham hotel that afternoon and expected to arrive mid-evening, after supper.

Sophie. He felt slightly guilty that he hadn't thought about her much over the last twenty-four hours. They would have been engaged for three years in a week's time, and he still hadn't fixed the date. Not that she'd pushed. He'd been working on it, though. She was about seven years younger than him and had just turned thirty. He'd known her for ten years, although a crass decision of his had made that time something of an emotional roller-coaster.

A car horn brought his full concentration back to the road, and he acknowledged to the driver of the red Ford Fiesta that he had indeed ill-considerately left it tight as he'd rounded a parked car. He indicated, pulled into a pub car park, and found a quiet spot.

Picking up his mobile he sent a loving text to Sophie before Googling Julie Reid. Why hadn't he done that before? There were a number of biographical details and plenty of references to her footballing husband and their celebrity lifestyle: Jonny and Julie at a celebrity party; Jonny and Julie on the beach in Mauritius; Jonny and Julie and their two children in Disneyland.

Then there were some articles in a slightly different vein: Jonny outside Solihull Magistrates Court following a driving ban for doing more than 120mph on the M42 early one Sunday morning; gossip pieces regarding model-like girls, including a rather compromising photograph of Jonny with a mystery blonde at a London night club a couple of years ago.

He clicked on a Wikipedia page for Julie. It was brief with many citations missing. Her date of birth made her thirty-five when she died. Two children – Billy, now aged nine, and Kitty, now seven. But an *only child* of Graham and Lindsey Harrison. There was no reference at all to any alleged brother. What was Jonny on about? He'd let the question go since Jonny hadn't exactly been in the mood for anything further – that had been obvious. Her "weird brother". If anyone knew, it would be Jonny. Or Julie's friend, the one she was staying with when she died.

He tossed his mobile onto the seat, switched on the satnav and stared out of the windscreen ahead of him as he tried to think, to remember. A young couple walked past hand in hand, returning to their car. He hardly noticed them. He thought back to the meeting in David's office. What was the name of the road where the friend lived, where Julie had died? He should have written it down. Think. He didn't want to ask Caroline; it would lead to premature questions. There was more to do first. Horse racing, it had something to do with horse racing. Epsom Street, that was it. The memory was a curious thing. No number, but recent activity would be bound to guide him. He bent forward and entered the street name into the satnav. After a swift pushing of buttons, he started the car and moved off.

He would just see where this took him and hoped, as a matter of pride, that he was ahead of Grant. Guy didn't do second place. The silver medal was for others. If this led nowhere, no one would be any the wiser and he could return to Shropshire. If he flushed something out, he could leave it as a gift for Grant and also walk away. This truly was not his fight, whatever David had alluded to. But what he found interesting was that his mind was already working out how he could play the next episode. That meant an element of him was up for the task, didn't it? Who was this supposed brother of poor Julie's? One more step, and one more step *only*. Decision made, come what may.

THIRTEEN

It was late afternoon when Guy reached Epsom Street, one of many terraced roads that had sprung up on old manorial land as Aston had industrialised in the Victorian era and early 1900s.

The two long rows down either side created a closed environment into which the sun was only now just reaching. There was a lot of shade, but it was still warm. The walls of the houses presented a line of front doors, displaying the variety you'd expect to find in any half-decent showroom. Cars were parked along the length of the street making passing a challenge, the competition for space an unplanned consequence of the supremacy of the combustion engine and the national rise in living standards.

Guy was conscious that his Morgan looked somewhat out of place; it attracted looks from a couple of elderly pedestrians who were making their way up the pavement. Guy accelerated slowly and eased his way down the road, glancing at the houses on either side as he went.

About two-thirds along a large gap appeared at the kerbside between the cars, and Guy noticed a burst of colour on the ground outside a house with a royal-blue door and a larger-than-average satellite dish nosing skyward. He pulled into the empty space and parked, then leaned forward to study the house through the windscreen. The curtains at all three front windows – one on the ground floor and two upstairs – were drawn, singling the home out in its row and giving it a distant, isolated look. Julie's friend was either away or she was very much keeping to herself and avoiding the prying eyes of neighbours and inquisitive strangers – a class, no doubt, in which she would place Guy.

Guy stepped out of his Morgan, locked it and walked the few paces to the silent front door. Through his peripheral vision to the left he noticed a net curtain slip back into place in the window of a neighbouring house. He looked down. Half a dozen bunches of bright flowers wrapped in cellophane or patterned shop paper lay at the side of the door, stretching out to below the window. He couldn't stop himself from reading a couple of the hand-written cards. They expressed shock, sympathy and love for Julie, wife and mother.

He rang the bell and glanced about him. The street was quiet save for a single car. The door remained steadfastly closed. It looked like a dead end. No friend of Julie's, no further means of gleaning information about Julie and her death.

Three teenage lads wearing baggy, low-hung jeans and carrying small bottles of lager swaggered past him, talking loudly and crudely, their attention drawn briefly to the Morgan.

One, sporting an Eminem tour t-shirt, turned to Guy. "That your car, mate?" he asked with enthusiasm, swigging flamboyantly from his bottle.

Guy nodded and smiled.

"Cool," the other two lads said in unison, and they started to amble off down the pavement.

"One minute, lads," Guy called. "You live round here?"

They stopped and turned to look at him.

Eminem said, "Who's asking?"

"A guy who needs to see the lady at number forty-nine."

"Linda?"

"Yeah, Linda," Guy said. "You are local, then. Know where she is?"

Eminem glanced briefly at his mates before turning back to Guy. "Might do. Depends." He appeared to be the group's alpha male.

Guy studied them as they stood there like a spread of hired gunfighters waiting for something to give. "You all look pretty thirsty." He dipped his hand in his pocket and pulled out three £20 notes. "Want to get yourselves some refills?"

Eminem walked back to him and took the notes. "Arr, might just do that," he said, waving the notes gently. "We'd invite you to join us, but guess you'll be busy visiting number twenty-three. Babs there takes in all kinds of waifs and strays." He smiled at his self-perceived cleverness, and the three of them mooched playfully down the street again, sharing out the money and talking loudly, palpably pleased with their good fortune.

Guy looked at the house numbers and walked up the street in the opposite direction.

Number twenty-three was on the same side of the road, with a varnished front door in need of some urgent care and attention. There was no sign of a doorbell, just a brass horse's head knocker, which Guy rapped briskly. After a few moments the door opened a short way, slowly and carefully, and a woman peered out. She was mid-thirties with long, dyed-blonde hair, dark roots very evident. She studied Guy, her pale blue eyes assessing the visitor. Guy knew it was either Barbara or Linda – the cautious way in which the door had been opened took him in one direction only.

"Linda? You don't know me. My name's Guy, Guy Sterling. I know Jonny and have just been chatting with him. Can you spare five minutes? I appreciate I'm just crashing in."

The woman didn't move, still holding the door as if she needed it for support. But she hadn't closed it. "How did you know I were here?" Her brow furrowed.

Guy gave his best reassuring smile. "I have friends, too. We all need them at times of crisis – and tragedy, like now. Barbara's been one of the best, I guess."

The woman looked a little surprised. "You know Babs?"

"By reputation. You've chosen your friends well. Can I have a few minutes with you, please? I'm here for Julie, I suppose."

Linda appeared to relax slightly, and she stepped back, opening the door slowly as she went. Guy looked in from the street and saw a girl aged about seven or eight appear in the narrow hallway. She was clutching a biscuit and had chocolate smeared liberally around her mouth.

"Come on in," Linda said. "Babs is out, but she'll be back soon." She turned to the girl. "Go play upstairs for two or three minutes, Kylie."

"Don't wanna," Kylie pouted with a challenging look.

"Upstairs now!" Linda snapped, and the girl

made her way moodily up the staircase, stamping her feet and staring accusingly at Guy as she went. *This was all his fault.*

"Sorry about that," Linda said. "She's usually a good girl. Come on through here anyways."

She led Guy into a small, dishevelled sitting room where a tatty armchair and sofa, strewn with toys and magazines, were lined up to face the vast television screen that dominated the room from its corner. Linda cleared the chair, muttering apologetic excuses, and offered it to Guy with a guiding hand. As he sat down, Linda perched on the edge of the sofa and looked expectantly at him.

How could he start? He knew nothing of her, nothing of Julie. The house was silent save for the sounds of Kylie moving about in the room above, still moody. He needed to get through this and learn what he needed before Barbara's return.

"I'm really sorry about what's happened," Guy began. "Awful, awful stuff."

Linda nodded thoughtfully. "How is Jonny? He must have talked to you – you being a mate of his and everything."

"He was full of emotion when I last saw him." Guy leaned forward, his elbows resting on his knees, his fingers steepled. "I guess you knew Julie well." He paused to allow her to speak.

"About thirty year. We met at school, first day of term and was mates ever since. She come from round here, she did. One of us, she was – so was Jonny, come to that. You wouldn't know it to hear him speak now, mind. Right posh he is now, if you know what I mean."

She paused and glanced at a photograph of Jonny and a brown-haired woman given pride of place on the mantlepiece by Barbara. A couple of white lilies had been placed around the bottom of the frame, creating a protective nest – a small, loving shrine. "Thick as shit is our Jonny, but can't half move a football – and there's more money in that than the frigging academic stuff, isn't there? Pardon me French."

Guy silently had to agree, and he nodded outwardly. "Childhood sweethearts, huh?"

"Least he knew she wasn't after him for his money. Them was together long before he got rich."

Guy said, "Why did she come to stay last week?" Linda shrugged her shoulders. "Dunno. She never said, really. She just rang me, she did, and come over." Guy gave her his most reassuring look. "She'd done that before then – just turned up like that? Jonny never said anything about that to me."

"Arr, usually when Jonny and her had had a spat, as it were. You know, one of their rows. There were several of those, 'specially in the last few months. She got hurt twice, if you know what I mean. She knew she were always welcome at our house, though, and Kylie gets on well with her kids…" She paused and seemed to drift away into thought.

Guy leant forward to draw her attention. "I never knew much about her family. Are her parents alive?"

"Well, her mom's dead, God rest her soul. Pneumonia it was, almost twenty year ago now. Julie was seventeen, eighteen – something like that, any road. Never knew her dad. Ran off with some wench when she was well small. He was living up in Scotland when Julie last heard."

"Siblings?"

"You what?"

"Brothers and sisters. Did Julie have any brothers or sisters?"

Linda paused and appeared to study Guy a bit closer. "Why you asking?"

Guy realised he might have pushed the questioning too far. "Well, despite knowing Jonny, I feel I hardly know Julie – you know, now she's gone; it takes something like this to make you reflect, don't you think?"

Linda seemed to relax and leant back into the sofa. "Arr, I guess so. Don't you know about her brother, then?"

"Jonny told me once she had a brother, but never went into much detail. He gave me the impression he was – how shall I put it? – a bit weird."

"Wouldn't say weird exactly. He's well successful now, of course. They fell out years ago – he's much older than her, isn't he?" She scratched her ear with her left hand, displaying a wedding ring and a gaudy, thick engagement ring. "Let me see, we was still at school. We must have been about fifteen, maybe sixteen come to think of it as it were exam time – what a waste of time they was. She never told me what happened, even when she was pissed. Tight-lipped about it she was, and I was her best mate, if you know what I mean."

Guy sensed movement at the front of the house and suddenly heard the sound of a key in the front door.

Linda said, "There's Babs now."

Guy asked quickly, "You said her brother was very successful now – at what? Whenever I've looked for information there's nothing about a brother. Wikipedia says she was an only child."

Linda laughed. "That's because she never talked about him, never let on, 'specially him being a celebrity and everything. And he don't talk about her, neither."

"A celebrity?"

"Blooming heck, I thought you would know that much, you being a mate of Jonny's and everything."

The sitting room door swung open and a large, elderly woman with untidy grey hair and a billowing, flowery dress entered. She was clutching two heavy shopping bags that pulled her arms straight down her sides. Placing them on the floor, she turned to Guy with a look that he read as saying, *Who the hell are you and what are you doing here in my house?* He stood up.

"Who are you?" she asked Guy before looking at Linda. "You okay, Linda?" She turned back to Guy with a thunderous face.

"The name's Guy Sterling and I know Jonny. I just wanted to speak to Linda –"

"A bloody reporter, no doubt. Don't you come tricking your way into here. Now get out of my bloody house before I call the coppers. Go on, scram."

"He's okay, Babs. Honest," Linda said, looking embarrassed.

"You can't see the trees for the bloody wood, Linda. He's trouble – believe me, his sort always are." She looked angrily at Guy. "Go on, shift I said, and be sharp about it."

Guy turned to Linda. "I can see I'm not

welcome for some reason," he said. "I've no wish to cause a problem so I'll go, of course. Thanks for your time anyway, I appreciate it. Take care now."

Linda looked even more embarrassed and stood up as Guy wove his way past Barbara and made for the front door. As he opened it, Linda followed him down the hallway. Kylie was sitting near the top of the stairs, chin resting in her hands, taking in the drama with interest as if her petulant stance had been vindicated. Linda took the door and made to close it. Guy suddenly spun round on the pavement and caught her eye.

He said in a low voice, "What's her brother's name?"

Linda gave a quick, self-conscious look over her shoulders, leaned forward slightly and said in a stage whisper, "He's that comedian. You know, the one that does game shows on the telly – Simon Stewart – the bleeding 'national treasure' and all that, if you know what I mean."

She smiled at him conspiratorially and closed the door tight shut.

As Guy pulled away from the kerb, a silver Audi A5 parked further up the street also edged slowly out and followed him. The male driver, a baseball cap pulled low on his head, dialled his mobile from the car's controls and reported that he was on the move.

FOURTEEN

Guy returned to his hotel in central Birmingham. It was now early Sunday evening and the weekend was drawing to its natural close. The automated voice in the lift announced its arrival at the twenty-second floor; he exited the doors and made his way down the carpeted corridor to the Arden suite, with its contemporarily decorated airy rooms and panoramic views over the city.

Having ordered supper from room service, he helped himself to a bottle of Malvern mineral water from the cocktail bar and picked up a hotel-branded notepad and pencil. Settling on the sofa with his feet up, he placed his iPad on his lap and connected it to the hotel wi-fi before looking up Simon Stewart on Wikipedia. There was a lot of information he was already aware of, but some of the detail added to his knowledge.

Simon had been born in the Aston area of Birmingham, and according to Guy's calculation, the stated birth date meant he was now forty-eight years old. Thirteen years older than Julie, which would have made him about twenty-nine when the pair fell out, if friend Linda had got it right. Simon was a struggling actor at the time, landing occasional roles in pantomime but little else. There was no mention of any siblings, but the page detailed how he'd crawled along the stand-up comedy circuit before he'd edged his way onto television and become a minor celebrity panellist some ten years ago.

A DVD of his live show recorded at the Alexandra Theatre in Birmingham a year or so later had suddenly attracted critical acclaim and it had rocketed up the chart as the must-have, all-time best-seller of its day.

In modern terms, it had gone viral. Simon had become a ubiquitous television host, fronting awards ceremonies and game shows until he devised, produced and presented the phenomenally successful quiz show, *Twist or Bust*, which had achieved global franchise sales. As well as making Simon Stewart extremely famous, it had also made him very wealthy.

Guy's research was disturbed by a knock on the door, and he roused himself from the sofa. A young waiter carried a tray into the suite – a supper of wild mushroom risotto, green salad and some Italian bread. Guy thanked the waiter, tipped him, and settled back on the sofa, juggling the warm plate and iPad before sliding back into the world of Simon Stewart.

Whilst Simon was busy getting rich with *Twist or Bust,* his wife, Sally Stewart, had become a television celebrity chef with her ground-breaking series, *Sally's Kitchen.* The celebrity couple was adored by society magazines and pursued by the tabloids, who rarely left them alone until they finally accepted that their twenty-five-year marriage was solid with no hint of scandal. *OK!* magazine had carried a sizeable feature on Simon and Sally earlier in the year to mark their anniversary, with photographs taken at both their London and suburban Birmingham homes.

As he finished his supper, Guy browsed some more sites but found nothing else of significance save that Simon was presently recording a new series of *Twist or Bust* at the BBC's studios in Birmingham. The amount of information that was so readily available on the internet never ceased to amaze him – although in this case, it seemed, not everything was there if Linda's comment had been accurate.

Guy leaned back into the sofa and closed his eyes to reflect and to plan. He was tired, though, and neither inspiration nor answers came to him. There was, however, another knock on the door. He snapped out of his reverie, placed the iPad on the square wooden table in front of him, and walked back down the hallway to the door. After peeping through the spy hole, he smiled broadly and opened the door.

"Hi, Soph," he said. "Great timing."

Sophie walked into the room and they exchanged kisses as she passed him. At a willowy five feet nine, she only had to lift her face slightly to connect. She was dressed in tight designer jeans, a plain cotton blouse and a pink cashmere cardigan, and carried a small, pink overnight bag. Guy inwardly admired her perfect model figure as she walked by and he took her bag from her.

"You got my text this afternoon, then, girl? You said you wouldn't need anything to eat – still the case? I could order something for you if you want."

He followed her through the hallway into the sitting room and placed the bag on the floor by a wall. Sophie looked at his empty plate on the floor by the sofa and said, "I'm fine, thanks. I had something earlier. I'll just have a glass of whatever you're having, please."

"Mineral water, ice and lemon."

"Sounds perfect, that'll be great. Thanks."

She stood and watched him fix her drink, taking it from him as he carried it over to her. "How was your day?' he asked, standing straight in front of her and looking into her deep brown eyes. He ran his hand through her long, brunette hair and then rested it gently on her narrow waist. He wanted the contact.

"Oh, you know," she replied with a jokingly weary sigh. "Mother and lunch, then a nap, then some housework, then a snack, then… then here. Is there no end to the excitement on a Sunday?" She paused, sipped her drink and placed it on the table next to Guy's glass. She stretched up to give him a kiss on the lips and squeezed his hand. "This is the best bit, though," she added and kissed him again. They embraced and held each other in silence for a few moments, their hands gently caressing, as if exploring for the first time.

"I'm looking forward to our week back in Shropshire, Guy," she said softly, as she stood with her face buried under Guy's chin. "It's actually been a hell of a week at work. The charity might want me to go back to Darfur in about a month to sort out issues from there. Early start tomorrow, right?"

Guy felt slightly guilty. He knew Sophie loved the work she did and was passionate about it, but she did need time out. They'd planned the week at Hofton a month or two back and he'd promised her several days of relaxation and pampering – and time together. He also wanted to put forward the plans he'd been working on for their long-awaited wedding.

He hugged her closer to him. "Could be a challenge, Soph. I've been brought into a new project here in Birmingham. I may need to spend some time here tomorrow."

"What project?" she said, pulling away slightly and looking up at him.

"I'll tell you, but I'd like you to get back to

Hofton and I'll join you as soon as I can. George is there and all the staff, so you'll be fine."

She frowned slightly. "That wasn't the deal, Guy. First thing on Monday, you said. I can go, but *you* won't be there. What's going on?"

"I'll be there as soon as I can – I promise."

It seemed to placate her. "So, what's the project?" she said, with an interested smile.

"It's complicated."

She grinned. "For me, a mere woman, to understand?"

"You know I don't mean that." He smiled back at her.

Sophie suddenly pulled back playfully but kept hold of his right hand. "Okay. How about a bath, then?" she said with a laugh, her tumbling hair dancing as she moved, animated and excited. "You can tell me all about your new project and what you've been up to today, *Sir Guy Sterling*." She stressed his name with mock importance, giving him an enormous grin and a flamboyant bow.

"Good idea," Guy said, enjoying the moment.

Sophie crossed the room, picked up her bag and carried it to the bedroom. Guy followed her, proceeding through to the marbled master bathroom where he filled the large bath, splashing in some bath foam. The room filled with relaxing scents and inviting warmth. As he bent over and stirred the water Sophie entered, naked, gathering her hair up into a crocodile clip as she walked. Guy turned his head and couldn't help but watch her. She was slim, toned and gorgeous.

"Bath ready, then, boy?" she demanded in a

deep, brisk voice.

"Nearly, ma'am," Guy said, and then he laughed and added: "Go on, get in, you."

Sophie stepped cautiously into the bath. Guy stripped, leaving his clothes in a careless heap on the floor, and also climbed in. They settled, legs intertwined below the surface, facing each other.

"So, lover," Sophie said. "What's been happening?"

Guy summarised everything that had happened since he'd been at David's club dinner just the evening before. He described his meeting with David, with Caroline Grant, and the highlights of his fledgling enquiry. He by-passed the run-in with Scarface – there was no need for excessive drama. Sophie listened intently, chipping in with the occasional concerned question.

"What does Superintendent Grant say about the Simon Stewart connection?" Sophie asked.

"Not actually told her yet."

"But shouldn't you?"

"Yes, that will be my parting gift tomorrow," Guy said. "She can wait to hear from me. After all, she says she has *far* better things to do with her time than talk to me – you know, *proper* police work."

"Naughty," Sophie said with a smile, and reached out and caressed his face with her fingers.

They finished their bath and dried off before meandering back into the bedroom wearing the hotel's soft white bathrobes. It was a relatively modest room with a modern black-and-white four-poster bed, illuminated by the comforting glow from one of the bedside lamps.

In bed, they touched and kissed and made love. It was romantic, gentle and very intimate.

Afterwards they lay together, Sophie resting her head on Guy's chest, her eyes closed. He twisted round to switch off the light, plunging the room into darkness, and Sophie turned to lie with her back to him.

"Love you," she said softly.

"More adventure tomorrow," he whispered with a slight laugh.

"I thought you were done with all that after the army," Sophie said sleepily. "But I'll support whatever you decide to do."

He kissed the back of her head. "I've already decided. You and our future come first. Nothing is going to jeopardise that – not the future, not the mystery of the past. You are my world – end of."

He kissed her again and settled down for sleep, spooned against her. Tomorrow he'd speak to David and return to his estate, to his own world, and start his future with the woman he loved knowing he'd done something to help David with his own challenges.

As Guy and Sophie fell asleep, the Audi driver was on his mobile. "Is that what Arman has instructed?" he asked, his accent betraying his Egyptian origins.

"Exactly that," the sniper said on the other end of the line in similar tones. "Can you do it?"

"Is the Pope Catholic? Consider it done."

"Ring me afterwards and I'll take the next step.

Don’t fail. Arman won’t like that.”

“Do you have PhD in stating the fucking obvious?” the Audi driver asked. “I call you.”

FIFTEEN

Guy was flying. Literally. He loved the way he could leave the ground at will with just the slightest movement of his arms. Those standing nearby always watched in awe and surprise. It was a great feeling. Now he was over London, the buildings and city streets some one hundred metres below, an azure-blue November sky above. He felt warm sun on his back and barely a whisper of cool breeze on his face.

Whitehall was filled with people – members of the public who lined the street, silently watching the military parade. The youths and pensive veterans who took part now stood to attention around the tall, Portland stone Cenotaph. The Prime Minister was laying a wreath in remembrance of the fallen, watched by senior members of the royal family, politicians, dignitaries and visiting representatives of various Commonwealth countries.

The explosions were sudden and dramatic. Several blasts in the heart of the gathering, ripping the heart from the nation. A huge fireball hurtled up towards him. He tried to turn, to avoid the searing heat, but lost the power of flight. He was falling, falling downwards to meet the terrifying flame rising fast towards him. He woke with a start.

The room was dark and Guy was lying on his back, his pillow damp with sweat. He glanced at the luminous digital clock on his bedside table, which told him it was 3.05am. He'd been asleep for just a handful of hours. To his right Sophie lay perfectly still; as usual, he could hardly hear her breathing. He recalled the first time they'd slept together when, with alarm, he'd woken her up due to his concern about the lack of vital signs. He searched for her hand and held it gently. She didn't stir.

The dream – the nightmare – that had woken him was familiar. A couple of years before he'd deduced it occurred when he was stressed and wound up – worried about something. And he knew its origins. Despite his efforts to resist, he returned in his mind to that bleak, bare room when the price for sweet victory was his darkest moment.

That room, with its concrete, windowless walls and two modern strip lights, was no more than some ten metres square and contained a single, macabre piece of furniture. The solid metal door was firmly shut, ensuring no noise could leave its confines. The barely conscious Moroccan was slumped in that piece of furniture – a chunky wooden chair in the middle of the floor. He was naked, his hands tethered to the chair's arms and his ankles strapped to its front legs. The chair itself was secured to the dusty lino-covered floor. Neither human nor object were going anywhere.

Guy took a couple of strides over to the man and studied him. His face was inflamed and bruised, with deep cuts and blood - both dried and fresh - covering his dark skin. His head was roughly shaved and there were razor nicks on his scalp and ears. Glancing down he noted the broken fingers, bruised torso and an unrecognisable mess between his legs. The man groaned, opened his eyes momentarily and then faded away.

Guy turned to his sergeant, a giant of a man standing close by. "He's better off out of it, Sergeant."

The sergeant nodded slowly. "It doesn't matter that he's unconscious now, does it, sir?" he said in a Devon drawl. "We have what we need."

"*If* he was truthful," Guy said.

"Do you doubt it?"

Guy shook his head gently, then exhaled loudly and slowly. "No, Sergeant. It doesn't take my experience to know that was the truth – he gave it up. No doubt, no doubt at all."

The door opened and a well-built, broad-shouldered man in his early fifties entered, immaculate in a colonel's uniform. His eyes lingered on the Moroccan before he looked at Guy. "The general's just come back to me, Captain. They're satisfied with what you've got. Apparently, it's the last piece of the jigsaw and fits in nicely. Everything else was worthless without a target, and you've got it."

"Thank you, sir. Wasn't straight-forward."

"So I see."

"Will it still go ahead?" Guy asked, brushing dust from the sleeve of his uniform.

"It can now. It had them all in a spin, though. Cancelling the ceremony would have been a victory for terrorism and a shock for the nation. The Prime Minister was hell-bent on going ahead, but we now know what the consequences would have been. Great work, Captain."

The colonel turned to leave, putting his hand on the worn doorknob. He paused and looked back at Guy before saying in slow, sincere tones: "What you did was the only way to protect what's precious to us, Captain. You do know that, don't you?"

Guy nodded, not looking at the Moroccan. "Of course, sir. We faced anarchy. The threat of losing the monarch, senior royals and the government required such extreme steps. I understand that, sir."

The colonel turned towards the sergeant. "And Sergeant – you follow that?'

"Of course, sir. It's why we joined the unit."

The colonel gave a half-smile. "Good man," he said.

"And now, sir?" Guy asked, indicating the prone Moroccan.

"Now?" the colonel said as he opened the door. "Now, I leave that to you. We can dictate the post-mortem report, if we need one." He paused before adding, "And I suspect we will need one, don't you, Captain? Better that way." He left the room, closing the door quietly behind him.

Guy stepped in front of the Moroccan who was breathing noisily, bubbles of blood foaming in his nostrils. "This animal would have killed so many people, Sergeant. So many important, well-loved people." He walked round to the back of the chair and stared down at the wretch. "I guess no one will ever know."

"We'll know, sir."

"Then it's our secret to keep." Guy seized the Moroccan's head and with one quick, twisting movement broke his neck. The crack seemed to vibrate and echo. "Accidents happen, Sergeant."

As he lay there in the dark, Guy could still hear that crack. It would haunt him forever. But that was army life and the role he had in it, he told himself. It was necessary then to protect his beloved country. Things were different now. The civilian world was a whole new place. The violence of that part of his life was history. An image of Scarface sitting by the fence nursing his broken arm suddenly crashed into his mind. That was self-defence, he thought. A one-off. He dismissed it.

He rolled onto his side, wrapped an arm over Sophie's narrow waist and tried to get back to sleep. Guy's final thought before dreams enveloped him was to recall that, less than a month after the death of the Moroccan, he had been promoted to major.

SIXTEEN

The morning was still fresh as Guy stood in his running gear at the window of the suite's sitting room. The pale dawn sky only just allowed him to see across the waking urban landscape. Far below, the odd car drove past as some early birds travelled to work ahead of the Monday rush hour.

As he finished his text and pressed the 'send' key, Sophie entered dressed in a light pink and white jogging suit.

Guy turned to look at her. "Is that new?"

Sophie smiled. "I'm going to take this jogging thing seriously. Try and keep up with you. It's not overly flattering though, is it?"

Guy took a few steps towards her and gave her a hug. "Looks great to me, especially knowing what's under the wrapping. I love it, and the contents." He stepped away. "By the way, I've just texted George at the manor. He'll meet you off the train in Shrewsbury."

Sophie nodded. "Okay. Time for the run. I've slipped a fiver in my pocket; I'll get you a paper on the way back."

"Thanks, you'll make a great paperboy."

"Girl."

"*Girl,*" Guy acknowledged, giving her a wink. "Which reminds me…" He moved towards her again.

Sophie recognised the look. *"No."* she said, with jokey firmness. "We promised ourselves we'd go jogging each day this week, so come on."

"But there's no eighth baronet yet."

"No need for one quite so soon," she said.

"I'd like to see a small one in waiting."

"Me too, but there's a wedding first, isn't there? That's what we said."

Guy nodded. "Of course. We need to get on with that." He picked up the room's key card and slipped it into a pocket. "Right, come on then."

They took the stairs rather than the lift, agreeing that they would probably need the easy option on their return. They set off up Broad Street at a gentle pace towards Edgbaston, running side by side. The pavement that ran alongside the shops, hotels and restaurants was still quiet at this early hour, although there were other running enthusiasts out and about.

For the next forty-five minutes they pounded along steadily, side-by-side, reaching suburban streets with a variety of modern and traditional houses and low-rise blocks of expensive apartments. The pavement was usually wide, the roads tree-lined. They rested together by a sign that declared this was Wheeleys Road, standing hands on hips, each taking a deep lungful of the morning air.

"There," Guy said. "You're doing pretty well. I'm proud of you."

Sophie smiled and nodded. "Guess I'm fitter than I thought – or maybe it's just this snazzy gear I'm wearing."

Guy leaned over and gave her a kiss. "It's all down to you. The gear just makes you look great – why do you think I sometimes run behind you?"

"Cheeky."

"Exactly…Ready? Race you to the next junction down there. After three – one, two…" And Guy took off down the pavement.

"Hey!" Sophie called after him. "That's cheating." She set off after him at jogging pace.

Guy sprinted to the junction, stopped and turned around. Sophie was at least a hundred metres behind, jogging slowly towards him.

"Come on," he called. "You can do better than that."

It was then his attention was caught by the car moving up the road towards the junction where he was standing. It was accelerating in a way that was quite excessive for the suburban street. He recognised it as a silver Audi A5 – sleek and powerful.

He felt uncomfortable. *What's that idiot driving like that for?* The noise of the vehicle and its high revs had attracted Sophie's attention, too. That was unsurprising; humans are wary of loud noises from birth, and this was very definitely out of place. Guy watched as Sophie paused, now about fifty metres away. She turned to look at the car, which accelerated even more. She started to step away from the kerb and towards the lawn of an adjacent red-brick house.

Then, to his horror, Guy saw the Audi mount the pavement. It was just ten metres behind Sophie – she had no time to move or protect herself. The car hit her full on, hurling her into the air and across its sleek windscreen where she bounced, all arms and legs. She fell off to the side, hitting the pavement hard and awkwardly. Guy almost felt the thud; he certainly heard it. The Audi pulled itself back on to the road with a jolt to test the strongest shock absorbers and shot past Guy as he started back down the pavement towards his fiancée. He looked at the car as it passed, but the windscreen, cracked and lined and crazed where Sophie had hit it, made seeing the driver difficult. His impression was that it was a male, but the balaclava the driver wore did its job effectively. The car wheeled left erratically at the junction and disappeared, but not before Guy noted its registration plate details. He ran to Sophie, who was lying still where she'd landed.

"Sophie! Are you okay?" he panted, kneeling beside her prone body.

She didn't stir. He felt on her neck for a pulse, crying out with relief when he found it. Weak, but definitely there.

A woman in her mid-forties, dressed in a nightie and dressing gown, came hurrying out of the red-brick house. "Is she okay?" she asked, concern in her voice. "I saw what happened. I was looking out of the front window. I've called the police and an ambulance."

"She's out cold, but she's alive," Guy said. "Have you got a blanket?"

"One minute." The woman hastily returned to her house.

Guy straightened a wisp of Sophie's hair, but didn't dare move her for fear of causing further injury. Her pink and white jogging suit was ripped and marked, giving flashes of grazed and dirty skin around elbows and knees. It was stained with blood in several places. She continued to lie utterly still, her eyes tight shut, her breathing very faint. More blood suddenly appeared, spilling out from under her head, mixing with her tangled hair.

"Come on!" Guy shouted, mentally begging the

ambulance to hurry. The woman from the red-brick house reappeared, carrying a blue blanket which she passed to Guy. He carefully threw it over Sophie and tucked it around her tenderly. Still kneeling, he asked the woman for more detail of what she'd seen, but she could add little that Guy didn't already know. Some other residents started to appear, attracted by the commotion and the sight of Sophie on the ground. They moved away respectfully on learning there was nothing they could usefully do to help.

A few minutes later a police patrol car arrived with two male officers, followed closely by an ambulance. Guy made way so the two paramedics could check Sophie over and gave some basic information to the police, including his and Sophie's identities, what he'd witnessed and the Audi's registration number. One officer wrote everything down in his notebook, while the other spoke to the woman from the red-brick house. Throughout, Guy glanced anxiously at the paramedics as they assessed and treated Sophie.

After what seemed to Guy to be little short of an eternity, they stretchered her into the back of the ambulance, an oxygen mask over her face.

One of the paramedics came over to where Guy was standing. "Are you her husband?"

"Fiancé."

"I'm sorry," the medic said. "But this is pretty serious. We'll take her to A&E at Queen Elizabeth's. You can ride in the back if you like."

Guy turned to the police officer. "I should go with her," he said, gesturing towards the ambulance with a slight roll of his head.

The officer nodded. "We have your details. We'll be in touch very soon."

In the back of the ambulance, Guy sat as close as he could to Sophie while around him the vehicle rocked as it made its way through the urban streets, the sound of its siren reverberating in his ears. One of the medics sat with them, keeping a constant eye on Sophie, who to Guy's eyes was deathly pale. *What was happening?*

He jumped as a text alert made his phone buzz. An unknown number. He opened the message and read thirteen cruel words: "*Sir Guy, let that be a warning. Don't interfere. We can do more.*"

SEVENTEEN

Late Monday afternoon found Guy in the intensive care unit at Queen Elizabeth Hospital, pacing restlessly. Other than giving a fuller statement to a visiting police officer in a quiet corner of the deserted waiting room, he had done nothing other than stride up and down the corridor and sit impatiently on well-worn NHS chairs. He couldn't face eating and had no wish to be anywhere other than as close to Sophie as the nurses would allow.

"Sir Guy?"

Guy looked up as a middle-aged male doctor he'd seen rushing about in his traditional white coat earlier entered the stark waiting room. He stood up.

"How is she?" he asked anxiously, his eyes scanning the doctor's clean-shaven face for any message.

"Please, take a seat," the doctor replied, sitting opposite him as Guy followed the instruction. The doctor leaned forward, arms resting on his legs, palms pressed together. "I'm sorry, Sir Guy, but it's extremely serious. She hasn't responded to certain treatments and we've been obliged to use propofol to put her into an induced coma to protect her brain from swelling and inflammation. It's a normal procedure, although not without risk, and it's going to plan so far. It's difficult to tell exactly how she is, but she does have a severe head injury – you must be ready for that." The doctor paused, his eyes never leaving Guy's face. "She's in good hands, I can assure you of that – we're very experienced at treating such trauma."

Guy sat back in his chair, his hands twisting in

agitation. "What's the prognosis, doctor? How long will she be in a coma?"

The other man sat back, shrugging slightly. "I wish I could tell you. She's certainly likely to be this way for several days. But we wouldn't induce for more than a couple of weeks, particularly as there is an increased risk of serious chest infection as her coughing reflexes are reduced. We are constantly monitoring her and will routinely reassess, but it could be weeks – maybe longer." He paused before adding, "Her left arm was fractured but, as you were told, we operated on that earlier. There should be no difficulties there. The cuts and bruises will heal, the one above her left knee will take the longest."

Guy was finding it hard to focus. "Will she recover?"

The doctor said nothing.

"Well? Will she?"

The doctor leaned forward. "Look, the effects of injuries such as these are notoriously difficult to predict. I really wish I could tell you more – indeed, I'd love to give you some encouraging and positive news – but I can't. There's no point in either raising your hopes or depressing you. It's a case of one day at a time. Sophie has a true fight on her hands, and we'll do all we can to help her win it."

Guy thought for a moment. "I understand, really I do," he said. "Can I see her?"

"Of course."

The doctor guided him through the intensive care unit, then respectfully stepped aside so Guy could enter the single room alone.

She was lying on her back under a cover, an oxygen mask strapped to her pale and bruised face. Her eyes were closed and her body was rigidly still, her left arm resting across her body in its recently fitted plaster cast. Guy was conscious of the medical machinery, of small coloured lights and tubes and bleeping sounds that gave life and positive reassurance in that warm, windowless room. But his attention was on Sophie. His heart went out to her and he fought tears as he saw her battered and pitiful state. He crossed over to the bed and gently touched her right hand, mindful of the cannula that was securely bandaged into a raised vein. It was this that allowed an infusion pump, set up on a nearby stand, to administer precisely metered doses of propofol.

"I'm so sorry, Soph," he said quietly, gently caressing her fingers.

He continued to stand there, watching her gentle breathing, ever conscious of the mechanical devices keeping her safe, even alive. "I'll be back," he promised, "and I'll bring you some news."

He kissed her softly on her forehead, gave her hand a final loving stroke and left the room.

A nurse was waiting in the corridor, clutching a white plastic carrier bag. She held it out to him. "Best if you take these personal things, Mr Sterling," she said.

As she turned, he thanked her and peered into the bag. On the top were remnants of the pink and white jogging suit. He took a deep breath, fought the tears and muttered, "Bastards."

*

Back in his hotel suite, Guy telephoned David Richardson and broke the news of what had happened. David said he had no idea and appeared shocked.

"This is dreadful, Guy. There's no reason for this hit-and-run to have landed on my desk," he said. "Those involved in investigating and reporting would have followed the usual channels. I can only assume you went to see Jonny Reid – was that it? It rather points to him after all, doesn't it?"

Guy reported his encounter with Reid the previous day, the subsequent trip to Aston to see Linda, and his discovery that Julie Reid's brother was Simon Stewart, the comedian.

"It's possible that Reid is responsible for Julie's death as a simple one-off, David, but having spoken to him I don't buy that, whatever Superintendent Grant might think. What we now appear to have is a choice of two – Jonny Reid and Simon Stewart. Both wealthy, both connected to Julie in line with your theory, and the matter causing angst to the Home Secretary. Everything tells me that Simon Stewart is the essential direction of travel."

"Can I ask what you're going to do?"

"Do? I'd have thought that was obvious, David. I decided yesterday to simply report in to Grant with an update and then leave you all to it. Not my fight, David, not my fight at all."

"You're not going to help?" There was obvious disappointment in David's voice.

"That was the case, but not now," he told his friend. "Now, I'm going to find out who's hurt my Sophie and, believe me, I'm going to hurt them. We have a common cause, David."

"But what about the threat – you know, the text you received?"

"Bring it on. Sophie is behind everything I do. By the time she comes round, by the time she's awake again, this will be sorted, believe me. Whatever it takes. You can take that to the bank, David."

EIGHTEEN

The next morning, it had gone eight o'clock before Guy was dressed. He'd endured a wretched and restless night alone in his hotel suite. He'd hugged and smelt the pillow that Sophie had lain on the night before and slept fitfully, waking often. He'd called the hospital soon after 3am, and again at seven. No change, he was told. He realised he was being unfair on the staff, but he needed to know.

His mobile rang, the name on the display showing it was Caroline Grant. He went to answer but changed his mind. There was something else he wanted to do before he spoke to her again.

Guy shifted the breakfast tray to one end of the glass dining table and set up his iPad. On searching for the BBC in Birmingham, he discovered its studios were in the Mailbox complex, not far from where he was staying. Picking up his mobile, he telephoned the reception number given on the web page. Introducing himself, he asked to speak to Simon Stewart.

"Mr Stewart? Is he expecting your call, Sir Guy?" the receptionist asked.

"No, no he's not. Is he available?"

"I'm afraid I can't say. Would you care to leave a message with his PA?" She sounded friendly and efficient.

"It's an easy one – just with you if I may, please. Will you ask him to call me as soon as he can? Tell him it's about Julie."

"Julie? Is that all? Will he know what you mean?"

"I believe so."

Guy gave her his mobile number and rang off.

*

It was about 11.15am when his mobile rang. Guy put the newspaper down on the floor, next to his cup of fresh coffee, and answered.

"This is Stewart. You rang me." Short and clipped.

Guy tried hard – and failed – to catch a hint of the popular, familiar voice from the television. No cameras, no media voice it seemed.

"We need to meet, Simon. This isn't a conversation for the phone." Guy waited. There was silence; Simon clearly needed time.

"Okay," he said eventually. "I'm in Birmingham. You?"

"Very close to you. Five-minute walk. Anywhere at the Mailbox that'll do?"

A pause, then Simon said, "Chamberlain Bar, seventh floor, ten minutes – I can give you five, max."

The line went dead as he rang off.

NINETEEN

Mailbox Birmingham, to give it its correct name, lies just off Birmingham's inner ring road, a long stone's throw from the city centre, and is the redeveloped Royal Mail sorting office. Formerly Birmingham's largest building, it's now a multi-purpose site that houses offices, designer shops, hotels and luxury apartments, as well as the BBC studios and a variety of upmarket restaurants and bars. It remains an impressive, distinctive edifice of modern glass and bright-red facing, reflecting its historic background.

As Simon only had to move between floors of the building, Guy was unsurprised to see he had already arrived and was seated at a remote table. The Chamberlain Bar was quite spacious with an open layout. It was also pretty quiet, so Guy was able to see and recognise Simon Stewart straight away from across the room – even though the celebrity was wearing casual jeans and a checked, open-neck shirt rather than one of the trademark loud suits for which he was renowned.

As Guy approached the table, Simon looked up from his *Daily Telegraph* crossword and at him with bright blue eyes. Guy noticed the man's face was devoid of the wit and humour with which he had made his name and fortune, and his well-groomed, dark brown hair held not even a hint of grey. Admittedly, that could have been thanks to science and the services of a good hairstylist rather than youthful genes. Despite exuding the supreme confidence of a successful man in the public eye, Guy could see a weariness underneath the façade that was working hard to erode the gloss.

Guy stretched out his hand, but Simon remained seated and studiously ignored the gesture. "Coffee?" Guy asked as he sat down opposite him at the small, cloth-covered table.

"I'm here to talk, not socialise," Simon said, placing his elbows on the table and resting his chin on his hands. His eyes never left Guy's face. "Does the name 'Arman' mean anything to you?" he asked.

Who was Arman?

"Nothing. I haven't a clue. Who is he?" Guy responded. His bewildered reaction must somehow have dealt with the query satisfactorily, because Simon sat back and folded his arms.

"Well," Simon continued. "Why are we here? What's this all about? Who's Julie?"

Guy showed no emotion as he said, "Your sister." His turn to observe the reaction to his words. A direct hit, if the look on Simon's face was anything to go by.

"Who are you?" Simon asked, eyes flicking rapidly over Guy's face.

"Someone who's trying to help. Have the police spoken to you?"

Simon looked impatient, almost annoyed. "Look, I don't know who the hell you are or what on earth you're doing," he said, "but you're not who I thought you were." He sat forward with both hands on the chair arms as if about to stand but remained seated.

"Who did you think I was?"

Simon said nothing.

"I'm not the police. I'm an ex-SAS major. Someone's asked me to help, get involved. I've seen some pretty rough stuff, done some pretty rough stuff come to that, and I'm on your side. You can trust me." He waited, but Simon's face remained blank. "Look, it was a professional hit, Simon. Cold-blooded and no mercy. This wasn't some Shakespearian crime of passion, there's a deeper, wider story here. Tell me then, what do you actually know about Julie's death?"

Still Simon said nothing, staring at Guy as if weighing things up. He relaxed his arms.

"I'm going to take a flier here, Simon. But it's based on some pretty firm foundations. Hear me out. You know, sometimes in life, we can't do things alone. I think you're trying to do just that. It's not a sign of weakness to get support now and then. Some people never seek it, some never have it offered. You're being offered it right now. A team is stronger than its individual parts. I can help you solve this – you are not on your own.' He paused, and then leant forward on the table. "I believe there's something more – I *know* there's something more. I've spoken to Jonny and he knows nothing, but that's not news to you, is it? *Is it*?"

Still no response. Just more staring.

"Jonny's bewildered, but you're not. You're solid; you have the aura of a man who has seen some, but not all, of the cards. For whatever reason, you're hiding something. Here, have this." Guy passed over his business card and placed it on the table in front of Simon. The comedian didn't even glance at it. "As I say, I can help you if you'll trust me. I can make this problem go away, but you need to let me in, Simon."

Suddenly Simon leaned forward to bring his face closer to Guy's. He looked thunderous, flushed. "I don't *need* to do anything, okay? Julie and I were estranged. She's been dead to me for years so what's just happened is irrelevant, right? You can just butt out, got it?" He stood up, sub-consciously straightened the bottom of his shirt, and started to walk towards the exit.

Guy turned towards him, placing his arm on the back of his chair for support. "Who did you think I was, Simon? A colleague of Arman's?"

Simon paused momentarily and then turned slightly to look at Guy. "I've nothing more to say to you." Then he left, swiftly, without a further glance back.

Guy was reassured. His experience told him he was right. Simon's body language had betrayed him, however hard he'd tried to contain himself. Sure, in his mind Guy had hoped the easy path would be taken, that Simon would open up and use Guy's shoulder to offload the sorry tale. At the least, he'd have liked an invite to a pity party where the depths of despair could be plumbed and examined. That hadn't happened, so Guy would have to up the pressure on Simon. A couple of memories flashed through his mind; darkened rooms, people suspected of such utter evil that even fiction-writers would discard them as too unbelievable; the Moroccan sitting lifeless in his chair. Force had been required then, but Guy reminded himself this was the civilian world. The military approach was in the past, and not required here.

As he sat on his own at the table, he reflected further. He had no other immediate leads, no one else to talk to. Linda in Aston had a large and ferocious gatekeeper, and probably little more to say in any event.

Going back to Jonny was out of the question and, in Guy's view, irrelevant. Without co-operation from Simon, there was nowhere else he could go right now unless he sought further information from Grant about the other deaths and used whatever the police had done to date. Not something he felt would be easy, but an image of Sophie drifted through his mind. He would do that for her, give and obtain an update, but ideally he wanted to work alone. The only real way forward was through Simon Stewart. He needed to talk further with him, extract information, through whatever technique was needed.

Then he noticed his business card had vanished.

TWENTY

Back in his hotel suite at a little after midday, having rung the hospital, Guy dutifully telephoned Caroline Grant. It wasn't what he wanted to do, but he owed it to David, and it was after all what he'd agreed to when the arrangement had been made on Saturday, just three days earlier. And, to be fair, Caroline had tried to call him. He paced the suite with his mobile.

"Grant here."

"Caroline, it's Guy Sterling. I thought we ought to catch up with each other." Guy attempted to be light, almost jovial, anticipating the usual hostile reaction. He didn't get it.

"Thanks, Guy. I tried calling you earlier. I was so sorry to have heard about your fiancée – how is she?"

He was taken aback by her friendly tone and concluded he'd been given the sympathy vote on this occasion. "No change, but thank you. It looks like it'll be a long process."

"I was going to let you know I'm being kept posted on the hit-and-run. The Audi was found burnt out. False registration, which actually belonged to a legitimate lorry. Officers are still working on it, though."

"And the main event? Have you spoken to David recently?"

"No, not recently," Grant said slowly, and Guy detected the slightest change of tone. "We interviewed Julie's friend, you know, the one she was staying with in Aston – a woman called Linda Wakefield. Nothing of particular interest there."

"What did she tell you?"

"As I said, nothing of particular interest. Nothing we didn't already know."

Guy sensed she was starting to clam up. "What about Jonny Reid?" he asked.

"Sure, Mr Arrogant. Two thoughts there. Either he's some sort of victim in the wider criminal activity we touched on with David, or this is a distinct and isolated incident in which he is more than heavily involved."

"You mean he had his wife shot? That's quite a statement."

"Wouldn't be the first time. Didn't you ever read any Agatha Christie? You may remember I told you on Sunday that when we went to his house in the morning there was some girl there about half his age who clearly hadn't just turned up for a late breakfast. Enquiries give the distinct impression she's not the sole focus of his affections, either. The amount of money he has slopping about will give him a variety of options, but then you'll know about that, of course."

Guy let it go and simply asked, "You re-interviewing him too?"

"Tomorrow."

"What about forensics from the flat in Bolton Street?"

"All clean," Grant said, "but then we know we're dealing with a pro."

Guy said, "I need to get home later today, Caroline, but I'll be back on Thursday. I'd like to visit the flat before I go – early this afternoon, if that suits."

"If you must," Grant answered. "I'll arrange for an officer to meet you there. I'll pre-warn them that

Sherlock's on his way." She gave him the address, which Guy wrote down with a shake of his head as he ignored her rudeness. "In the meantime, we're looking at all local CCTV for both the Tuesday and the previous couple of days as there's likely to have been some sort of reconnaissance."

"No point going back much beyond Monday if that's when Julie moved in, unless the actual decision to move was taken and communicated earlier."

"Exactly," Grant said. "And it raises an obvious question: how did the sniper know she was there?"

Guy paused by the suite window and gazed out across central Birmingham. There were a number of ways the sniper could have known – through Linda or someone local to her, through someone Julie had told, through being followed – or through Jonny.

"Anyone else on your list?" he asked.

"Not at the moment. Who've you got in mind?"

"Julie have any relatives?"

"Mother's long dead, father's in Glasgow. The two kids, obviously."

"Brothers, sisters?"

Grant paused and then said, "Don't think so. Seems to have been an only child. Jonny's down as next of kin. Why d'you ask?"

Guy realised he was facing a dilemma. How open was he going to be?

He said, "Just thinking aloud."

"So, how about you – any news or information?" It was said in a tone devoid of underlying interest. Grant clearly expected the answer to be 'not a lot'. It wasn't.

"I've met with Jonny –"

"Really?" An unguarded note of genuine surprise. "And…?"

"He may have a curiously detached approach to what's happened, but my instinct says he's not involved. He says it's just his way of handling it."

"Is that what he said? Well, there's a surprise. And you believe him?"

"Frankly, yes," Guy said, straightening a picture on the wall which to his mind was slightly crooked. "I've learned to trust my instinct. I've used it a lot, in the past. It's never let me down."

"Really? I think you're too trusting. I've learnt to be more sceptical. Heard too much during my career."

"Sounds like none of us is perfect. Well, you're entitled to your view, Caroline, but I don't share it. I also talked to Linda Wakefield –"

"And she spoke to you?" Grant interrupted, with further obvious surprise.

"Yes – that's how we managed to have a conversation, Caroline. What I've learned through both Jonny and Linda is that Julie had a brother, and a well-known one at that." Guy walked over to the sofa and sat down, resting his elbow on its arm.

"Not so well-known that it's common knowledge or readily available." Grant sounded defensive.

"True. By well-known, I mean that he's famous – one of our country's cherished celebrities. Simon Stewart, no less."

"You're joking!"

"I do joke, but not on this occasion," Guy said. "They've been estranged for about twenty years, since long before he hit the big time. I don't know what the fall out was about, but it led to them both effectively ignoring each other's existence completely. Treated each other as if they'd died. I've met up with Simon and talked with him –"

"Already? You've had a meeting?"

"Well, meeting may be an over-the-top description, but yes, we met up. In my view, Simon knows something – although he wouldn't say what."

Guy stood up and started to pace the room again.

"Maybe you're imagining it. If they've been estranged for that long there can be very little connection between them, certainly nothing for any third party to take advantage of – even if they knew about the relationship."

"Or maybe I'm not imagining it. I think you should speak to him too." Guy waited for the inevitable choleric reaction of kicking back on an instruction.

"Oh, so you think I should speak to Stewart?" Grant sounded almost offended. "Thanks for the advice. I think that would be another classic waste of time."

Right again. "Decision for you to make," Guy said, "but I would consider it a good use of your time – more useful than talking to Jonny again."

Grant's tone hardened. "Guy, this is my investigation, okay? I certainly won't be running it on the basis of your…advice. Now, is there anything else or can I tick the box on David's sheet to confirm we've spoken?"

"Tick away, Caroline. Just don't tick the box that confirms you've listened objectively and dispassionately to my update. That would be misleading, wouldn't it?"

He ran a hand through his hair.

"You just don't get it, Guy, do you? Your involvement is an unnecessary nuisance, a pain in the bloody neck, okay? I hear what you say, and I take the view you're barking up the wrong tree, so just let me get on with it – all right?"

"Of course. You get on with it to your heart's content and let me know whether Jonny cracks under pressure with a full and detailed confession. I somehow doubt it. Cheers, Caroline."

Grant muttered something, but all Guy caught before she rang off was a brief goodbye, in one form or another.

TWENTY-ONE

After a quick sandwich in the hotel, Guy drove to Bolton Street in Aston where he was shown the abandoned apartment by a CID officer, DC Baxter, who was waiting outside the damaged front door when Guy arrived. As he endured the damp and musty smell that pervaded the various rooms, Guy appreciated the choice of location as ideal for the murderous task that had been performed – its height, distance, positioning and anonymity were perfect. Well selected. Professional indeed.

DC Baxter, although not directly working on the investigation, shared Guy's view of the effectiveness of the location and confirmed that, as far as he knew, nothing of any investigatory use had been found there by forensics. Guy was however a little surprised by the young detective's slightly outspoken views of Grant as the officer leading the enquiry. He was evidently not optimistic of a successful outcome as he reckoned his boss was "overrated, having climbed the greasy pole by using her female attributes rather than any investigative ability." Guy tactfully avoided passing comment.

From Bolton Street, Guy called in at the hospital and spent half an hour at Sophie's bedside. He brought her up to date with what he had been doing and could only imagine and hope that, despite so little sign of life, she could, through some medical and human miracle, actually hear him.

By late afternoon Guy was well on his way home. He drove his AeroMax round the Shrewsbury bypass before turning south onto the A49, towards the rough beauty of Caer Caradoc and the Long Mynd hills. He slowed the silver sports car with gentle pressure on the brake pedal and, easing down the gears, took a minor, grey-asphalted lane, along which he accelerated quickly to the village of West Hofton. It was very straight and single-tracked, the stubborn remnant of a long-forgotten Roman road that cut through the valley floor centuries ago. But Guy didn't notice the views of his childhood; his mind was instead back in the Bolton Street flat. The open window, the distant garden, the conversation with DC Baxter. There was something sinister crouching in the place where an assassin had committed murder a week before.

A battered sign and a gnarled veteran ash tree marked the entrance to the village. Guy reached a shaded junction where, across the open green with its heavy lime trees and worn paths, stood the Sterling Arms pub, a black and white ancient affair with a riot of colour from many hanging baskets. The village had a late Tuesday afternoon stillness as Guy turned left and drove up the high street which, as it ascended, narrowed into a lane just wide enough for two careful vehicles to pass each other safely.

The houses thinned as the village reached its natural end and, ahead of him to his left, stood a small copse of oak trees through which emerged the driveway to the Hofton Manor estate. Guy steered the Morgan off the public road and into the wide entranceway, relaxing as it funnelled towards the pillared and arched gateway ahead of him, the Sterling family crest emblazoned on the apex. High stone walls ran either side, over which could be seen the quarried-slate roof top of the gate lodge and its twisted brick chimney. Guy slowed as he pressed the button on his key fob and watched the large and ornate wrought iron gates swing effortlessly inwards, revealing still further the open asphalt driveway and the vista of the estate.

As he drove through them, a youth emerged from the low wooden gate at the bottom of the path that lead to the lodge's white-painted front door. Guy slowed and brought the car to an idling stop, wound down his window and called out to the lad with a cheerful wave.

"Everything okay, Jack?" he asked. "Anything to report?"

Jack strode over and stood by the car. He was twenty-two years old, short in stature and mischievous-looking. He had closely-cut dark-brown hair and several tattoos on both forearms, prominently displayed thanks to the short-sleeved Shrewsbury Town football shirt he wore with baggy jeans and scruffy trainers. By employing him on the estate, including in his duties the care of the cars, Guy had without argument saved Jack from an increasingly self-destructive life of crime. The young man was blossoming.

"All's good, sir," Jack answered, a broad smile lighting up his face.

"Great," Guy said. "I'll catch up with you later." And he pressed the accelerator gently to take the Morgan into the estate.

Despite living here all his life, this part of the home-coming never failed to stir him. After a quarter of a mile of historic parkland, the driveway turned and took Guy between two magnificent cedar trees, and close to the gatehouse. The Elizabethan manor house was constructed of red brick with black wooden beam work in the prominent gables. Castellated and turreted in parts, its small, stone-framed windows glinted as the sun reflected off multiple panes of aged glass.

The principal drive led Guy through the gatehouse, with its symmetrical windows and Dutch gables, and into the large outer courtyard, lawned and treeless. A mere hundred metres took him through the low stone archway and into the inner courtyard around which the manor was built. Here he parked. Save for some well-manicured lawns and thin, colourful borders around the perimeter, the courtyard was gravelled. Its central focal point was an ornate fountain with two leaping and well-lichened fishes constantly spraying water from their open mouths.

He strode to the ancient front door, which opened ahead of him to unleash two animated black Labradors who greeted their master with unfailing adoration and boundless excitement. Guy wished he could share their love of life, but at that moment in time it was not as he'd planned, and action was required.

As Guy was arriving at Hofton Manor, the sniper lay on an unmade bed with a cheap burner phone pressed to his ear. The voice on the other end of the phone was deep – the same person who had instructed him to undertake the shooting of Julie Reid the previous week.

The deep voice said, "So he's definitely bitten, Mehrak?"

"No doubt," the sniper replied, a degree of relief

and pride in his voice. A job well done.

"Good. That's a large investment into the scheme, but it looks like it should bring lucrative returns. The next few days will tell."

"I believe so, Arman. But I'll keep a careful eye on this new investment, to ensure he maintains his side of the agreement."

"And if he doesn't?" Arman asked, checking the sniper had taken everything on board.

"Then he's finished," the sniper said, simply. He paused and added: "But I suspect I'll take the view he's finished anyway."

"I like the way you're thinking," Arman said. "It may give us both some entertainment."

TWENTY-TWO

After a decent cup of tea, Guy left the manor through the east wing and walked down the back drive to the stable block, which lay to the south-east of the house and adjoined the south garden. Built at the same time as the manor house on a quadrangle design, the stable block had originally contained a brew house, but most of these buildings had fallen into serious disrepair by the mid-1900s. Guy's father had set about the restoration with relish, converting the ailing stables and abandoned lofts into a magnificent multi-garage, workshop and small leisure complex consisting of an indoor swimming pool and gym. The two large, white-faced clocks with their black Roman numerals, set on either side of the stubby brick tower above the entrance arch, now each displayed the correct hour and, after many years of conflict, finally moved in unison.

Guy walked through the quadrangle and had almost reached the swimming pool door when it opened ahead of him. A giant of a man dressed in blue overalls appeared, making even Guy look small. Despite his oily clothing, he had a composed demeanour and erect posture. His dark hair, with its slight hints of grey, was neatly cut and correctly gave the impression that he was ex-army; indeed, he had been Guy's sergeant in the SAS and HUMINT. They shared the truth about the Moroccan's death. George had followed Guy out of the army to become the estate's handyman and take care of security.

"Good afternoon, George," Guy greeted him. "All well with you?"

George stopped and seemed to be pulling his thoughts together, a serious face replacing his customary smile. "Welcome home, sir. I got your messages. I'm so terribly sorry – how is she?" His voice was deep with its Devon drawl.

Guy updated George on recent events as they stood in the quadrangle, the sound of doves flapping and calling above them as if a late-summer normality was trying to fight its way through the sudden turbulence.

"How long are you stopping, sir?"

"Just a couple of nights, George. I have an essential trustees' meeting here tomorrow, so I'll return to Birmingham on Thursday. There's something I need to collect in any event, which only I can do. Betty's done me some supper."

"Good, she said she would. It's strictly her day off today of course, but she said she'd sort something out before going to visit her brother."

"I really appreciate that." Guy paused. "I've had a text from my sister, Lucy. She's threatened to visit – thinks I need some support or something. It's very sweet, but not really necessary. She'll be here sometime on Thursday, just her. I've told her I won't be here, but she was always the stubborn one of the three. Ruth would have taken my hint, but there we go. Let Betty know will you, George? Now, I'm off for a swim and some time in the gym."

As he swam lengths in the warm pool, Guy's thoughts returned to the death of Julie Reid and the work he'd undertaken at David's request in the face of Grant's strong opposition. In his mind he ran through key names and characters – Julie and Jonny Reid; the mystery teenager seen by Grant at Reid's house; the Aston friend, Linda Wakefield; the evasive Simon Stewart. And who was the 'Arman' Simon Stewart had mentioned? He realised how far he was from identifying those behind both Julie's death and, apparently, several others. He reminded himself he'd need more information from Grant or David about the earlier deaths if he was to explore those avenues.

Later in the gym he followed the programme set by his trainer and noted that on almost every piece of equipment he had to reduce the weights. George had evidently been exercising earlier, which came as no surprise. He recalled how, as Guy's sergeant, George had started every morning with an early gym session – he was one of the fittest men Guy knew. His physical abilities, together with his courage, guile and unquestionable loyalty, had made him an easy candidate to lead security on the estate and generally help out.

It had just turned eight o'clock as Guy finished the Betty-prepared supper, which he ate at his desk in the study. Save for the security room with its practical furniture and high-tech equipment, this was perhaps the most modern room in the manor. The mid-Victorian, mahogany, twin-pedestal desk and leather Chesterfield chair – the pride of Guy's grandfather – had been respectfully re-located to the Sterling library, to be replaced with contemporary furniture and the necessary electronic trappings of the 21st century office. Two large sash windows, simply draped, looked out to the west and the rising parkland of the estate. Guy loved the room for its contrast, its summer evening light, and the solitude it afforded him when he needed it.

He had spent some time over supper on his computer, researching. He Googled Caroline Grant and picked up various articles where her exploits as a detective were recorded. He found her profile on both LinkedIn and Facebook. She appeared to have risen quite spectacularly through the ranks. Recalling DC Baxter's comments earlier that day, if she was overrated, which seemed to fit Guy's experience of her, then her rapid promotion could point to a bigger story. Now, though, Guy viewed that more as gossip than of information with any practical value.

He stretched his arms out, yawned and stood up. The wall opposite was lined from floor to ceiling with beech shelving, all filled with contemporary books; a range of novels, biographies and travel guides. He walked over to the left-hand side, knelt, and removed about thirty centimetres of books in a single wedge from a low shelf. Placing them carefully on the thick, cream carpet, he looked at the resulting gap. The wall behind was decorated in the same lightly patterned wallpaper as the rest of the room. Guy pressed his fingers gently on the rear of the shelf and heard the familiar click as a section of hinged wall swung outward by about a centimetre. He pulled the door fully open, revealing a traditional safe door with a central dial lock.

Guy twisted and turned the dial in compliance with the pre-set code, until the door popped open and a light came on in the safe cavity, which was no bigger than an average microwave oven. This was one of three secret safes in the manor. Guy stretched his hand over some documents, cash and a couple of passports, and withdrew a compact and lidded cardboard box, which he placed on the floor. He closed the safe, replaced the books and returned with the box to his desk. Other than the trustees' meeting, this is what he had come back to the manor for. Seated at the desk, he opened the box and took out the dark Glock 17 Gen 4, leaving a silencer and ammunition in the container. He had been delighted that, shortly before he gave up his commission, the British army had bought these models to replace the older, heavier Browning 9mm. Strictly speaking, this particular Austrian-manufactured pistol, whose frame, magazine body and various components were made from specially-formulated plastic more resilient than most steel alloys, still belonged to the army. Evidently, though, the quartermasters hadn't missed one from the 25,000 or so pieces originally purchased.

Semi-automatic, with each larger magazine carrying up to thirty-three nine-millimetre rounds, Guy admired its performance and checked it over. He had it 'on loan' from the army for his own defence; at least that's how he saw it. He smiled – yes, he was still the Maverick who did not follow all the rules, but enough of them, and publicly enough, to get where he wanted to be. Maybe one day he would return it. He'd certainly never envisaged using it as an aggressor. But then he hadn't expected to find himself in his current position.

With his elbows on his desk, he aimed the weapon at a vase on the mantlepiece, knowing its three safety mechanisms would prevent any discharge. Once those were removed, however, it would be a different story.

TWENTY-THREE

On Thursday morning, Guy stood in the Great Hall of Hofton Manor and put on his green Burberry jacket. He noticed that one of the trustees from the previous day's meeting had left his hat on a side table. The grandfather clock in the corner of the room struck ten with its traditional solemnity.

He could hear Betty clearing away the late breakfast in the small dining room used by the family when there were no guests. He'd missed the traditional English breakfast while abroad, although its return now meant he would have to spend extra time in the gym.

He walked to the doorway of the small dining room and leant in. Betty paused and looked up, wiping her hands on the front of the white apron she wore neatly over her grey uniform.

"Thanks for the breakfast, Betty – as good as ever. And thanks again for looking after the trustees so well yesterday – best sandwiches in the whole of Shropshire."

Betty beamed. She had a very friendly face and took great pride in her appearance, as reflected by her perfectly set grey hair. "Any news from the hospital, sir?"

"No, but thanks for asking. As of this morning, no change at all," Guy said. "It's going to be slow progress, but we'll get there, I'm sure of it."

Guy returned to the Great Hall. Betty had always been in his life. Now in her sixties she'd joined the manor staff as a maid some forty years before, taken on by his late grandmother shortly before she died. Betty had married an older village man, Len, a couple of years later and they'd lived in one of the cottages on the estate. Len became the estate's odd job man and occasional chauffeur. A widow for the past ten years, Betty had opted to take some staff rooms in the manor and quietly got on with her duties with dedication. She always seemed to be in good humour and was an extremely popular figure in the neighbourhood, often spending time caring for her disabled brother in West Hofton.

Guy summoned his two black Labradors, flicked his tweed cap onto his head and stepped out of the ancient, oak front door. There was a promise of warmth in the air and the sky appeared to be clearing of some scattered white cloud. He stepped up the pace and strode after his Labradors as they trotted ahead with all the assured determination and controlled enthusiasm only contented large dogs can display.

Once out into the parkland, Guy picked up a short stick from the long grass and, gaining his dogs' undivided attention, launched it like a boomerang far into the air. The dogs ran in a frantic race for their quarry. In their temporary absence, Guy turned and looked back at the impressive manor. A vision of Sophie completing that day's crossword, her legs folded beneath her, passed through his mind and brought him back to reality. She wasn't there.

The dogs returned with their stick, dropping it duly at his feet. He could not resist the way they stared so intensely at their new toy so he bent down, picked it up and hurled it again as far as he could. They set off, and he followed slowly.

His mobile rang and he took it from his jacket pocket – a withheld number. He answered simply, "Guy."

"Guy Sterling? This is a humbled man ringing with a huge apology. This is also a very desperate man. It's Simon Stewart here."

The name brought Guy to a sudden halt and he felt a twist of excitement in his stomach. This was out of the blue, totally unexpected.

"Simon, good to hear from you. No apologies necessary, none at all," Guy said jovially, empowered by the thought that the brick wall might be starting to crumble.

There was some hesitancy in Simon's voice. "That's very generous, Guy, but I regret they are. I was extremely rude to you a couple of days ago. I realise now you were trying to help, and I slapped you in the face – metaphorically speaking, of course."

The voice was distinctive, more like the Simon Stewart Guy knew from the television. Guy had a sudden mental image of a press photograph he'd seen from a couple of months back – Simon striking one of his trademark poses outside Buckingham Palace after receiving his OBE from the Prince of Wales.

Simon continued. "You know about my connection with Julie – not many do, so you've found that out. You're not a policeman, and you seem a decent, honest sort who wants to help for some reason."

"I'm looking into Julie's death, but, as I said to you, I think there's a bigger picture, Simon."

"I don't know about that. I want a further meeting with you. Soon as you can. I see from your card you’re based in Shropshire.”

“That’s correct. But happy to travel – where are you?”

“Four Oaks, edge of Birmingham. I’ll text you the address.”

“Why the change of heart, Simon?”

“I’ll tell you when we meet, if I don’t change my mind. But something awful’s happened, and I don’t know where else to turn.”

TWENTY-FOUR

It was turning twelve forty-five when Guy locked the Morgan and strode across the driveway towards the imposing Queen Anne house. It had been an easy drive to the affluent Birmingham suburb. The deep-red front door swung open ahead of him and Simon Stewart, dressed in casual jeans and open-necked shirt, stood there. He welcomed Guy with a firm handshake.

"Great timing, Guy. You found us all right, then?"

"Satnav did all the work."

Guy followed his host into an impressive hall and through to a large drawing room, opulently furnished, with wide French windows that looked out onto a sizeable lawn and secluded, well-kept garden.

Sally Stewart rose from a deep sofa, part of a seating arrangement that formed three sides of a square in front of an open fireplace, currently protected by a wood-mounted, tapestry screen. Guy crossed the room to shake her hand. He knew from his morning's research that she'd just turned forty-four but was shocked to see up close that she looked some ten years older. Beneath the short blonde hair he expected to see the bubbly personality from the television screen, seen cheerfully cooking in her famed rustic kitchen. Instead, even professionally-applied make-up couldn't disguise the fact Sally had recently been crying.

"Welcome, Guy. So good to meet you. I hope you're the answer to our prayers." Her voice was quiet, sincere, but with a quiver of emotion.

"I do hope so. What a beautiful spot you have

here."

"It's our bolthole. Grab a seat," Simon said, motioning towards a sofa as he joined them in front of the fireplace. They all sat, each taking a separate side of the three-quarter square, and Simon continued while Sally poured coffee from a pre-set tray on the low central table. "We have our place in London and a villa near Florence; however, this is away from the pressures of the capital and convenient for when I'm recording in Birmingham, which has been quite frequent of late. Sally's focus is really London, sometimes Salford, and she's here when she can be. The neighbours leave us in peace and there are a couple of quiet pubs nearby – so what more do we need?" he added with a weak smile.

"Our family," Sally said suddenly, answering Simon's rhetorical question.

"Of course. Our family – goes without saying."

"But shouldn't…"

Guy heard a slight edge in Sally's voice. "What's happened?" he asked.

Simon and Sally glanced at each other. Guy detected a degree of uncertainty.

"We have two children," Simon said, throwing a further quick glance at Sally.

"Freddie and Jenny," Sally added. "The photo up there was taken about two years ago by Carlos Gray."

Guy recognised the name – a leading London photographer and first choice for the wealthy. His recent official portraits of the monarch and senior members of the royal family had won much critical acclaim.

He glanced up at the large family photograph that hung proudly above the white Adam fireplace.

Simon and Sally were seated on simple armchairs, holding hands and beaming at the camera with professional smiles. To the left, seated on the arm of his mother's chair and with his left arm stretched around the back of it, was Freddie. He was a handsome lad with his father's good looks and fair hair inherited from his mother. He looked confident and self-assured, a hint of a smile on his lips.

On the right of the shot was Jenny, mirroring her brother's pose. Strikingly beautiful, she had long, curly dark-brown hair that reached well below her shoulders, and deep-brown, almost black, eyes. She had an innocent, delightful smile. The whole family looked relaxed and at ease with a shared closeness, a love that had been expertly captured by the photographer.

"Freddie was eighteen and Jenny sixteen," Sally said, nodding towards the picture.

Guy responded, "It's very fine. What's Freddie doing nowadays?"

"Drama at Warwick," Sally replied. "He loves it, although I'm not sure how much time he spends actually studying. Seems to have a new girl in tow every time we see him. Still, he's happy and that's all I care about."

Simon nodded and stared straight ahead.

"How often do you see him?" Guy asked.

"Not that often, to be honest. He and his new flame, Emma, were here very briefly over the summer and have now gone to Thailand for a week or three. We'd obviously like to see more of him, but we're the aging, uncool parents. Our work schedules have been pretty hectic, too, which hasn't helped. I've been recording a new series of *Sally's Kitchen* in London and

Simon's doing *Twist or Bust* in Birmingham. We don't see much of each other, if it comes to that."

"That's why we're still married," Simon said, and threw his wife a brief grin. She tried to smile back, but clearly wasn't in the right frame of mind.

Guy said quickly, "So, tell me about Jenny."

"That's why I've rung you," Simon said.

"She's eighteen now," Sally said. "She did her A levels this summer at Cheltenham Ladies – she was head girl, you know. She did pretty well and has a place at Oxford to read German and Spanish – she's always been good at languages…" Sally's voice tailed off and she took a tissue from the sleeve of her pink cardigan. Tears formed in her eyes.

Simon stepped in. "Look, here's the thing. Jenny's gone missing. She hasn't come home and we're deeply worried. She hasn't been gone long, but it's completely out of character."

"Tell me more," Guy said, leaning forward.

"Jenny and I are very close. She talks to me – probably more than to Sally, to be fair. Always been a bit of a daddy's girl has our Jenny. She decided to get casual work after school before starting at university this autumn. She based herself here and I think she quite liked being at home again after having boarded for so long. She had always been a good girl, Guy."

"Had?"

Simon glanced at Sally, who was wiping her nose. "Yes," he said. He paused for a beat before adding, with more than a hint of irritation: "Until Sergio came on the scene." He started to drum his fingers on the arm of the sofa.

"Sergio?"

"I believe he's her first serious boyfriend, if you get my meaning. He's twenty-nine and a bit of a wide boy, to be honest. She got a job in this restaurant in Birmingham, the Latin Rose, and met him there. Not a lot we can do about it as she's eighteen – eighteen for Christ's sake, and he's almost bloody thirty. It's not right. He's all over her, and she seems to have fallen for him completely. Sally and I have both warned her, but you know what teenagers are like – they know it all, don't they? She's always been a bit headstrong, doesn't take advice easily. We had him checked out and he's got form. Drugs."

Sally said, "That was at least ten years ago, Simon."

The defensive comment clearly irritated him further. "Sure, Sal – ten years since he was last *caught*. Who knows what he's into now? We've heard about these parties, Guy. Not good, especially for impressionable, un-streetwise girls. She tells us something about them when she gets back. 'I'm sure you did the same thing at my age, Dad,' she says. As it happens I didn't, but that doesn't matter. It's her we care about, that's all that matters."

Guy looked at them both across the low table. "And now she's missing," he said. "Tell me what happened – when did you last see her?"

Simon stood up and walked across to the French windows where he stood with his hands in his pockets. Staring into the garden, he said, "Not seen or heard from her since yesterday morning…"

"One day, five hours and twenty-three minutes

ago," Sally interrupted.

Simon glanced at her, gave a gentle nod and said, "Quite so. She left here yesterday morning to go to her restaurant job. The manager says she was there all day and left about eight o'clock in the evening. She told us she'd be back this morning as she had this party to go to last night – with bloody Sergio, of course. She made the party, that we know, but she's not been seen since. She usually sends one of us a text when she's out, but we've had nothing."

Guy said, "Have you called the police?"

"No, not yet. We've called you. You see, she didn't come home this morning when she said she would. I was here, Sally was out. Despite her absences, she always tells us when she'll be back, even if it's in three days' time. She's always faithful to that – or at least she rings us if there's any change. She knows we worry about her – well you would, wouldn't you? Do you have children, Guy?"

"No, not yet." Guy shifted on his seat to get more comfortable. "What efforts have you made to contact her?"

Simon said, "We tried her mobile, but no answer. Switched off or something. I've been round to Sergio's place in Moseley this morning, grim as it is, and got what I could out of him."

"Where was the party?"

Sally blew her nose and Simon glanced at her before continuing. "At Mike Burns' place."

"Mike Burns?" Guy said, finishing his coffee with a final tip of the china cup. "The entrepreneur?"

"Do you know him?" Simon asked.

"Well, I met him for the first time last Saturday as it happens, at some dinner. So I only know him a touch."

"Big around here, is Mike Burns. Mainly property development as well as other sidelines – like his sand and gravel company. That's how he got himself started. Not the easiest of guys to be with. You may have found that."

"Meaning?"

"I also met him once. He came up the hard way. A successful businessman, I guess, but did seem to have a fairness about him, to be just. A lot of hangers-on, of course. Millions in the bank – bottom end of The Times annual rich list. Sixty, seventy million –"

"Seventy-five," Sally interjected.

"Yeah, something like that. Still, he had a party last night and Sergio and Jenny went to that. He's got some big place the other side of Tamworth from here – rural it is, very rural."

Guy got to his feet and stood with his back to the fireplace, hands clasped behind him as if warming himself in front of a blaze.

He looked at them both and said, "So, who did she leave with? Sergio?"

"Who else?" Simon said.

Guy looked straight at him across the room. "So presumably they went back to Sergio's place?"

"No, and this is where I get very angry…"

Sally looked up at him. "Simon…"

"Well, really. He told me they had this row in the car, that she hit him and forced him to stop on some godforsaken country road. She gets out and he drives off. *Drives off.* Who leaves an eighteen-year-old on a country road at frigging three in the morning?"

"Simon!" Sally said sharply.

"Sorry. But who would?" Simon paused as if taking a mental breath. "He claims he turned round after five minutes and went back for her, but she wasn't there. Claims he looked and looked. He says he thought she was, and I quote, 'pissing him about' so he just went home. *Home.* Didn't even bother to find her this morning – seemed to have a bloody hangover. So it was down to us poor parents to try to sort it out when she didn't come home as promised. Bloody idiot he is."

Guy swept his hand through his hair. "So why haven't you contacted the police?" he asked, noting a further exchange of swift glances between them.

"Because they're always bloody useless, and we don't want the avalanche of publicity," Simon said. "From what I know about the police, they'll tell us where she's not rather than where she is. You know, 'She's not at Burns' place' or 'She's not at Sergio's flat' or 'She's not on the bloody country road' – I don't want to know where she's *not,* I want to know where the fuck she *is*."

"Come on, Simon," Sally said. She turned to Guy. "That's why we contacted you, Guy. We need something to happen. We want to find our baby. The police would say we should launch a public appeal and we will do that soon, but the publicity won't be good for us."

"But surely the priority is her safety?"

"Of course it is, Guy," Sally said. "We're friends with Laurie Whittall – you know, the publicist – and we talked to him this morning. His advice is not to go public yet – make it a last resort. Await developments. Publicity could attract the wrong attention, he said, could put Jenny at risk."

"With respect, I'm not sure I agree with that," Guy said. "Personally, I'd get an appeal out and get photos round. Use the Missing People charity, for example. Still, it's your call until the police are involved, I guess."

Simon said, "You're the compromise, Guy. Discreet enquiries, no fuss. We want your full attention – will we get that?"

"Of course," Guy said. A thought struck him. "What about friends?"

"How do you mean?" Simon asked.

"Well, could she be with a friend now? Could she have called someone from the roadside?"

"She would have rung and let us know by now," Sally said. "Besides, most of them are old school friends, living at home and at least an hour or two down south. I've put in some subtle calls to her best and closest friends and asked for discretion, but nothing."

"We can only think of a couple of close friends living locally and neither know anything," Simon added.

"Okay, park that for now," Guy said. He paused; it was time for progress. "Now, can I see her room and have you got a recent photo? I'll also want details about Sergio, the restaurant and Burns' place. I can assure you that I'm going to find her – and bring her home safe."

"Promise?" Sally asked.

"Promise – and I keep my promises, all of them."

TWENTY-FIVE

Sally stood up. She offered to find a photo of Jenny and jot down some details while Simon showed Guy their daughter's bedroom. Guy followed Simon up the magenta-carpeted staircase to a wide landing, and then down a short corridor to a door that bore a childish wooden sign that read *Jenny's Room*. Simon paused a few moments as if summoning up some emotional courage, and went in.

It was an unremarkable room. Although large enough for a double bed, there was just a neatly made single with an array of teddy bears and stuffed animal toys around the pillow. The room was tidy and very feminine with a lingering smell of girlish scent. Simon picked up a small white teddy and studied it, lost in thought.

Guy said, "Simon, I'm obviously sorry Jenny's gone missing. I'm sure she'll be home soon. But you haven't said any more about Julie, nor explained your reference to 'Arman'. I won't pull my punches – is this awful development linked to that?"

Simon continued to look at the teddy, turning it in his hand as if he hadn't heard Guy's question. Finally, without looking up he said, "I've nothing to add, Guy. It's out of character for Jenny. Just find her. We'll pay whatever fee you want."

"Come on, Simon. I'm not police – that's the whole point. I can do things they can't and, unlike them, I'm not bound to set off chain reactions."

Simon stared up at Guy. "Just find our Jenny," he said slowly and firmly. And with that he placed the teddy gently back with its friends and turned to the door to leave. Guy moved swiftly ahead of him and closed the door.

"Sit down, Simon," he said firmly.

Simon looked almost shocked at Guy's actions. Slowly, more as a statement than a question, he said, "I beg your pardon."

"It's simple, Simon. I said sit. I mean it. I'm willing to help Sally and you, but you're damn well going to hclp yoursclvcs, too. And that means opening up."

"I don't know what the hell you mean," Simon said, his face turning red. A man of wealth and influence, he was used to ordering around countless lackeys who obeyed without question – and who certainly didn't tell him what to do instead. "Out of my way." He made to move past Guy.

"Shall I ask Sally to join us?"

Simon stopped. "Leave her out of this," he said forcefully, glaring angrily at Guy.

"As I thought," Guy said. "She doesn't know, does she?"

"Know what?"

"Whatever it is you know."'

"Which is?"

"About the threats from Arman," Guy said. He held Simon's stare and remained blocking the doorway.

Simon said nothing. He just crossed his arms and looked at Guy. For a second Guy thought he'd pushed him too far, but he wasn't going to back down. This was his game, his rules. Simon's body language alone told him there was more to be disclosed, and once again he was going to follow his instinct.

Simon began to relax, then stiffened. "For Heaven's sake, find our Jenny, Guy," he pleaded.

"I gave Sally my word that I would, Simon," Guy reassured him. "But I need to know what you know."

Simon nodded. "I've nothing more to say, now move, please."

Reluctantly Guy stepped aside, realising he was not going to open up Simon just then – but he felt he had progressed. "You're not helping anyone here, Simon, but I'll do it the hard way if that's what it takes."

Simon opened the door, and silently left.

Guy turned and swept the room with a final glance before he followed Simon downstairs. Sally was in the hallway.

"You two seem to have had a good natter," she said, as she handed the collated information and photograph of Jenny to Guy.

Guy thanked her with a smile. "Helpful to discuss matters," he said. "I'll be in touch."

He left the house with a steely determination to find Jenny and bring her home, not doubting for a moment that this was all somehow linked with what he'd got involved with in the first place. The picture might be bigger, but the goal was the same.

TWENTY-SIX

Guy decided to stay locally, rather than return to the centre of Birmingham. He booked into Sandbrough Hall, a former Georgian mansion that had recently been converted into a luxury country house hotel. It was located between Lichfield and Birmingham and gave extensive views across the Staffordshire countryside, including the spires of Lichfield Cathedral in the far distance.

Before he unpacked, he sat down in one of the armchairs in his suite and telephoned the hospital in an all-too-familiar way to ask for an update. No change. As he closed the conversation, he took the sheet of paper Sally had given him out of his pocket and found the mobile number he wanted. Following her handwritten digits, he dialled it, holding the phone to his ear for several rings before it was answered.

"Yeah?" The male voice was sharp, impatient.

"Is that Sergio?" Guy asked briskly. Who else would it be?

"Who wants to know?"

"Someone who hears he may be interested in a well-paid job – cash."

The magic word – the bait on the hook that never failed.

"And who's that?" A hint of suspicion.

Guy said firmly, "I asked if that was Sergio."

"And I said, who's asking?"

Guy said, "No matter. I've obviously got the wrong number. Sorry to have bothered you." *This is my game and you will be the fish on my line.*

"Hang on, mate. This is Sergio. And you may have heard right about my interests." The voice of someone backing down.

"Sure now?"

"Sure. What's it all about?"

"My name's Sam, Sam Granger, and I want to meet you. You home later?"

"Might be." Sullen again.

"Look, Sergio. I haven't got time to waste here. Are you in the market or not?" Guy spoke in an intolerant tone. "If not, just say – I've got a second name, but I was told you're good." An opportunity always looks more attractive when it's going away.

"Who gave you my name?"

"I'll give you all the details when we meet."

"So who was it?"

"I'll give you all the details when we meet."

Pause. *This is my game*.

"What the hell. Okay," came Sergio's resigned response. "I'll be at my flat from eight tonight. Want the address?"

"I've got it already – Moseley, right?"

Pause. That had taken him by surprise.

"Yeah – Moseley," came the slow reply.

I win, the fish has landed. "That's sorted, then. See you at eight-thirty, Sergio. One chance only. Oh, and Sergio…"

"Yeah?"

"Don't piss me about."

Guy rang off. *Game over*.

TWENTY-SEVEN

It was almost dark that Thursday evening, just coming up to eight thirty, when Guy reached Moseley. He had left his AeroMax at the hotel and, on Simon's recommendation, had contacted a hire car company in Sutton Coldfield. He now drove a blue Ford Mondeo. Guy had a soft spot for this workhorse of the road but, more importantly, knew it would attract less attention than the Morgan. There was also less chance of it being traced back to him. He had a feeling this wouldn't be a smooth meeting, not least because Sergio was expecting some kind of lucrative financial deal, and not an interrogation about his missing girlfriend.

In its day, Moseley village had been divided from the city of Birmingham by extensive farmland, but its many large, Edwardian houses now indiscernibly formed part of the conurbation. As the twentieth century wore on, the owners of those elegant dwellings had found them expensive to maintain and the in-coming working population, together with growing numbers of students, had provided a new market that led to many of them being converted into flats. A serious drop in Moseley's standing followed, coupled with a significant increase in crime ranging from car theft and burglary to violent disorder and prostitution. The new century had been kinder as the suburb recovered some of its former reputation, but its northern end was, in the main, still poor and deprived.

Guy turned into Stenham Hill Road, one of Moseley's more northern streets. He drove slowly, neck craning as he looked through the windscreen and side windows trying to identify house numbers. He quietly cursed that the numbers were placed erratically – sometimes on a gate post, sometimes on a door, and sometimes completely out of sight in what appeared to be some ludicrous game played out by the owners. The growing darkness and meagre streetlighting didn't help. He suddenly noticed number twenty-four out of his driver's window so at least he knew on which side of the road to look.

A few metres on he pulled up in a space by the left-hand kerb and looked across at number thirty-six. It was a large, late-Victorian, semi-detached house rising to three floors, red brick with some decorative black and white woodwork in the front-facing gables and above the door.

Guy stepped out of the car, put on his black leather jacket and zipped it up halfway. Locking the car via its remote device, he crossed the road. The house had lost its original front garden to an asphalt forecourt on which was parked a green Mini Cooper, an old Vauxhall camper van with a flat tyre, and a four-year-old white Audi TT. The Stewarts had told him Sergio drove such a car. He felt the TT's bonnet; it was slightly warm. Sergio had returned home not long before.

At the front of the house, on the left side, illuminated by the orange glow of the streetlights, Guy could see *36A* and an arrow, roughly daubed on the bricks in black paint. Guy knew Sergio rented the basement flat, so he followed the arrow round the side of the building until he reached a concrete flight of stairs leading down. There was a single, dim light halfway up the wall. More black paint had been used to number the green front door, which looked in poor condition with a cracked pane of thick frosted glass. The stairwell was littered with old beer cans, tatty pages of an abandoned newspaper and screwed-up fish and chip wrappers. Sergio clearly wasn't a house-proud man. Guy thumped loudly and firmly on the door to announce his arrival and stepped back, accidentally kicking an empty bottle of something as he did so.

A light went on and a shadow appeared in the door window. It leaned over to turn a stiff, simple lock before pulling the door inwards by about twenty centimetres. A head appeared and gave Guy a quick once-over.

"You Sam?" the head asked.

"What do you think?" Guy answered.

Sergio tugged the door open and Guy stepped into the flat. The stale smell hit him immediately and the brightness of the two neon ceiling lights made him blink slightly, but he remained alert to his surroundings. He stood in a rundown kitchen, the sink piled high with unwashed crockery. A further mess rested on a simple table that stood to one side accompanied by three cheap, plastic-seated wooden chairs. There was just about room for a worn two-seater sofa, wedged between some ailing kitchen cupboards, and a tall, overflowing swing-bin. The floor was covered in filthy linoleum tiles, worn and peeling, revealing in places the concrete foundations. Those parts of the walls that were visible were discoloured from years of cigarette smoke and cooking fat.

The door grated slightly across the floor as Sergio pushed it shut before turning to Guy.

"We'll talk in here," he said. "There's no sodding room anywhere else."

Guy moved to one of the chairs and stood behind it, placing his hands on its railed back. He looked at Sergio, a metre or so away, leaning on a kitchen work surface that was as dirty and messy as the rest of the pigsty. He wore designer jeans, decorative cowboy boots and a cotton shirt with the top buttons undone to reveal a heavy gold chain lying against a hirsute chest. He had effeminate hands, and two of his right fingers bore deeply ingrained nicotine stains. Black hair, deep-brown eyes and tanned features, with a day's stubble for good measure. He was good looking though, almost handsome. He looked at least his twenty-nine years and could have passed for thirty-five – the result, no doubt, of a stressful and hedonistic lifestyle.

"You Spanish?" Guy asked. He stared at Sergio without emotion, a blank canvas betraying a hint of intimidation. Just enough to show Sergio he was in control.

"I'm told my dad was," Sergio replied. "My mum had a holiday fling with him on the Costa Brava. Mum's a Brummie – lives in King's Heath now, just down the road." He picked up a cigarette packet off the counter and took one out before making to throw the packet across to Guy. "Smoke?" he asked.

"No."

Sergio shrugged and tossed the packet on to the counter. He flicked open a cheap, yellow disposable lighter, throwing it down after the packet as the cigarette caught. He pulled on it deeply, drawing the smoke into his lungs before exhaling flamboyantly.

He turned back to stare at Guy. "So, what's this job then?"

Guy held his gaze. "How old are you?"

"Twenty-nine – thirty next month."

"Married?" Guy asked.

Sergio smiled and took another drag. "You're joking, huh?" he said, breathing out smoke that gathered densely around him. "Not getting caught in that frigging game. I'm a free agent, me. I like girls, Sam, and…" he pulled at length on the dwindling cigarette again, "…they like me."

"Got a girlfriend now?" Guy asked. He found the smoke strong and unpleasant, and his eyes tingled.

Sergio smiled as he exhaled. "What do you think?" he said.

Guy shrugged. "Means nothing to me, but any number between zero and three, I suspect," he said.

"Correct," Sergio confirmed with a boyish grin.

As if on cue, the door behind Sergio opened to give Guy a view of an untidy bedroom with an unmade king-size bed, a duvet hanging off it. A girl entered the room wearing only her bra and knickers. She had long, light-brown hair and was young and slim – Guy guessed she was aged no more than twenty. She was very pretty. She barely glanced at Guy as she stretched out behind Sergio, picking up the cigarette packet and lighter before returning to the bedroom and closing the door behind her.

Guy said, "Well, at least one then."

Sergio said nothing but smiled smugly.

"I think we know someone in common," Guy continued.

"Yeah, I asked you that on the phone. Who did give you my name?" Sergio asked as he sucked again on his cigarette.

"I'm referring to Jenny."

Sergio exhaled rapidly through his nose and mouth, his eyes narrowing. "Who are you? I thought this was about a bloody job," he said coldly.

"It doesn't matter who I am," Guy said calmly, "I'm here, just focus on that."

"Like fuck I will."

Sergio suddenly turned, dropped his cigarette and snatched a black-handled kitchen knife from a wooden holder behind him. It had a fifteen-centimetre blade. Guy had anticipated the move after seeing the knife set earlier and, as Sergio turned towards him and brought the knife around, he lifted the kitchen chair he was leaning on and swung it up, hard. A light chair in strong arms, the movement was quick and had a lot of momentum. It caught Sergio's outstretched hand squarely and with force; with a look of surprise and a yell of pain he released the knife, which clattered to rest on the floor by the table.

Guy took advantage of his counterattack. He threw the chair at Sergio's feet, grabbed him by the arm and hurled him towards the sofa. At six feet four inches tall, Guy was considerably the larger of the two men, and fitter. Sergio's feet and legs became tangled in the upturned chair; he tripped and stumbled across the floor until he found himself on his back on the sofa, his legs hanging to the floor.

Guy knelt heavily on Sergio's chest with one knee, pinning him to the sofa and staring down at him.

He pulled the Glock from his jacket pocket, silencer fixed, and pointed it at Sergio's forehead, watching as beads of sweat appeared. The man looked terrified. Guy was suddenly conscious of the strong scent of expensive aftershave. The bedroom door behind them opened and the girl he'd seen earlier stepped cautiously into the kitchen. Guy glanced at her while keeping his gun firmly aimed at Sergio.

"Get out and shut the door," he ordered.

She seemed to take in the situation rapidly and retreated quickly back into the bedroom, almost slamming the door behind her. The noise echoed around the dingy room – the only sound, save Sergio's heavy breathing.

Guy turned back and stared Sergio in the eyes, noting the fear in them. "So, where's Jenny?" he demanded.

Sergio swallowed hard and his eyes flicked rapidly between Guy's face and the weapon. "Look," he said, "I…I don't know who the hell you are, but I've told her dad all I know. There's nothing to add, honest."

"But I'm not her dad, am I?" Guy said, slowly and firmly. "So you haven't told *me*, have you? And in this game, I play by different rules – so you'd better tell me now." Narrowing his eyes, a determined expression on his face, Guy continued to stare at Sergio.

"I haven't seen her since early this morning, not since we left the party. That's the truth."

"What happened at the party?" Guy said.

"Nothing," Sergio said. "Just one of Burnsy's normal dos. Jenny and I left together in my car at about one o'clock, but she hit me and got out."

"Where was this?" Guy asked.

Sergio attempted a shrug from his prone position. "I don't know exactly," he said with a hint of annoyance. "It was bloody dark, wasn't it? Somewhere between Burnsy's place and Tamworth. She just got out on the verge and I drove off."

"Quite a man, aren't you? Leaving a girl like that," Guy said, for some reason suddenly conscious of the repulsive odour emanating from the overfilled bin.

"I went back for her, but she wasn't there," Sergio said. "I drove up and down the road a couple of times, but nothing. I thought she was hiding from me, pissing me about, so I guessed she hadn't learnt her lesson."

"What lesson?"

"Not to piss me about."

Guy said, "What did you do then?"

Sergio tried to move. "Are you going to let me get up?' he asked. "This is bloody hurting."

"Shame," Guy said slowly. "I told *you* not to piss *me* about, but you chose the stupid option. Seems you've still got a lesson to learn, too." Guy pressed more firmly into his chest and Sergio groaned. "I repeat – what did you do then?"

Sergio looked at him. "Came back here – what else?" he said. "Drank some whiskey and crashed out through there." He nodded his head in the direction of the bedroom.

"Alone?"

"Yeah, of course. Who do you think I am?"

"We've established that, so it was a fair question," Guy said. He paused for a moment. "What then?" he asked.

"In the morning her dad called round – you know, the comedian. Wasn't telling jokes though. Asked where she was so I told him, just as I've told you. He wasn't too happy. I can't change the facts though, can I? I've no sodding idea where she went and, frankly, I don't give a toss."

Guy restrained the deep urge to hit him. His instinct for the truth was also kicking in big time.

"You're lying, aren't you?" Guy said forcefully. "What proof have you got? Who saw you at the party and who saw you leave with her?"

"Plenty of guys," Sergio said. "Place was packed. And there's CCTV at the front door, we'll be on that."

Guy relaxed slightly, trying to work the youth out. Was he making it up? He seemed confident in his version of events, but then he'd had time to work on it. It was also what he'd told Simon. Same detail, same story. Guy didn't know Jenny, but he could see it might add up. And yet…

"You met her at a restaurant? The Latin Rose?" Guy asked.

"Yeah," Sergio said. "I'm mates with the manager. I help out in the kitchen now and then. Jenny got a job as a waitress there. Better class of bird than usual so I couldn't stop myself, could I? She liked me and I liked her, so we got together – it was all consensual, okay? I didn't force nothing."

Guy shifted slightly and looked down at him.

"How do you know Burns?" Guy asked. "What does a multi-millionaire entrepreneur want with an arsehole like you?"

Sergio paused and looked steadily at Guy. "He's a friend of a friend," he said. "Burnsy comes from round here, right. Some of his family arc still here - the ones he doesn't like that is. He gave me some work up at his house."

"Doing what?"

"Odd jobs."

"Long way to go for odd jobs," Guy said.

"The guy's loaded. He pays well."

"So what's the odd job man doing at his party?"

Sergio swallowed hard. "We hit it off, didn't we? He might have money and be a big shot now, but he's still from round here, right? Went to the same school as me, although bloody ages before I went there. He talked to me about it. It was a different place then. He's okay with me."

Guy stared at him then said, "Well, Sergio, if you know Burns' place so well, you're going to do me a favour, right?"

Sergio looked wary.

"Who's in charge of security there?" Guy asked. "Someone like that, with CCTV and probably more enemies than friends – he must have someone on site."

Sergio attempted a nod, not easy from his position. "Yeah, he does," he said. "A guy called Vince, big bloke. He's not permanent, mind – turns up for parties and every now and then, and to check the system."

"Get on with him?"

"We're okay."

"So, here are your instructions," Guy said. "You

have a nice little word with Vince if he's there and get a copy of the CCTV recording for last night. Any cameras you can to prove to me you were there with Jenny – and left with her. Ask him for it. Or download it on to USB sticks and nick it whether he's there or not. I really don't give a toss how you do it – but you'll do it. You said there were cameras at the front, so I want to see your and Jenny's happy faces on it, right?"

"What if he's there and he won't give it to me – you know, if he's awkward about it? What if I can't nick it? He's a big bloke."

"So am I, Sergio," Guy said. "And I'm the one who's going to make your life hell, got it?"

Sergio went quiet.

"Well?" Guy prompted.

"Okay, okay. I'll have a go."

"You do it tomorrow," Guy said. "Then you take the copy to your restaurant. Put it in an envelope and leave it with the front of house manager for collection by Sam Granger. Got it?"

Sergio looked miserable but nodded as firmly as he could.

Guy leaned closer to him and pressed the end of the silencer into his left temple, pushing the skin into a reddening dent. As he did so he stretched over and picked a mobile out of the mess on the near-by table and placed it right in front of Sergio's face.

"Yours?" Guy asked, tipping his head slightly to emphasise the query.

Sergio gave a nod.

"Code?"

Sergio stared at him in evident confusion.

"I said, what's the code, arsehole?" Guy pushed the silencer firmly into Sergio's temple again.

Sergio told him. Guy tested it and, as the phone lit up, turned it off.

"There, that wasn't difficult, was it?" Guy slipped the mobile into his own pocket. "Mine now."

Sergio frowned and started to speak, but Guy cut in. "Before I go, Sergio, I've got one final question for you." Guy focused on him, ready to notice any – and every – facial reaction. "Where can I find Arman?"

"Who the fuck's Arman?"

"Not good enough." Guy pressed the gun even harder into the man's temple.

Sergio's eyes moved wildly. "For fuck's sake. I swear on my mother's grave; I don't know who the hell he is."

"Your mother's alive and well and living in King's Heath, you said."

"Whatever. I still have no bloody idea what you're on about. I don't know anyone called fucking Arman."

Guy could see no signs he was lying. Not a guaranteed assessment, but good enough for present purposes. He eased off the gun's pressure on Sergio's temple. "Now listen, Sergio, and listen good. I think you're a pile of crap. I'm going to leave you now, but I'm not finished with you. I want those memory sticks at the restaurant tomorrow. And I'm putting someone on you, so watch your back. Get yourself a new mobile and text the number to your old one tomorrow. I'm going to keep in touch with you, be your new friend. So, if I want to talk to you again, you'll come running, right? All meek and mild, else you'll notice things in your life starting to change – like the brakes on your TT go seriously non-existent at just the wrong time, or you need the fire escape to get out of this bloody shithole. Understand?"

Sergio nodded. He looked worried.

"My mate's lurking somewhere outside now, so you just get back to your girl and stay away from the door," Guy said. "I don't reckon you'd like him, and I know for certain he won't like you. Get it?"

Sergio nodded again. He still looked worried.

Guy stepped back, the Glock pointing at Sergio's head. Sergio brought up his right hand and rubbed his chest hard. He started to sit up, to regain some posture. Guy walked backwards, avoiding the fallen chair, and kicked the kitchen knife further under the table. He reached the door and opened it, grateful for the sweet smell of the fresh, evening air as it washed over him. It felt good. He took the key out of the lock, stepped out and locked the door behind him, leaving the key in place.

Taking the outside steps two at a time, he returned to his car. He pulled away from the kerb and set off back towards his hotel, damp shirt sticking to his back.

Further down the road a dark-skinned man who looked about forty years old with a neat, dark moustache was walking quickly towards number thirty-six. He strode with a purpose, as if summoned. He wore a smart raincoat, fully done up, and a coordinating trilby hat.

He saw Guy's swift departure and noted down the Mondeo's registration number.

TWENTY-EIGHT

Guy stopped at a pub on his way back to the hotel for something to eat, even though it was late. He ordered a steak with all the trimmings and settled at his dark-wood table with a large glass of their best red wine. The pub restaurant was relatively quiet, which pleased him – it gave him a calm environment in which he could think and try to enjoy the wine, such as it was.

He could understand Simon and Sally's dismay at their golden girl daughter taking up with Sergio. Not the man Simon would have wanted for daddy's girl. Yet Sergio seemed adamant about what had happened on the night Jenny disappeared. He'd noted, however, that there'd been no emotion over the sudden, unexplained loss of his girlfriend; indeed, Sergio had expressly said he wasn't bothered. And the presence of the other girl rather confirmed his view that Sergio had the looks, the ability and the gall to keep a handful of adoring girls in his thrall, each believing they were the chosen one. For him, losing Jenny was probably more of a relief than a matter for tears or worry. The relationship probably hadn't yet become an inconvenience – save for visits from an irate father and now a maniac with a Glock, of course.

As Guy drank his wine, he reflected on how the army had taught him how to handle weapons such as the Glock, how to fight unarmed, and how to engage the enemy. The SAS had taught him finer skills and given him a harder edge. With them, he'd learned how to survive in all circumstances and seen physical action in many countries, from Afghanistan, Iraq and Bosnia to more discreet and classified missions in North Korea and Libya.

But he'd always been part of a team, a well-trained, well-drilled band of experienced, professional soldiers thoroughly versed in army tactics and army code. His more recent work with HUMINT had taken things to a darker level where those codes had been broken, but for a good cause.

Now he was on his own, a civilian, bound by English law, and he realised he was already straying outside several of those in a way that was reminiscent of the past. It was easy to react angrily to the low life that was Sergio, but that didn't make it right. Yes, he was trying to find someone to pay a price for Sophie and to find a naïve, possibly spoilt young girl who could be in danger – or dead – but did that justify him playing *Dirty Harry* in a Birmingham suburb? And was it necessary here in civilian life?

But he felt he couldn't stop – maybe, after all, he had to slip back into the old ways so alien to his public persona. He needed to win at any cost, just as he always had. It was becoming easy to do so when he was on his own. Who was he when no one was looking?

Guy took Sergio's mobile out of his pocket and examined it. The code worked, so at least he'd told the truth about that. Although the call history revealed a lot of traffic, Sergio obviously wasn't much into texting; there were only a handful of unimaginative and unsuspicious texts. Unless any had been deleted, of course.

Guy pulled up the contacts information. This was busier. The names listed ranged from individuals such as Mike Burns and Jenny herself through to companies and businesses, including the Latin Rose restaurant where he'd met Jenny. But no mention of Arman. Guy pulled out a small notebook and pen from his pocket and methodically went through them all, creating a sizeable list in his book.

A middle-aged waitress appeared with his steak and, as he set about it, he reviewed and considered the information.

Was there anything there to act as a stepping-stone to Jenny? And was he not travelling away from Julie's death and his agreement with David? He somehow felt the answer was no. Regardless of Simon Stewart's reticence to discuss 'Arman', Guy was convinced a connection existed between Julie's death and Jenny's disappearance. Two such dramatic events couldn't be a curious coincidence, and Simon was the common link between them. He was wealthy, in line with David and Grant's theory propounded in Lloyd House the previous Saturday night. Finding Jenny would therefore assist him in finding Arman, which in turn would solve Julie's murder and give David his blaze of glory.

The theory, if true, was straightforward. But that was the easy bit. The challenge was to make it happen.

TWENTY-NINE

The man with the dark moustache, raincoat and trilby was in Sergio's flat, and was evidently not Guy's non-existent mate. His raincoat and hat were now on the back of the sofa. He was dark-skinned with dark eyes, almost black. The features of an Egyptian. He was leaning against the worktop, taking the occasional swig from a half-empty bottle of beer. He'd spent the last few minutes talking to Sergio, who had already downed two large whiskeys and was sprawled on the kitchen chairs by the table. The girl had stayed in the bedroom on Sergio's instructions. She had at least got dressed.

"When you asked me to help, Mehrak, I hadn't appreciated it would lead to all this hassle," Sergio moaned, and noisily took another mouthful of whiskey. "I dig the money from Arman, but still…"

"Stop the bloody whining," Mehrak said, irritated by what he regarded as a pathetic reaction. "I need to let Arman know what's happened here."

"I'll tell him myself if I ever get to meet him," Sergio sulked.

Mehrak took out his mobile and called Arman's number. "Arman?" he said when the call was answered. "I'm with our little investment." He related to Arman what had happened in the basement flat following the visit by Sam Granger.

"Who the hell is Sam Granger?" Arman asked.

"We don't know for sure. I do however wonder from the description whether our little baronet friend still hasn't quite got the message yet. Sergio's sitting here with another whiskey and still can't add anything. He just keeps saying he's done what we asked of him and he wasn't expecting all this hassle," Mehrak replied.

Sergio nodded as he lounged in his kitchen chair, his outstretched arm on the table gripping the glass tumbler, his feet resting on a second chair. He turned to Mehrak as if tuning in. "Tell him he just forced his way in here, waving his gun and everything. I never knew him before. He must have been waiting for me to get home. I didn't tell him nothing and agreed to nothing neither. He didn't scare me, that's for sure."

Mehrak repeated the message.

Arman said, "He sounds like unwanted trouble. We need to confirm who he is, and quick."

Although he was on the phone, Mehrak nodded and smiled. "I've got his car number plate, Arman," he said. "I rang Ed so we could get official data quickly. He did the police check thing and called me back. He says it's registered to some hire company in Sutton Coldfield. I'll get it checked out in the morning – won't be anyone there at ten o'clock on a Thursday night."

"Let me know straight away," Arman said. "I believe Stewart's signed him up rather than risk the cops. Find out who he is and then get round to his place and sort him out. And for Christ's sake take some guns with you – if he is who we think he is, he knows what he's doing."

"Sure, okay. First thing tomorrow."

"Good. And one more thing…"

"Yeah?"

"Tell Sergio not to go opening doors to fucking strangers."

THIRTY

Mehrak walked along a side street in Sutton Coldfield the next morning, still disguised as a forty-year-old gent. It had passed rush hour and the Friday commuters were all dutifully at work in the city. His mobile was pressed tightly to his ear as he looked down and watched his measured pace along the concrete pavement.

"That you, Steve?" he asked.

"Yeah, Mehrak. What you found at the car hire place?"

Mehrak started to speak but paused as a mother with a child in a pushchair came past him at some speed, as if late for an appointment.

Once they'd gone, he said, "Bugger all. Notice on the door says it's shut all day because of an illness and a funeral – I thought one followed the other, not came as a job lot. Anyhow, I can't safely progress anything, so we'll approach this a different way. You listening?"

"Yeah," Steve said. "What's the plan?"

"This guy who knocked Sergio about wants the CCTV recording of him and his girl leaving Burns' party."

"So?"

"Sergio reckons he can get it today. I want you to get yourself to the Latin Rose restaurant and be there when this guy collects it from reception. Take a photo of him, and then follow him – see where he goes, who he meets, what he drives, anything. I want everything, right down to his shoe size and whether he picks his nose. Got it? Just get detail, okay? Then call me."

"What if he doesn't show?"

"Then you can't do any of that fucking stuff, can you? Then just ring me. But he'll show, he wants this recording, doesn't he, right? So why would he not show?"

Steve said, "You not going to stop him having the copy, then?"

"Not just our call, is it? It's going a slightly different route to what Arman planned, but he's cool about it. We'll just let Sergio do his thing – give him some rope. Probably be the same result in the end, so makes no real difference."

"The Latin Rose, then. What time?"

"Be there for about five. If he doesn't show or you mess up, Steve, it looks like I'll be back here in Sutton tomorrow when hopefully this car hire place will be open – so long as everyone's well again or safely cremated. I'll then be able to – how shall I say? – make some gentle enquiries." Mehrak smiled grimly to himself. His enquiries always got the answers he needed. He'd now seen the layout of the place and its location. Research, always research.

Steve said, "You still there, Mehrak?"

"Sure. Now get into the city centre and keep me posted."

THIRTY-ONE

The girl sat on her bed. It wasn't so much her bed, but rather the bed that she'd been given. It was a simple black-painted iron frame, heavy with no castors. The headboard was integral, a looping thick metal tube with small vertical rods lined up some ten centimetres apart, like window bars. The mattress was, however, comfortable – deep and modern. There was a traditional pair of sheets, two pillows and plenty of blankets in various hues. They had pretty much kept her warm for what she felt must have been a couple of days now; she was starting to lose track.

Despite the warm cardigan she was cold, and she pulled a yellow blanket over her jeans and up to her shoulders. She looked round the room – or rather her prison. But this was surely worse than prison? At least there'd she'd get visitors, mix with other prisoners, have recreation time. She'd seen it on the telly. Here there was none of that. Nothing and no-one, except the guy in the cloth hood.

The room was bare, save for an incongruous modern toilet in one corner and a shelf bearing a random selection of books which was secured to one of the whitewashed walls. Even the floor with its small, central gully, dry and dusty, which disappeared into the narrowest of drains at the foot of the rear wall, was plain, time-worn brick. There was no window and no natural light. The single electric bulb, which hung forlornly on slightly bent, dirty-white wire that protruded from the centre of the ceiling was the only light – and it was permanently left on. The whole room felt subterranean – a chill, damp cellar with no heating.

There was a small grille in the white-painted door, through which blew a gentle draught. And the sound of crying. At least, the girl thought it had been crying; she couldn't be completely sure. Perhaps her mind was playing tricks. It was distant and could have been the wind in this desolate place. She couldn't investigate, though, not with the door kept locked. She wanted to call out, but the hooded guy had made it clear that she was not to speak, not at all, or there would be no food. He hadn't spoken, either – he'd written it down on a scrap of paper, let her read it, and made her nod to show she understood. She had, so now she didn't dare call out to try and discover whether anyone other than the wind was unhappy.

At that moment, she heard approaching footsteps. She drew her legs up and wrapped her arms round them, resting her chin on her knees, feeling the coarseness of the blanket on her soft skin. She stared at the door as the footsteps stopped. There was always a pause, and then the hooded figure would suddenly appear in the small grille where he'd stand, looking at her. She pulled her legs in tighter and hugged them more firmly.

The face disappeared and she heard the latch turn. In the wall to the right of the door, about half a metre up from the cold floor, was a metal hatch about thirty centimetres wide and of similar height. It looked like it had been installed recently. The girl knew that in a moment the hatch door would swing open into the corridor, and it did. Gloved hands pushed a brown plastic tray through the gap, placing it on a short brick pillar that had evidently been put there for that purpose; it, too, was new.

On the tray was a plastic jug of water and a fresh, clean polystyrene cup. There was also a paper plate holding some brown, meaty stew, crumbling boiled potatoes and long green beans. Again. Oh, and bread. Lots of bread. No cutlery; she knew there wouldn't be. There never was. She had learnt to use her fingers, and the bread. When the tray came to rest, the hatch swung shut and she heard the latch again. There was a pause, and then the sound of departing footsteps.

The girl kicked the yellow blanket from her slim legs and crossed the narrow room to pick up the tray of food. She carried it hastily back to the bed, where she sat cross-legged and looked at it. Faint steam curled and twisted slowly from the plate, drifting away to nothing. She picked up a piece of bread and made to break it, but instead stopped and just held it. Although she was hungry, she felt a sudden, strong and violent emotion. The girl burst into tears and cried loudly for her former life.

THIRTY-TWO

The brown envelope with 'Sam Granger' scrawled across it lay beneath the small reception desk at the Latin Rose restaurant in Temple Street, just off Birmingham's New Street in the very centre of the city. It was almost six o'clock on Friday evening and the duty manager, as a favour to Sergio, had placed it there about an hour earlier ready for collection. Sam Granger would apparently call in for it that evening.

The restaurant was gradually filling up – a mix of office workers out for a group supper and couples who wanted an early dinner before moving on to the cinema or theatre. It was busy even for a Friday night. There was, however, one man sitting alone, not far from the door, nursing a drink with an open menu on his lap and apparently waiting for a delayed friend. He was a short, large, fit man in his early fifties. Steve was fulfilling his instructions, but Granger hadn't appeared yet.

Steve leaned back confidently in his seat, legs outstretched, and took another swig of lager. He glanced around the restaurant. It was quite a posh affair, in his view. Solid, dark wood tables, large, green plants plunging into richly coloured pottery tubs, patterned wallpaper and Italian floor tiles all combined to create an intimate, inviting atmosphere. A couple of young waitresses moved around the tables efficiently, watched over by a head waiter in his forties who would stride to the front desk to greet new customers, like a true maître d', as they ventured in.

A young girl aged no more than eighteen, with

shoulder-length, brunette hair and wearing a McDonald's uniform entered the restaurant. The head waiter was now standing at the reception desk, a pensive expression on his face as he flicked through a clipboard of forms. Steve eyed the girl, who was slightly overweight but not unattractive, and glanced back at the menu a little guiltily when she looked across at him. At this rate he'd have to order something, he thought; he could be there all evening. The door opened again, and he looked up to see the girl leaving, a brown envelope in her hand. With a start he stood up, dropped the menu on the seat and hurried to the desk. The head waiter looked up with a slightly puzzled air.

"Yes, sir?" he asked.

"Was that Sam Granger?"

"She said so." The head waiter hesitated, attempting to hide his incredulity as he asked, "Was she the friend you were waiting for?"

"Sorry, change of plan," Steve said. "I have to go. Take this."

He dropped a £20 note on the desk, walked hastily to the door and exited onto the pavement. He looked up and down the relatively quiet street and saw the girl turn into the McDonald's outlet some twenty metres down his side of the road. He ran as quickly as he could, almost colliding with a tall, blond-haired man leaving the fast-food restaurant.

Inside, it was busy. Steve pushed his way towards the counter, searching for the girl, although he was struggling to remember what she looked like. The shoulder-length, brunette hair stuck in his mind. He received some withering glances from those queuing for their supper, but he didn't care about that. He made it to the shiny metal counter and stared into the hectic kitchen that was awash with youngsters rushing around in their bespoke, but unfathomable, roles. A guy of about thirty in a white shirt, with a look of supervisor, if not manager, about him caught his eye and stepped towards him.

"Can I help?"

Steve glanced at him briefly, then continued to scour the kitchen. "I'm looking for a girl," he said.

"Aren't we all?" the manager guy answered.

"No – a brunette, a teenager, she works here."

"Look, mate, if you want a girlfriend try the internet or the local rag. We're a fast food restaurant in case you haven't noticed - so, unless you want a burger, hop it."

Steve knew he had to persist.

"Don't get cheeky with me, son," he said. "Her name might be Sam Granger. She's one of your staff, a girl, and she's just come back in here. Just this minute. You must have seen her come in. I need to speak to her."

"Well, unless you have a warrant or news that someone here's won the lottery, I'm really not interested. There's no girl called Sam working here, okay? He's a Sam, that spotty kid over there." The manager guy pointed out a pasty, skinny lad. "But he's not a Granger, and he's probably not your type. Now, my staff are working, and I'd like them to stay that way, if it's all the same to you. So, I repeat, unless you want one of our burgers or a boxful of nuggets, please leave."

Steve was conscious that the busy staff immediately behind the counter were doing their best to serve customers while at the same time listening with interest to the exchange. Customers too were casting furtive glances whilst maintaining a very English distance from any involvement. He looked around once more, but realised he was beaten. He turned to leave.

The manager guy said, in a louder voice, "And if I see you lurking outside, having made your intentions towards teenage girls on my staff all too clear, I'll call the cops – got it?"

Steve reddened and looked over his shoulder. "Don't worry, I'm off," he said.

He pushed his way through the melee and left.

The manager guy walked into his small office by the side of the counter and closed the door behind him. The girl was sitting on a white, wooden chair, picking her nails. She didn't seem to have a care in the world.

"Okay?" he asked.

She nodded, still focused on her nails. "Yeah, fine. I gave it to him," she replied.

"I know, I saw. Now, back to work. And Annie…"

"Yeah?"

"Remember that's not how we usually treat our customers."

"Sure."

"And here's your half."

The manager guy gave the girl a £50 note, retaining its twin for himself. Easy money, courtesy of the tall, blond-haired gent.

THIRTY-THREE

Guy had been waiting patiently inside the door of the McDonald's. The girl – Annie, he recalled – had passed the brown envelope to him as she'd entered and carried straight on to the manager's office as planned. Guy had tucked the envelope in his jacket and almost collided with a short, stocky man in his early fifties as he'd left. He'd paused in the street outside, peering back in through the large window just long enough to take in a description of the man who had by then barged his way to the counter. He had been right to be careful and put precautions in place; this man had evidently followed Annie from the Latin Rose. For one hundred pounds, all had gone to plan.

Guy walked down the pavement into New Street and paused at the corner to peer back at McDonald's around the edge of a shop wall. The short stocky man was still in there. He had no doubt the manager would play his part and play it well. He took the envelope out of his pocket and peeled it open. Inside were two red USB memory sticks. He replaced the envelope in his pocket and glanced back at the burger outlet again

Three teenage lads exited McDonald's, followed closely by the short, stocky man. Guy instinctively pushed himself back against the wall, although he calculated that only part of his face was visible from Temple Street. He saw the man pause and look about before turning away from Guy and walk up the rising road towards St Philip's Place and the cathedral. Guy watched him go and then slipped in behind a group of middle-aged businessmen who'd turned past him. The short stocky man pulled out his mobile as he walked and appeared to be having an animated conversation. Guy watched as he turned left at the top of the street and disappeared from view.

Upping his pace, Guy stepped into the roadway to overtake the suits who had given him temporary cover. His mind was working quickly. He hadn't known what would happen at the Latin Rose, but despite his threats to Sergio he didn't trust the creep and had yet to determine in whose camp he truly belonged. Evidently not Jenny's. The short, stocky man he was now following could only have known about the drop from Sergio, who must therefore have told someone about Guy's visit to the squalid flat. And the only reason for coming to the restaurant would have been to see who collected the envelope – to find out who Sam Granger was, possibly to speak to him, probably to threaten him.

If that was the case, there could be two scenarios. The first was that this short, stocky bloke was innocent of Jenny's disappearance and was just a mate looking after Sergio, with the intention of sorting Guy out for unwanted aggression to his pal. Possible, but not completely plausible. It would have been easier for Sergio to have simply set up a further meet with Guy, using some excuse, and had Guy sorted out there and then at a quiet, private place of Sergio's choosing.

The second scenario was that Sergio was involved in Jenny's disappearance and the short, stocky man shared that guilt and was now on a mission to find out who Guy was. If that was the case, the short, stocky man was a link who might take Guy closer to Jenny. It would also necessitate a complete review of everything

Sergio had said about Jenny, as nothing he'd said could now be trusted.

As he reached the top of the street, he saw the short, stocky man crossing the central square past the cathedral, near the spot where Guy had sat with Grant the previous Sunday morning. He was still on his phone. Guy continued in pursuit some two hundred metres behind. The more he thought about it, the more he wanted to speak to him, and his delay in following had put him too far behind. He started to jog.

It then occurred to him that if Sergio had connections with Arman, what exactly was in his pocket? What was on those memory sticks, and were they just opportune bait to reach Guy? Were they shop-bought and unadulterated, or carrying relevant evidence?

He saw the short, stocky man reach Colmore Row, a broad, one-way street that ran the length of the large open space containing the cathedral. Suddenly, the man waved his hand and, as Guy started to gain ground, he saw him climb into a black taxi cab and take off down the road. From his distant viewpoint, Guy could only watch him go.

Guy paused by the side of the cathedral before taking his mobile out of his pocket and calling Grant. She answered with her usual abruptness, and Guy told her he wanted to meet.

"…and where are you?" Guy asked.

"Where do you think? Working, of course. Lloyd House." She sounded as hacked off as usual."

"I'm not far away. Ten minutes?"

"If you must," Grant answered, ringing off.

Guy made his way towards the police

headquarters, annoyed with himself for not thinking his actions in relation to the short, stocky man through quickly enough. He was rusty and needed to sharpen up back to his old self. He was also becoming increasingly hacked off at Grant's attitude towards him. He sensed another heated scene approaching, despite the possible progress in his pocket.

THIRTY-FOUR

Grant came into the reception area to greet him. Waiting in the doorway to the lift lobby, she caught Guy's eye and nodded in a mechanical way. Guy walked over from the reception desk like a gladiator entering the Coliseum. Grant moved back into the lobby, holding the door but making no attempt to give a customary handshake. She summoned a lift, a set of doors opening promptly as if they'd picked up the mood, and they entered. There was no one else in it. Grant pushed the button to the sixth floor with force, almost thumping it. They didn't speak.

The lift suddenly halted, and an electronic female voice announced this was the second floor. The doors slid open and a casually dressed young man stepped in, clutching a small file. He carefully pressed the button for the fourth floor and the doors closed.

"Stairs not working, Ben?" Grant asked.

Ben looked embarrassed. "Was in a hurry, ma'am."

"Stairs keep you fitter – faster, too, with effort."

"Yes, ma'am," Ben said. "Next time for sure."

He looked up at the lights that indicated which floor they were on as if willing the lift to speed up. As it halted on the fourth floor, Ben scuttled out like a frightened rabbit and the heavy silence resumed.

When the lift stopped again, Grant strode out, crossed the short lobby and pressed a code into a door lock. It was so automatic she hardly looked. Guy followed her down a narrow, office-lined passageway until she stopped by a door bearing a plate with her name on it. Grant paused in the corridor and, with a wave of her right hand, directed Guy into the room.

The office was a reasonable size with two windows that looked out across Colmore Circus to the modern Wesleyan Assurance Society building, all brick and glass. There was a large desk with three chairs in front of it. Shelves with books and papers, and three slightly dented, grey filing cabinets with four drawers each. And tidy, very tidy – even the desk. No photographs. Guy heard the door close behind him as Grant walked to her desk and sat down. He took one of the facing chairs.

Grant looked across at him. "So, what's new, Guy?"

Guy leaned forward. Time to turn the attitude, get her to answer first. "That was my question to you," he said. "You seen Jonny again?"

She said nothing for a moment, seemed to be weighing things up. She picked up a pencil from the desk and fiddled with it, as though she was working out how to hold a chopstick. "Rearranged for tomorrow," she said. "Nothing on forensics, didn't expect there to be." The apparent decision to say more was accompanied by the pencil being dropped purposefully into a black, plastic holder to her right. "We have, however, found the killer." Her eyes never left his face.

Guy was impressed. "Really? Tell me more."

"When I say 'found', we have pictures," Grant clarified. "An old tramp forced his way into the empty flat in Bolton Street. We've tracked him on CCTV footage making his way there, including from the camera that covers the outside balcony. Old guy with a long holdall. Folded-up rifle size. Shuffles along he does, seventy or eighty if he's a day."

"Disguise?"

"Without a doubt," Grant said. "He'll be young and fit and unidentifiable. He's a pro who knows exactly what to do and how to play the system. Knows who's watching – and who isn't. In a city like ours you can be pretty anonymous if you want to be."

Guy leaned forward. "What about afterwards?" he said. "Can you trace his route from street cameras? Where did he go?"

"We've got the start of his journey back," Grant said. "Quite the actor, he is. Also hot on research. I reckon he was parked up somewhere around Stanley Street, an area where the street cameras are few and far between, if indeed there are any at all. No coincidence, right? Busy roads, could have been in any car – and one that is no doubt hidden somewhere or burnt out – untraceable back to him, in any event." She leant back in her chair and crossed her arms. "What about you?" she added in a tone that barely even registered as disinterested.

Guy was ready for the arrogance and endeavoured to keep his response in check. It wasn't easy. "Me?" he said. "There's little point in updating you as you clearly don't give a damn about what I've been doing. You're focusing on Jonny; I'm looking at Simon Stewart. One of us is right or neither of us is right. I prefer my version, especially with recent developments."

Grant placed her elbows firmly on her desk with a sudden air of apparent interest. "Recent developments?"

Guy said, "Look, I've seen Stewart and his wife – you know, Sally Stewart, the TV chef. Simon denied any knowledge about what happened to his sister, but I don't think he's being straight with me. I think someone is putting him under pressure. Something's going on."

"If that's the case, why doesn't he come down here and tell me?" Grant asked.

"I think he would," Guy said. "But something's happened that's preventing him from doing so."

"Which is?"

Guy paused. How much should he divulge? "Look," he said eventually, "this needs to be confidential at the moment. I'll tell you because we've agreed to share information, but it's for our debate, nothing else."

Grant leaned back again and crossed her arms, pulling them in tight. "I'm not making any promises," she said. "I investigate crime and I'm the SIO here. It's my show. I don't negotiate like some two-bit politician. You tell me what you know, and I'll handle it as I want to." She paused, her eyes challenging him.

Guy decided to go on the offensive – he needed to make things happen. "There's a daughter missing," he said, watching her closely.

He had clearly caught Grant off-guard.

"A daughter? What are you on about?"

"I told you on the phone that Simon Stewart had met me at short notice. What I didn't mention was that he seemed to think I might be connected to someone else – a guy called Arman. When he realised I wasn't, that was when he left. Took my card though and then rang me yesterday morning. In a state he was. I met up with him and Sally at their home in Four Oaks yesterday afternoon. His daughter, Jenny, has gone missing. He felt he could talk to me because of who I am and because I'm not a policeman. Here, look at this."

Guy took the photograph of Jenny out of his pocket and slid it across the desk to Grant. She casually picked it up and gave it a dutiful glance before dropping it back down in front of her, as if looking at a newly dealt card in a poker game.

"She's eighteen," Guy continued, and summed up Jenny's position and thc circumstances of her disappearance as he understood it.

Grant gave an almost Gallic shrug – unimpressed, her momentary interest seemingly gone. "What's this got to do with the murder of Julie Reid?"

Guy, irritated by her attitude, felt he was wading through treacle. "Because I think someone's putting pressure on Stewart," he said. "First killing his sister, and then doing something with his daughter."

Grant pulled a pained expression and slapped the desk with the palm of her hand. "Look, just because she's not turned up after a party with her boyfriend doesn't mean she's a victim," she said. "There are all sorts of reasons why her parents haven't heard from her – staying with her boyfriend, or a new boyfriend, making a show of independence, fed up with parental control - need I go on? If her parents are so concerned, why haven't they reported her as missing and not just summoned the great Guy Sterling?"

Guy stayed focused. He was almost used to her poor approach by now. "They've been advised not to at this stage by Laurie Whittall –"

Grant looked scathing. "I thought he was a

publicist," she said. "Unusual for him to advise 'no publicity'. No money in it for him either. Anyhow, there we are then. The parents are on the ground, they know her, and she's probably a typical child of celebrities – you know, drugs, alcohol and wasting the parent's wealth in true second-generation style."

Guy felt a growing frustration. The room seemed to be warmer. "But she's clearly missing, Caroline. It doesn't matter who her parents are, a young girl is missing, and the father's sister was shot dead in Aston."

"There are thousands of daughters missing, Guy." Grant waved her hand roughly towards her filing cabinets. "Sons, too. Over two hundred thousand people go missing in the UK each year, and of those just one in seven thousand become homicides. Most just go home having stayed with friends or when they realise sleeping rough is even less fun than following their parents' house rules. Especially in winter."

Guy said, "I think Jenny is at serious risk of becoming a one in seven thousand."

Grant rose, picked up a file from her desk and walked over to one of the cabinets where she dropped it noisily, cardboard to metal. She turned to Guy, who'd been watching her. "Bit early to predict, but I doubt it. Like Lassie, Jenny will come home, mark my words. Now, what do you want from me, Guy? Until Jenny is reported missing officially, I'm not interested. My priority is Julie."

Guy insisted, "I think they're one and the same."

"Oh, do you? I don't agree. One was a professional hit, the other is a girl who's gone missing after a night out with her boyfriend. I know about Mike Burns' parties."

"Tell me."

"Food, music, booze, girls – probably some for hire – and no doubt some products from warmer climes. All wrapped up in money and extravagance, fit for the children of our monied celebs," she said as she returned to her desk. "So, I repeat – what do you want from me?"

"Your opinion on the disappearance – as a detective."

"My opinion as an experienced detective is that a spoilt girl has done a bunk. She has a hefty allowance and pin money from the restaurant. I reckon there's an element of attention-seeking here."

"But the lack of publicity is surely wrong," Guy said, working to get Grant on-side.

The police officer returned to her desk and appeared to relax a little. "I'm with you on that," she conceded.

"Okay, but what happened in your view, Caroline? Cut the crap and work on the basis that I might actually be right."

Grant picked up a coffee mat, playing with it in her hands as she spoke rapidly. "Rich girl meets poor, petty criminal. Sexual attraction. Petty criminal takes rich girl to celeb party. Row on way home. Rich girl runs off. Petty criminal has a bad case of the egos and goes home. Rich girl has a greater case of the egos and runs off to some friend for adoration and shelter."

"That's pretty cynical."

"I've seen it before."

"Many celebs' daughters go missing in the West

Midlands, then?"

She said nothing.

"But what if you're wrong, Caroline? What if she's in trouble somewhere, or dead?"

Grant flicked the coffee mat gently back on to her desk and leaned back in her chair, her chin resting on the apex of the pyramid created by her hands and arms. She looked at Guy. "If she's dead then we'll find her in due course and the only urgency is the parents' peace of mind. If she's in trouble, we'll find her in due course and then give the parents peace of mind. My money's on one of those two." She gazed challengingly at Guy.

Guy said, "I have doubts whether she even went to this party, let alone left with Sergio. It may be the case, and she may have been abandoned at the roadside, but I need convincing. Having met him, I think he's making it up, but I've limited options of investigation."

"You'll need evidence then – witnesses at the party and so on. But you're wasting your time. Chances are this girl and her Romeo were there and she's even now with friends or a new beau making this Sergio and her parents sweat."

"That doesn't sound like Jenny."

"Suddenly know her well, do we?"

Guy said nothing. He didn't know her, of course. Grant could be right.

"Look," Grant said, "I can't just crash into Burns' life demanding the guest list, can I?"

Guy said, "There's CCTV at the front of the house. That would either record them leaving or not."

"Same issue, Guy. I can't get it even if it still exists – not without co-operation or a search warrant."

"It does exist."

"How do you know?"

Guy produced the envelope. "Because there are copies in here."

Grant looked genuinely surprised. She leaned back again into her chair and thought for a few moments. "How the hell did you get that?"

"I've got it, that's all you need to know. What I want to do is play them, see who's right; so let's try that, shall we?"

THIRTY-FIVE

They used the PC on Grant's desk. Grant moved the monitor screen so they could both see it from either side of the desk, leaning in towards each other. Closer than Guy would have liked, but he had a job to do. Guy placed the photograph of Jenny by the monitor as a point of reference. Grant inserted one of the two USB sticks into the computer, manoeuvred the mouse and, with a series of clicks, galvanised the small memory stick into action.

The copy ran with all the grainy familiarity of colour CCTV footage, although the quality was, Guy accepted, pretty good. But then the owner could afford it.

"Well, the date's correct. Wednesday night, 11.38pm and counting." Guy recalled his earlier thoughts that Sergio might have passed on any old recording, or indeed unadulterated sticks, just to get Guy off his back. He knew that would have led to howls of derision from Grant.

"There's nothing to say it's Burns' house," Caroline pointed out, looking at the screen.

The first, silent recording was taken from inside an elegantly furnished mansion and picked up a busy bustle of casually dressed guests, laughing, talking and drinking. It switched between rooms, including a large hallway. It looked like a very animated, jovial environment.

Guy stared intently at the screen. "Now, where's Jenny?" he said in a low voice, almost to himself.

"No sign of your truant yet. Camera shy, is she?

You may have been sold a pup here, Guy, for all I know."

Guy ignored her and watched a moment longer. "It's 12.04am on the Thursday now," he said, pointing at the timer. 'Sergio claims they left about 1am. Wind it forward to shortly before then and we'll see what's picked up in the hallway, if it's shown."

Grant used the mouse to fast-forward the recording and the picture moved rapidly, almost at comical speed. People sped across the screen in swift, jerky movements making it look like Euston station at rush hour. She allowed it to play normally again at 12.58am, and they saw it showed the hallway. Guy leaned in towards the picture, willing Sergio and Jenny to appear.

"There!" he exclaimed, pointing to two people descending a wide staircase in the corner of the screen. "Pause it now, quick."

Grant moved fast and clicked to pause the film.

"That's them, surely?" Guy said. "Those two right there, heading towards the door."

The frozen frame showed Sergio quite clearly. Although he didn't have a photograph, Guy recognised the man without any doubt. He had after all spent some time recently staring into the man's dark-skinned face during their encounter at the basement flat. He looked at his companion, flicked a glance at the photograph again, and then back to the screen.

"I'm absolutely certain that's Sergio, Caroline."

"I wouldn't know, would I?" she said in a tone that Guy read as her accepting his analysis.

"And he's with Jenny. I'm sure that's her. Look,

compare the photo." He lifted it up.

Grant was silent for a few moments as she peered at the girl in the classic, plain-black cocktail dress. She then said, "I think you might be right. It certainly seems to be her."

Guy said, "Can you enlarge her face?"

Without replying, Grant played with the controls and suddenly the girl's face dominated the screen.

"It's her!" they exclaimed in unison.

Guy felt tremendous relief. No pup, just irrefutable evidence that Jenny had been at the party with Sergio. It was only a start, but a good start.

"Play more," he urged.

Grant clicked the mouse again, and the scene showed Sergio and Jenny standing and chatting cheerfully with a young man whose back remained permanently towards the camera. At one point Jenny laughed, turned to Sergio and kissed him on the cheek, and then held his hand. After a further minute or so the picture suddenly stopped and there was just a blank screen.

"Looks like we need the other stick," Guy said.

He took the second USB memory stick from the envelope and swapped it with the first one.

After a brief moment a new scene appeared. This footage was from an outdoor camera that must have been fixed some three metres up the front wall to the left of the guests as they exited the house. It captured the front door and showed part of the driveway running diagonally across the top of the picture. The footage showed couples leaving in differing states of control, with a variety of cars rolling out of what must have been a parking area off-screen and then moving on towards the drive and, presumably, the gates.

"Advance it to about 1am again," Guy said.

Grant did so. They watched occasional guests departing, singularly, in pairs and in small groups. A couple walked out of the front door and Guy leaned forward. Here they were, surely; he recognised the clothing. The man was on the left, nearest the camera, his right arm draped round the girl's shoulders, just touching the top of her black cocktail dress and pulling her into a tight, romantic hold. She was holding a coat and a clutch bag. They stopped suddenly, the man turning to look over his left shoulder as if someone standing in the doorway behind him had said something. It was Sergio. He held his pose, mouthed something, laughed and then turned to move forward again.

Guy said, "Run that again and hold it as he's looking round."

Grant replayed the film. As Sergio was holding his position, talking to the unidentified third party behind him, she paused it. Guy studied him. He looked relaxed, normal – just going home with his girl. Was that smugness in his face? Part of him was disappointed. If Sergio had left on his own, this recording would be clear and irrefutable proof that the toe-rag had lied to him. But that wasn't the case. The recording showed boy leaving with girl on his arm. Another part of him, however, was pleased that he'd at least established Jenny's whereabouts at this late hour, although it still left him with the challenge of where to go next.

Guy could understand Simon and Sally's concerns about both the parties and the boyfriend, and their impact on a naïve young girl. He watched the screen and focused on her. As the third party attracted Sergio's attention, Guy saw that she paused too, partially twisting her head over her right shoulder back towards the door. Her long brown hair, however, was trapped under Sergio's right arm as it ran round her shoulders; she appeared to give up the attempt to turn and simply returned to snuggling into her man, waiting for him to finish his exchange and walk forward again.

With Grant's help on the controls, Guy watched the moment several times. He felt there was always something eerie, almost sinister, watching someone's final moments on CCTV when the viewer knew the person was walking through the last few minutes and actions of their life. But was this the case here? He watched the couple walk forward together across the gravelled forecourt in the direction of the parking area.

"Well," Grant said. "Your Sergio may be a minor villain, but he seems to be telling the truth."

Guy sensed a softening of tone. He said, "This may show them leaving together, but it doesn't support what he claims happened next – the row, leaving her by the roadside, coming back to look. This shows they were at the party and left together, no more."

"But more than you thought was the case," Grant said neutrally.

"Yes, if I'm honest."

Once the couple had moved away, the camera maintained its all-seeing and unblinking eye on the forecourt. A man meandered out of the house and paused as a white Audi TT drove at speed out of the parking area, across the front of the house, and into the funnel to the drive.

"That's his car," Guy said.

"Back to the drawing board then, Guy?" Grant said and switched it off.

Guy stayed silent, leaning back in his chair as he reflected on what he'd seen.

Grant asked, "Anything else?"

Guy replied: "Any other theories?"

"No. She'll turn up in the next day or two. But I'll think about it."

"And if she doesn't?"

"Then, Guy, we're both in the shit, aren't we?"

And Guy realised that for the first time she'd seen they had something in common.

THIRTY-SIX

It was eight-fifteen on Saturday morning when Mehrak reached the small, brick office building at the front of the Royal Sutton Car Hire Company. He was once again a middle-aged man with a neat, dark moustache, smart raincoat fully fastened, and wearing a coordinated trilby hat and leather driving gloves.

As he entered, a traditional shop bell rang above the door, and an elderly man holding a small screwdriver turned and looked down at him from the top of a stepladder.

"You doing some dusting?" Mehrak asked light-heartedly, closing the door behind him.

"Camera's on the blink again," the elderly man said, reinforcing the information with a gentle wave of the screwdriver. "Times are tough enough without having to pay for an engineer." He descended the ladder, and, placing the screwdriver on the counter, turned to his new customer with a friendly smile and appeared to draw on his go-to greeting. "Anyhow, enough of that. I'm Jerry Stamford, owner of the best car hire business in Sutton – here to help and here to please, so how can I assist you?"

Mehrak paused and then said, "I need to hire a car, and you've been recommended."

Jerry beamed. "That's good to know. We do our best. Now, what are you looking for and for how long?"

"Just a small car, a Punto, a Clio, something like that. I need it until Tuesday."

Jerry stepped behind the reception desk, sat down and opened the computer. "You're bright and early," he said. "First customer of the day. No prizes though, I'm afraid. One moment and I'll check what we have available. Won't be a sec." The screen reflected off his glasses as he worked the system. "A Punto, you said? That shouldn't be a problem. And since you *are* my first customer, I'll do you a special deal after all. Blue okay?"

Mehrak smiled. "Colour's not important. Just something reliable."

"They're all reliable, sir."

"Of course, I wasn't implying anything. It's just that I saw one of yours broken down near here on Thursday night – a blue Mondeo."

Jerry looked up at him with a surprised expression. "Really? I didn't know about that. We had to close yesterday. I was at a funeral, and my receptionist was ill. First time I've had to close like that in over thirty years. But all customers have my mobile, and there's roadside emergency cover on all our vehicles. Most unusual…"

"Sounds odd, but I took the registration number – there was a reason."

Mehrak gave Jerry the number and watched as he carefully typed it into the keyboard, clearly too concerned and pre-occupied to query how Mehrak had linked the car to his business.

As he stared at the screen, Jerry said, "Let me see… Here we are. No, nothing's been reported here."

"A nice guy had hired it," Mehrak said. "I'd lost my wallet and he was standing by his car. I asked him the way to the police station, and he gave me directions and lent me some cash for a taxi. I would very much like to write to him to say thank you and repay the money.

May I take his name and address?"

Jerry shook his head slowly as he stood up and returned to the counter. "That's really thoughtful," he said, "but I'm ever so sorry, sir, I can't do that as we keep our customers' details confidential. I've always taken great pride in that – and it's the law now, of course. I'm sure you understand."

"That's a shame."

"Well, you could leave your details here with me, and I'll ensure he gets your message. You can rely on me."

Mehrak paused for a beat before putting his hand into his coat pocket and pulling out a small wad of £50 notes. He looked Jerry straight in the eye as he held the money out to him. "Would this help?" he asked.

Jerry stared at it as if it was more money than he'd ever seen in his lifetime. He repeated: "As I say, I'm really sorry, but I can't tell you anything. I have my reputation. I really can't do anything improper."

"Then how about this?"

Mehrak suddenly produced a handgun from his pocket. It was short, stubby and fitted with a silencer.

Jerry froze and then raised his hands slightly, palms out. He just stared in silence at the gun. He appeared to go weak and quickly lowered his right hand to seek support from the wooden counter.

"Well?"

"I…I don't know… please…"

Mehrak gave him a callous, almost inhuman, stare with his dark Mediterranean eyes and said, "Simple decision to make, old man."

Jerry didn't move, didn't speak. It was as though

he was literally petrified.

Mehrak sighed heavily. “Enough’s enough, you senile old git. I’ll take that as a ‘no’ shall I? Yeah? Time’s up.”

Mehrak fired twice into the elderly man’s chest. Jerry collapsed backwards onto the floor, knocking the desk chair sideways, all life gone.

“I’ll do it myself then, loser,” Mehrak said to Jerry, as the blood stain grew rapidly on the front of the dead man’s blue shirt.

Returning the gun to his raincoat pocket, he rounded the counter, seized a notepad and pen and looked on the screen, still open on the Mondeo hire page, as Jerry had left it. He wrote down the name Guy Sterling and the Hofton Manor address and shoved the notepad into his pocket. Then he snatched the keys to the blue Punto off the counter where Jerry had placed them moments before and read the registration number on the fob.

Mehrak walked briskly to the front door and locked it. He turned the ‘Open’ sign to ‘Closed’ and pulled down the short Venetian blind. He strode back behind the wooden counter, stepped over the prostrate body and slightly opened a metal latched window in the side wall before swiftly moving into the back of the building where he found a darkened storeroom. It didn’t take him long to locate a five-litre can of petrol; shaking it, he estimated it was well over half full. Returning to reception, he sprinkled the fuel liberally over Jerry and the surrounding area, shaking the remnants of the can onto his handkerchief and carelessly throwing the can itself into the back-office room.

The rear door took Mehrak into a narrow yard, evidently used for washing and cleaning the fleet, judging by the taps and the neatly rolled yellow hoses systematically placed on the walls. He turned right and walked hurriedly, but with poise, until he reached the far corner where he dropped his handkerchief on the dry ground.

A few more steps and he joined the rough, concrete driveway up to the car park's double gates. Unclipping them, he pushed them open and strode methodically around the assembled clean cars until he found the blue Punto that matched the registration on the key fob. He unlocked it and sat in the driver's seat. It started first time. Easing it into gear, he drove it gently through the gates and stopped on the concrete driveway at the point where it passed the side of the office building.

Leaving the car idling with the handbrake on, he stepped out and crossed to the corner of the building where he picked up his handkerchief. He took a lighter out of his pocket and, holding the material at a respectful distance, he set it alight. The flame took rapidly and, with his back to the brick wall, Mehrak calmly reached out and threw it like a grenade through the window he'd opened earlier. There was a sudden, resonating rush of fire; within seconds, the reception area and office were burning fiercely.

Mehrak got back into the blue Punto and set off through the main gate, Guy's address in his pocket as if he had no cares in the world. He never even bothered to look back at the blazing funeral pyre that was the remains of Jerry Stamford's life's work.

THIRTY-SEVEN

After visiting the still-unconscious Sophie in hospital, Guy spent the rest of Saturday morning walking around the city of Lichfield's more scenic areas. Thinking and planning seemed a more worthwhile use of his time than rushing about aimlessly. He needed to piece things together – to see the whole picture.

The sky was slightly overcast, although occasional breaks in the cloud enabled warm sun to light the surroundings. As Guy paced along the side of Minster Pool, admiring the imposing presence of the cathedral as it rose above trees and houses across the water to the north, he reflected on his meeting with Grant the night before. He would not find himself in the shit, as she'd put it; of that he was quite determined.

Julie was dead, killed by a professional sniper. Her footballing and apparently younger-girl-loving husband, Jonny, although appearing quite callous, seemed to be as much in the dark as he was, not that Grant seemed to see that. Simon Stewart looked to be telling some but not all of the story. Where did he go from here? Overshadowing everything, for Guy, were his poor Sophie and someone warning him off. Arman, whoever he was, must somehow be behind the threat, but it would carry no weight with Guy. Running Sophie down had had the opposite effect to what was intended.

A sudden burst of squawking behind him made him turn. An elderly lady with a cheap, nylon shopping bag was tossing pieces of bread to a dozen mallards in the water, leading to a Darwinian fight. The water shook and wings beat as hunger or greed created an unseemly spectacle of frenzied mass-feeding.

Guy walked on. The CCTV footage supported Sergio's story. If Jenny's disappearance was unrelated to Julie's death, then Sergio's testament gave credence to a wicked coincidence. However, Guy struggled with coincidences; it was always the first place to dig deeper. The only person he hadn't spoken to whose name had been cited so far was Mike Burns. He had of course met him as a fellow guest at David's club dinner, and he'd seemed a decent enough bloke. He put Grant's description of Burns' parties down to jealousy, the same negative emotions she'd displayed towards Guy himself and his own wealth. Since Jenny had left the party with Sergio, what could Burns add? The only connection was the fact he'd hired Sergio as an odd job man, but then that had been explained, and in turn it had determined Jenny's presence at one of his parties. So what? He would need to park Burns for the moment, which left only Sergio as a way forward.

And he was no nearer linking any of this to his family's car accident. Was that just a fantasy, a clever initiative by David to manipulate him into assisting? He needed more information about the other deaths David had referred to.

He sat down on a metal bench, lost in thought and heedless of his surroundings. He needed to run all this past someone. Not Grant – she was heading stubbornly down what Guy strongly regarded as the wrong road. Chasing evidence to prove her pre-determined theory, irrespective of actual facts. George. George always talked objectively, sensibly and was never afraid of considering or voicing a view, even when his own opinions roundly contradicted Guy's. He'd been a sounding board on several occasions when they'd served together in the SAS.

He pulled out his mobile and called George, who answered promptly as ever.

"Hi George, all well?"

"Fine, sir. How's Sophie?"

"No change, but thanks for asking," Guy replied. "Look, I need your help. Can you get yourself on to a train today to Birmingham? Soon as you can. I'll meet you by the ticket barriers at New Street Station. Check the train times and text me when you'll be there."

"No problem, sir. You sure everything's okay?" He sounded concerned.

"Just want your support, George. A hint of the old days. Text me."

Guy rang off and looked up across the murky water. A strategy and planning meeting – just like the old days indeed.

THIRTY-EIGHT

Mehrak concluded his phone call, snapped his small laptop shut and walked from his bedroom back into the kitchen of the dowdy, Birmingham flat. Steve was lounging at the table playing cards with a thin, middle-aged guy who sported greasy, fair hair and a drawn complexion. They were waiting for something to happen and looked up expectantly as Mehrak entered.

"Well?" Steve queried. "Any news while I thrash Tony at cards again?"

"I did some research on him and made some interesting calls," Mehrak said. "All you need to know is that the bastard doesn't do as he's told. I've discussed it all with Arman, and he's keen on what we have to do. We have his instructions."

"And who is he?" Steve asked.

"A baronet called Sterling from Shropshire. Posh, landed gentry type with a family pile north of Shrewsbury. Possibly more to the point, he was a major in the SAS until about three years back. No other reference to a security or detective role so, for some reason, he may be out of his comfort zone."

"Still," Tony pointed out, "he's not your average civilian. Comes with some ability, no doubt."

"What does Arman want us to do, and what's in it for us this time?" Steve asked.

"Usual money, unusual job," Mehrak answered.

"Do we need your crazy brother?" Tony asked.

"Not this time." Mehrak smiled as he spoke.

"Okay, what kind of job then?" Tony persisted.

"Does it matter?" Steve said, folding his cards

on to the table. "Would you argue with Arman?"

Tony snorted. "Get real. Fancy the use of my knees too much."

"You thinking of John?" Steve asked.

"John?" Mehrak queried, looking across at them both in turn.

"Yeah, John," Tony said. "Steve and I knew him before you came on the scene. Big guy was John. Must have been at least six foot six and built like a bloody brick shithouse. Builder, he was. One socket short of a set though. Joined the team but forgot to read the small print, particularly the bit that says you don't fuck up."

"What happened?"

"Fucked up some job by getting pissed the night before. We weren't involved. His bad luck was that Arman was in one of his moods. Took it to heart, he did. They found John's body by the Thames. Both knees blown away and nothing to breathe with."

There was silence in the room.

"Well," Mehrak said, "there'll be no fucking up this time, right? We need to point out to Sterling the error of his ways and get him to back off. And, if he declines, then we'll demonstrate again why that was the wrong decision."

"Again?" Tony asked.

"Long story," Mehrak replied. "Now, I'm not sure where Sterling is at present, but he's not at home and not expected back today. His sister's staying at his house, though."

Tony said, "How do you know all that?"

"Because I rang Hofton Manor – that's where he lives – and asked. He runs some kind of charity, so no problem getting the information as a trustee wanting to speak to him," Mehrak said.

"If he's not there, where are we going to find him?" Steve asked. "We can contact him by mobile, but we can hardly exert pressure that way."

"That would depend," Mehrak said with a smile. "He's very likely to take notice with what I have in mind. Let's get going and I'll fill you in on the way. We're leaving now, so listen carefully to what you need to take."

THIRTY-NINE

With abrupt awareness, Jenny realised she'd read a whole page of her book without taking in a single word. This wasn't the first time it had happened; her mind was on other things – memories, people and deep wishes. She closed the paperback and lay back on the bed, her head resting on the two pillows.

She still wore the same white blouse, jeans, and pink cardigan that had been piled on the bed for her when she'd been pushed into the cellar room and the blindfold removed. Same underwear, too, but at least that was her own. She felt dirty and unclean. Her scalp itched and her hair was disheveled. She hadn't showered for what must have been days. She could imagine herself stretched out, not on the bed as she was now, but in a luxurious bath, immersed in sweet-scented hot water, as hot as she could take it, with bubbles kissing her cheeks and chin, fizzing and popping and chattering in her ears.

The actual number of hours and days she'd been in the room had become incalculable; she had no window to see light or dark, no watch, no calendar. She could only track time in terms of meals, the highlights of her day and the only remaining vestige of normality.

Her eyes roamed the room. The light was still on; it had never gone off, not for a moment. She couldn't find a switch – it was controlled from outside, like the rest of her life. She scanned the familiar brickwork of the ceiling, dusty, scarred, and rich with cobwebs and spiders of differing sizes each lost in its own world and unaware of the lost soul in their midst. She recalled how the largest spider she'd ever seen had crossed the room determinedly and slid effortlessly under the locked door in a demonstration of freedom and choice that had made her cry. She'd cried a lot recently – for her parents, for Sergio, for the loss of her life.

Sergio – where was he? She wanted to be in his arms, to feel the wonderful and skilled touch that brought her whole body to life, that made her kiss him, want him, open herself up to him for their mutual pleasure.

She tried yet again to recall what had happened, how she'd ended up in this repugnant prison. She remembered a party at Mike Burns' house. She remembered music, noise, and the throng of people. There'd been a band playing in the garden and a temporary, boarded dance floor filled with young and old alike enjoying the music, dancing stiffly or flamboyantly under a warm, summer night sky. There'd been playful, scantily-clad girls laughing and singing along to familiar lyrics that evoked memories and made the moment timeless.

She recalled entering the French doors from the garden, feeling alive and energised and excited from the animated dancing. She could remember it clearly, seeing herself in her mind's eye as though she was some remote observer. She was holding Sergio's hand as they pushed their way through the melee in the sitting room, past people holding drinks and chatting earnestly, heading once more for the dining room with its tables laden with food, alcohol and tempting excesses.

After that, events blurred into a montage of scenes. Try as she might from her miserable present, she couldn't piece together her recent past. White wine – had she drunk too much? She could remember weaving her way up the staircase and standing in the hallway of Burns' house. She could remember being in Sergio's Audi TT; she could remember draping her arms around his shoulders and kissing him long and hard; she could remember kneeling in front of him behind the locked door of an upstairs bathroom. Why wouldn't it all become clear? It was so frustrating. She sat up on the bed, feet on the floor, and glanced across at the door, which was forever shut. *Let me out. For God's sake, let me out.*

Jenny picked up her book and hurled it across the room. It smashed against the wall and came to rest on the floor, spread-eagled, its spine stubbornly rising towards the ceiling. She stood up, walked across and kicked it, hurting her foot in the process. The book careered into the door and this time fell closed, a torn page sticking out like a bookmark. Despite the pain, she took a step and kicked it again, sending it speeding beneath the bed. She leant her back against the door and slid down it until she was sitting on the floor.

She was about to grab her knees and wrap her arms around them tight but stopped herself. She was more than this. Her parents were Simon and Sally Stewart, after all. She stood up, crossed the cell, and rescued her tattered book from under the bed. It was covered in dirt and cobwebs. She stared at it, then shifted her gaze to the bottom of the door. If a simple spider could escape, so could she – couldn't she?

FORTY

Guy glanced at his Omega Seamaster watch. It was 3.15pm on Saturday, almost a week to the hour since he'd attended the Bull Club dinner. The concourse in front of the main ticket barriers at Birmingham's New Street Station was busy with a stark contrast between those hurrying to catch trains and those, like Guy, who alternately stood and paced around as they waited to meet someone.

The sound of his name being called made him look towards the ticket barriers. George approached, effortlessly swinging a small holdall in his left hand. They greeted each other with a brisk handshake.

"What's new, sir?"

"I'll update you in the car. We'll go back to the hotel and review. I'm in a multi-storey – a little bit of a walk."

"Sounds good," George said. "I could do with a stretch. Not overly spacious, those carriages."

They walked out of the station and through to Corporation Street. On the corner of the wide pavement a street vendor sold copies of the *Birmingham Herald* from a small, mobile kiosk. The day's headline proclaimed: '*Local businessman dies in fire tragedy*'. Guy bought a copy and tucked it under his arm.

The journey out of the city was straightforward, and Guy was able to update George with everything relevant that had happened – from his visit to the Stewarts' home in Four Oaks through to his encounters with Caroline Grant and Sergio.

Back at Sandbrough Hall, George checked into

his room and the two men met in the deserted lounge, an ornate room with a high ceiling and picture windows offering excellent views of the well-tended gardens and countryside beyond. They ordered a tray of tea and sat either side of an elaborate marble fireplace; the log fire hissed and flickered gently, emitting the relaxing aroma of burning cherry wood. Not strictly needed in terms of the weather, but it gave the room a homely feel.

George replaced his teacup onto its saucer, his giant hands making it look as though it had been designed for a doll's house. "Where's this all leave us, then, sir?" he asked. "I guess the priority at this time is finding Jenny – if her disappearance is connected with Julie's death, then that would be a bonus. That's how I see it. So, are we any nearer?"

Guy had been staring into the fire and continued to watch the dogged flames licking the wood as he spoke. "Not much, George, if truth be known. Jenny's still missing and her whereabouts remain as indeterminate as ever. Last seen apparently in a country road in the middle of the night."

"And the delightful Grant reckoned she was hiding out with a friend – attention-seeking?"

Guy smiled. "That's how she sees it," he agreed. "Right. You argue her corner; let me try to prove my point." He scratched his chin. "I asked Simon and Sally about Jenny's friends. Most of them are further south apparently, old school friends from Cheltenham Ladies'."

"Of the friends the parents know about," George said. "Are you telling me the parents know *all* her friends? She's a teenager, after all."

"I think with someone as honest as Jenny seems to be, they probably do, yes. Why wouldn't she tell them about any other good friends she has? After all, if she can confess to Sergio as a boyfriend…" Guy's voice trailed off.

"And have they contacted all the friends? Every single one of them?"

"Sally said she'd rung round all the key ones – you know, the closest ones who would know something," Guy said. "She asked for discretion."

"But if one of them is sheltering her, they're hardly going to say, 'Oh, Mrs Stewart, she's actually staying with me, but I'm not to tell you'," George pointed out.

"I know what you mean," Guy said. 'But this 'staying with friends' thing just doesn't make sense to me. Okay, I haven't met Jenny…"

"You don't need to have done – she's a celeb's daughter," George interrupted. "The daughter of two celebs, come to that. Headstrong and determined – evidenced by the fact that she can date Sergio in brazen opposition to them."

"True. But here's a girl who's also innately responsible. She was head girl at school and has always kept her parents informed of where she is and when she'll be back – she even updates them if there are changes, and even if Sergio is involved. So for her to simply take off is as likely as a palace guard going AWOL, or indeed even moving." Guy paused. "So, what did happen on that country road, George? Let's take it that slime-ball Sergio did drop her off in the countryside at one fifteen in the morning. Where would she go? She was dressed for a party. She might have had a coat, as seen on the CCTV, but she also had high heels. Not designed for walking any distance or yomping across fields. If Sergio did have a shot of guilt and returned for her, where was she at that point? Hiding?"

"But why hide, sir? If he drove for five minutes before deciding to go back, he'd have left her for ten minutes. Maybe fifteen, tops. That's time for her to work out that she had limited options, and that pride or no pride she was better off in the car than shivering on the verge."

Guy ran a hand through his hair. "She could have called one of these famous friends to come and fetch her and then hidden from Sergio knowing the cavalry was on its way," he said. "But then we've established that her friends aren't involved –"

"No," George interrupted. "We've established that no friend *so far asked* has confessed to knowing her whereabouts."

Guy nodded slowly. "Fair enough. But remember, her friends are seventeen and eighteen, mainly living at home with parents according to Sally, so not well placed to drive out in the middle of the night at short notice. Besides, other than a couple of friends in Sutton Coldfield and Four Oaks, all the others are an hour or two away at least."

As he poured them both another cup of tea, George said, "Again, that's of the friends we know about. She may have an older, local friend."

"Fair comment, George. But let's assume for a moment that no cavalry came to rescue her. What if instead she was picked up by a stranger as she waited in the hope that Sergio would see sense and return? That's the unspoken fear, isn't it?"

"In which case, sir, she could be anywhere, dead or alive. But what are the chances of someone with such evil intent driving down that rural road in those ten minutes?"

"Remote, but then don't forget she has actually disappeared," Guy said. "And we're involved because it could be that one-in-a-million case." He stood up, picked a couple of logs out of the wicker basket and placed them strategically in the grate. Turning back towards George, he said, "Okay, what if there was no row? What if she wasn't dropped off there? After all, we only have Sergio's word that's what happened, and that surely has limited value."

"You mean if he brought her back to Birmingham, to Moseley?"

"Yes."

"But if she's disappeared and Sergio is somehow to blame, why go through all the fiction of a row, sir?"

"Because in reality he took her somewhere in Birmingham, or she was collected from his flat by Arman or whoever's kidnapped her. 'Disappearing' miles away would throw the police off the scent. If he said he'd brought her back to his flat and that she simply left in the morning, gone when he woke up from some alcoholic stupor, it would have been simpler – and maybe more believable – but would point the police to Birmingham."

"Where can the evidence come from, sir, to support the theory that he actually brought her back to Moseley, or even Birmingham? Because if that was the case then he's lying about the row – and why would he be doing that?"

Guy thought for a moment. "Well," he said slowly, "we can get it from the same technology we're partly relying on to date. I'm going to ask Grant if she can get someone to look at the ANPR database to see if and where it picked up Sergio's TT on the roads into Birmingham – from Tamworth right through to Sergio's squalid little flat."

"ANPR?"

"The Automatic Number Plate Recognition system. All police forces have access to the database and can track a particular number plate, so long as it passes operating cameras of course. I think I'm right in saying it photographs those in the front seats, too. That would show if anyone was in the car with Sergio," Guy explained.

"Think she'll do it?"

"I can but ask. If not, I'll have a quiet word with David. I'm going to get it, George, come what may – I feel the results are going to be really interesting."

FORTY-ONE

Grant answered her mobile straight away.

"Caroline," Guy said, not bothering with pleasantries, "I need you to look into something."

"And what would that be?"

"Look, we've established Sergio left Burns' party with Jenny – you saw the CCTV footage too."

"Go on."

"Well, we only have Sergio's word that the row happened and Jenny disappeared like a victim of a conjuror's trick. As I see it, that 'evidence' needs to be weighed against the fact he's a palpable slime-ball and to go missing like this is so out of character for Jenny. It could also be a cover for her actually being taken in Birmingham, even from Sergio's flat."

"Okay. Let's run with that for the moment."

"Right. So, he says he left her on a road near Tamworth and went home. He told me he was alone there, save for a bottle of whiskey. If he returned to his flat, we can fairly presume he travelled a standard route back to Moseley – why wouldn't he? If he didn't, he took her somewhere else in the city. If his 'row' story is correct, then one white Audi TT with a single occupant should have hit Birmingham any time from 1.45am, probably nearer 2am, allowing for any alleged search of the roadside. If the row never happened and Jenny remained in the car, they'd have reached Birmingham any time from say half one – and then we'd have a white Audi TT with two occupants."

"You mean if he's lying about the row, he could be lying about his destination as well?"

"Exactly, although Simon Stewart went round in the morning and confirmed Sergio had been drinking."

"Doesn't mean he was drinking at home. Could have gone home later." Grant said.

"His car was there – would he have risked drink-driving?"

"I thought you said he was a slime-ball. Besides, someone could have driven him."

"All good theories, Caroline, but what would really help would be if you could arrange to get some road CCTV checked through the ANPR database. See if you can track his car, his journey. See if there was a passenger when he came into Birmingham. Can you do that?"

There was a long pause.

Eventually Grant said, "I can – even an inspector can authorise that as it's fewer than ninety days ago – but it's a lot of work for some poor sod, and all on a whim which, in my view, has nothing to do with the murder of Julie Reid –"

"But everything to do with a missing girl. Come on, Caroline. As I understand it, the database also stores photographs of the driver and any front seat passenger. Is that right? If so, it'll prove this matter once and for all. No passenger, he left her; passenger, he's lying."

He heard Caroline sigh.

"Okay, okay," she capitulated. "I'll put it in hand. But don't hold your breath. It'll depend on whether he passed any cameras – which is likely – and whether those cameras have been converted to the ANPR system; not all have. And the picture quality isn't always razor-sharp – it's often not much more than a blur."

"But at least it'll show whether someone's in the passenger seat, won't it?" Guy pointed out. "And if there is, wc know who it is already, don't we?"

"You're more persistent than I gave you credit for, Guy. I'll cut you some slack – but only a little. Okay?"

"Thank you, I really appreciate that. Timescale?"

"When it's done." Grant paused and then added, "I don't know – twenty-four hours? It'll take what it takes, but I'll push it, okay?"

"Thanks, Caroline. Anything new your end?"

"No, not yet. How's your fiancée?"

The question threw Guy for a moment. "No change, but thanks."

"Let's hope there's some good news soon."

Guy hesitated a moment and then said, "I don't want either of us in the shit, Caroline. Let me know what you find."

He rang off.

FORTY-TWO

On Saturday evening, Lucy lounged on the deep sofa in Hofton Manor's snug Red Drawing Room. She turned a page in her book, absent-mindedly twisting the ends of her long, blonde hair with the fingers of her left hand. Her mind drifted from the story as she reflected she'd returned to her family home to support her older brother in his hour of need, but she'd not even seen him yet.

That said, as an independent, newly-single thirty-year-old, she could go where she liked – and at the end of the day, spending time at the manor with all its comforts, nostalgia and associated activities was about as good as it could get. It was certainly a positive contrast to her life in London. She finally gave up on the book, put it down on the sofa and glanced at her watch. Ten past eight. She rubbed her eyes. A sudden deafening noise took her by surprise, and it was a few moments before she realised two large concrete planters had crashed through one of the French windows. They'd taken out the entire pane of glass, leaving just a jagged necklace around the inside of the frame.

As she started to unfurl herself from the sofa, three men stepped quickly but carefully through the shattered window into the room. Each wore a black balaclava and black leather gloves, and each held a handgun. She heard the dogs start to bark beyond the Great Hall, but the drawing room door was shut.

The leading man pointed his gun at her. "Don't move a bloody muscle," he said firmly. He turned to one of the others. "Get the door, Chas."

Lucy froze as the short, stocky man called Chas

crossed the room to the light oak door.

"What do you want?" she asked quietly.

"Shut it," the leading man said sharply. "I said don't move. Anything, Chas?"

Lucy turned to see Chas easing the door open and looking through the gap. The sound of barking became louder.

"Someone's coming, Andy," he said.

"That'll be…" Lucy began.

"I said, shut it," Andy growled menacingly.

Chas moved behind the door as it swung open and the elderly housekeeper, Betty, entered looking flustered and alarmed in her customary grey tunic and white apron. She stopped as soon as she saw Andy and started to scream, but Chas shoved the door shut, came up behind her and wrapped his left hand across her mouth. Pulling her into him, he pushed his gun into her right side and hissed at her to be quiet. Betty froze.

"Sit down on the sofa," Andy ordered, motioning towards the settee with flicks of his gun. He turned to the third, taller man. "Bill, stay by the French windows," he said.

Chas frog-marched Betty to the sofa and pushed her firmly down next to Lucy. Chas stood to one side. The third man, Bill, sidled over to the broken window.

Lucy looked at the lead man, trying to see his eyes as they peered through the balaclava. They were dark, cold and threatening – she could sense that without any facial clues. *Help me, Guy*.

As she stared, Andy said, "Any more noise from either of you and the other one gets a bullet in the leg. Understand?"

The two women nodded and risked a quick glance at each other. Lucy noticed Betty was shaking; not surprising, given the circumstances.

"Is there anyone else in the house?" Andy demanded.

They both shook their heads.

"That's better. Let's get down to business. Who are you?" He looked at Lucy.

"Lucy, Lucy Sterling."

Andy nodded. "Right. Sister of Guy Sterling, huh? You look like your picture."

Betty shot her a glance.

"We want to get a message to him," Andy continued. "Where is he?"

"He's on business in Birmingham. We're expecting him back soon."

"Well, if he's not here, we'll have to ring him, won't we? Where's your mobile?"

"Over there on the table, by that chair," she said, pointing. "I'll get it." She started to rise.

Andy turned his head to follow her line of vision and then looked back at her.

"Sit down," he ordered, and then paused as if a thought had occurred to him. "Actually," he decided, "yes – you fetch it. Let's have Lady La-di-da do the running around and waiting on me. Get it and give it to me."

Lucy stood and walked over to the table. As she leaned over to pick up the mobile up with her right hand, she appeared to trip; she put her left hand out to the edge of the table to stop herself from falling.

"Pissed, are you?" Bill asked.

"Sorry. Pins and needles in my leg."

Lucy stood up holding her mobile and, as she did so, took her left index finger off the panic alarm button that was fixed under the table's rim. It was the first time it had ever been used. *What if it wasn't working?* She knew there'd be no audible signal in the room – it would be received in the security room, the gate lodge and – most vitally with George away – in the local police control room in Shrewsbury. She didn't know how long it would take for the police to respond – the manor was, after all, rural and set well back from the main road. And the estate's electric gates were closed, but they should have the code. Was Jack in the lodge?

As Lucy returned to the sofa, she tried to give Betty a discreet, reassuring look. She hoped Betty would realise the panic alarm had been activated and that, with any luck, help was on the way.

FORTY-THREE

Having returned to his hotel room after an early supper, leaving George in the bar, Guy settled down in an armchair with his notebook and pen to review all the developments in the case. How he missed Sophie.

His mobile, which lay on a small table next to him, burst into life. He picked it up, glancing at the caller ID as he did so.

"Hi, Luce. What's new?"

There was no response, just silence.

Guy continued, "Lucy? You there? Can't hear you." He pushed the phone hard against his ear.

A man's voice replied, "Lucy's here, but so are we."

Guy paused for a second. "Who the hell's that?"

"The name's Andy, and I'm the guy who's standing in one of your sitting rooms pointing a gun at your little sister."

Guy said nothing. *He'd left her exposed.*

"You still there, Guy? I hope so, else things are going to get pretty messy at this end."

"Of course I'm still here! What do you want, money? You can have money – just leave her alone."

"I'm not after your money, Guy. I'm looking for some – how shall I put it? – commitment."

"*Commitment*?"

"Exactly," Andy said. "You sound puzzled, so let me spell it out for you. I do favours for lots of different people. Some you'd like, some you certainly wouldn't. You certainly won't like my friend who's asking for a favour today."

"Who's that?"

"Shut up and listen," Andy snapped. "I understand you're doing the rounds in Birmingham, asking rather too many questions. My friend doesn't like that. He's already tried to tell you – and that reminds me, how is Sophie?"

Guy felt a wave of anger but forced himself to stay quiet.

"Nothing to say, Guy? Never mind. Now, my friend thinks you're asking about things that don't concern you. He thinks it really is time for you to stop and go home. Are you going to agree this time?"

"I've a job to do."

"And so have I, but it seems mine can be done quicker. I'm here already; a couple more seconds and my job's complete."

"Leave my sister alone. She's not involved in any of this. This is my errand, not hers." He hurried over to the room safe and opened it, still holding the mobile to his ear. He removed the Glock, slipped it into his pocket and closed the safe.

Andy went on, "Got Betty here, too, Guy. She your maid or something? Looks like she's in the frame at this end as well." He paused for a moment. "I haven't heard any commitment from you yet, Guy, and I'm a man with very little patience. My fault and a bit of a bummer in situations like this, but, hey, what can I do about it?"

"What commitment are you looking for?" Guy snatched up the Morgan keys and made for the door.

"Simple," Andy said. "You stop interfering, I leave you in peace."

"I don't take instructions from lunatics," Guy replied as he left the room and hurried downstairs.

"Wrong answer, Guy."

"Look, just leave the women alone. I'll come home right now. You hear me? Just pack up and go, okay? You've got what you wanted, tell your friend that. Right?' Guy glanced into the bar, caught George's attention and beckoned him urgently.

"I think you're moving in the right direction, Guy, but you're in no position to give orders, are you? We'll go when we want to go, and that isn't quite yet."

"You're messing with the wrong person," Guy warned. He unlocked the Morgan and both he and George climbed in. "I'm not someone you want to fall out with. Won't end well for you, believe me."

"Think you're a tough guy, do you?"

Guy accelerated hard on to the main road, showering grit from the hotel drive onto the neatly mown verge. The mobile switched to hands-free.

"You wouldn't be able to research the half of it."

Andy's voice echoed around him. "Sounds like you're driving, Guy."

"Correct. I'm leaving Birmingham, as I said. I'm coming home, and I'm not in a good mood."

"It's a long way, Guy. We'll be gone by the time you get here."

"You'll have run away, you mean? I'll find you, believe me I will. I won't sleep until I do."

"Seek if you dare, Guy, but you'll be on a fool's errand." Andy paused for a beat. 'You know, your attitude has really hurt me, it's hurt me very much indeed. I suspect you don't realise how serious I am, so

I'm going to show you."

Guy said nothing. There was something evil in Andy's voice, in his tone. He glanced at George who was listening intently.

Guy said slowly, "What do you mean?"

Andy's voice came clearly down the line. "I'm going to play a game before we leave."

"A game? Are you bloody mad?"

"Language, Guy. I'm getting a little annoyed with your 'big man' attitude. Let me remind you I'm the one with a gun in my hand, I'm right here, and I could kill these two pathetic women in the next five seconds. So I'm the one who's doing the talking – calling the shots, literally. So yes, a game. Listen up. One of the two women in front of me will be today's example. The other will be the example if you dare to carry on interfering."

"What are you on about?"

Andy hissed, "Listen, you stuck-up piece of shit, and listen good. I've two decisions to make. First one – where do I put the bullet, leg or chest? Second one – who receives it, Lucy or Betty? Choices, choices, huh?"

"You bastard!"

"I know. But life would be so dull if I did a nine-to-five for a small packet of beans, wouldn't it? Chas, come here."

There was a pause and Guy strained to work out what was happening. He couldn't hear Andy, but he could hear a woman starting to cry.

"Right, here we go Guy. Sitting comfortably? I've found a way to choose. If we were on telly, I would show you my charming assistant, Chas. However, you can't see how fucking ugly he actually is as he happens to be wearing a rather fetching balaclava. Say hello, Chas."

Guy heard a second male voice grunt a hello.

"Now, Guy, my lovely assistant is right next to me and he's got a coin. He's going to toss it now, aren't you Chas?" There was silence. "Chas just nodded, Guy. Right, toss the coin, catch it and turn it onto the back of your hand. Heads it's the chest, tails the leg. Go."

Another pause.

"Well, well. That's interesting, Guy. Sadly, under the rules of this wonderful game, I can't tell you whether that's a head or a tail – and we must follow the rules, mustn't we? Now, toss it again, Chas. That's it. Heads it's the rich bitch, tails it's the old bitch. Well caught, Chas. Let me see. Well, well. I'd love to tell you what I'm going to do next, Guy, but, hey, seeing as you know the rules of the game now, you're not expecting me to, right? Time to remove the silencer so you can join in the fun. And just before we close and see this through, let me remind you – if you decide to play detective again and upset my very good friend, the other bitch will have it in the chest within seven days of your indiscretion. Got it?"

Guy yelled down the phone, "You're a dead man, Andy. The hunt starts now!"

As he spoke, there was the loud crack of a gunshot and then the line went dead, just as a woman started to scream. As the echoes reverberated around the car's cabin, Guy realised with deep frustration that, due to its sheer terror, he couldn't even identify its source.

FORTY-FOUR

Arman lounged on the sofa in his London hotel suite, one foot resting on the distant arm, the other on the floor. He wore a bathrobe, which hung nonchalantly off his bulky frame, and he felt relaxed after a calming massage in the basement spa. He could still smell the oils, feel the satisfying, feminine touch.

He wrapped up a telephone conversation on his private mobile. The line had not been good.

"Sure, sis, I'll be home in the next day or two. You'll just have to cope a little while longer. I know you can do it. You can, can't you…? What…? I said in a day or two. Just keep doing what you're doing, and all will be fine. I'll ring you in the morning, okay?"

Another mobile started to ring from the floor by his side.

"Look, I must go, someone's calling me on the other phone… The other phone, I have two, okay? One's for business, one's for you. Love you, bye."

He rang off, answering the second as he snatched it up off the floor.

"Yes, Mehrak. Latest?"

"Job done," Mehrak informed him.

"Where are you now?"

"Heading home."

"And the great detective?"

"Heading home too. I reckon they must have had some sort of alarm, or the cops were quick off the mark when called because we passed a blue lighter speeding in that direction as we got on the main road. They're going to find an interesting sight. Played the game."

"Like Manchester?" Arman asked.

"Yeah, it's fun all round."

"You sad bastard. Tell the lads I'll arrange for the money to be paid. I'll bring it up to date. And pay your brother, too. Keep available for any follow-up; we want his stuck-up lordship to back off. He's sticking his beak in too many places and we can't afford any trouble now. There are some things you can't spend your way out of. Now, get out of Shropshire and check your alibi."

"That's sorted, Arman. I'm not an amateur."

"I know that, Mehrak – if you were, you wouldn't be so fucking expensive."

Mehrak laughed. "Worth every penny, Arman. Paying for amateurs is a false economy."

"Don't I know it."

"What are you doing now?"

"Me? I'm staying in London for a couple more days, then heading home. Just rung my sister. Everything's okay there but go and check, will you? You know what she's like."

"Sure. I have an interest in all this, too."

FORTY-FIVE

Guy was already on the motorway by the time he tried Lucy's mobile for the third time, but it still wouldn't connect. With a heightened sense of frustration, he telephoned the manor's landline. After several rings the phone was answered – by Lucy. She sounded dreadful.

"Guy. You need to get here quickly."

"I'm already on my way. Have they gone? How's Betty? How are you? I can't get through on your mobile."

"They stamped on it."

"How's Betty? What's happened?"

"She's... she's been shot. There were three of them. They just burst in..."

"Is she okay?"

"Not really. The guy shot her in the left leg, just below the knee. I've tried to stop the bleeding and called an ambulance. She's being really brave, but she's in a state of shock. The main guy pointed his gun at me and then, at the last moment, turned it on Betty. He dropped my mobile on the floor and stamped on it, then made further threats, then they left through the garden."

"Poor Betty. You're not hurt?" Guy asked as he pushed the Morgan to ninety miles per hour.

"I'm fine."

"Thank God for that. Were you able to press the panic alarm?"

"Yes, but the police aren't here yet. No sign of Jack either. What's happening, Guy?"

Guy knew what was happening. The threatening text he'd received came back into his mind. They had brought the fight to his home.

"Who were they, what did they look like?"

Lucy described them. "It was like something out of a Hollywood film, Guy. Utterly unreal, shocking. This Andy bloke had the coldest eyes I've ever seen – and it was all I could see of him. Dark, almost black they were." She paused. "As well as Andy, there was a Chas who tossed the coin. And the third one was…was…"

Guy heard Betty mutter something.

"Yes, that's right, Betty, it was Bill," Sophie said. "I'm sorry, Guy, but I can't tell you much else."

"Hey, you've done brilliantly," Guy said, "George and I will be home soon."

"Are you staying?"

"For as long as it takes to sort Betty out and get you home," Guy said.

"And then?"

"Then I'm back to Birmingham. I have a job to complete, and now an Andy to find, too."

FORTY-SIX

The following morning Guy, George and Lucy ate a light breakfast sitting around the large, wooden kitchen table, its surface worn with decades of use. The atmosphere was subdued, each reflecting on the previous evening's events.

As Guy ate his toast, he recalled Lucy's bewilderment that the police had asked very little, had said statements would be taken 'sometime soon', and had left when Betty was safely in an ambulance. It was no mystery to him. On the drive home he'd called David and explained what had happened. David was evidently being kept in the picture by Caroline and told Guy to leave it with him. He'd obviously sorted something. No fuss from the police, by David's command. Guy was being allowed time to resolve things himself.

George interrupted his thoughts, breaking the silence. "Thought any more about the plans we discussed last night, sir?"

Guy looked across at him. "Nothing further, George. You stay here. I'll drop you, Lucy, at the station in Shrewsbury, and then I'm going to make contact with Mike Burns. You never know, he may have something to give, and we have limited leads at the moment. Jenny was at his party after all, and he apparently knows Sergio – although I do struggle with that one. Perhaps after that I'll put some further pressure on Sergio – let's see what Caroline comes up with."

"Sure you'll be okay?" George looked slightly concerned.

"I'll be fine," Guy reassured him. "I'll feel a hell

of a lot better knowing you're minding the shop here. If I carry on, it's highly likely they'll come back. I need you here, George. I'm not taking any more chances. Do whatever you think is necessary to keep the place safe."

They finished breakfast and Guy drove Lucy to the station to catch the London train. After they parted, he sat in his car in the station car park and rang a local florist to order flowers for Betty, who had been detained in hospital for observation. He also ordered yet more freesias for Sophie; they were her favourite flowers. Then he pulled out his notebook, which he'd left in the car, and flicked through the pages until he found the list of telephone numbers he'd made from Sergio's mobile – it seemed an age ago. He found Mike Burns' number, which had a Tamworth dialling code. He was about to call when his phone rang; it was Grant. He braced himself for the next skirmish and hoped he could avoid an all-out battle. *Keep cool, be relaxed, polite.*

"Morning, Caroline."

"David told me what happened last night, Guy," she said in a concerned tone. "I was so sorry to hear. How's your housekeeper?"

Guy updated her. "Thanks for asking, Caroline. Anything new at your end?" He was struggling with her amicable tones, which were so alien to him. Sure she was brisk, that was her usual style, but on this occasion he detected a softer edge to her tone – or was that just wishful thinking?

"I've got some feedback on the ANPR enquiry you asked me to carry out. Remember?" she was asking now.

"Of course. That was quick," Guy said sincerely.

"We are efficient here, Guy."

"And what have you found?"

"We tracked the car along the obvious route back into Birmingham and Moseley from Tamworth. M42 and M6 motorways, followed by the Aston Expressway. It tootled into Birmingham all legal and proper. Could say it was an exemplary drive, especially for the early hours of the morning. By the way, I can confirm it's registered to your Moseley Sergio – Sergio Thomas Robinson, believe it or not."

Guy felt a strong sense of excitement. "Not wanting to attract attention, then?" he asked, almost rhetorically.

"Maybe, maybe not. Who knows?" She paused briefly before adding, "It's difficult to get a clear shot of the actual driver, Guy –"

"What could be seen?" Guy asked, interrupting her in his enthusiasm to hear the results.

"I was just going to say," Grant said. She paused, seemingly enjoying the moment – Guy wanted answers, and she had them. "Looks like a young lad. Coincidence if not your Sergio, wouldn't you say?"

"I agree," Guy said. "And Jenny? Could you see Jenny in the passenger seat? Or was it empty, in line with his version of events?"

"As I recall, you said she had long brown hair? You left with the only photo on Sunday."

"Correct," Guy said. "So? Was she there or not?"

Grant answered smoothly. "Well, as I warned you, always difficult to tell who's who with present technology, Guy. But what I can say is this: Sergio was not alone on the Aston Expressway. There's a long-haired girl in the passenger seat. Seems like your missing girl is in Birmingham after all, Guy, and Sergio has some more questions to answer."

FORTY-SEVEN

Guy's mind began to process the new information. Had he expected this news or not? If Jenny was in the car and was taken back to Birmingham, possibly to Moseley, then Sergio was lying. Lying about what happened that evening. Lying about the row. Lying about abandoning Jenny at the roadside in the early hours of the morning. It raised several further questions. Why was he lying? Why make himself look a complete jerk about abandoning her in such a way when he hadn't? Where did they go in Birmingham? His flat? And, most important of all, where was Jenny now? One thing Guy was certain about was that he had to speak to slime-ball Sergio again.

"You still there, Guy?" he heard Grant say down the phone.

"Sure, yes, I'm here."

"Puts a different light on your missing girl case then?"

Guy could sense the re-emergence of Grant's trademark smugness.

"True. But a girl's still missing, Caroline, with very concerned parents. It's not a happy situation whatever the detail. I'll need to speak to Sergio again."

"Want me involved?" The question threw Guy – she almost sounded sincere. Maybe she was slowly coming round to his way of thinking.

"Give me time to work on it. I'll speak to Simon and Sally; see how they want to play it. I'll advise them again that whatever advice they've had from Laurie Whittall, it must surely now be time to talk to the police

– bring you on board."

"Okay, speak to them. If they want help, call me."

"Thanks. Appreciated."

"It's for the sake of the girl, and the parents, not you," she said quickly. Back to the Grant of old.

"Noted."

Grant rang off.

Guy leaned back in his car seat. He now had two calls to make. Before Grant had phoned, he was about to call Mike Burns. He contemplated waiting until after he'd visited Sergio, but then he didn't know when he might get to see the multimillionaire businessman. Better to at least get something in the diary. Sergio was the priority for a meeting though.

He telephoned the number he had for Mike Burns and settled back. A woman picked up.

"Murdoch Hall."

"Good morning. My name is Sir Guy Sterling and I was hoping to have a word with Mike Burns, please. Is he available?"

"Mike's not here at the moment, I'm afraid. I can take your number and ask him to call you, if you'd like. Will he know what it's about?" She sounded elderly and a little hesitant. Guy was grateful that his Betty had more about her.

"Would you just give him my name and number and say that I could do with some advice – just five minutes of his time? Remind him I met him at the last Bull Club dinner. Who am I talking to?"

"This is Valerie Burns," came the reply. "You'd better let me have your number then. What is it?"

Guy felt embarrassed he'd assumed the woman was a housekeeper. He hadn't checked into Mike Burns' background, nor had he asked him for details – there hadn't been the need, and the topic hadn't come up when they'd met at the dinner. No reason why his wife wouldn't answer the phone after all. Guy gave her his mobile number.

"You'll be sure to pass it on, won't you?" he said. "It's important. When do you think he'll be back?"

"I'm not exactly sure," Valerie answered, "but he won't be long, not long at all. I'll make sure he gets your message in any event, Mr… erm, Sir Guy."

Guy thanked her and rang off. Not much more to do there for the moment.

He ran his fingers over his mobile and dialled Sergio's number. It rang four or five times and, while it resounded in his ear, he pictured Sergio's untidy, rundown flat with its worn floor, overflowing bin and putrid smell.

"Yeah?"

Guy said, "Getting used to your new mobile number, Sergio? Sounds like you're driving. Where are you?"

"What's it to you, Sam?" Sergio replied in a confrontational tone.

"That needn't concern you. What does need to concern you, however, is whether or not you answer my question: where are you? It's not a tricky one, is it?"

Pause.

"Going home. Why?"

"Because I want some help from you. This time there might be something in it for you – as long as you're sensible and don't piss me about."

"You told me last time there was something in it for me. There wasn't though, was there?" Sergio sounded belligerent rather than angry – having a go at someone who had mildly cheated him.

"That's because you pissed me about, Sergio," Guy said firmly. "Like you said Jenny pissed you about."

"This about Jenny again?" Sergio verbally squared up to Guy.

"No, it's about you, Sergio, not Jenny. I've moved on from Jenny. Reckon she's holed up somewhere with one of her girlie mates, playing silly buggers. You know what these celeb kids are like – just want attention. What do you think?"

Sergio suddenly sounded more upbeat. "Too right, Sam. She used to do my head in." He paused. "Okay, I'll meet you. Where?"

"Your flat again. When will you be back?"

"About dinner time."

"I'll be round at about one thirty then. Put the kettle on."

FORTY-EIGHT

Sergio let himself into his basement flat and shut the door behind him, oblivious to the tortured sound as it scraped on the floor – the noise was so familiar to him it no longer registered. He looked at his watch. Twelve fifty. That maniac Sam would be round in forty minutes or so, but somehow he felt more relaxed about the prospect. Sounded like Jenny was no longer of interest. Maybe he'd impressed the bloke, maybe he was going to get hired after all. He noticed the mail on the floor and kicked a couple of brown envelopes under the table. Bills, most likely. Sod them. They could wait until he'd earned something from Sam.

He crossed the kitchen to his bedroom. The bed was untidy, unmade – as it always was, unless he was entertaining. He eased his small backpack off his shoulder and tossed it on to the duvet, then took his wallet out of his pocket and checked it. A couple of fivers left. He could do with the cash. As he replaced the wallet, he reflected money never lasted long – just like snow in the desert or whatever the bloody expression was. He smiled. Spoiling pretty girls was expensive. They always preferred the rip-off doubles to singles in a nightclub.

He opened his rucksack and tossed a half-empty packet of condoms onto the bedside table. He smiled again. The doubles made them more pliable though, easier to get into bed. Stupid tarts. Yes, it had been a good night. He tried to remember the girl's name and failed. Could only picture her adoring face looking up at him as he'd lain on top of her naked body. Yes, a really good night.

Walking back into the kitchen, Sergio pulled open the door of the fridge that sat under a grimy work surface. No light came on – that had bust months ago. The shelves were pretty bare, and what was in there looked rank and dubious. Stooping down, he grabbed a bottle of lager from inside and shoved the door shut. The small fridge shook. He snatched a packet of salt and vinegar crisps and a bottle opener from the worktop and slumped heavily into a chair at the table. Resting his feet on a second, he scraped it back across the floor to find the perfect position, legs were fully stretched. Metal met metal, and there was the hiss of released gas as the top flew off the beer bottle. The solid disc hit the laminated surface and rolled like a punctured wheel for a few seconds before rattling to a stop with a miniature drum roll.

Sergio took a long swig of beer, grimacing as the cold, fizzy liquid hit the back of his throat. It felt good, though. He placed the bottle on the table and belched loudly before picking up the crisp packet, ripping it apart and stuffing a handful of crisps noisily into his mouth. At that moment he heard footsteps descending the stairs outside, followed by a sharp knock on the glass panel in the door. *Shit, Sam was early.*

He dropped the crisps on the table, lifted his feet from the chair to the floor in a slow, deliberate movement and walked the few steps to the door, opening it with force and confidence.

It wasn't Sam. For a few brief moments he was thrown – the trim beard was new and the Yankees' baseball cap was pulled tight down over his visitor's head.

"Mehrak. Wasn't expecting you."

Sergio stepped back into the kitchen to let Mehrak enter. He was casually dressed in jeans and a blue denim jacket with black leather driving gloves. He turned to face Sergio, his eyes even darker than his host recalled.

"I'm expecting Sam," Sergio said simply.

"I know, you rang and told me – remember? Did what you were told again."

"He'll be here soon."

"I know, one thirty. I do listen." Mehrak glanced round before looking back at Sergio. "Anyone else here?"

"No, I just got back from Manchester. Why?"

Mehrak stepped further into the kitchen. "I want you to take me somewhere," Mehrak said, pushing the door closed behind him. "Important meeting, and I could do with your support, if you get my meaning. We need to collect something on the way."

Sergio straightened up, standing as tall as he could. "You don't own me, you know, Mehrak. I've done what you asked with Jenny. Whatever's next is down to you and Arman. Sam's out of it too, he said so, so I'm a free agent again now, aren't I? Can take a job from anyone, right? And Sam's offering me cash." He stared defiantly at Mehrak.

A dark look crossed the other man's face. "You don't seem to have heard me, Sergio. I want you with me, *now*. You'll get double what Arman's already paid you. Better to take an actual offer rather than another of Sam's games."

There was logic in that statement, Sergio reflected. Hard cash was king at the end of the day – here was a bird in the hand and all that. But there was something in Mehrak's look that scared him.

"Look, Mehrak, I don't want to let Sam down. What will I say to him?"

"You won't be here to say anything if you're doing a job for me, will you? And you will be doing a job with me, won't you? Arman asked for you in particular – I can't go back and tell him you refused, can I? Not good for my reputation – and certainly not good for you."

Sergio started to feel even more uncomfortable. He started to tune in to his instinct. The person here with him now was the greatest threat. Sam might be a maniac, Sam might have a gun, Sam might be able to throw him around – but Sam wasn't here. Mehrak was.

"No," he agreed slowly. "I guess I won't be here – I'll be with you, won't I?"

"You've got it." Mehrak seemed to relax. "We'll take your car. Get the keys."

Sergio nodded and went into the bedroom. Mehrak drifted over to stare into the messy room as Sergio fished his car keys out of a small side pocket on his backpack.

"Still get many visitors?"

Sergio turned, keys in his hand, and smiled. "All I need. One wants her own key."

"Could be tricky."

"Yeah, my thoughts exactly. Means I have to string her along. If she pushes, she's history."

Mehrak laughed. "Ever the romantic," he said.

"Come on, then."

As they left the flat, Sergio locked the door with as much of a flourish as he could muster when pitted against a protesting lock. Together, the two men strode up the steps and climbed into Sergio's white Audi. He reversed it quickly off the drive and took off down the road at a steady speed.

As he did so, a red Land Rover Discovery with two men on board pulled away from the kerb and headed in the same direction.

Some twenty minutes after Sergio's Audi had departed, a black taxicab dropped Guy off in Stenham Hill Road. Guy paid the driver with a £50 note and took no change.

"As I said, stay here for half an hour or so," he told the man. "And here's a deposit for the return journey." He handed over a further £20 note and turned to walk up the street towards number 36A. He did wonder why on earth Sergio had agreed to another visit from the madman with the Glock but assumed his tactic of putting him at ease had misled Sergio enough to want to meet up again. The lure of easy cash was irresistible to someone like him.

However, the absence of the Audi TT was a surprise. Guy trotted briskly down the steps to the tatty door. He knocked. And waited. No movement in the kitchen. He thumped on the door again. Still nothing. Guy tried the door; firmly locked. Pulling his mobile from his pocket, he selected Sergio's number and let it ring out. There was no reply and it clicked through to voicemail; Guy hadn't heard the handset ring in the flat, either.

Guy pocketed his phone and kicked at a McDonald's bag on the floor. It hit the wall and a small cardboard burger box fell out. He had evidently underestimated Sergio, and something in him was surprised. He'd felt sure he'd had his measure.

FORTY-NINE

Sergio's mobile rang out as he drove. He turned his head quickly to glance at Mehrak in the passenger seat; the baseball cap remained firmly in position and he was looking straight ahead. Great make-up – that beard looked like the real McCoy.

"It's Sam."

"Leave it," Mehrak replied brusquely. "He can call another day."

"You said we had to collect something. Which way?"

"I'll show you, don't fret," Mehrak said sharply, still staring ahead. "Lichfield and then right. A51. Just keep going."

They skirted the edge of Lichfield and headed away from the city on the A51. It was rural, taking them past the occasional pub and a golf course. There was an army barracks on the left. Sergio glanced in his mirror.

"Mehrak," he said cautiously, "ever since we left Birmingham, there's been a red Discovery following us."

"You mean taking the same route?" Mehrak said blandly, showing no interest in the observation.

"Well, yeah."

Sergio noticed Mehrak didn't glance back, which he'd have expected if the man was concerned. But he didn't even glance in the wing mirror; just kept his eyes on the road ahead.

"Maybe it's going to Tamworth, too," Mehrak suggested. A large wooded area had appeared on the horizon. "Popular market town. Even got a castle for tourists."

Sergio went quiet and kept driving. He glanced frequently in the driver's mirror. The red Discovery was still there. "Curious, though," he said, more to himself than his companion.

"Depends," Mehrak said.

"On what?"

"On who they are."

"Looks like two blokes, but they're too far back to see."

"Let's lose them then," Mehrak said, as they neared the crest of a hill, the woods now closing in on their left. "Hopwas Wood coming up," Mehrak continued. "Slow down, there's a sandy track on the left. Take it, and we'll see what happens."

Sergio saw the entrance and slowed without indicating. He swung the Audi off the main road. It really was a sandy track. Badly maintained, it ran between two high grass banks that were studded with silver birch trees of varying sizes. Sergio slowed to negotiate the ruts, mindful of the damage they could do to his car. He was so busy concentrating that he forgot to look in his mirror until he reached a fork.

"Shit. They've turned up here as well." He started to feel panicky. He looked at Mehrak, who continued to stare ahead. Why was he so calm?

"Turn right at the fork," Mehrak instructed. "Follow the track. I know what we'll do. There used to be a house up here, demolished now. It's private land in the heart of the wood, peaceful. We'll have them in the open there and it'll be our game."

Sergio nodded, reassured. Mehrak evidently

knew what he was doing.

The surface of the track improved. It was still sandy but firmer, like a proper driveway, as it twisted its way through a woodland of planted fir laced with ubiquitous silver birch. The Audi objected to the rough ground; it wasn't a comfortable ride. Sergio glanced yet again in the mirror. The red 4x4 was enjoying the off-road terrain and was catching them rapidly. It was much nearer now, and Sergio could see he'd been right – there were two men inside. The Audi entered a clearing that held the remains of a ruined house, as Mehrak had said. There were larger trees here – the vestiges, Sergio surmised, of a once-glorious garden.

Sergio looked out of the windows, assessing the terrain and location. He felt out of his depth again, scared. Mehrak still seemed perfectly calm.

"Now where?" he asked loudly.

"Just pull over, for Christ's sake," Mehrak snapped irritably. "Let's deal with this once and for all."

Sergio brought the car to a stop and turned off the engine. He kept his foot on the brake, though he was unsure why. Mehrak dipped his hand into the pocket of his leather jacket and pulled out a handgun with a silencer. Sergio felt a rush of relief, although he'd had little to do with guns. They weren't his game. But Mehrak seemed comfortable with it, and that reassured him.

"Come on. Let's get out and sort it." Mehrak opened the passenger door. Sergio applied the hand brake, released his seatbelt and opened his own door. As he stepped out of the car, he looked behind him and glanced at Mehrak across the low roof of the Audi – the other man remained calm, hands down by his sides. The red Discovery had pulled up some twenty metres back. Sergio was conscious of the sudden silence as its engine was switched off. There wasn't even any birdsong – just the murmur of a distant car, way back on the main road.

The doors of the Discovery opened and two men got out, apparently unarmed. Relieved, Sergio glanced at Mehrak again. He'd moved to the rear of the Audi, the gun in his right hand pointing nonchalantly at the ground but visible. Sergio took a couple of strides to join him; it would show them he was with the bloke with the gun. He was on the winning side. The men closed the doors and walked towards them.

Mehrak moved beyond the rear of the Audi, closing the gap a touch more. He gave Sergio a reassuring look and waved him over.

"Come here."

Sergio walked confidently to his colleague's side.

"Do you know them?" he asked, as the men approached – one tall, one shorter.

"Yeah," Mehrak replied. "I know them."

"So, what's going on?" Sergio gave Mehrak a nervous look. "Weren't we picking something up? What do these guys want? If they're delivering something, why the gun?"

Mehrak turned to face him. "They've come for you," he said slowly. His eyes narrowed, dark and cold; he raised his gun and pointed it at Sergio.

This wasn't real, surely? Sergio was suddenly more frightened than he'd ever been in his life. He looked to the two men for any sign of hope but saw only malice. Surely Mehrak wasn't going to let anything happen to him? Not after all he'd done to help with Jenny. Who were these guys? What the hell was happening? Sergio threw a look back at the driveway, but the two men were in the way. He looked around the clearing at the tree line – it was too far. There was no chance he'd reach safety, not with Mehrak and his gun there.

Mehrak was tracking his panic.

"You're going nowhere, Sergio," he growled. "At least, nowhere you know. You'll stand right where you are - *right there* – or else I'll take one knee out at a time and then put a slow bullet in your gut when you hit the ground."

Sergio felt his face pale. His legs felt weak and his eyes flickered wildly as he tried to go over his options. There were none – he was at the mercy of this mad Egyptian.

"Put it on, Steve," Mehrak directed.

The shorter of the two men stepped forward, taking a thin piece of plastic from his jeans' pocket. He walked behind Sergio.

"Put your hands behind your back, Sergio," Mehrak ordered.

Sergio could hardly move. He felt numb and sick.

"Look, Mehrak," he stammered in pleading tones. "You don't need to tie me up, I won't run, I *promise.* I'll do whatever you want, go wherever you want, honest."

"Hands," Mehrak repeated sharply. His voice was cold, different to anything Sergio had heard before.

But he couldn't move.

In one quick movement, Mehrak lowered his gun and fired. There was a soft sound and a burst of sandy soil exploded between Sergio's feet, making him jump. He looked up at Mehrak, terrified and unable to speak.

"The next one's in your right foot," Mehrak said in a low, menacing voice. "Hands!"

Sergio quickly put his hands behind his back, his right hand seizing his left wrist as if seeking support. Steve stepped up close and he felt plastic wire encircle his wrists and hands, wrapping round them like the coils of a snake. The cord was pulled tight and fastened; it cut deep into his skin. When Steve stepped away, Sergio's immediate reaction was to test the firmness of the grip. It was tight, very tight. His hands were firmly, uncomfortably locked together. He felt his freedom ebbing away.

"Get it, Tony," Mehrak instructed, walking over to Sergio and standing close in front of him. Sergio felt cold metal through his shirt as the barrel of the gun was pushed into his stomach. Mehrak's eyes were just centimetres from his face.

"You're a tosser, Sergio, you know that? One of life's little pieces of shit. Sell out to the highest bidder. You've done all we need you to do and now you're a liability, a loose end. Can't trust tossers and pieces of shit, can we?"

Sergio was still struggling with his fear and confusion. He was stunned. His head swam and he felt faint. Acid burned in his stomach. He expected Mehrak to pull back, but the Egyptian stayed right in front of him, staring impassively into his face.

"Oh, one more thing," Mehrak said, bringing his knee up sharply into Sergio's groin, rapidly and without warning. Sergio took a sharp intake of breath and doubled up as the pain shot through him, barely stopping himself from tumbling to the ground. "That's from all those wretched girls you've screwed, bullied and dumped over the years. There'd have been a queue of them wanting to do that to you from here to fucking Lichfield, believe me."

Sergio focused determinedly on a patch of earth as he waited for the pain to ease. He saw Mehrak's feet walk towards the Audi and heard him say: "We'll use that one, Tony."

He felt Steve's hands grab him, the henchman pulling him roughly across the clearing. Randomly, he noticed a chipped and weathered house brick lying abandoned in the grass. He hobbled along, still bent over and breathing hard. All dignity was gone. Hearing his Audi's engine, he raised his head – was Mehrak leaving? He saw the car reverse slightly before taking a slow, wide arc towards the tree line, in the same direction Steve was guiding him. Then he saw the taller, lanky guy, Tony, and stopped. A further rush of panic shot through his body. Tony had thrown a rope over a high tree branch and now it dangled freely – a swinging noose on the end of it.

"No!" Sergio screamed, and stepped backwards. He felt Steve increase his grip and a second pair of hands take him from the other side, forcing him forwards. Mehrak was back at his side. He felt the gun barrel in his ribs.

"Walk," Mehrak commanded, "else life is going to get so painful you'll be begging to die."

Sergio found it hard to generate movement in his legs. He was in a state of confused panic. The blood rushed in his head and thumped in his ears. He attempted to struggle but it was useless – he was caught like a fly in a web.

The three of them eased nearer to his car, parked beneath the gently moving rope. When they were about a metre from the Audi, Steve and Mehrak spun him round and shoved him violently against the side of the bonnet. Sergio felt the wheel and its arch press into the back of his legs, the momentum forcing him over the bonnet so his only view was the blue sky. Without the gripping hands, Sergio suddenly felt free, like the cloud he could see, but as he raised his head and started to straighten up, he saw Mehrak and his gun in front of him again.

"One for the journey," Mehrak said, once again bringing his knee up firmly into Sergio's groin. The pain was intense, extreme; he brought his head down and bent over in agony, supported by the edge of the bonnet.

The Audi rocked and Sergio realised that both Steve and Tony were now standing on the bonnet and the sloping roof. Once more he was seized and dragged upwards, the windscreen wipers scratching his back. He kicked out with his legs but couldn't prevent the upward movement. He was pulled onto the roof and, as he was forced upright, he felt the noose encircle his head. It slid down over his face and tightened at his neck, biting into his Adam's apple. Sergio stood on the car's roof, his instincts screaming at him to keep still and retain his balance; easier said than done with his hands tied, a burning sensation in his groin, and the tightness at his neck.

As he steadied himself, he suddenly felt all the hands that held him let go. The car rocked slightly as Steve and Tony jumped to the ground. Sergio strained to free his hands, but it was useless. He stared at the ground below, almost losing his balance. Somehow, his legs were automatically holding him up. He tried desperately to stop himself spinning. The panic was intense – this couldn't really be happening. *I'll wake up soon. I've always survived.*

"Steady, Sergio," came Mehrak's callous voice from the ground. "We don't want an accident now, do we?"

The sound of Mehrak's laughter was loud, mixed with sycophantic chuckles from Steve and Tony. Sergio's mind was racing as he desperately tried to keep his balance. He tried to plead for mercy, but the rope was too tight on his throat and he could only utter some stifled mutterings.

"The Casanova begs," Mehrak screeched, hooting with laughter which suddenly died away.

There was a moment's silence. Sergio shifted his feet, ever mindful of his predicament. His head rolled slightly, and he could see a large white cloud moving over the blue above the woodland clearing. He noticed the other end of the rope had been tied to a strong, low and ancient bough. He strained to see what was happening on the ground below him. The brief quiet was broken by Mehrak's cold and emotionless command: "Go, Steve."

The car's engine started, the vibrations travelling

up Sergio's legs and making his position feel even more precarious. Suddenly the roof was moving, slowly, gently, steadily. Sergio's feet angled away from him forcing him to take two short, sliding steps down the Audi's sloped roof as the rope tightened mercilessly around his neck. And then he was falling, groundless.

FIFTY

Jenny didn't know what time it was when she heard the footsteps return to the corridor outside her prison door. Her watch had been taken from her, a pale band of skin where it had been on her left wrist a constant reminder of this frustration. As she sat on the bed, her back against the slightly chilly whitewashed brickwork, someone approached with brisk, steady strides. She could still feel her last meal in her slim stomach, so she was surprised the masked guy was returning so soon.

She slowly closed the book she'd been reading and raised her head to watch the grille in the door. The footsteps stopped. There was the usual pause and then the hood appeared and stared at her for a few seconds. Although familiar now, that look and his total control still made her feel very vulnerable, even threatened. She had to toughen up. She heard the key turn and the door opened into the room. It was rusty and heavy, almost medieval. She felt a draught and wrapped her arms together in front of her for warmth – a subconsciously defensive pose.

The man stepped into the room and placed a small cardboard box on the stumpy pillar by the hatch. From where she sat, Jenny couldn't see anything inside save for some sheets of paper sticking up at one side. He pulled the door closed behind him, glancing quickly at the girl before he took a key out of the pocket of his jeans and locked the door. The key returned to his pocket and pushed in deep. She noted which one.

There was something in his deliberate movement that caused her some concern. She wondered what she'd do if he tried to molest her, and the thoughts and fears she'd lived with over however many hours and days it had been came rushing back. She was helpless. She was slim, weak and – save for her intelligence and her agility – defenceless. She was young, and she knew she was attractive – Sergio had made that evident to her. Goosebumps rose on her skin and she felt her heart start to beat faster to the rhythm of her fears.

The man dipped into the box and withdrew a large kitchen knife. It had a black plastic handle and was aggressively sharp. A professional blade. She drew her legs up and stared at it. The fear pressed again, stronger than ever.

"What…what are you doing?" was all she could say, her mouth dry.

The man lifted his left index finger to where she guessed his mouth was beneath the cloth hood and signalled to her to be silent. She put her hand across her mouth and nodded vigorously. She would do what he commanded. No argument. No trouble. No choice. For now. He slid the knife carefully into the back pocket of his jeans. Right side.

The man turned back to the box and took out the small sheaf of papers. She could see some words in a large font typed on the top one as he positioned them in front of him. And she noticed for the first time he was wearing yellowish-coloured surgical gloves. He took a step towards her and held out a single page. Waggled it up and down with a gesture that meant: "Take this." With a slightly shaking hand, she took it, turned it round, and read it.

"I have a series of written instructions for you. How well you come out of this will depend on whether you cooperate. It is your decision whether you live or die. You have seen my knife. I have killed many people. You'll just be the next. You will follow my instructions to the letter and immediately. Nod if you understand."

She looked up at him and swallowed hard, nodding clearly and firmly in an exaggerated way. He placed the sheet of paper at the bottom of his small wad and passed her another one.

"Your parents have failed to do what was asked of them. That is a shame. Everything that will now follow is because of their lack of love for you. Everything that follows will be their fault. The guilt is theirs and it will stay with them for the rest of their pathetic lives. I am absolved from blame. Nod if you agree."

The girl slowly lowered the piece of paper. Looked at the man. She knew how she felt, what she thought. She didn't need to be told. She nodded, nodded hard.

The man picked up the box from the stump and placed it on the end of the bed. From where she was sitting, she could just see a small food container made of clear plastic with a grey lid. It was empty save for some tissue. He passed her the next sheet, taking the previous one back.

"If you're not standing up, stand up. When you are standing up, take off your cardigan and then your blouse. Place them on the bed. You have one minute to

do this or else you will suffer. Nod if you don't want to suffer."

She could feel her stomach tightening as she placed the sheet of paper on the bed. Were her worst fears coming to pass? The man stretched round to his rear jeans' pocket. The right one. He produced the knife and held it in front of him. She nodded vigorously and started to stand up. *I have no choice. Where are you, Dad?* Her legs were stiff, but she eased round and placed her feet on the floor. She had no shoes, just socks that had been on the bed when she'd arrived, like the cardigan, like the white blouse – warmer than the black dress she'd been wearing. She stood up a metre or so from the bed and looked at him.

The man tapped his wristwatch with the blade of the knife. Its steady chink echoed gently in the room, but with all the resonance of an alarm bell. She moved more quickly, undoing the large buttons and pulling her arms out of the pink cardigan. She placed it on the bed and hesitated. There was no choice. The buttons on her blouse were smaller, fiddlier, and she struggled to unfasten them with her nervous fingers. She needed several attempts at each single button. One, two and then the third. The blouse separated as she went, revealing the tops of her breasts and her delicate white bra. She didn't look up, didn't look at the man, but she could feel his eyes on her, watching. She hated it. She heard him tap his watch again with the blade of his knife. A warning call. She moved faster; more errors, more buttons open. She yanked the blouse out of her jeans, peeled it back over her shoulders and dragged her arms out of the sleeves, turning them inside out as her hands caught on the narrow cuffs. She tossed it on top of the cardigan and stood up, straight. She tried to put dignity in her pose and finally looked straight at the man. She could see his eyes through their holes in the hood as they flickered over her. She knew she was in good shape – narrow waist, toned stomach, modest breasts.

As she stood there, he replaced the knife in its pocket and dipped his hand into the box, taking out a folded sheet of plastic. Clear, clean and new. He walked over to the stump, almost three metres from her, and opened it up, placed it there like a tablecloth. As he smoothed it out, eradicating the wrinkles and pressing it down as it crinkled under his touch, she launched.

In a couple of silent strides on her socked feet she was behind him, snatching the knife before he even turned. She backed away quickly to her bedside, waving and stabbing it towards him with quick, jerky movements as if it was a sword. She could feel her heart pounding, beating hard, and beating quickly.

"Stay back!" she screamed. "Stay back!"

The man turned to face her, a five-metre space between them. The vile hood hid all expression save for the eyes that stared at her intently. She tried to resist their almost hypnotic control. He took a short step towards her.

"Stay where you are," she said. "Toss me the door key."

He said nothing and took another short step towards her.

"I mean it!" she shouted, and poked the knife towards him with a series of vigorous thrusts. "Give me the key!"

He took another short, deliberate step. She could feel the cold bedstead pressing into her legs. There was no retreat. She swallowed hard. He took yet another slow and purposeful step. He was a couple of metres from her, not far beyond the outstretched, swinging knife. He paused. A rush of hope ran through her. He'd realised the control the knife gave her. She had won. He slowly put his hand in his pocket and extracted the key. It lay still in his open palm. She stared at it, taking in the freedom it represented. She would be home soon.

"Toss it on to the bed," she said. "Go on, do it, and then step back."

He lowered his hand slowly and the head turned slightly to her left, looking down at the mattress and bundle of blankets. Then with a quick, sudden movement, he threw the key hard and fast towards her face. She could see it coming, knew what it would do if it struck her. She cringed and ducked and dodged it – and felt his hand encircle her right wrist with growing pressure. The key hit the wall behind her with a metallic ring and fell to the bed. Her arm was twisted round, and the knife fell to the floor. Two hands pushed her forcefully backwards, and she sat down firmly on the bed. The man stepped forward and slapped her hard in the face. She clasped her cheek in a pathetic attempt to relieve the pain.

The man picked up the knife and pointed it at her.

"Leave me alone!" she screamed. "Don't touch me!" She pulled her legs up tight and hugged them, staring at the man and willing him to back off.

He straightened the hood and approached her, the knife pointing dangerously towards her head and neck. She looked around wildly, but there was nothing other than her book. She picked it up and threw it mindlessly at him. Despite the short distance, she missed. It crashed harmlessly to the floor and lay there, open and useless. He was now right by the bed. The knife came towards her; it was just centimetres from her throat. The hood was leaning in very close, so close she could smell the musty fibres of the cloth.

Suddenly he stretched out his other hand and plucked the key from its resting place before shoving it back into his pocket. He stepped back, the knife still evident, and still pointing towards her menacingly. There he stood watching her, as if planning his next move.

He returned to his box and took out another sheet of paper. Turning back towards her, he silently motioned with his hand, indicated that she should walk over to the stump. Part of her wanted to resist, to stay where she was, but the more rational part of her realised she had lost the battle. She was determined, however, that the war would be a different story. She took the few steps necessary, guardedly keeping what distance she could as though, like a hunting cat, he might spring again at any moment. She stopped and looked at him. He held out the new piece of paper, which she took. She read the further instructions.

"Kneel down and place your hands flat on the tray shelf, on the plastic sheet. What I am going to do now is going to hurt, hurt a lot. This is where you make

a true decision of life or death. Do as I say, and you will survive. You will be hurt, but you will be alive. Fail to do as I say, and I shall stick my knife in your stomach and leave you. Your choice. You have one minute to decide – and then I shall act, guided by your decision."

She let the piece of paper drop to the ground and felt like following it. Her legs felt weak, her mouth dry and every cruel possibility raced and fought its way through her mind, activated by her boundless imagination.

She desperately wanted to run as her personal nightmare went from worse to worse. A locked door, a strong man with a knife, and no one to help. She was as vulnerable as a new-born chick, as terrified as a squealing pig at slaughter. She heard the irritated tap of the knife on the watch and in response, almost like Pavlov's dog, she dropped to her knees and placed her hands on the plastic sheet. Flat, as commanded. She closed her eyes in the same way she used to do as a child – *I can't see you so you can't see me; the nasty things will all go away.*

Without sight, her hearing intensified and detected every little sound. The footfall as the man stepped towards the bed and then returned. He seemed close to her now, but rather than opening her eyes to see, she screwed them tighter still. *It will all go away, please make it all go away.* She could sense his closeness, hear his heavy breathing. She could smell a hint of male deodorant, a suggestion of sweat. It was heady, suffocating, crushing. He was near her, very near. She jumped as she felt his hand touch hers, but kept her eyes tightly closed. He held her hand, his breathing seeming to grow louder, more rapid. Deodorant, sweat, her thumping heart; the floor, feeling icy beneath her knees. Her head spun. *Daddy, where are you?* Suddenly, she felt the cold, hard steel blade on one finger, followed by a sharp pain.

She opened her eyes, saw the blood and screamed.

FIFTY-ONE

Guy spent until late Sunday afternoon at Sophie's side, watching her as she lay there breathing gently, the focus of so much medical equipment. He held her hand and talked to her, read a few chapters to her and shared her silence with her. He tried to find her consultant for an updated prognosis, but he was not on duty.

Later, back in his hotel room at Sandbrough Hall, he made a couple of calls. His brief conversation with Grant had been just that, but then he hadn't expected it to be otherwise. The pressure on her was clearly mounting, presumably piling down the food chain from on high. She'd nothing of significance to report. Neither did he, come to that, other than Sergio disappearing off the face of the planet. When he had telephoned Grant about that earlier in the afternoon, she'd suggested he was off visiting Jenny in her hide-away – lovers having time away from family, friends and hassle. She had told him that enquiries were continuing around Aston, with much time spent on watching CCTV footage. Theories had been expounded, followed up and dismissed about how the sniper – or whoever engaged him – had known of Julie's stay in Aston. Jonny had not been questioned further other than a short telephone call to query some date or other. Grant was no nearer a resolution. And the press were starting to push, although the embargo on the story was holding – just.

Guy had also telephoned Simon, who'd made little comment on Sergio's disappearance and no suggestion the lovers had high-tailed it to Gretna Green. In answer to Guy's question, he said he'd nothing further to say that might be helpful. Both he and Sally would be at home in Four Oaks for the next few days; they'd been due to have a few days in Venice but had cancelled the trip for obvious reasons.

There'd been no response from Mike Burns, Guy realised, picking up the telephone to call him. Then, hesitating, he changed his mind. That could wait until morning.

FIFTY-TWO

Simon Stewart stood at the kitchen window of his home and watched a breakfasting blue tit as it clung tenaciously to the mesh bird-feeder that swung gently on the tree branch. Giving up was not an option for the twitchy little thing, he thought; it had to fight to survive. Every day was a constant struggle, every day held risks and dangers. Simon could relate to that.

He took a swig of his tea and felt the hot liquid trickle down his throat. It was Monday morning. Was it really five days ago that Jenny had come charging into the kitchen as he'd sat there eating a piece of toast, enjoying a late breakfast before leaving for the Birmingham studios to record two further episodes of *Twist or Bust*?

"So, what are your plans this evening?" he'd asked.

Jenny had said she was going to some party with Sergio, leading to an inevitable confrontation as he played the protective father at the mere mention of his nemesis. He felt some guilt, knowing they saw things so differently, and this was a rocky topic. But it burned his soul so much it hurt; he couldn't stop once he knew Sergio was in the arena. He recognised that the challenge came because the degree of hatred he felt was diametrically opposite to the love he had for Jenny. It was an emotional conundrum.

"All these nights stopping out," he'd said.

"I'm eighteen, Dad, for Christ's sake. *Eighteen*. I'm not a baby anymore. I'm an adult, a woman, and it's my life. Don't do the moral bit with me."

"Don't be so selfish, Jenny, you're still part of this family. We care about each other, think about each other's feelings. You know very well what the media, the press, are like. We need to be careful; our reputations are at stake."

"*Your* reputation you mean, Dad." She crossed her arms, regarding him with narrowing eyes. There was anger in her voice. "*That's* what this is all about. You're not concerned about *my* welfare or whether *I'm* happy – you're just worried I might damage the shining reputation of the great Simon Stewart!"

"That's not fair, Jenny. Look, let's talk about it tomorrow."

She moved smartly into the hall, bag swinging from her right hand. She turned her head to glance over her left shoulder.

"No point, Dad," she said more gently. "I love you, but you're not going to persuade me, okay? Now just get off my case and drop it – *please*."

And with that she'd marched out of the house to catch her train into the city. He could still hear the door slamming.

He hadn't heard from her since. He felt his eyes starting to well up, and he sat down on a wooden stool at the breakfast bar. The blue tit sped off as a great tit arrived to try its luck. If only life could be rewound and played out again with the benefit of future knowledge. But that would be too easy. Safer though.

A shrill sound rang out from a white, plastic box on the kitchen wall. He walked over to it, straightening his checked dressing gown. On the small screen he could see a motorcycle courier; he pressed the button that allowed the gates to open and returned to his tea. Hearing Sally come down the stairs he rose again and went over to the kettle, filling it at the sink before placing it on the side and easing down the switch. A mental picture of Jenny thumping it as she dashed for the biscuit barrel, running late for something, played in his mind and caused a smile to whisper across his face.

Sally entered the kitchen, wearing a red tracksuit and white Nike trainers, with no make-up and her hair tied back.

"Tea?" Simon asked as the kettle started to build up steam.

"No thanks. Just a glass of water, please. I'm going to pop downstairs to the gym for half an hour or so. What are you doing?"

"Tea and thinking."

"Tea and sympathy more like. Five days today, right?"

Simon looked at her and nodded.

The doorbell rang.

"That's a courier. Probably some scripts. I just let him in," Simon said.

"I'll go." Sally turned and left the room, her trainers complaining gently with every step across the hallway. Simon was pleased to see her looking a hint brighter. She was still pale, tired and distressed, but for the first time in five days she wasn't crying.

Simon heard her exchange brief pleasantries with the courier, then the front door closed and she returned to the kitchen clutching a small package, which she placed on the breakfast bar.

"Something to be signed for, I presume?" Simon asked. "Doesn't look like scripts."

Sally looked at the label. "Addressed to us both," she said.

Picking up the package again, she began to unwrap the brown paper. Simon took his tea back to his spot by the window. The great tit had gone. The bird feeder hung abandoned and peaceful, resting until the next onslaught.

"Curious," Sally said, almost to herself.

Simon turned. She'd opened the package. The brown paper lay in torn pieces, recklessly removed. She held a plastic container.

"What is it?" Simon asked. "Wedding cake?"

"I don't know."

Sally placed the container in front of her and removed the grey lid. Simon could see a wad of tissue paper, which she removed. He was starting to cross the room when his wife suddenly let out a loud scream and put her hand to her mouth. She stepped backwards away from the counter, dropping the tissue paper as she went. Simon saw something unravel from it and fall, hitting the breakfast bar before it came to a halt. He stepped over to look, unsure at first what he was seeing. Then, with a sharp intake of breath, he realised that lying on the polished granite surface, still and macabre, was a small, bloody, feminine finger.

FIFTY-THREE

Guy picked up the blood-soaked finger with the tissue and placed it back inside the small plastic container. It had been left where it had fallen for almost an hour; neither Simon nor Sally could bring themselves to touch it. He folded the tissue paper over it and, using a piece of kitchen roll to avoid forensic contamination, replaced the grey lid before setting it down on the granite work surface. He wiped the counter down with some more kitchen paper, dropping it deep in the bin afterwards, then washed his hands at the sink before drying them on a patterned towel.

"I'm really sorry, Simon," he said, turning to look at the television star. Simon was sitting in a wicker chair near the kitchen window, but he'd twisted it round to look toward Guy. He was wearing old, sloppy jeans and a striped blue golf shirt, which gave the impression of having been thrown on in haste. Guy walked across the quarry-tiled floor to sit in another wicker chair close by and studied him. Simon looked tired, ashen, emotionally drained. He'd evidently been crying. Guy's heart went out to him. He struggled to comprehend what a parent must feel in such terrible, traumatic circumstances. It was all so unreal, a nightmare from which there was no waking.

Guy crossed his legs and settled further into the chair, his eyes never leaving Simon. The other man leant forward, his forearms on his knees, and stared at the floor.

"I think it would be best if you let me in, Simon."

Simon continued to gaze at the floor. He neither moved nor spoke, not even appearing to hear what had been said. Guy had witnessed such trauma before. His colleagues in the SAS had been tough to the point of cliché, but he could still clearly remember that day in Libya and always would. Corporal Davies had become separated from the covert mission in Gadaffi's own back yard and was captured. Through sheer audacity and determination, they'd rescued him before he could be paraded on state television – but not before he'd been brutally maimed through barbaric torture. The condition of the corporal had shocked them all, and Guy had spent time on the subdued flight home counselling those soldiers who'd been worst affected.

"You heard me, Simon. If you want my help you must let me in. You've called me over, so tell me what you know, tell me what's going on. You're holding out on me – I know you are, it's screamingly obvious – and I can't help you if you won't open up."

Simon pulled a handkerchief out of his jeans pocket and wiped his nose, then leaned back in his chair as he manoeuvred the square of fabric back into place. Returning Guy's gaze, he said, "Sally's taken it very badly. Who wouldn't? She's lying down upstairs. I could say nothing to console her. She kept wondering whether Jenny was alright and agonizing over what she must have gone through. Would they have anaesthetized her? What drugs is she getting now? What animal would do this to a defenceless eighteen-year-old girl? Where the hell is she? I have no answers, and I just feel useless." He swept his hand through his hair.

"Simon, when you first asked me to help you, I

asked if there was anything else you knew. Anything you hadn't told me. When we first met at The Mailbox in Birmingham you said something about an Arman. When you showed me Jenny's room and I pressed you on that, you refused to answer. I let it go. But I can't let it go any more, Simon. I've always had the strong impression that you're holding something back, not giving me the full picture. Am I right?"

No reply. Simon stared at the floor again.

"If you think keeping stuff to yourself is going to help, you're wrong – hopelessly wrong," Guy continued. "I appreciate you're grieving for Jenny right now, but I'm going to be brutal. I'm on your side – remember that. We need to share information – both relevant and irrelevant. Who knows when something will become important? We have the same aims, the same goals. Julie's dead and Jenny's missing – who's next? If you keep taking the same approach, how can it change? How can things get resolved? Holding back may have put her at risk, may have led to the present crisis. What harm is there in –"

"Okay, okay, stop there." Simon raised his hands in surrender and looked at Guy, who noted a look of resignation, almost relief – as if a burden was about to be lifted. Guy paused and sat back, hoping he'd got through to the man at last.

Simon nodded slowly. "Yes, there is more to tell. I haven't told you because I thought it would cause more difficulties, not help the situation. If I'd thought telling you earlier would have saved Jenny from this dreadful ordeal I'd have done so, believe me. But I thought not telling you would protect her – keep her, and all of us, safe. It hasn't worked out like that. You're right, Guy. It's time to draw a line and move forward."

"Who's Arman, Simon?"

Simon shook his head and looked at him. "I don't know."

"*Simon*."

"Look, Guy, I honestly don't know who the hell he is. That's the honest truth. If I knew who he was it would all be much easier, right? But I don't, I really don't."

Guy studied him closely. From his experience of interrogation, he could see Simon was displaying all the signs of someone speaking honestly. He'd held Guy's gaze without flinching, without even blinking. He was sure he'd witnessed relief when he'd agreed to a new approach, had agreed to open up to Guy and share the burden. No point in making that emotional decision and then reneging on it moments later, however tough the question.

"Okay." Guy nodded slightly. "Tell me what you do know, then. There was a moment, I guess, when you'd never heard of him, and now you have. How did he come into your life?"

Simon rubbed his fingers across his mouth and let them come to rest on his chin, which he stroked gently, subconsciously as he spoke.

"Suddenly and without warning. He rang here two weeks ago today, Monday of the week Julie died. I made a note of the date; it's in the office. I've kept a file on all this. It was a mobile number and I tried to find out who owned it through some contacts of mine, but it's unregistered, and they couldn't trace the owner – pay as you go, a 'burner' phone or something like that."

Guy was unsurprised by the details. "What did he want?"

"What they always want, of course - money, and lots of it."

"Be specific."

"Try a million."

"For what?"

Simon let out a sigh. "For my family's safety," he said bluntly. "Look, it went like this: pay him a million and my family would be safe – no one would come to any harm. If I refused, someone would be harmed and the price would go up. It would continue that way. He said he never stopped – he always got what he wanted in the end. He said it sometimes took a 'hit or two' for someone to cotton on, but he was a patient man. He told me he used professional hit men, and added that once someone was on his list, they would always be on his list."

"His list?"

"Yeah, his list of targets. Once he'd selected you, there was no escape. He would kill and harm until you paid. No police or else he would punish the family. And he said that threat would continue even after payment was made. No more demands, just 'punishment' if we ever let on to the police."

Guy thought about what Simon had told him and then said, "Police protection schemes?" It felt lame as soon as he said it.

"Get real, Guy. Sure, they might be able to provide a safe house for a short period of time, but what good's that? You can't like that live forever, even if they've got the funds. At some point you'll be vulnerable, and members of your wider family will always be at risk – like Julie. They can't protect everyone."

Guy ran his hand through his hair - *things were starting to fall into place*. He said, "So Julie was the example, so to speak? You refused to play ball."

"Of course I did. Told him to fuck off, the bloody crank," Simon said. He paused as if thinking, then continued. "Arman had this smoothness, this cold edge to his voice – and yet he would also show an angry side now and then. He seemed completely unfazed by my response. Now I see why. He had me over a barrel – I had no options. He told me he'd selected a victim – my sister, Julie. He must have done a hell of a lot of research beforehand, because not many people know about the connection. We fell out with each other completely when she was about sixteen. Hadn't spoken since, and I mean that literally – at least, until very recently. We didn't even acknowledge each other's existence, it was such a massive bust-up. But Arman knew."

Guy realised this was information for Grant. He refused the temptation of feeling smug or justified that he'd been right. Right in his assessment of Jonny Reid, right in his judgment that the trail led to Simon Stewart, and right in his decision to dogmatically and carefully explore that trail. All that was for another day.

"You warned Julie, didn't you?" he asked.

Simon nodded. "Yeah. Rang her up. She knew it had to be serious as we hadn't spoken for all those years. I just told her there was a threat, a real threat on her life from a nutter who wanted money. I said I needed time to sort it and she had to go somewhere quickly – you know, to a friend's house or somewhere. If she hadn't had her kids, I suspect she'd have gone further, abroad maybe. But she stayed local and went to stay with one of her best mates, an old school friend."

"My guess is that they were ready for that. Probably ready to follow her the moment Arman rang you. As soon as she took off, they were on her tail all the way to Aston. Then it was just a matter of working out the logistics of the hit. She had no chance."

Simon looked thoughtful. "I thought I'd given her a chance, that's the point, but as it turned out, I placed her in danger," he said regretfully.

Guy leaned forward. "You weren't to know that, Simon. You did what you thought was best, what anyone else would have done. You can't blame yourself for that. As you said, Arman could have been a crank. It could have been an empty threat with no intention or ability to see it through if you didn't cough up."

Simon stood up and walked to the patio doors where he gazed unseeingly into the garden. "Well, turns out he is a crank, but of the lethal and merciless kind," he said. "And now he has Jenny..."

"Did you speak to him after Julie was shot, before Jenny disappeared?"

Simon nodded. "He called me. It was like he was gloating that Julie was dead and he'd successfully carried out his threat. I still wouldn't budge. I refused to pay his demand, which he'd already said would go up. He threatened my daughter, but I still wasn't going to be pushed around. I'm too bloody arrogant, that's my problem. I was going to warn Jenny, but what could I say? Then we had this big row last Wednesday and I haven't seen her since. I had the opportunity and didn't take it. All this is my fault. I should've done more."

Guy shook his head. "No, Simon. This isn't your fault. This is all down to Arman and no one else. Jenny may be injured, but at least she's alive –"

"For the moment."

"What do you mean?"

"There's a time limit. A strict one."

"How do you know?"

Simon paused and then said, "Because this was also in the plastic container."

With that, Simon pulled a folded piece of paper out of his back pocket and walked over to Guy with it. Guy took it and leaned back in his chair as Simon returned to the patio doors. It was a piece of standard A4, folded twice and now quite crinkled. He opened it. The typed text was in a large, clear font and covered over half the page.

"I trust the enclosed proves once more to you that I'm serious. Jenny is alive, bandaged and crying for you. She accepts what has happened is your fault, as you have not done what was asked of you. This is your final chance to save her. There will be no quick bullet for Jenny, as there was for Julie. Instead, her death will be slow and painful. Again, this will be your fault. Jenny has been told this. You know from our first conversation when I set out the rules that the price has gone up. It is now £1.5m. When Jenny is dead it will go to £2m or another family member will die. I am a patient man, but my patience has a limit. You've nearly reached it. It is

now Monday morning. I will ring you later today. I will make one call, and if you fail to answer you will not hear from me again - until I want £2m. I want the money by noon tomorrow, Tuesday. Fail, and the process of Jenny's death starts then. It will take several hours, maybe days – who knows how long someone can last without food and water? But what is certain is that you will never see her again, nor know where she will forever lie. Arman."

Guy lowered the paper and looked across at Simon. "At least we know she's alive, Simon. But this is a cast-iron threat with a very short fuse. We must consider the options."

Simon looked bemused. "Options?" he said, turning to Guy. "There are no options, Guy. The bastard has me. I need to pay up and save Jenny. I put a call into my accountant this morning. He's sorting out the money, so it'll be ready first thing tomorrow morning. I just want your help to see it through, make sure that when I've paid I get my Jenny back."

"What makes you think that even if you pay up he'll let Jenny go? She'll have a tale to tell, an injury to explain."

Simon looked thoughtful and crossed his arms. "That's a risk we've got to take, isn't it? If I refuse, she's dead. If I pay up, there's some chance he'll honour his word – seems wrong to associate the word 'honour' with this bastard, huh? But at least it gives us hope. The money's not important, never has been. We've plenty of it. I just hoped he'd back off – but I see there's no prospect of that now, none at all. It's just a matter of waiting for the call, seeing how he wants it done and ensuring it happens – to the letter."

"And the police?"

"I can't involve the police. Not now, not ever. I just want us to be left alone, as we were before all this happened. Will you support us – just a little longer?" He looked pleadingly at Guy.

"How much of all this does Sally know?"

"I kept some of it back for a while, but as of this morning she's aware of it all and shares my view on the way forward. She would have paid from the get-go – she's not exactly happy with me. Will you help us further?'

"Of course. I said I'd help, and I will, for as long as I'm needed. We must go along with Arman today, but let's review once we hear what he says."

Guy stood up and started to pace the room. It was surely time to explain a bit more. Simon had opened up and things were falling into place. It was a judgment call – one he had to make right now.

"Simon, there's something more I need to tell you."

Simon looked up at him expectantly.

"The police are obviously looking into Julie's death. They haven't spoken to you yet, but I'm aware of how they're doing."

"How come?"

Guy leaned back against the worktop, hands in his pockets, and looked directly at Simon. "I was contacted by the chief constable, David Richardson, shortly after Julie's death. He and the Sterlings go back a long way – he knew my father. David wanted me to assist the detective on the case, be a sort of maverick outsider who could go places and do things which, if official, would get the formal enquiry into – well, let's just say hot water and bad PR."

Simon looked surprised. "Just over Julie's death?" He thought for a moment. "Oh, I get it. Arman really is a serial extortioner, and Julie was his latest hit. They've worked it out."

"Sort of. At least, I'm pretty sure that's what the chief constable thinks, but, for some reason, they've put a detective superintendent in charge called Caroline Grant, who's turned out to be incredibly headstrong and opinionated. I give her my theories – she ignores them. She spent several hours talking to Jonny Reid, which in my view was a complete waste of time, and so it's proved to be. They seem to have appointed the most useless police officer ever. The chief constable's belief – if he still maintains it – is that Julie's death is one of a series linked to a particular person or an organization. Everything you've told me today rather confirms that. I guess it's Arman who's been at work for a few years. Choosing wealthy people, threatening them, taking their money and killing their loved ones if they don't play ball. It may even be that my late father was a victim."

"Your *father*?"

"Long story; let's park it for now. The point is this: the more astute members of the police force believe, you could say *know*, that Julie's death was because of an 'Arman'. If Grant finally gets it, even with what I've advised her so far, they could come here innocently as part of those enquiries. Maybe they could turn up in the next hour. What if Arman is having this house watched, which seems highly probable? He might think you've reported Jenny missing."

Simon looked thoughtful. "But surely in those circumstances the police wouldn't actually come here, not if her life was threatened if we reported her kidnap?"

Guy nodded. "True, but they don't know about the threat, do they?" Guy ran a hand through his hair. "Arman appears to be beyond rational. So the challenge we have is there's a risk Arman will react if the police come here."

"But surely it's inevitable they'll turn up eventually – once they've made the connection between Julie and me. I suppose I'll have to hope they call first, and then I'll just have to play dumb and meet them elsewhere if all else fails. Not very public-spirited, I guess, but I must put my family first. I haven't, to date, and look where it's got us." He paused as if a thought had struck him. "But where does that leave you?" he asked. "You're right in the middle of all this. What do you tell the police?"

"To be honest, Simon, it doesn't seem to matter what I tell Grant. Her attitude seems to be changing, to be fair, but I have no confidence in her and whether that will last."

"Okay, so the police may or may not get involved. For now, I just want to focus on Jenny's safe return. What's your plan?"

"A good question," Guy said. He sat down on his chair once more.

"Do me a favour, Simon – just give me five minutes to work this through."

Simon stood up. "Sure. I'll go and check on

Sally. Give us a shout when you're ready. I'll keep my mobile close by in case Arman rings." He picked up his phone and left the room.

Guy settled in his chair and closed his eyes for a few minutes, running various options through his head, looking for ideas and possible solutions.

Then he heard a mobile phone start to ring upstairs.

FIFTY-FOUR

Guy reached the bottom of the stairs just as Simon arrived on the landing above, an outstretched arm holding the mobile phone. It was still ringing, the tone mimicking the old rotary dial telephones of the previous century; the summons of choice for nostalgic mobile users of a certain age. Right now, though, it sounded loud and ominous rather than reassuring and friendly.

Sally, her hair unbrushed, appeared behind Simon wearing a long, kimono-style dressing gown patterned with bamboo. She was tightening the silky belt around her waist. Simon waved his arm back and forth, highlighting the phone and its steady call.

"It's Arman!" he said, almost – illogically – in a stage whisper.

"Answer it then – go on, quickly," Guy said, starting up the stairs two at a time.

Simon pressed a button and lifted the phone to his ear. As Guy reached the landing, he could hear a male voice on the line.

"No, Arman," Simon was saying. "There's just Sally and me. No one else. I understood what you said before. She's standing next to me; I'll put you on speaker so she can hear, if that's okay?"

There was further muttering, then Simon pressed a button on the handset and held it out in front of him. Guy and Sally instinctively drew closer.

"You've got a pretty daughter, Sally." Arman was well-spoken, his words slow and deliberate.

Guy noticed that Sally, her eyes already red and tired, was starting to well up.

"I just want my baby back," she said quietly, dabbing her eyes with the white, already-damp tissue she clutched tightly in her hand.

"Of course you do," Arman's voice was soft, soothing. Then, in harsh tones: "And all at the same time no doubt, not in a steady flow of pieces."

"Bastard!" Simon's curse was sharp, sudden and loud. Guy looked at him and saw by the other man's helpless expression that he'd immediately realised the error of such an involuntary reaction. There was silence. They all looked at the mobile in Simon's hand; the line was open, but there was no sound. After fifteen agonising seconds of silence, Arman's voice came again, as steady and controlled as before.

"That was naughty, Simon. I suggest you apologise quickly before I ring off – because believe me, I will. Then there will be no more about Jenny. No university this year. No walking your daughter down the aisle. No more hugs or kisses. In fact…no daughter at all."

"I'm sorry, Arman. I apologise. I'm very stressed – surely you can understand that? Please don't harm our girl. I'm sorry, I really am." Simon's tone was pleading, and he addressed the mobile as if it held power over his whole life. There was a further silence. A tear rolled down Sally's cheek. Ten seconds passed, slowly and painfully. The trio on the landing waited anxiously.

"That's better," came Arman's voice suddenly. "Your apology is accepted." His voice remained calm, assured and in control with no hint of emotion. "Now, how's the money situation, Simon?"

"It's all in hand. I was on to it straight away.

Should have it in cash tomorrow morning."

"One and a half million?"

"All of it, to the last penny."

"Good. I'll contact you tomorrow morning after ten o'clock with detailed instructions, but I'll give you some general information now. The money is to be placed in two strong suitcases. They must be identical and blue in colour. Are you feeling strong, Simon? Do you know how much they'll weigh?"

"I haven't a clue."

"A total of almost thirty-five kilograms, Simon. Surprising, isn't it? Just as well I want fifties, huh? Twenties would be nearer fifty kilograms. Aren't I thoughtful? So - two evenly weighted suitcases, strong, secure and unlocked. Oh, and don't try any fancy tracking devices – I will be scanning them for signs of such naive stupidity and then the deal will be off. Got it?"

"Got it," Simon replied.

"Now, make sure your car has a full tank of petrol. There will be no opportunity to fill up. You will be following the instructions alone – there is to be nobody with you, do you understand? No Sally, no police – and no Guy Sterling. Got it?"

Simon looked up at Guy with a start. He started to nod, a faraway look in his eyes, before realising that wouldn't be communicated via the mobile. "Yes, Arman," he said hurriedly. "I've got it. No problem, I'll do whatever it takes, okay?"

"Good. Until we next speak, then…"

Sally interrupted, "Arman, is Jenny okay?"

Silence.

For a few seconds.

"Until next time," Arman continued. "And don't miss my call – any time after 10am tomorrow."

He rang off.

FIFTY-FIVE

Guy spent the rest of the day with Simon and Sally, and then suggested he stay overnight

"Would you do that?" Sally asked.

"Of course. It makes sense, as long as I'm not in your way. I always keep an overnight bag in the car – it lets me be flexible and gives me options."

By the evening, Simon had filled the fuel tank of his silver Mercedes SLS AMG to capacity and purchased two sturdy blue suitcases from a store in Sutton Coldfield. His accountant had confirmed that he personally would deliver the cash to the house in the morning. Discreet arrangements had been made with Simon's bank; the money would be delivered without any security measures which might draw attention to it. It would be dropped off more like a home-delivery of groceries, rather than in a security truck with someone riding shotgun.

Later, the three of them sat with their after-dinner coffee around the ornate fireplace in the lounge, beneath the family photograph. Neither Simon nor Sally had eaten much of the Chinese take-away so Guy, although ravenous, had tactfully eased off to an empathetic pace.

Placing his mug on an occasional table, Simon looked across at Guy with a determined expression. "Guy, this morning after Arman rang off, I asked how he knew you. You seemed surprised he did. Any more thoughts on that? I think we should know." He waited expectantly.

Guy ran a hand through his hair and sank back

into the sofa, beating a gentle and silent rhythm on its arm with his fingers. He was conscious he hadn't told them about Sophie but knew he couldn't keep the information in his back pocket for long. He needed to give them something though – just not everything at once. At this stage, he judged it would create additional anxiety for them. A step at a time.

"I'm not sure I have the answer, but Sergio's curious disappearance has rather pointed me in a certain direction," he said, slowly. "I've still not been able to reach him on his phone. I haven't told you this, Simon, but on Saturday evening some rather unpleasant types paid a visit to my home in Shropshire…"

"*What?*" Simon exclaimed in surprise and alarm.

"It's okay," Guy reassured him. "They were armed and threatened that if I didn't back off, then they'd harm my family."

Simon looked aghast. "For Christ's sake you shouldn't be here. You should be at home. These guys are evidently madmen, merciless." He made to stand up.

Guy raised his hand to calm him. "Look," he said. "I appreciate the concern, Simon, I really do. But we've increased our security and we're just getting on with what we want to do, not what Arman and his lackeys tell us."

"I hadn't appreciated the sacrifice you were making," Sally said.

"No sacrifice, Sally, but thank you. I take a very positive message out of the threat – I'm on the right track. Arman's call this morning is the ultimate proof, let alone Saturday's visit to my home, which had to be on his orders. The question I've been wrestling with, though, is how did Arman know of my existence, my interest in this matter?"

"And what's your conclusion?" Simon asked.

"Initially my money was on Sergio, but something happened before I met him."

Simon and Sally listened with shocked expressions as Guy told them about the hit and run and the subsequent text he'd received.

"But who knew you were involved at that stage?" Sally asked.

"Well, ironically, I wasn't – I was still making my mind up but doing a bit of digging as a sop to David. So at the time, as I see it, there were the chief constable and his deputy, the superintendent, Jonny, and anyone I talked to in Aston."

"One of them knows Arman then, surely?" Simon suggested.

"But that seems so unlikely," Guy said. "I thought Sergio was the only person I'd had dealings with who was involved with Arman, but he knew me as Sam Granger. I don't see how he could have known my true identity. I didn't even visit him in my own car – I hired one from that place in Sutton you recommended. Oh – shit…" He broke off. Simon and Sally looked at him questioningly. "Sorry," Guy said, "but I've just thought of something. That hire company was burnt down and the friendly old chap that ran it was killed. What if that wasn't the accident it's been reported as, but murder?"

Sally said, "But that's dreadful – how far will these people go?"

Simon leaned forward. "So Sergio saw you leave

and got your registration number?"

"He couldn't have done. I locked him in his basement flat – he had no view of the road. And he didn't see me arrive, either. He could have used a window to get out, but why? And he'd have to have been quick. I can't see him going the extra mile if he didn't have to. Besides, I told him someone was watching the house. The kid's a coward, he won't risk any heroics. No, I think there's another explanation. I had no further direct contact with Sergio, so if he didn't see my car that evening, someone else must have done."

"A neighbour?" Sally asked.

Guy shook his head. "Not round there. It's not exactly Neighbourhood Watch territory – that would be a full-time job. No, someone else was there – someone who knew to make a note of it. I suspect that Arman, or more likely one of his guys, was outside that evening. Maybe Sergio asked them to be there because he was suspicious of my call, but I don't buy that. I have no doubt he thought I was going to offer him a job, a one-off task. And his reaction when I first mentioned Jenny is the final proof that I took him by surprise, as far as I'm concerned. Which means either someone was arriving by coincidence or they were the summoned cavalry, and that would have to have been by one of Sergio's girlfriends who was in the flat –"

"*Girlfriend?*" Simon exclaimed.

"That's for another day, Simon, but you shouldn't be surprised. The key point is that someone noticed my car and then traced it back to the hire place despite the fact it wasn't branded in any way. A visit a couple of days later, strongarm tactics, information extracted, then torch the place – owner and all."

"That poor man," Sally said. "But if the car wasn't branded, they could only have traced it through the number plate – and I didn't think just anyone could do that."

"You're right, Sally," Guy confirmed. "The only people who can trace registration plates within so few hours are the police – with a quick, telephone enquiry."

"Which means we're back to someone within Arman's crew being a policeman," Simon said.

"Possibly. Or they at least have an accessible and accommodating mate they can call on for help."

"But that's only a theory," Simon said.

"What's a viable alternative?" Guy asked. "My only question is why they took forty-eight hours to get my name and address from the car rental place."

"We may never know," Simon said.

Guy shrugged. "True. But I intend to do my best to find out."

Sally looked concerned. "You mean Sergio is one of Arman's gang? And he's been here, in our home!"

"I never trusted the bastard from the start," Simon said. "Corrupted Jen, he did. Look how she's changed. Look what's happened to her. This is Sergio's work for sure – and now he's gone into hiding."

"You can say that, Simon," Guy said, "and I agree he's not one of the world's saints, but my issue is this – how come he's in Arman's camp? Was he always there? I doubt it. I wondered if he'd picked up your daughter deliberately, as part of the grand plan, but that seems unlikely. There was no guarantee she'd be interested, and the way they met at the Latin Rose would have been hard to engineer – he was there before Jenny was. They've been seeing each other for a few months now, too. No – I don't think he was originally an Arman man. My belief is that, somewhere along the way, he's *become* an Arman man."

"When?" Simon asked.

Guy nodded thoughtfully. "Good question. Recently, I'd guess. Sergio's a fickle chap – likes money and girls and has no morals as to how he gets either. In my view, Arman decides to target you and then makes all the necessary enquiries, including the whereabouts and movements of your children. I believe they'd have approached Sergio after finding out he was Jenny's boyfriend and enlisted him for thirty pieces of silver – or whatever the going rate is nowadays. It must have been wonderful for Arman to have discovered such a weak link – and a very worthwhile investment of a pretty small sum. A lucky break and a piece of good fortune. The question remains, though: where did he take her in Birmingham?"

"And why the fabricated account of the row by the roadside. You know – saying he abandoned her in the night," Sally interjected.

Guy nodded. "Clearly he was under instructions. The lad can certainly fabricate stories well enough to keep several girls strung along, but I doubt he's up to planning that sort of detail. When Jenny failed to come home on time, Arman would have known you'd go and see Sergio. In a worst-case scenario for them, it could have been a visit from the police. Sergio needed to be ready with a story for whoever came asking. First it was you, then me. Both visits would have been reported to Arman."

"He's got a lot of questions to answer," Simon said grimly.

Guy nodded. "He sure has. And it's my intention to ask them, politely or otherwise – as soon as I can track the clown down, that is."

FIFTY-SIX

Early next morning Guy, dressed in jeans and an open blue shirt, let himself out of the patio doors onto the extensive wooden decking, where he took in the Stewarts' well-tended garden. The sky was cloudless, but there was a slight chill in the air that suggested, subtly, that autumn was coming. He took a long swig of tea from his mug. He'd woken a little after four o'clock and, despite all efforts to get back to sleep, he'd lain there thinking about Sergio, Jenny and how best to outmanoeuvre Arman.

There was a lot hanging on this. He had to get it right. Falling back on his army training, he tried to place himself in the mind of the enemy, to see things as they did, to view the options they had. Communication was key. Guy had obtained an anonymous mobile for Simon from a local supermarket the previous afternoon; although Arman was using Simon's business phone, he didn't want Simon to risk using his personal number in case Arman had extracted it from Jenny. An engaged tone during the drop process would not be clever when Simon had been ordered not to communicate with anyone.

With Jenny's life on the line, they couldn't afford to be seen to be disobeying any of Arman's instructions, whatever they may be. What they did know was that Simon would be told to deliver the money in the blue suitcases somewhere in his car, perhaps some distance away. They had no idea how Arman would set out his men, so they couldn't risk anyone being in the car with Simon in case someone was watching. Simon had suggested that Guy hide on the back seat or even in the boot, but this was fanciful; not only did it increase the risk of compromising the operation, it would also restrict Guy's options. Guy had worked things through using his own instincts and had made some constructive decisions of his own.

The sound of the gate buzzer rang out in the kitchen behind him, interrupting his thoughts. He looked at his watch – a quarter past nine. Trust an accountant to arrive at exactly the appointed hour. He finished his tea and walked back into the house, entering the hall just as Simon opened the front door.

"Arthur!" Simon exclaimed in a jovial tone, stepping back to let his guest enter the house.

Arthur was a short, overweight man of about fifty, breathing heavily with the effort of carrying a large brown suitcase from his Audi 6. He was dressed in a slightly ill-fitting plain grey suit that had seen better days. Arthur shook hands with Simon, who offered to bring in the second case. With an expression of grateful thanks, Arthur bumbled across the hallway with a nervous smile and stretched out his hand to Guy.

"Arthur Ward," the accountant stammered, giving Guy a quick once-over without making eye contact.

"Guy Sterling. I'm assisting Simon in this project."

"That's what I understand. A lot of money," Arthur said. "I trust you know what you're doing. It's most unusual."

Simon evidently heard this as he returned with the second case. "Arthur's always been a bit of a worrier, Guy – haven't you, Arthur?"

Arthur grinned and looked sheepish, uncomfortable at being the centre of attention. "Well, I've been your accountant for what – eighteen and half years now, Simon, and I've always known all about your financial affairs. You haven't told me what this is all about and it took a hell of a lot of string-pulling to get the bank on side. I trust it's all legal – I wouldn't want to be involved in anything improper."

Guy could see the accountant was genuinely concerned as he loosened his tie slightly and threw searching glances at his client.

Simon stepped forward and put an encouraging arm around the man's shoulders. "You can be assured there's nothing improper on my part, Arthur. Having said that, the less you know for the moment the better – I don't want you worrying unnecessarily. I'll fill you in when the time's right, but that's not now." He removed his arm.

Arthur seemed to relax slightly and gave a weak smile as he straightened his already-straight glasses.

"There is one more thing you could do for me, though," Simon continued.

"And what's that?"

"Guy here needs a lift down the road – can you help?"

"Of course – it's a somewhat easier task than what I've done for you so far this morning."

"Excellent. That's settled, then."

Guy said, "We need to transfer this money to two different suitcases so you can take yours back, Arthur. Can you fetch them, Simon?"

Simon went swiftly to the dining room, returning with the two blue suitcases he'd bought the day before.

"Oh, there's no need for that," Arthur insisted. 'Keep them, for heaven's sake. They're something and nothing."

"Thanks, but we'll do the swap," Guy said firmly.

Between them they transferred the tight bundles of £50 notes into the new suitcases and, at Guy's suggestion, placed them in Simon's Mercedes while Arthur returned his empty cases to the boot of his car. They were now somewhat less valuable than when they'd arrived. Back in the hallway, Guy grabbed his beige summer jacket and looked at his watch. Just gone 9.35am. Arman had promised a call any time after 10am.

"Right," Guy said. "Thanks for all that, Arthur. Time to move on."

Arthur nodded, shook hands with Simon and started to walk towards his car. Guy glanced at Simon; he looked nervous, like a boy about to go to a new school. "You'll be fine, Simon," he told him. "You've got everything ready and we've been through it plenty of times. Just keep in touch with me as planned – okay?"

Simon gave a weak smile and nodded. "I'll be okay." He paused. "But are you sure Jenny will be? This is all about her. I want her home, Guy."

"I know," Guy said, soothingly. "It'll be fine, believe me."

"I do," Simon replied, simply, and the two men shook hands. "I'll open the gate," he added, walking back towards the kitchen.

Guy caught up with Arthur just as the accountant was getting into the driver's seat of his Audi. Guy opened the back door on the passenger side, catching Arthur's slightly bewildered expression as he climbed in.

"It's okay, Arthur," Guy said reassuringly. "On this occasion it's best if I'm in the back. I'm going to keep a low profile, so please ignore me."

"I see," Arthur said. "Well, actually I don't, but never mind. Where to, then? I was going back into Birmingham to my office."

"Could you drop me in Oaklands Road?"

"Where's that?"

"A few hundred metres from here - just over the Lichfield Road. If you could go down, say, about three hundred metres and then pull over just round a bend there, that would be terrific."

"This is a strange day," Arthur said out loud to himself. "No problem." He started the engine.

The gates opened ahead of them as they approached, and Guy lay flat on the back seat with his legs curled up. He had no idea who might be watching Simon's house. Possibly nobody, but he didn't want to take any chances. There was too much at stake. Arthur was trusting, pliable and eager to please, and Guy had no doubt he would not seek any explanation for the strange goings-on, but he'd listen intently if one was offered.

After a few minutes the car pulled over. Arthur dropped Guy off and drove away, office-bound. Guy crossed the road to where a black Range Rover Sport was parked up, a young man wearing a plain t-shirt in the driver's seat. Guy opened the passenger door.

"Morning, Jack," he said. "Good journey?"

Jack sat with his hands on the wheel and smiled broadly at Guy.

"All's gone to plan, sir," he said. "Left the gate lodge dead on time. There was little traffic, and I parked up an hour ago. I've been reading my book. What now, sir?"

"Now? Now we sit and wait. And keep our fingers crossed."

FIFTY-SEVEN

The call came through at about 10.35 am. It was from Simon's new, anonymous mobile, which Guy answered through the Range Rover's speakers.

"Has he rung?" Guy asked.

"Just – he's such a callous bastard."

"What did he say?"

"I'll give you the edited version. I'm to leave the house now with the money. Alone, he said."

"Where to?"

"Towards Good Hope Hospital."

"But that's just down the road, isn't it?"

"That's right. Look, Guy, I've got to dash. I'll leave this phone on and I'll put it on my lap in the car. I've got to be there in ten minutes."

Guy could hear him scurrying across the driveway, opening and closing his car door. The engine started, smooth and powerful. Reverse, then forwards. Guy could picture it approaching the opening gates and turning out into the road.

"Start up," he said to Jack, before stepping out of the passenger door and climbing into the back. He lay down again, feeling the large car vibrating gently to the hum of the engine. As he lay on the rear seat, he picked up the *Birmingham A-Z* which had been placed there ready for him and opened it at the marked page. "Go up to the top of the road and then left," he instructed. "You should see Simon's Mercedes coming out of the road opposite, turning right."

"Cool," Jack replied.

The black Range Rover pulled away, rounded

the short bend and took off at just legal pace to the junction with the Lichfield Road.

"He's already on the Lichfield Road, sir," Jack informed Guy. "About a hundred metres up and moving away."

"Follow, but remember to keep your distance like I told you," Guy said, running his finger along the map and identifying the hospital site, firmly within the Four Oaks and Sutton Coldfield suburb. "Why there?" he wondered.

Jack drove steadily, a running commentary keeping Guy informed of where Simon's car was, what it was doing and how far it was ahead – never more than two hundred metres, never less than a hundred.

Guy strained to listen to the sounds from Simon's car. Then he heard the sound of a mobile ringing, loud and sure through the Mercedes speakers. Simon answered.

"I'm coming, I'm coming," he shouted.

Even with the protracted chain of communication, Guy recognised Arman's deep voice. "Well done, Simon. There's a good boy. Everything necessary on board?"

"Yes, in the boot…"

"And nothing unnecessary?"

"No."

"Now this is where I want you to go." Arman proceeded to give directions and rang off.

A few seconds later, Simon's voice came through to Guy, who was pleased Simon had followed his instructions and kept the new phone muted while Arman was on the line.

"Did you catch that?" Simon enquired.

"All of it. We'll keep a couple of hundred metres behind you."

The cars continued along the suburban road for several minutes, pausing for traffic signals and other vehicles. Guy remained lying on the back seat, his horizontal position affording him glimpses of blue sky, clouds, trees, and the tops of buildings. He studied the A-Z map. From the road names Jack was feeding him, he realized they were heading into a more rural area.

Through the cheap mobile on Simon's lap, Guy and Jack heard Arman ring again.

"You in Withy Hill Road yet, Simon?"

"Just."

"There's a motorway bridge not far ahead, you'll know it. Cross it and then park up on the next bridge – it crosses over the dual carriageway."

Guy whispered, "Pull over when you can, Jack, and we'll wait."

After a few moments, Jack parked up on the side of the road, and left the engine running.

Arman's voice came through again, "Good work, Simon. I can see you – you're about ten metres onto the bridge. Any misbehavior and the deal's off, right? And you know what that means."

"I'll do what you want," Simon said, dully. "I haven't come this far to mess up."

"Good boy. Here's what you do next. When I tell you to, you get out of your lovely car and go round to the boot. Take the suitcases across the bridge at your end to the opposite side – I'll be able to see them better. Once I'm satisfied, I'll send a car for them, a dark blue

Audi 8. It'll draw up next to you and the boot will open. Place the suitcases in the boot, close it and step back. Don't say anything to the driver, don't even look at the driver. Got it?"

"Got it."

"Right. It's nearly time, Simon. You're so much closer to your daughter now, closer than you can even imagine." Arman paused. Guy felt suddenly uncomfortable. "Now, final instruction. Pick up your mobile in your right hand, hold it to your ear, shut the driver's door and then keep your left hand empty and stretched up above your head. I want to see it empty – and believe me, I will see it. Then collect the suitcases as instructed. Now, out."

Guy heard a rustling followed by the sound of the car door shutting. There was a distant creak – he guessed it was the car boot opening. More rustling, and then the boot slamming shut. Then silence. With the cheap mobile phone left on Simon's seat inside the car, there was no communication. No sound, and certainly no visual. Now what?

"Shit," Guy said. "Keep your eyes open for the dark blue Audi, Jack – it should come towards us after the drop." Guy raised himself slowly and carefully peered out. They were surrounded by hedges and fields. After a few minutes, Guy felt agitated and useless.

He was on the point of concluding something was seriously wrong when suddenly Simon's voice came over the mobile. He sounded desperate and spoke loudly and quickly. "Guy, he's got the money. Where the hell are you?"

"Parked down the road behind you. Where's the

Audi?"

"Sod the Audi. There is no fucking Audi. While I was waiting like a dickhead on the bridge this low-level truck – you know, like a builder's lorry – pulled up directly below me on the dual carriageway under the bridge. Arman told me to drop the suitcases off the side onto the back of the truck. Couldn't miss, straight down and in. As soon as the second case landed, the truck sped off up the road towards Lichfield. I'm back in the car now – what are you going to do?"

Guy found himself taken completely by surprise. He grabbed the map.

Simon spoke again. "If you come across the bridge and turn left, Guy, it'll take you up to a large roundabout. The only other way he can go before that is onto the motorway, but that would be a nonsense – there's no escape route. If you're very quick, you might beat him to the roundabout or at least catch up, but you'll have to really motor."

"Jack, get going. Quickly!" Guy ordered. "Simon, we're on it. Stay where you are, we're coming past you." He glanced up. "Be my eyes, Jack, until we're at the roundabout."

Even as he spoke, Jack was galvanized into action. The Range Rover accelerated forwards, gravel and loose stones spinning from beneath the wheels as the car felt for grip. As it drove on, Guy was aware of them negotiating some gentle bends.

"Keep it steady over the bridges, Jack. Simon may still be under surveillance," Guy warned.

They sped down the lane. Guy propped himself up on one elbow as he sprawled across the back seat, legs dangling into the foot well.

"Bridges ahead, sir. Mercedes on the left. Passing it now. Simon's in the driver's seat," Jack recited. "Junction ahead."

"Take a left," Guy said. "Then just follow the road. Tell me when you see the roundabout."

The Range Rover slowed and then suddenly accelerated through a sharp left that made Guy roll on the back seat. A car horn sounded loudly to his right.

"Sorry, sir. I didn't make myself popular there, but there was a whole queue of cars coming – we needed to get ahead of them." The car powered forward for a few moments, then Jack spoke again. "Roundabout ahead, sir."

Guy sat up and looked out through the windscreen. A pub came into view on the right side of the road, standing adjacent to the roundabout with a road to the right leading to its rear car park. Guy looked ahead, watching for the builder's lorry that should have been entering the roundabout from the dual carriageway to their left. No sign. They must be too late. Then he looked again at the road to the side of the pub and saw it.

"Quick, Jack. Turn right by the pub. It's there."

Jack hardly had time to indicate but swerved off to his right and pulled up. A builder's lorry was parked on the verge, a little way before the entrance into the pub car park. This was clearly the old road, superseded by the adjacent improved highway that now carried traffic away from the roundabout and towards Tamworth. Guy observed the truck; there was no sign of life. He felt the reassuring weight of the Glock in his jacket pocket and stepped out of the Range Rover.

"Stay here, Jack," he said over his shoulder.

He moved quickly up behind the truck. There were no suitcases – the back was empty. He eased round to the cab, but there was no driver. He looked around but could see nothing out of the ordinary. *It's probably the wrong bloody truck.* An elderly couple in their late seventies came out of the pub and looked at Guy.

"Did you want the driver?" the woman asked, squinting through thick glasses.

Guy smiled at her. "Why do you ask?"

"Well, it looks like you're looking for him," she said. "He's gone, though."

"Gone? Did you see him?"

"Oh yes, dear, I did. Through the window. He took two suitcases from there," – she pointed to the back of the truck – "and then got in a big black car. Left with his friend, he did."

"Which way did they go?" Guy asked.

"Oh, that way, dear." The woman gestured to the old roadway. "They drove very quickly; I was a bit worried for them. I'm sorry you missed them."

Guy signalled to Jack to join him, then turned back to the couple. "Thank you for your help. Would you mind if my friend takes a note of your name and address? You may just have witnessed something very important. There may be a reward."

"Of course, dear."

Guy left Jack to take the details while he called Simon. He told him where they were and arranged for him to join them. It was pointless setting out after a 'big black car' that could go in any of five directions from the roundabout.

Simon's Mercedes pulled in behind the Range Rover. Guy walked over and climbed into the front passenger seat. Simon looked bewildered and shaken.

"What's happening, Guy?" was all he could say.

"Well, they've got your money, Simon, but then we knew they would. What I'd hoped was that I could at least follow them, get some clue as to who they are and where Jenny is. Obviously, that hasn't worked out. But the good news is, as far as Arman is concerned, you followed his instructions. We can only hope he'll release Jenny now. If he doesn't, then I hate to say it, but he never intended to in the first place."

"I'd better ring Sally."

Before Simon could do so, though, his phone buzzed into life, the ringtone echoing around the car.

"It's Arman."

"Answer it," Guy said. "I'll sit quietly."

Simon pressed the button. "Yes, Arman? Have you got the money?"

"It looks like it, Simon. I'll need to have it checked though, of course." Arman's voice was cold.

"When can we see Jenny? Will you keep your promise?"

"Oh yes, I'll keep my promise."

Guy felt an overwhelming sense of relief. He glanced at Simon and thought he read similar emotions in the man's face.

"Tell me, though," Arman continued. "Did you keep yours?"

"You have the money."

"So it seems, but there was more to it than that, wasn't there?"

Simon looked bemused. "What do you mean?"

"Oh, come on, Simon. Don't play the innocent. You haven't kept your promise at all, have you? Just you, we agreed, didn't we?"

Simon looked worried and Guy felt a chill of anxiety pool in his stomach.

"A black Range Rover Sport driven by one Jack Williams, no doubt with Sir Guy Sterling hiding in the back was not what we agreed. Was it?"

Simon stared at Guy, lost for words. Guy felt dizzy.

"Can you hear this, too, Sir Guy? I'm guessing you're there – am I right?"

Guy said nothing.

"Answer me for fuck's sake!" Arman screamed, before adding quietly and slowly: "If you know what's good for you and Jenny."

"Yes, I'm here," Guy replied, reluctantly.

"Young Jack from the lodge, wearing a white t-shirt. You disappoint me, Sir Guy. You see, I've done my research. I would've thought with your soldiering background you'd have taken more care in the face of the enemy."

Guy said nothing. His mind was racing. What had he done?

"You fouled up, Sir Guy. Big time. There's going to be a lot of suffering, a lot. And Jenny's not coming home, Simon. As I just said, I will keep my promise – the promise that if you disobey me, she dies – a slow, slow death. Thirst and starvation. That starts now. You've seen her for the last time. Such a shame. No more fatherly hugs, no father of the bride. You'll no longer have a daughter in a few days, Simon – and then I'll be wanting two million pounds."

The line went dead.

FIFTY-EIGHT

Guy lay on the sofa in the tower room at Hofton Manor and stared out of the large window. The room was a traditional den – the preferred place for his father and his card-playing friends, as they'd enjoyed its seclusion and the panoramic view across the estate. A full mug of tea sat next to him on a dark-oak occasional table. It was cold – it had been there for a while. His Glock was packed back into its box and lay under the sofa. It seemed irrelevant, almost macabre.

This room was the ultimate retreat for Guy when he needed his own space. The card table still stood in the centre of the oblong room, accompanied solely by the large, red leather armchairs set in pairs at strategic angles, and the sofa on which Guy now lay. All the walls were lined with books from floor to ceiling – old, leather-bound tomes in blocks of colour. Some of the works were priceless, among them several first-edition Dickens and early copper-plated manuscripts dating back to before the Reformation. However, for Guy, their value wasn't in their financial worth but the deep nostalgia they held after being part of his family for several centuries. Right now, though, they meant nothing. He could think only of Jenny, and the position she was now in.

The mug of tea was cold because Guy was thinking. Hazel, the assistant housekeeper, had urged him to drink it earlier that Tuesday afternoon after his return from Birmingham, but it had stayed there, unmoved. The rest of the manor was quiet; Lucy had returned to London and Betty was still in hospital.

Guy had given Hazel strict instructions that he was to be left alone – no, he hadn't had any lunch and nor did he want any. If anyone called, they should be told he wasn't there, and nor was he expected back. In short, he wanted space, room and time alone so he could reflect on the situation and work out what he could do to save Jenny.

He closed his eyes to focus on the options, but try as he might he could not clear his mind of the image of Simon Stewart's angry and disappointed face. That Arman had outmaneuvered Guy had been frustrating, the loss of one and a half million pounds disappointing to him – but the promised loss of his daughter was devastating. Arman had described Guy as a jerk and Simon had warmed to the name, berating him as they'd sat in the Mercedes after Arman's call. He reminded Guy that he'd just wanted to protect his daughter and that Guy had interfered for his own purposes.

Guy knew the accusations were unfair, but it was not the time for debate. He would have liked to remind Simon that they'd fully discussed the risks, and that all three of them had decided the previous day to run with Guy's plan. It could have worked, but instead it had failed; the consequences, much considered, were now reality. But he understood Simon's reaction and raw emotion.

George had tried to reassure him. "You did what you thought was best, sir," he'd said on Guy's return to the manor. "We know well enough from the past that not everything goes to plan."

"Doesn't make it any easier though, George. I've never met her, but that girl's become quite a part of my life, and whatever that bastard Arman has planned, she doesn't deserve it. I feel I've really let her down, just when we seemed to be on to something. I'm going to take some time out, George. Reflect, reassess and create a new strategy. I'll sort this - I have to. I'm not going to let a wretch like Arman hurt this girl or my family's reputation. We will succeed."

George had left him alone and had returned to the security room.

But there'd been more negativity to come. Grant had called while he and Jack drove home in the Range Rover; Guy had intended to ring her when he got back to the manor, but she'd pre-empted him. Her tone was passive, going through the motions.

"What's new with you?" Grant had asked.

Guy could picture her sitting at her desk in Lloyd House, playing with a pencil or a coffee mat or some other make-belief executive toy as she paid lip-service to the orders of her chief constable. Guy had felt obliged to put her fully in the picture. When he'd finished, there was silence.

"Are you still there, Caroline?" he'd asked eventually.

"Shit. Bloody shit," came the response.

"And you still think this is a rich celeb's daughter seeking attention?" Guy tried – and struggled – to avoid sarcasm.

"Of course I bloody don't," Grant snapped. "I need to go and see the Stewarts as soon as possible. They may not have reported that their daughter's missing, but I'm treating you as their agent whether you've been sacked for incompetence or not. You've allowed this to get out of control, Guy. This is right at the heart of the Aston investigation – you should have told me earlier."

"Like you'd have listened."

"Of course I would!"

"Well, that would have been a first."

"Whatever. I need to get on, so I'll catch you later – I'm going to need a full statement from you. You're driving – going home?"

"Yes, to regroup."

"Don't. Just stay out of the way. No more stupidity else I'll have you arrested. Understand?" And she'd rung off. The telephone cradle was probably shaking even now, the random executive toy no doubt hurled across her office.

Guy shifted a cushion, lifted his hands behind his head and attempted to think as he stretched out on the length of the sofa, conscious that both time and life were slipping by.

FIFTY-NINE

The nondescript white Ford Transit van was making its way up the M6 – away from Birmingham and towards the junction with the M54, the motorway that took traffic west and into Shropshire. At shortly after two thirty the traffic was surprisingly heavy, and the journey was taking longer than expected.

"Bloody traffic," Steve muttered, inching the van through a particularly heavy patch.

Tony reclined in the front passenger seat, long legs stretched out as far as he could within the constraints of the cabin, his arms crossed.

"We're part of the problem," he observed, idly.

Steve flashed him a glance. "You what?"

"We're part of the problem," Tony repeated, scratching his ear. "We're in a vehicle, aren't we? Therefore we're part of everyone else's traffic."

"How come you've gone philosophical all of a sudden?" Steve asked. "You started reading them books again?"

"No – just makes sense though, doesn't it?"

They were silent for a while. Then Steve said, "Are you okay doing this without Mehrak, Tony? You know, on our own?"

Tony detected a hint of nerves, but that was only to be expected in the circumstances. He said, "We've done stuff on our own for years, Steve. Remember, Mehrak's relatively new on the scene – so's Arman, come to that. Of course I'm okay. And besides, Mehrak's got other stuff to do. It's not as if we haven't been to this mansion before, is it? At least we'll know our way about. And Sterling's away."

Steve turned to look at him. "Yeah, you said that when we were sorting to go – how do you know?"

"Did what Mehrak did, didn't I?" There was a hint of smugness in Tony's voice. "I rang the place to speak to his lordship and was told he was away, not expected back. Simple. Probably still traipsing around Birmingham with his sidekick – Jack wasn't it? – trying to work out what he's done wrong."

"Interfering, that's what," Steve said with some force. "How do you know the rich bitch will be there?"

"I don't," Tony replied, watching the traffic through the dirty windscreen. "But if she's not, there's bound to be someone about – you know, what with a house that big and posh. The woman who answered the phone, or that housekeeper might even be back from hospital by now. There'll be someone."

More silence. Then Tony continued: "We'll show Mehrak we can do just as good a job as he did – better even – and it's daylight this time. Perhaps we'll even get a bonus from Arman if we impress him with our initiative."

"We're not telling him, then?"

"Only when it's done."

"What about the dogs we heard?"

"Probably just your average estate dogs. You know, like ones that go on them pheasant shoots. They won't touch us, unless we come over all dead, of course." Tony paused. "We'd better stick to Bill and Chas again," he said. "Just no Andy this time. As Mehrak said, as easy as ABC."

Steve smiled. "Sure."

"Like the job," Tony added.

"What do you mean?"

"Like the job. You know, easy as ABC. Into the house, find the rich bitch or the old bitch or whoever's about. The lucky one gets a bullet in both kneecaps and then we're out of there. Sterling was warned and Arman would want it seen through."

Steve grinned. "Great – home for supper then?"

"You bet."

Tony leaned forward, restrained by his seat belt, and opened a supermarket carrier bag that lay in the footwell in front of him. At the bottom of the bag were two black nine-millimetre Berettas. Keeping them low and out of sight, he checked them both over expertly, releasing each magazine and sliding them in again so that each of their fifteen rounds were at their beck and call.

Once satisfied, he left the bag alone at his feet and thought no more about them.

SIXTY

It was mid-afternoon when Guy decided he needed some gentle exercise and took the spiral staircase down from his garret and entered the morning room. He unlocked the French windows and stepped out into the formal Elizabethan garden of patterned parterres and walkways within high brick walls.

Where was Jenny?

Other than Sophie, he'd thought about nothing else. The gravel on the path shifted begrudgingly under each step as he walked. Back to basics. If Sergio had brought her back into Birmingham, where would he have taken her if not to his flat? Arman clearly had a team around him, so they could be based anywhere in Birmingham. The bedroom of a flat somewhere, even the cellar or basement of some old Victorian house. The options were legion, and there was no time.

But why the lie about the row? If she could be hidden so easily in Birmingham, there was no need to mislead people by telling them Jenny might be in the countryside somewhere. And yet Sergio had been adamant about the story. Guy was frustrated that he still hadn't managed to contact him – *or was that by design?*

As he neared the morning room windows, he noticed a black and white cat threading its way along the far end of the high wall. At first he thought it was Betty's cat, but on looking more closely he realised it was the recently arrived stray – it looked similar enough to fool the casual observer but had slightly more white on its chest. He was reminded that Betty would be home soon.

Re-entering the morning room, Guy decided to go to his study. He needed to go back to the start of the evening when Jenny went missing. That meant contacting Mike Burns and visiting his place in rural Staffordshire.

He sat at his desk and was just about to ring Burns when the door opened and George burst in.

"Quick. Intruders, sir. I've just picked them up. Two of them, armed. They're almost at the south side, approaching the walled garden. Same route as before."

Guy leapt up from his desk. "Damn, I've left my gun upstairs. Go and grab a shotgun from the cabinet, George. I'll get to the tower room –"

"But there won't be time - they're coming that way..."

"Shit, I've left the French windows in the morning room open, too. I'll take the back route, George. Put your mobile on silent and we'll liaise in the Great Hall – and be careful."

George turned obediently and ducked out of the study.

Guy hurried back to the Great Hall, but instead of bearing left towards the main staircase and the morning room, he opened a light-oak door under the minstrel gallery to enter the private parlour. The richly decorated room still retained its original oak panelling on which hung many family portraits, including one of the first baronet, Sir James Sterling.

Guy twisted his way quickly through the scattering of occasional furniture to the far wall. He knelt and, with experienced fingers, located a small, metal handle. He pulled it, gently. A low section of panelling, no more than sixty square centimetres in size, eased forward with the faintest of clicks. Guy felt a steady draught exhaling through the gap. He hastily pulled the hinged door open and the light from the room picked out a bare, stone floor. He sat down on the blue carpet and eased his feet and legs through the small opening and then, placing both hands on the back of the entrance way's lintel, pulled himself through.

Guy found himself kneeling on the cold flags in a darkness broken only by light from the private parlour. It was enough for him to locate and pick up a small rubber torch from its usual corner – the modern version of the old oil lamp that had previously hung from the wall, ready to help any fugitive who came that way. He switched it on. The beam wasn't strong, but it was sufficient; he needed to see the floor, not the stars. Guy pulled the wall door closed, hearing a metallic click as the brass locking mechanism, still faultless after centuries of existence, secured the access.

From his crouching position, he flashed the beam around him. The tight stone antechamber was around a metre square and maybe one and a half metres in height – no more than a large crate, with a dusty floor and cobweb-infested ceiling. Opposite, breaking out of the crate, was a very steep stairwell, no more than half a metre wide, which disappeared up into the inky blackness. The atmosphere was fusty and damp; neither natural light nor fresh air found its way into this most secret of escape routes. This was an original part of the manor, designed for politically darker days, as well as being the secret to one of his frequently used childhood tricks when he would leave many a boyhood friend alone and baffled in the Tower Room above.

He shuffled forward and eased himself onto the first step as quickly as he could and began to climb the straight staircase, hunched like Quasimodo heading for the bells. He trod carefully but confidently, the torch picking out the neat stone steps carved and created with dedication and discreet planning. He had no idea whether the passageway had ever been used for its original purpose of aiding a Protestant priest to escape a martyrdom by flames or axe. In later times, perhaps, it might have abetted the escape of some Cavalier, on the run from Cromwell's army of regicidal Roundheads.

Guy's shoulders rubbed along the gloomy walls and his heart pounded from the exertion, but such was his determination to reach the tower room and his waiting Glock that he barely noticed. With his leg muscles burning he reached a small landing halfway up, with a 180° turn to the second-floor level. He brushed round it, holding the cold central support with his left hand as he focused on the second stage of the hasty ascent.

Finally, he reached the last riser and found himself in an antechamber even smaller than the one at the foot of the staircase. The passageway had not been designed for someone of his build, but he could still use it. Guy shone the beam down in front of him to reveal a dark-panelled wooden door, its brass closing mechanism the twin of the one on the entrance below. He leaned down carefully, mindful of knocking his head on the unforgiving stone wall, and eased the lever upwards until it clicked. The wooden door swung outwards, carrying with it the various volumes of mounted books that camouflaged it among the genuine bookshelves.

Crouching forward, he coiled himself through the cramped gap until he found himself sitting on thick pile carpet. Leaning forward, he pushed the hidden door closed until it once more became part of the colourful library.

He pulled his mobile out of his pocket and called George, holding the device tight to his ear. He pictured the screen flashing silently on George's phone.

"Sir?" came George's whisper.

Guy spoke in a low voice. "I'm in the tower room, George. You?"

"Security room, sir. They're in the Elizabethan garden, right by the morning room. One's holding back, the other's about to enter. He's a short bloke – in his fifties? He's got a hand-gun – looks like a Beretta."

"I'll deal with him, George. You watch the other one."

Guy moved quickly and quietly across the room. Dropping to the floor, he slid his hand underneath the sofa and pulled out the small box. Kneeling, he placed the box on the sofa where he'd sat earlier that afternoon and took off the lid. The silver Glock lay ready for him; he removed it and pushed in one magazine, sliding a spare into the back pocket of his jeans. Holding the gun in front of him, Guy took silent, purposeful strides to door of the room, which stood slightly ajar.

He stopped and listened. Silence. Holding the Glock almost at face level, pointing it straight at the ceiling, Guy kept his back to the wall at the left of the door as he slowly pushed it fully open. He knew any sound from a complaining hinge would echo excessively down the barren stairwell. The hinges behaved; Guy released a breath he hadn't even been aware of holding. Bending his knees, Guy slipped through the door and onto the buttressed stone landing above the spiral staircase, lowering his gun and glancing down though the stair's metal rails as he went.

He paused. Still nothing from the morning room door two floors below. The short bloke would be in there by now. Guy didn't want him to come further into the house – unless, of course, he was controlling whcrc the man went. Dipping a hand into a pocket, he extracted a penny coin and tossed it into the stairwell. He lost sight of its flight, but heard it ricochet off the spiral stairs as it fell. As Guy melted back into the tower room, he glimpsed a figure, silenced gun to the fore, moving slowly into the bottom of the stairwell far below. Guy dropped to his haunches just inside the room, leaned back on the wall by the open door, and waited.

Guy felt as relaxed as anyone could in such a situation. He was on home territory – literally. He knew every inch of the manor, all its secrets. He'd explored it as a child and had played all over it as he'd grown up. His instincts were as alert as ever as he waited. He was relying on sound, his ears straining to hear the slightest noise. He knew precisely what he was waiting for. The fifth step. The modern spiral staircase, built over the fatally-worn original stone steps, was made of quality materials, but the fifth step from the top retained its own bespoke creak.

He could picture the short man on the stairs, treading slowly, one careful step at a time. His gun would be clasped in both hands and held ahead of him, probably slightly raised, ready for the potential quarry above. He would be climbing the circular staircase almost sideways, crab-like, with his back to the wall. He'd be conscious of the open door at the top, but also very aware of the one below, through which he'd just passed. Was he the hunter or the hunted? Despite his positive advance, he wouldn't be sure, and he was on unfamiliar territory – the manor's layout, its unique characteristics were all unknowns to him. But how good was he, Guy wondered. What training had this armed intruder had that gave him the balls to take on this situation with such brazen confidence?

The signal from the fifth step came a few seconds later – not loud, not overwhelming, but distinctive and obvious to those who knew it. Guy did. He launched himself out of the tower room, diving horizontally as he'd been trained to do with his arms straight ahead and both hands wrapped tightly around his Glock. Like a goalkeeper, the issue of landing safely came second to the critical task in hand. The top of the staircase was a couple of metres from the doorway across the veranda-like landing and, as Guy flew through the air, his target was in view. The short man was almost at the top of the stairs, some three metres away, his head about a metre higher than Guy's trajectory. He'd been glancing downwards when Guy made his dramatic entrance, and the unexpected appearance made him turn, adjusting the direction of his gun. Guy was prepared. He'd known almost exactly where his adversary would be standing.

There was a quizzical look on the man's face, but he had little time to react as Guy let off two quick shots. He felt the strong kick as the gun recoiled, but he was trained to cope with that. He watched as the pair of lethal shots punctured the man's forehead with a single dark hole, his head flipping back like a coconut on a fairground shy. The man's legs buckled, and he collapsed backwards.

As Guy landed harmlessly on the stone landing, he saw the man rolling and falling backwards down the staircase, crashing into the white walls and metal railings in an unrestrained descent, arms and legs flailing uncontrollably. Even in death the body moved, obeying the laws of gravity. The unfired Beretta hit a single step, slid between two metal rails and fell to the floor at the foot of the tower with a loud clatter, bouncing twice before settling on the edge of a small, circular rug in the centre of the flagstones.

The dead man came to rest about halfway down the staircase, stretched out with his feet above him, his head twisted at an unnatural angle and caught in the upright where a wooden step met the painted stone wall.

SIXTY-ONE

Guy lay flat on the floor at the top of the stairs, his gun pointing down at the door below, aware George had warned of two men. The one spread out on the staircase was of no interest to him now. Keeping his eyes on the door, Guy reached into his pocket for his mobile. There was a missed call from George, who answered promptly when he returned it.

"You okay, sir?"

"I'm fine. One down. Where's the other?"

"He's just fled, sir. High-tailed it, heading for the kitchen garden and the parkland."

"Right. Grab the Morgan, George, and get up to the gate. I'll follow him. I want him alive if possible – but that's second to our own health, okay?"

Guy slipped the mobile back into his pocket and stood up. He descended the stairs two at a time, noting the blood stains on the white walls and the larger pool of sticky redness around the twisted head with its unseeing eyes. He didn't bother to feel for a pulse; he knew when someone was dead from his experiences in uniform.

Running into the morning room, his natural caution prompted him to pause by the French windows. He noticed the tall, green wooden side-gate in the wall to his right had been forced open, so he ran along the gravel path and went through it, gun in his hand and shoulders forward in a low, level dash. The path took him around the side of the all-weather tennis court to a formal, pillared gate that led into the kitchen garden. This, too, was open. Guy noticed marks on the ground – the signs of someone in a hurry. He heard the Morgan start up in the inner courtyard behind him.

Bearing left, he followed the carnage that took a straight line across the beds of lettuce and radishes to the rusty, metallic kissing gate that led into open parkland at the far end of the garden. Guy vaulted it easily, placing his hands on the top and swinging his legs over. He landed in the longer grass and looked up. A man was running several hundred metres ahead of him, taller and slimmer than his adversary on the stairs. Guy could see this second intruder was tiring – he wasn't moving quickly. Guy took off after him, avoiding the occasional dead branch long-since fallen from the scattering of trees. The thin grass brushed against his trousers, unprotesting against his hasty footfall. Keeping his eyes on the man for signs of counterattack he started to make up the ground but was still too far away to be sure of a debilitating shot from his Glock.

His opponent suddenly stopped, having evidently noticed Guy. Instinct made Guy slow up as the man spun round and dropped smoothly onto one knee, raising his gun with both arms outstretched in front of him in a single, swift motion. If the bloke had another Beretta, Guy was confident it would take a more-than-fortunate shot to hit him at that distance; however, the man was too far away for him to be sure, and Guy wasn't going to leave the issues of the man's skill and training to chance. He threw himself against a large sweet chestnut as three shots rapidly dislodged large pieces of bark from the trunk near his head. Silence.

Guy picked up a rotten stump of wood and threw it away from the tree. It landed awkwardly in the grass before coming to rest. Nothing. Carefully, Guy eased around the tree, breathing heavily. The man was off and running again; Guy followed but had lost another hundred metres or so to his quarry.

The man was approaching the estate wall. He leapt at it, and Guy could just make out the line of a rope that started to strain and shake as the man pulled himself up. Guy quickened his pace, but by the time he reached the wall the man had gone. The rope was still swinging gently like a pendulum.

Hearing a vehicle starting up on the other side of the wall, he grabbed the rope and started to climb. Peering over the top, he saw a white van completing a dramatic U-turn off the wide verge. Its gears crashed, the engine over-revved and its whole body rocked as it spun on the rough surface, before it settled onto the asphalt and accelerated towards West Hofton. Guy leapt off the wall, rolled on the verge and knelt to catch his breath as he watched the van's escape. Standing up, he smiled to himself as he began to jog down the lane after it.

It was heading straight for George.

SIXTY-TWO

Approaching the arched gates and lodge house in the Morgan, George pressed the fob button and slowed to allow time for the gates to swing open. He drove through and brought the car to a sharp halt, sliding slightly on the loose surface where the entrance to the estate joined the public highway.

To his right, the lane ran to West Hofton; to his left was the old route along the side of the Long Mynd hills. George got out of the car, stood still and listened. The road was quiet. He thought about the options. There had to be a vehicle which had not only brought the gunmen to the manor, but which would also be waiting to aid their escape. Two men had entered the estate. Only one was leaving, but was there a third in the car? On the previous occasion, there had been three men; was the other one acting as driver this time? He strained his ears, but there was still no sound. There was nowhere else to park up, confirmed by the fact that the tall guy had taken off in a westerly direction towards the parkland and the lane. If there was a car, he ought to be able to hear it from where he was standing. If it went away from West Hofton, he would hear it start and he could follow. On the other hand, if it came in his direction…

George leaned into the Morgan and pulled out the shotgun. Breaking open the double barrel, he checked again that two circular bronze and red cartridges were lodged securely in place. He snapped it shut, and at the same moment heard an engine start some way up the lane. He craned his neck and concentrated. Gears crashed and wheels screeched. Then acceleration. It was coming his way, there was no doubt. He heard it pick up speed and lifted the shotgun. Drawing it level with his eyes, he readied himself.

The white Ford Transit van burst into view around the bend – less than fifty metres away and moving fast. He could see the driver staring straight ahead, almost willing it on. Suddenly, the man turned his head slightly and noticed George, simultaneously realising his mistake in choice of direction. He yanked the steering wheel down hard right and tried to swerve towards George, who held steady and fired two quick shots at the front tyres before leaping out of the way. Two hits. The driver lost control; the Ford Transit careered past, crossing the top of the driveway diagonally and crashing into a large oak tree by the estate wall. The impact crushed the cab, the rear of the van forced momentarily into the air before it bounced down on to the surviving rear tyres. Silence returned, save for the creaking of metal and groans from the cab.

George reloaded the shotgun and went over to the driver's door. The frame was bent dramatically and there was glass everywhere, small diamond shards strewn on the ground and throughout the cab itself. The shape of the cab meant the driver was probably trapped, his legs likely crushed in the footwell. George looked through the window. The driver's face was covered in blood, his dark hair parted to reveal a deep gash.

Hearing the sound of someone coming towards him, he lifted his head to see Guy approaching.

SIXTY-THREE

Guy jogged past the rear of the damaged van and saw George standing near the driver's window. He noticed the off-side tattered tyre and assumed, as he'd heard two shots shortly before the sound of the crash, that the near-side was damaged too. He carried his Glock ready in his right hand but relaxed on seeing George's calm face.

"Nice shooting, George – what's the status?" Guy asked, flicking his head towards the van's cabin.

George tugged at the driver's door. The handle lifted, but that was all. The hinge end next to the bonnet was badly dented from the collision and refused to give. George placed his left foot against the side of the van and pulled again, straining with outstretched arms, leaning backwards to reinforce the effort. With a jolt the door suddenly jerked open.

Guy stepped forward and peered inside. The driver was slumped forward, his face on the steering wheel, angled towards the open door. His arms hung down limply, reminding Guy of the rope at the estate wall, and his eyes flickered open occasionally. Blood ran down from a bad cut on his forehead, dripping down the side of his nose and around his mouth to fall from his chin in droplets onto the grubby cab floor. The man was making low groaning noises, seemingly drifting in and out of consciousness. Guy's attention fell on a silenced 9mm Beretta which lay in the damaged passenger footwell, along with a single black driving glove.

"Watch him, George," Guy instructed. "Although there's not much to watch, the state he's in."

George stepped close to the open door, pointing the shotgun at the stricken driver, as Guy walked quickly round the back of the van to the passenger side. He yanked firmly on the handle and, after some little effort, the door succumbed. It seemed the collision had thrown everything forward onto the floor; as well as the gun and the glove, there were two packets of cigarettes and a silver lighter. Guy picked up the glove and pulled it onto his right hand – not a perfect fit, but good enough. He picked up the Beretta with his gloved hand, then stepped back and pushed the door closed. It bounced against the frame and came to rest slightly ajar.

Re-joining George, he checked the Beretta. There were three shells gone from the magazine, a round had been chambered, and the silencer was screwed tightly in place.

"Right. Time for a chat, I think," Guy said, motioning George to move back.

He grabbed a sizeable chunk of the driver's hair and pulled his head sharply up and back, away from the steering wheel. The man groaned and opened his eyes. Guy shoved him back into the seat, pleased to note he was fit enough to support himself in an upright position. Blood still oozed from the gash on his forehead and the man slowly raised his right hand, wiped it across his face and brought it down to study it. His forehead and right cheek were covered in a thick, sticky layer of his own blood, some of which was now smeared across the palm of his hand and fingers.

"That's a bad cut," Guy said, leaning into the cabin and resting his back on the inside frame of the van, facing the driver. "You need some medical attention. What's your name?"

The man said nothing, just slowly wiped his face again with his hand and stared at it.

"This is going to take time if you're going to ignore me," Guy continued. "And we don't have time, as I suspect you know. I'm Guy Sterling, but I guess you know that too. So, your name?"

While he waited for a response, Guy peered into the driver's foot well. It was creased forward, trapping the man's feet and legs beneath twisted metal. His right foot was caught under the accelerator pedal that protruded at an unusual angle. He looked back at the driver, who continued to stare at his hand in deep shock.

"Sorry, didn't hear your reply," Guy said coolly, resuming his position just inside the cabin.

"That's because I didn't say anything." The man spoke in a low, slow, sullen voice.

"Seems you can speak, though, so that's good news, isn't it? Looks to me like you're trapped in the van. Your legs and feet caught down the front. Accelerators are useful, but a nuisance at that angle." Guy paused. "I do need your name, though, and I've asked politely a couple of times now. My patience is good, but I can get a little upset in the face of blatant rudeness. Don't make me resort to the past."

The man raised his head slightly. "What do you mean?" he asked warily.

"It's a long story with much to tell, but in the SAS I was assigned to HUMINT where we interrogated people you really wouldn't like to meet. There were rules, but sometimes… Well, you know how it can be.

There are degrees of urgency and importance where the result is more vital than how we get there. I thought I'd left all that behind, but, seeing a young girl's life is now hanging by the narrowest of threads, I feel reluctantly pulled back. I may come across as Mr Nice Guy, but there's a side of me that's designed to deal with arseholes like you. Unfortunately for you, it's how I'm wired."

The man said nothing, staring into the footwell.

"So," Guy continued, "I'm going to ask you one last time, and if I don't get a reply, I'll have to see if I can get your legs out with a degree of force. Understand? What is your name?"

The man said nothing, instead raising his right hand slightly with some considerable effort to give Guy a half-hearted V sign. Guy backed out of the van, turned to face the man and then, lifting his foot, delivered a forceful kick to his lower right leg. The driver let out a piercing scream and leant forward, clasping his raised knee with both hands. It seemed as far as he was able to reach. The leg didn't move, but it was now evident to Guy that the right ankle was in a very damaged state. The man rocked on his seat as he handled the pain, his face reddened and screwed up in agony, eyes tightly shut. The blood appeared to flow faster from the gash on his head.

After a few moments, the wave of pain evidently started to subside. The man whimpered slightly, still clutching his knee, but he said nothing. He opened his eyes and gave Guy a defiant stare. Guy held on to the door and frame of the van and raised his foot again, as if aiming at the leg a second time.

"It's Tony," the driver said quickly.

"Nice try. That the first name you could think of? What about Andy or Bill or Charlie – that neat ABC trio?"

"It's Tony," he repeated in clear desperation, eyes on Guy's hovering foot. "Tony Lauder, honest it is. Those other names were made up."

"So you were one of the three tossers that threatened my sister and shot my houseekeeper?"

Tony said nothing and concentrated on his hand again.

Guy's foot suddenly lashed out again, like a striking cobra, hitting its mark near the shattered ankle. Tony screamed in agony again, writhing on the seat as he clutched his leg and fought back tears of pain.

As Tony recovered and quietened down, Guy leaned right up to him. "You work for Arman. Who is he and where can I find the little shit?"

A look of sudden terror crossed Tony's face. Guy had the distinct impression that although refusing to willingly give even his name was an issue of pride, principle and bravado, the topic of Arman was an altogether different and more serious matter. Tony was on very unsafe ground – the epitome of the cliché 'between a rock and a hard place'.

"I have the impression that talking about Arman is a problem for you. I'd guess he doesn't take kindly to snitches. I know, let's look at it this way, shall we? Your dilemma is this. On the one hand, Arman may or may not give you a decent slapping for not only getting caught, but also for telling tales. That won't be very nice, I guess. Am I right?”

Tony stared straight ahead.

“However, on the other hand, you’ve got me standing right over you now. You’re trapped in this shitty little van and, unless either George here or I decide to be generous and call for some professional help to get you out and treated, you’re going to stay here. And believe me, it won’t be a comfortable wait because I’ve got stuff to do, and if you’re not going to tell me what I want to know soon, I’m going to have to make you think and speak a bit more quickly. Understand?”

Tony said nothing.

Guy’s foot shot out again, and Tony once more spent a few minutes writhing in agony.

As he surfaced back into a state of calm, Tony said through gritted teeth, “Okay, okay, I understand.”

“Excellent,” Guy said. “Now we’re getting somewhere. So – who’s Arman and where’s Jenny?”

Tony’s dilemma at the mention of the girl’s name was written all over his face.

Guy continued in clear, deliberate tones, “Yes, Jenny. Jenny Stewart. The innocent eighteen-year-old you brave bunch of losers had the courage to kidnap. Must have been quite a dangerous assignment, grabbing a helpless girl like that. Tough guys, aren’t you? Here’s my main question, the one I want answered in the next few minutes. Where’s Jenny?”

“I don’t know.”

“Not good enough, Tony – or whoever you are. One more try.” Guy raised his foot.

“For fuck’s sake, I don’t know!” Tony cried.

Guy delivered the kick hard and low. Tony’s

scream was piercing and for a moment Guy thought the wretch was going to pass out. He clung to his knee as if his leg was coming off – the ankle was certainly looking dodgy.

As the noise subsided, Guy said quietly: "Well, you'd better tell me what you do know. I've not got all night and, looking at the state of you, I'm sure you haven't either. Let's start at the beginning, shall we? But no fairy tales, okay? I know time is running out for Jenny but believe me, it'll run out even quicker for you if you don't tell me what I want to know."

"Fuck off," Tony answered, then flinched in anticipation of another kick. It didn't come.

Guy stepped back from the door and turned to George.

"George, there's a copy of *The Times* on the passenger seat of the Morgan, could you fetch it for me, please? Then move the car back on to the estate, just down the drive a few yards, and walk back. Thanks."

George nodded and walked over to the Morgan.

Guy glanced at Tony who was looking confused. "Changed your mind yet?"

Tony said nothing.

"You will, trust me."

SIXTY-FOUR

Guy walked round to the van's passenger side and leaned in. Tony tried to turn his head to see what he was doing, but his injuries were too painful, so he went back to staring vacantly ahead. Behind them, the Morgan's engine started, and Guy could hear it being driven away. He moved back to the driver's door just as George returned and passed him the copy of the newspaper.

"Thanks, George. Now, Tony, are you going to tell me what you know about Jenny?"

No reply.

"George, do you know what percentage of cars catch fire when they crash?"

Tony turned his head to look at Guy; evidently, rotating his neck to the right was okay.

George shook his head slightly. "No, sir."

"Have a guess."

"Ten per cent?"

"Actually, it's less than that – some say as low as one per cent. Do you know what that means, George? You have to be pretty damn unlucky to be in an accident where your car catches fire. Not sure what the percentage is for vans, mind you. What do you think, Tony?"

Tony said nothing, just stared and tried to sit up straight.

Guy twisted the newspaper into a baton-shaped roll. "It's not the actual petrol or diesel that tends to catch fire," Guy continued matter-of-factly, addressing George again while he absent-mindedly frayed the top of the paper baton with his fingers. "They're actually relatively safe in liquid form. No, it's the fumes. Very combustible, are fumes. A single spark can set it all off, you know. Whoomph! Then, there's an inferno."

Guy transferred the newspaper to his left hand, reached into his back pocket with his right and pulled out the silver cigarette lighter he'd just picked up from the passenger footwell.

"Can you smell diesel fumes, George?"

"Funny you should mention that, sir, but I thought I could. Might be mistaken, but then this van has just had a bad accident – you know, coming off the road at speed and careering into this tree. Maybe the driver was drunk."

"I guess forensics will never know. Not sure you can do a blood test on a charred body, George – certainly couldn't take a breath test…"

Tony tried desperately to free his leg, but the stricken van stubbornly held its prey.

"Looks like the driver was trapped and couldn't get out in time, George," Guy continued. He flicked the lighter with his right thumb and a modest flame ignited and burned steadily, flickering slightly in the gentle breeze. "Let's see if we're right about the fumes. This should prove it one way or the other."

Guy waved the lighter slowly under the frayed end of the paper baton until the newsprint gradually caught light. It smouldered and burned, giving off curls of grey smoke and releasing small scraps of blackened paper into the air. Guy flicked the lighter closed and returned it to his back pocket. "Best starting point would be the engine, I suppose, George. It's pretty accessible with the bonnet all creased up and everything."

Guy took a couple of steps towards the front of the van. where it was crumpled against the oak tree. He held the burning baton in front of him waving it slowly as if he was exploring some darkened cave.

"No. Stop!" Tony shouted desperately, still pulling on his leg despite the evident futility of the endeavour.

"No fumes yet, George," Guy called, taking a further step towards the bonnet. He continued to wave the burning baton. "Have you ever thought about what Joan of Arc went through, Tony? Or all those Christian martyrs through the ages? Tied to a stake, unable to move while the flames ripped through their skin, their flesh – smelling yourself on fire, feeling the agony."

Tony tried to interrupt him. "Please, don't. Stop. I'll tell you what you want to know. I'll tell you all I can."

Guy turned and walked back to the driver's door, passing the burning baton to George. The flickering flames continued to slowly consume the paper, a few lines at a time.

He stared at Tony, whose face was now a macabre mess of smeared blood. The flow from the untreated gash appeared to have stemmed slightly. The man was a mess, but he surely held the information Guy needed to find Jenny and track down Arman.

"Okay, Tony. Where's Jenny?"

"I don't know –"

Guy pulled away. "You're a scratched record, Tony." He stretched an arm out towards George. "Give me back the newspaper, George."

"No, no wait!" Tony shouted. "Please, hear me

out."

Guy paused and turned back to Tony.

"Look," Tony said. "I don't know where she is, but I can tell you what happened. I wasn't there, okay? My mate Steve was, and he told me bits of it."

"Where's Steve?"

"He came with me today. I heard shots when I was just in the house – is he dead?"

"The short, fat guy? Hard to survive two shots in the forehead."

Tony fell silent for a moment.

"You were going to tell me what happened," Guy prompted, quietly.

"Yeah, okay." For a moment, Tony had a slight far-away look in his eyes before he seemed to snap back to the present. "Look, I can only tell you some of it. Steve and I have worked for Arman for a few years, on and off. We do 'heavy' work, so to speak. We get called in when he needs us, sometimes by Arman, sometimes by whoever's his lieutenant."

"Who's the lieutenant now?"

Tony clammed up.

"You were doing well, Tony. Don't stop now."

"Okay, okay." Tony's shoulders drooped, all attempts at posturing gone. "The lieutenant at the moment is an Egyptian bloke called Mehrak. I don't know his full name – I don't even know if that's his real name, but we all call him that. He must be late twenties, speaks fluent English with a hint of an Egyptian accent. He says he was educated in England – some posh school in the Midlands. His main skill is shooting though. He's a sniper, and a fucking class one."

Guy threw a glance at George who nodded, acknowledging that they were making progress. Guy felt confident from this last piece of information that Tony was being truthful, at least to some degree.

"Did he shoot Julie Reid?"

"Yeah." No hesitation. Tony was on a roll. Guy threw another look at George.

"So who's Arman and where can I find him?"

"I don't know."

"Tony…" Guy's tone was slow, deep and threatening.

Tony's fearful expression returned. "Honest to God and on my mother's grave, I've no bloody idea. I've never met the psycho, okay? He'll fucking kill me if he knows I've told you all this stuff."

Guy didn't doubt it. "And I'll fucking kill you if you don't. So where can I find him?"

"I've told you, I don't know," Tony said in desperation, glancing briefly at the burning paper baton in George's hand. It was still smouldering, giving off smoke and the occasional flash of flame.

"Ok, here's the big one again, Tony. Where's Jenny?"

"I don't know where she is now, honest I don't. I know Arman had her kidnapped because that Simon Stewart bloke wouldn't pay up, not even when Arman had his sister shot. All I know from Steve was that her boyfriend took this Jenny to some party. It was planned, right? They gave the boyfriend some money to help, bought him so to speak. I don't know how it happened. Steve wouldn't tell me more. Arman told him not to tell anyone how they got her, not even me. And you do what

Arman says, we've all learned that trick."

"Was this a party at Mike Burns' place?"

"Yeah, that was it. Out Tamworth way. I've not been there, but it's some big posh pad."

"Is Mike Burns in on all this?"

"Not that I know of. Never met the bloke. I think they just took advantage of one of his boozy parties that's all – Steve could have told you."

"Well, now he can't," Guy said. He tested Tony. "What's this boyfriend's name?"

Tony looked puzzled. "Sergio," he said slowly. "I thought you knew that."

"So why have you come looking for me? Sergio didn't know who I was, even though we had a nice chat. How did Arman get my name and address?"

"I don't know all of it. I got the impression from Mehrak that you were poking around, and they warned you off. I wasn't there, honest. Then you turned up at Sergio's flat. Mehrak said he didn't know for certain if it was you, but he saw you as you were leaving. He got your number plate and tracked it to some car hire place."

"How did he do that? Friend in the police?"

"Yeah, he knows some low-level copper who doesn't mind doing favours for cash. Got the owner's details that way."

"So Mehrak gets my details from the hire company owner, and then for some reason kills him and sets the place on fire. You mix with nice people, Tony."

Tony said nothing.

"Where's Sergio now? He's not answering his phone."

"Dead," Tony said.

"How?"

"I don't know – I wasn't there, was I?" Tony replied belligerently. He studied his hand. "Mehrak and Steve did it. Steve just said they'd taken him somewhere and killed him. Arman had said he was 'past his sell by date' or something like that."

Guy felt overwhelmingly that the man was lying, but he did believe the central theme – one way or another, Sergio had been killed. It made sense – he'd fulfilled his purpose and had become a potential liability. Still, the details weren't important right now.

"One final question then, Tony, for one last time. Where can I find Arman?"

Tony sat silent for a moment, breathing heavily, still in pain. Guy waited for a few seconds, watching him closely. Then, in a tired voice, he said, "I don't know, honest I don't. He spends a lot of time abroad. He lives off this racket and pays us well. I don't know how to find him. He contacts us through whoever his lieutenant is when he needs us. I say again, I've never met him – haven't even got his number. That's the fucking truth, I swear it is."

Guy looked into the pathetic face while he decided what to do. It was time to close – the guy was spent. On the whole, he felt satisfied. He recognised grains of truth in the shovel of sand Tony had thrown out. There was probably more, but he knew he'd extracted all he could using his current tactics.

He stepped away from the van.

Tony looked frightened. "What now? Are you going to get me out of here?"

"No," Guy replied. "Now you've finished

singing like the proverbial canary, we're going to torch this van."

SIXTY-FIVE

Jenny was lying on her bed in the cellar room. She was always either lying or sitting on the bed as there was nowhere else comfortable to be. It was part of her normal routine: three dull but welcome meals; exercise that meant walking round and round the small room until she was almost dizzy, or occasionally some sit-ups; and, in between, lying or sitting on the bed to read, think or doze. There was also some broken and fitful sleep – interspersed with many bad dreams – during what she guessed was night.

But today, whatever day it was, something was different. She'd had breakfast with a mug of tea – the container was plastic, of course – but lunch hadn't arrived. A plastic jug of water and polystyrene beaker remained permanently by the bed, refilled when she left it on the brick stump by the hatch. She'd finished the water jug during what she felt was the night and had followed the usual routine. But though the jug had been taken away, it had not been returned.

Her stomach told her that lunch, possibly even supper, were long overdue. The gentle twinges of hunger from a few hours before had become a strong ache. And she was so, so thirsty. She'd banged with her fist on the locked door, shouting out despite the hooded man's written instruction to stay silent. But what if he'd died, struck down by a heart attack or something? What if he was lying upstairs dead? Who knew she was here? Who would feed her, give her water? How long could she survive? *Where are you Daddy?*

She'd tried to think of any way she could

escape, anything she could use, but there was nothing. The door was locked, the hatch by the stump was locked, and there was no window. She was incarcerated by brick. She had nothing with which to pick a lock, even if she could work out how to do it. She had even tried working on other ideas, such as breaking the solitary light bulb to use as a tool or weapon, but the simple act of extracting it while standing on the moveable bed would leave her helpless in the dark. And if such a plan failed, she had no doubt the hooded man would leave her in the dark as punishment.

She'd tried snatching and wielding his knife, but that had resulted in failure. Force was the only way she could escape – except now it seemed there was no one to force. Surely the hooded man would return, peer through the grille as usual and open the door? Open the door. Jenny sat up quickly. She recalled how quickly she had closed the gap to snatch the knife. What if she waited until she'd been observed through the grille and then rushed to the side of the door to force her way out as it opened? Take the hooded man by surprise? A new hope ran through her, a new determination to win her freedom as she psyched herself up.

But first, she needed the hooded man.

Jenny stood up again and went to the door. She raised her right fist and banged on it as hard as she could, screaming for help until her chest heaved with exertion, her mouth went dry and her stomach ached even more. Despite her intentions, tears still welled up in her eyes. Overwhelmed by the effort and emotion, she stumbled back to the bed and collapsed heavily onto it.

Where was the hooded man?

As she lay there, she suddenly heard footsteps. It had surely worked. Her ears had become attuned to every noise in the draughty corridor as the days passed, and never before had the sound of footsteps been so welcome. She could picture the hooded man approaching, coming to find out what all the noise was about. Maybe he was bringing something to eat and drink, but most welcome of all he'd be bringing the key. She twisted onto her back so her head rested on the pillows, but her feet hung off the bed, and watched the grille. Waiting for the hooded man to make his routine viewing of both her and the cell.

This time was no exception. The footsteps stopped, there was a pause, and then the hooded man appeared and stood watching her through the door. They stared at each other. After a few moments he moved away, and she leapt up and raced in her socked feet to the edge of the door. Sure, she wanted food and drink to appear through the hatch door, but she wanted her freedom more.

The hatch didn't open. Instead, to her relief, she heard the key grate in the lock and, with their usual medieval protest, the hinges started to swing the heavy door open. As soon as the gap was wide enough, she hurled herself through it with as much force as her weakened body could muster. But the hooded man blocked her way, and she realised as soon as she saw him that he was different. Bigger, larger, stronger. This was a different person. As she crashed into his bulk, he seized her and forcefully pushed her back into the cell. She staggered and fell to the floor, landing on her back, propped up on her elbows.

She watched him enter and close the door behind him. As she started to edge back towards her bed, she observed him insert the treacherous key into the lock and turn it, stealing her freedom. He extracted the key and placed it carefully on the brick pillar. Still watching him closely, Jenny sat down on the edge of the bed, legs together, her bandaged hand resting on her lap. It dawned on her that she'd only seen the hooded man's whole body on a couple of occasions – the first when she'd been brought into the room and thc blindfold removed, and the second when he'd attacked her hand. Her right hand subconsciously embraced the bandage. Every other time, all she'd seen was the hood through the grille, or gloved hands delivering or retrieving the food tray through the hatch.

This man had baggy, blue slacks pulled round his belly, held up by the heroics of a straining black leather belt with a silver buckle. His modestly patterned shirt was open at the collar, revealing copious tufts of grey chest hair. He wore no gloves. From looking at the bottom of his neck, where it emerged from the hideous cloth mask, she noted his wrinkled skin was weathered and tanned – the result of persistent exposure to the sun and the ınevitable ageing process. She guessed he was at least in his sixties; the other man had been much younger, more athletic, with the rapid movement of youth.

Jenny stayed still on the edge of the bed, surreptitiously glancing at the silent key. The man stopped a metre or so away and stood looking at her.

"Lie down." His voice was deep, with a tone that appeared comfortable with control. She held his stare and then, very slowly, shook her head.

Before she could move, his right hand shot out and slapped her hard across the face, forcing her to turn to her right. Her cheek stung as she turned back to face him, eyes defiant.

"Lie down," he repeated. She didn't move. With a speed that seemed alien to his size, he suddenly grabbed her shoulders and forced her back on to the bed. As she fell, she raised her knees, her legs clamping together. She lay, head on the pillow, staring up at him as he stood over her with his hands on his hips. She was suddenly conscious that her blouse had pulled out of her blue jeans, exposing a narrow section of her shrinking midriff. It caught his attention and he sat heavily on the edge of the bed, facing her. The old iron bedstead hardly moved as it accepted his weight.

Reaching out, he placed his right hand flat on her exposed stomach. She tried to push herself up onto her elbows, but he slapped her hard again and forced her back down. His hand returned to her stomach and caressed it lightly. His fingers followed the smooth curve of her slim waist, and then returned to the flatness of her midriff, stroking gently back and forth, slowly taking in the soft firmness of her femininity. She froze, unable to move. She found his touch terrifying and threatening but knew it would be having a very different effect on him, just as it had with Sergio.

Suddenly, he withdrew his hand and leaned forward, close to her face. The cloth hood smelled pungent with masculine sweat. The man spoke in a quiet, deep voice.

"Your parents have failed you, Jenny. No one is

coming for you."

Jenny started to lift her head again to sit up, but he pushed her back.

"No. Don't move and don't speak. I don't want to have to hurt you, but I will. Lie still."

Jenny's thoughts were in turmoil. She didn't believe this dreadful man – and yet where were her parents, where was Sergio, where were the police? Surely no one gives up on a missing girl – no parent gives up on a missing daughter? She wanted to speak so badly, to ask questions and seek answers, but the man's threats and menacing appearance, his all-conquering power and authority, overwhelmed her.

The man pulled back but continued to perch on the edge of the bed, looking at her face. She could see his eyes through the holes in the hood as they surveyed her. His right hand lifted from her stomach and moved up, touching her, tracking her, coming to rest on the top of her forehead. She felt him try to run his fingers over her long brown hair, but they caught in the myriad of knots that bore witness to the fact that she had neither washed nor even brushed her hair for days. The experience seemed to bring his action to a premature end. The tips of his fingers left her hair and moved to the side of her face where they fondled her left ear lobe, caressed her cheek and ran a brief, exploratory mission over her dry lips. She swallowed and remained still, cringing inside and silently begging him to stop, but she dared not speak.

With a pointed forefinger he slowly drew an imaginary line from her mouth down over her chin, her neck and to the centre of her chest to the buttons of her white blouse. To her horror, his left hand joined its partner and he started to unfasten her blouse, one tiny button at a time. She pressed herself further into the mattress, tightening her muscles, but was unable to move. Her blouse now open, the man slid his right hand under her cotton top and manoeuvred it into the loose-fitting bra, wrapping it around her right breast which he gently gathered and caressed in his fingers and his palm.

Despite the threat, despite the danger, she could take no more. She had tried force, she had tried defiance, and she had only one weapon left. She looked hard at the eyes through the macabre hood. They flickered up from her chest and they connected with each other.

Jenny said in quiet, calm tones, "Please don't touch me. I'm just a young girl. I'm frightened and I'm hungry and I'm very, very thirsty, and I just want to go home to my mummy and daddy. I miss them, and they'll miss me." A single tear, a messenger of sorrow, rolled down from the corner of her right eye and slowly traversed her pallid cheek to fall in a single droplet onto the dirty white pillow. It left a snail-like trail across her perfect skin. Her eyes were watery, doe-like, and they looked up at him with innocence, with feminine weakness, with the resignation to accept his decision without complaint or grievance. But in them was also an appeal to his heart and soul for pity, for compassion, for mercy. Jenny spoke no more words; she let her eyes deliver the final, desperate petition.

The man's hand paused and rested on her breast. He sat there, staring at her for almost a minute before he slowly withdrew it and, in unison, his hands pulled the blouse together and straightened it out. Leaving the buttons undone, he stood up, paused momentarily as though about to speak, and then collected the key and let himself out of the cell. As the creaking door closed and the cruel key turned, Jenny rolled onto her side. Bringing her long legs up she curled into a tight foetal position and sobbed more tears than she'd ever cried in her life.

SIXTY-SIX

Despite the pain it caused, Tony continued to tug on his leg. It was a futile effort – he was firmly trapped. The threat to torch the van caused him to stare at Guy in horror and disbelief. "I've told you all I know, honest I have. Get me out of here, please," he begged.

Guy said, "But you've shown others no mercy, and as far as I can see you'd have happily killed someone in my home this afternoon if things had gone differently. I don't go a bundle on that, Tony." He stretched out an arm towards George. "Pass me the newspaper, please, George."

George hesitated and gave Guy a hard stare. Guy caught the look and winked. George appeared to relax slightly and handed the coil of paper to Guy. It was about a third of its original size, still smouldering, but with no obvious flame. Guy took it in his right hand and blew gently on the lit end. The paper glowed, and fragments of charred paper and grey ash took to the late-afternoon air.

"Still burning," Guy observed, looking at George.

"Seems to be," George replied. "Should still do the job."

"No! Don't, please don't!" Tony wailed despairingly.

Guy took a few strides towards the crushed bonnet and then paused. He had Tony's full attention. Giving him a quick glance, he dropped the newspaper on the ground and stamped out the flames. Tony sank back in his seat, sweat now mixing with the blood on his face.

Quietly, he said, "Thank you, Sir Guy."

Guy turned to George. "Right, take the Morgan back to the manor, fetch the flatbed tow truck and get back here as quick as you can, okay?"

"Yes, sir." George spun around smartly and walked quickly back to the Morgan.

Leaving Tony, Guy walked to the back of the van and opened the doors. Inside there were boxes, some clothing, a variety of tools and a traditional emergency kit for winter driving that included a wooden-handled shovel. He climbed in and poked around, but there was nothing to pique his interest and certainly no clues to point him towards either Arman or Jenny. He sat on the floor of the van, legs hanging over the edge so his feet touched the ground. Taking the Beretta out of his pocket, he studied it; not a bad weapon, but he preferred his Glock any day.

His thoughts were disturbed by the sound of a car travelling up the lane from the direction of West Hofton. The road was typically quiet, now limited to very local traffic. Guy tucked the Beretta under a blanket in the rear of the van, climbed out and closed the doors. A white Honda Civic drove past, the young male driver not slowing despite the wreckage of the van. As the car disappeared up the hillside, the lane fell silent again; the only noise was an occasional moan from the cabin.

After a few minutes, Guy noticed a yellow flatbed tow truck coming up the estate drive towards the gates, which opened at its approach. Guy had bought the vehicle a couple of years earlier for use on the estate and as a cheaper, more local alternative for his West Hofton neighbours when they needed it.

He watched as George spun the truck round and, the reversing alarm sounding, backed it up to the rear of the van. Guy helped George fasten the winch securely, then walked back to Tony.

"Right, listen up. You stay nice and still now because George is going to winch this wreck up onto the flatbed, okay? Then you'll have a little ride back to the manor and we'll take it from there, right?"

Tony said nothing, just nodded slowly with a defeated, deflated air.

Guy shoved the driver's door closed as much as he could. The winch strained and the van was dragged, grating and complaining, backwards onto the low vehicle. As George secured it for its short journey, Guy inspected the oak tree. It was marked but showed no sign of giving up on its next two hundred years of life.

Guy hopped into the tow truck's cabin for the short journey back onto the estate, reflecting on what Tony had told him and thinking about what his next move would be. He'd learned a lot, but it seemed Tony wasn't privy to all Arman's plans and secrets. Guy was confident that what he'd been told was the truth, perhaps with some inaccurate minor detail. Pulling on deeply buried memories, he knew more than most that anyone placed under the same duress and pressure as Tony had been would struggle to find multi-tasking straight-forward. They would inevitably fall back on elements of truth, much easier to relate and remember than inventing some fiction or other. But while Guy now knew some of the background and was aware of his opponents' brutality, he still didn't know where he could find Arman, the Egyptian sidekick or – most importantly –

Jenny.

There was also another dilemma. Grant. Should he update her on the apparent facts now in his possession? He did after all now know the identity of the sniper who had shot Julie Reid almost two weeks ago, and why, and this was at the centre of Grant's investigation. A number of theories had been confirmed. But what if Tony was making it up? It could make Guy look a fool once again, and he wasn't prepared to allow that to happen. In addition, although elements of the past had been verified, no real answers or direction for the future had been given. If he were to ring Grant, he could imagine how the conversation would go.

"Good news, Caroline. I've caught a bloke who works for Arman. He's told me a lot of stuff, although it was under the threat of becoming a Guy Fawkes' impersonator."

"No duress, then?" Grant would say, wryly. "Where's Arman, then?"

"I don't know. But he's a violent man."

"No shit, Sherlock – let's tell them to hold the front page for that one, shall we? Okay, so who did shoot poor Julie Reid?"

"Some English-speaking Egyptian called Mehrak – although that may not be his real name."

"Okay. And where's he?"

"I don't know."

"But at least you've found out where Jenny's being held, right?"

"Um – no."

It didn't sound impressive. He was also aware of Grant's instructions that he should stay at Hofton Manor or face arrest. There was no way he could do that. He watched the parkland roll by and looked towards the rocky hilltop of Caer Caradoc. No doubt Grant would have been to see the Stewarts by now. With her attitude towards him and the Stewarts' belief he'd let them down – indeed, that he'd endangered the life of their daughter – he couldn't see himself being the hero in their conversation. He had to do more, find a way through this treacle. He thumped the dashboard of the truck hard with his fist.

"Sir?" George questioned, glancing at him.

"We've got some of the answers but not all, George. I keep running and re-running all we know through in my mind, but even with Tony's confessions confirming some of what we thought, it doesn't yet come together. I feel we're so close we can almost smell it. *Where* did Sergio take Jenny? It's all so bloody frustrating." He paused. "But we're not going to fail, George. That's not the Sterling way. We have to find Jenny before she dies, and we're talking literally hours."

"You're taking it very personally, sir."

"Of course I am – that's how I'm wired! Sterlings lead from the front and win. We always have, always will. Any denting of that is an attack on me, my very being. I'll fight back – I've no choice."

"How this time?"

"Another roll of the dice. Mehrak warned me not to look for Jenny, or something like that. That's a gauntlet thrown down if ever I've seen one. I've already picked it up and I'll continue to hold it until the task is complete, whatever it takes. The next step will come to me – I know it will."

George drove the tow truck through the archway under its guardian clock tower and parked up in the stable yard. As Guy climbed down from the cabin, his attention was caught by Betty's black and white cat strolling across the yard; he felt for him – it had always been an affectionate creature who'd known Betty since he was a kitten. He must be missing her. The cat stopped suddenly and turned slightly towards Guy, revealing its white, furry chest. More white fur than Betty's cat. It was just the stray again, last seen in the Elizabethan garden.

As Guy swung the truck door closed, a thought struck him like a lightning bolt.

Suddenly, things became very clear.

"George!" he shouted. "For fuck's sake, we've been led a dance! I see it now. I think I know where Jenny is!"

SIXTY-SEVEN

George came to the front of the lorry, a quizzical look on his face as he saw how animated his boss had suddenly become.

"I'll tell you soon, George, but I've got to go, right now. This is the plan. Do what you can to get that piece of shit out of the van – a decent crowbar under the pedal might do it. Check his face, dress his wound and get a couple of aspirin down his throat. That'll tide him over until a doctor can look at him. Shove him in one of the cellar rooms for now – lock him in with some bread and water, and we can hand him over to Grant soon. Oh, and you'd better tidy up Steve, too – he's languishing on the tower staircase. Shove him in the cellar room with Tony, as he seemed to miss him. It'll also be a reminder for him to behave."

"Shouldn't we get a doctor to him sooner, sir? He's in pain."

Guy hesitated, then said, "You're probably right, George, but the priority now is Jenny. Tony can put her first this time. Besides, we're going to get a grim reputation if Tony turns up at A&E in that state so soon after Betty."

George nodded.

"Ring Jack and get him up here – he'll be with his mum in the village this afternoon. Brief him. I don't know what resources Arman has or how quickly he can mobilise them, but he's going to be pretty pissed off when he doesn't hear from these idiots, so I want someone here, okay? Give him the shotgun, he's pretty handy with it. I feel sure, though, that if we move quickly enough, we can head any response off at the pass."

"Okay, sir. And the superintendent?"

"We'll ring her soon, but first we're returning to the Midlands. I'm going now in the Morgan, and I've got a small job for my sister, Lucy, to do – I'll call her. Once you've sorted things here, follow me in the Maserati straightaway. We can talk more when we're driving – you know, directions and things. Got it?"

"Yes, sir." George hastened towards one of the outbuildings to fetch a crowbar. Guy jogged quickly up to the manor and went to his office. He located the memory sticks Sergio had left for him and shoved the first one into his desk computer, fast-forwarding to the section of film where Sergio and Jenny came downstairs to the hallway. Then he inserted the second one and studied what he'd already watched several times before. He smiled.

As he crossed the Great Hall to return to the courtyard and the Morgan, he heard an unfamiliar mobile ring out. Hurrying into the morning room, he followed the sound through to the stairwell of the tower room. Steve's crumpled body still lay on the staircase. Guy climbed the steps two at a time and found the ringing mobile in the dead man's pocket. The caller's number was recognised, the name spelled out in six letters on the display. Guy answered the call.

"Yes, Mehrak?"

There was an uncertain pause. "That you, Steve?"

"No, it's not," Guy replied. "Steve doesn't look too good at the moment – I guess two bullets in the head aren't great for anyone's health. This is Sir Guy Sterling, and frankly it's not much of a dare to find you. Be on your toes, Mehrak – I'm coming for you."

Then he rang off.

SIXTY-EIGHT

Guy halted his Morgan on a quiet side road in the hamlet of Murdoch, not far from one of the more remote walls that encircled the Murdoch Hall estate. He glanced at his Seamaster – just after seven o'clock. The journey from Shropshire had taken the best part of two hours and the evening light was starting to fail. He had followed the directions on his satnav and, during the journey, had received the awaited call from George who was now following behind. Guy had told him his destination.

"What's the theory, sir?" George had asked.

"I think we've been set up and used, just like Sergio. They bought him – right? – and got him to bring Jenny to Burns' party on the Wednesday evening."

"Okay. We know she was there from the CCTV."

"Agreed," Guy acknowledged. "But I don't think she ever left."

"But we saw them leaving on the CCTV footage, sir – the Audi and everything."

"That's what we were meant to see, George. That's why Sergio could get the film for us so easily. It was meant for the police, but we asked first. When you look carefully, the girl Sergio was with on the front step as he left never showed her face. It looks natural – but it was deliberate. *Because it wasn't Jenny.*"

"Then who was it?"

"I reckon it was his other girlfriend – the one I saw in his flat. Not identical, but similar enough to Jenny. There was a slight difference in their hair length and that's what I confirmed by looking at the real Jenny in the hall. Angles can be misleading – like when you're identifying cats."

"You think she was in on it too?"

"I've every reason to think so, George. Someone else took her to the party – perhaps this Mehrak character – and she was the lookalike to fool us into thinking Jenny had left."

"But why the story of the fight and leaving her in the lane?"

"It was believable, wasn't it? No doubt Arman or Mehrak realised the police would also recognise Sergio for who he is and see such a crass move as entirely in character. It would leave Jenny's whereabouts a complete mystery, but certainly not at Burns' place."

"Okay – then what's Arman got to do with Burns?"

"That I don't know," Guy conceded. "Sergio did say, however, that Burns wasn't at the party – that wasn't unusual, apparently. Maybe Arman is a friend who took advantage of his absence."

"But would she still be at Burns' place, then?"

"Something tells me she is - if not, it's a new starting point. We'll soon find out." Guy was silent for a moment, then asked, "How's our Tony?"

"Enjoying the hospitality of the manor alongside his mate, sir."

"No complaints, then?"

"I told him if he had any he should put them in writing to the management." George hesitated, then added, "His ankle's pretty bad, sir. He passed out going down the cellar steps. He'll need some medical attention soon, however much of a scumbag he is."

"I know. Soon, I promise. How far behind me are you?"

"About an hour, although I should make that up if the traffic continues to improve."

"Okay. If I'm not outside the hall when you arrive, you have my orders to advance with discretion, starting from somewhere near my car. But before you do that, ring Grant and tell her to bring some officers over. I'm going in first, just in case my theory's wrong."

Later, just as Guy was about to leave the M6, Lucy had rung him.

Guy said, "Hi again, sis, were you able to do the research, then?"

"Sure," Lucy said. "How's that for prompt service?"

"Great. And what have you found out about Murdoch Hall?"

"I've done what I can. Murdoch Hall's about five miles north-east of Tamworth. It's on the outskirts of the medieval village of Murdoch, now little more than a hamlet. Even the pub has closed – it sounds a bundle of fun. The house was owned by the Fulgrove family for generations, but about twenty years ago it was sold, together with its five tenanted farms, by the executors of Edith Fulgrove, the last of the line. She was an eighty-seven-year-old spinster when she died. The buyer was Mike Burns. So now you know."

"You're quite the historian, Luce" Guy said. "What's it like?"

"The house? English Heritage describe it as *"a small country house built by Thomas Fulgrove in the early eighteenth century*" – not personally, I'd guess; he'd have got some blokes in to do all the manual stuff." Guy smiled. "It then goes on a bit about structure and design and why there are certain pointy bits on the gables, all of which would no doubt send an architect into the highest of raptures. Anyhow, basically Guy, it's made from red brick and is pretty big."

Guy laughed. "You seem to have got bored with your research," he said.

"Well, it's not my field of course, but if you really want to know it says here that it's got 'hipped slate roofs, has had some major alterations and additions over the years, especially in 1824, and its principal alignment is roughly north-south, facing south. It's two storeys high with large pane sashes.' Do you really want more?"

Guy had laughed again and, after pleas from Lucy to be careful, he'd ended the call.

Checking his Glock and tucking it into the inside pocket of his leather jacket, Guy locked the Morgan and walked discreetly across the corner of an open field to the estate wall. Made of red and weathered house bricks with faded blue coping stones, it was some two metres high. No fencing or other security measures were visible. Using a thick fallen branch as a slight leg-up, Guy scrambled up and over the wall, landing athletically on his haunches in the shrubbery at the rear of the hall's garden.

He stayed low as he crept through some thick rhododendrons until the back of the house was visible in the dusk, about one hundred metres away. He mapped a sheltered route which would take him towards a glass-panelled back door and rear windows where electric lights shone out. He was not concerned about CCTV but did keep a watchful eye out for dogs. Although his Labradors at home would never make true guard dogs, a couple of German Shepherds or Rottweilers would be a very different story.

SIXTY-NINE

As he neared the back door, Guy could see an elderly woman moving around a large, modern kitchen. Her movements were unsteady and deliberate – she seemed to move almost in slow motion. The woman was making a cup of tea; once it was ready, she pottered slowly out of the room, switching the light off as she went.

Guy walked across a flag-stoned yard to the door and tried the handle. It was locked. Peering through one of the glass panels, he could see the key in the lock on the inside. Noticing some towels on a nearby washing line, he seized one and returned to the door. He wrapped the towel thickly around his left hand and, after waiting for a couple more minutes to make sure the woman was away from the kitchen, he smashed the panel nearest the key. The glass shattered easily, most of it falling inside and leaving a hole big enough for Guy to carefully stretch his hand through the jagged gap and turn the key. Trying the door again, he was frustrated to find it still wouldn't open; it was bolted as well as locked.

Holding down the handle, Guy pressed his right shoulder against the door. There was some give. Still with the handle down, he shoulder-barged the door with several quick, short runs. At the third, the door surrendered, swinging back on its hinges. Guy slipped into the kitchen and concealed himself behind the interior kitchen door, where he waited for the sound of approaching footsteps. Nothing. It seemed nobody was coming to investigate the disturbance.

Taking his Glock in his right hand, Guy moved stealthily into a gloomy corridor, which offered the choice of various doorways. He chose left, moving slowly towards an old, wood-panelled door. Gaps around the edges betrayed light shining on the other side. Glock raised, Guy turned the smooth knob and slowly opened the door a few centimetres before quickly pushing it fully open and stepping through.

He found himself in an impressive hall with an imposing crystal chandelier hanging from the centre of the ornately plastered ceiling. To his left was a sturdy, oak-panelled front door with heavy, floor-length curtains on either side, presumably concealing large windows. A handsomely carved, wide oak staircase rose elegantly opposite, naturally drawing the eye to the upper floor and the gloom of the landing. The floor, of dark grey flagstones, was covered in richly patterned rugs and led down a wide corridor to Guy's right, disappearing deep into the building. The house felt antiquated, with a musty smell and cold atmosphere that was anything but welcoming.

He noticed a small CCTV camera, fixed high on the wall facing the front door. Moving towards it, he turned to face the door and recognised the same general view he'd already seen. Then, there had been partygoers milling about in the hall, Sergio and Jenny among them. The house had been alive with people and merriment. It was very different now.

Suddenly, Guy heard slow and deliberate footsteps coming down the corridor to his left. He pressed himself against the wall, gun poised and at the ready across his chest.

SEVENTY

The woman Guy had seen earlier entered the hall, shuffling as she went. As Guy stepped forward, aiming the Glock straight at her, she turned slowly to face him. She showed no sign of alarm or concern.

"Oh, hello," she said in a relaxed tone, as though unexpectedly meeting a friend in the high street. "Who are you? Did you let yourself in?"

Up close, Guy was struck by her appearance. She was quite frumpy, a classic maroon twinset – probably cashmere – covering her frame with no finesse or style. A small string of pearls hung at her neck, and a large, patterned skirt emphasised her wide hips. Her face was heavily made up in an amateurish way and she wore thick maroon lipstick. Her hair, shoulder-length, was rather unkempt and was dyed a Gothic raven-black. Guy guessed she was in her early to mid-sixties, but there was a curious, disorientated air about her that he struggled to understand. He slipped his gun back into his jacket pocket.

"My name's Guy. Are you Valerie?"

"Yes dear, I am."

"We spoke on the phone. Is Mike in? Or anyone else?"

"Mike's out. I've locked the doors. He told me to – he's very particular about locking up," she explained. She was quietly well-spoken, her voice educated. "He's been concerned about security ever since we moved here. And I always do as I'm told – he's looked after me well."

"When will Mike be back?" Guy asked.

"He shouldn't be long. Would you like to sit down?"

Guy watched her closely, ready to note her body language. "Where's Jenny, Valerie?"

Valerie frowned. "Who, dear?"

Guy took a couple of steps forward. "Come on, Valerie, I haven't time for this. Where is she?" He studied her closely; her eyes blinked, and her face stayed blank, expressionless. *She's not all there.* Stepping forward, he put a hand on each of her shoulders. She began to move backwards, but he tightened his grip and held her still. "You've been told not to tell anyone, haven't you? Was that by Arman – or Mehrak, maybe?"

"Who?" She looked bewildered, puzzled.

"Arman. Look, don't worry about him. Where is she?"

"Who?" Valerie frowned again.

"The girl."

"Oh!" Understanding washed over Valerie's face. "You mean Jane?"

"Yes, Jane," Guy nodded. "Where is she?" He glanced at the front door. *Was that a car outside or was it the wind getting up?*

"Well, she's downstairs, of course. Follow me."

Valerie moved unsteadily across the hall and set off down the corridor. Guy followed, glancing around. He noticed the front door was bolted. Trying to control the urge to rush her, Guy knew he'd get more by going at Valerie's pace. Her mind was clearly fragile. Instinctively, his hand went to his jacket pocket, needing to feel the heavy, reassuring weight of his Glock. Part way down the cold corridor, Valerie turned left into a smaller, dimly lit passageway with no windows. The stone flags were bare, the cream walls displaying various hunting scenes.

"She's down here." Valerie had paused by a latched door, bolted at the top. She reached out purposefully and agitated the stiff bolt until it shot open, the metallic crack amplified as it reverberated in the passageway. She held the handle, pressed the latch with her thumb, and pulled it open. Guy glanced inside. Darkness.

"Are you sure she's in here?' he asked. It could have been an under-stairs cupboard, but the cool air and slight draft emanating from the open doorway gave the impression there was more to it.

"Oh yes, dear, I'm quite certain." Valerie stepped into the doorway, feeling to the right with her hand. A sudden click, and the darkness was illuminated, revealing some tired brick steps leading below ground.

"Please show me," Guy said.

Valerie started forward, firmly and deliberately placing her feet on each worn step as she descended. She carefully clasped a round, varnished handrail, drilled into the peeling, whitewashed wall with metal supports. It was decorated with spiders' webs and random smears of dirt and dust. Although slow, Valerie seemed confident about what she was doing. Guy hesitated a fraction before following her down the straight staircase, estimating they were a full floor level beneath the house. He stooped slightly; the ceiling was rather low for someone of his height.

At the foot of the stairs was a square metre of rough brick flooring, with a small drainage gully and a passage to the left. Valerie flicked a switch on the wall and electric light flooded out. Guy followed her as she turned left, focusing on the goal. Ahead was a long cellar corridor with several ventilated doors to each side. A series of bare bulbs hung at regular intervals from an arched, white-painted brick ceiling.

Guy's heart was racing at this turn of events. The more he thought about it, the more it made sense. As they approached the end of the passage, Valerie stopped by the last door on the right. It was painted white like all the others, but this one had a small grille in the centre near the top. Guy noticed that, while all the other rooms were in darkness, a light burned in this one. There was a large key in the lock.

"Is she in here?" Guy asked.

Valerie nodded, staring at the floor. Guy stepped forward and tried the door. It was locked. He made to turn the key, but it was stiff and wouldn't yield.

Valerie placed a hand on his forearm, looking anxious. "You can't go in there. You see…"

The key suddenly gave up its resistance and turned in the lock. Ignoring Valerie's pleading look, he pushed at the door, but it simply rattled. Pulling it instead, it opened towards him, creaking and protesting on its hinges. Medieval. Ducking his head beneath the low lintel, Guy stepped inside.

Valerie remained in the passageway and watched him. Her hand moved smoothly to the door.

Guy looked about. Save for some old shelving and a battered old wardrobe, the room was completely empty.

SEVENTY-ONE

Guy turned back to Valerie, who had stayed in the passageway. The elevation of the room allowed him to stand up to his full height, and he did so now. Her face was expressionless as she stared back at him.

"What's going on, Valerie?" Guy demanded. Glancing at his Seamaster he saw it was already quarter to eight – Mike Burns would be back shortly. This mad woman was messing him about. She looked perturbed, troubled.

"You said there was a girl staying with you. Jane? Well, she's not in here, is she? So, what are you talking about?"

Valerie shuffled into the room. "No, she's not in here," she said simply.

She walked past Guy to the battered, single wardrobe. Made of some dark wood, glossy and chipped, it rose almost as high as the ceiling. Valerie slipped her hand round the back of the cupboard as if she was feeling for something. There was a metallic noise, the sound of a clip releasing, and to Guy's surprise she pulled the whole wardrobe as though she was opening a door. It moved easily on solid castors and fixed hinges into the room, revealing another door behind it.

"It's this way." Valerie pushed the door open and switched on a light. Another brick corridor stretched ahead of them, shorter than the one they'd just walked through. Once more, Valerie set off and Guy followed, their footsteps echoing on the bare brick.

Valerie stopped after just a dozen paces or so; they were outside another painted white door with a central grille and a large key in the lock. There was a light on in the room. Guy stepped forward and tried the door – it was locked. *Déjà vu.*

“It’s locked,” Valerie told him in a matter-of-fact voice. “It’s always kept locked. But you can’t go in, not yet.”

Guy ignored her, seizing the key. It wasn’t quite as stiff as the previous one. He turned it and heard the locking mechanism shift. Pulling the door, it partially opened to the sound of protesting hinges.

Valerie grabbed his arm. “You can’t go in there like that,” she said earnestly. “You need this.” She reached up to a shelf on the wall behind them, removed something and handed it to Guy. Looking down, he saw it was a bizarre cloth hood with two holes cut out for the eyes. “I have to use it,” she told him.

Guy ignored her. Opening the door wider, he looked inside. A girl was sitting on a wrought-iron bed, arms wrapped tightly around her knees which were drawn up to her chin. Her dark hair was matted and dirty, her face grubby and streaked with tears. Her eyes were red from crying. She looked wretched and miserable, pallid and washed-out.

She didn’t move. Just stared at him.

SEVENTY-TWO

"Jenny?" Guy asked quietly, studying her face. The girl in front of him looked very different to the image he'd been carrying around in his head these past few days. That girl was beautiful, innocent, full of life and laughter; this one was almost unrecognisable.

She nodded slowly. "Yes. Who are you?" she replied softly.

"My name's Guy. I'm helping your mum and dad, Simon and Sally Stewart. You're safe now, but we need to leave straight away. Put your shoes on quickly."

Guy remained in the doorway, suddenly aware he was looking into a prison cell. Bizarrely there was a modern toilet in one corner and a shelf of books, but other than the old bed that reminded him of his prep school days, that was it. He moved back into the corridor, not trusting Valerie to leave the door open, not to lock him in. Finding Jenny was fantastic; ending up locked in the cell with her would be a disaster.

But Valerie just stood there holding the strange hood. "You should have worn this," she repeated, shaking it gently in her hand.

"It's all right – I don't need to use that," he said, gently. "The girl's name is Jenny – do you remember now?"

"Oh yes, Jenny – that was it. How did I forget that?" She nodded her head lightly, almost talking to herself.

"Okay, Valerie. Listen. Jenny would like to go home, so I'm going to take her with me. Let's all go back upstairs, shall we?"

"Is she going to help me with the gardening?" Valerie's face was serious.

"She might – would you like her to help?"

"Oh, I would, very much, dear – there's so much to do before it rains."

Guy looked back into the room. Jenny hadn't moved. "Jenny," he said firmly. "Come on. We have to go, quickly. We've got to get out of this house."

Behind him, Valerie said, "Mike will be back soon. He'll want to say goodbye to Jane."

Jenny remained motionless. "Can I trust you? What's my brother's name and who's his girlfriend?"

Guy's mind went blank. All he could see was the large family photograph hanging over the Stewarts' fireplace in their home in Four Oaks. They had to leave – Valerie was right, Mike Burns would be back soon. Guy would prefer to leave him to Caroline Grant. His priority was to get Jenny to safety.

"Jenny, we don't have time for this," he pleaded. He wanted to go into the room, grab her and get her out, but he was mindful Valerie could still choose to lock the door. He thought about taking the key from the lock, but from Jenny's attitude, he wasn't sure he could even force her to leave. Captivity plays funny games with the mind.

"I don't trust you," she said, tightening her grip on her legs.

"Your boyfriend's name is Sergio – he lives in Moseley."

She didn't move, and said again: "What's my brother and his girlfriend's name?"

"Jenny, you don't understand, we have to go. It's not safe here. If we don't…God, I can't remember…

Oh, Freddie! Your brother's Freddie – and Emma, that's his girlfriend. They've both gone to Thailand."

Jenny jumped off the bed. "I'm sorry," she said, kneeling on the floor and reaching beneath it. She withdrew a pair of black, high-heeled shoes.

"Is that all you've got?" Guy asked with some alarm. "They're not exactly practical."

"Of course it's all I've got – I was brought here straight from a party!"

"Okay, come on. We'll talk about that in the car."

Jenny slipped both shoes on and walked unsteadily to the door. Guy guided her through, gently. Valerie reached up to replace the cloth hood neatly back on its shelf and then followed her, with Guy bringing up the rear.

"Just follow the corridor, Jenny," he said.

He watched her pass through the door that was hidden by the wardrobe, which was still pulled back on its runners. He felt nervous suddenly, although reassured that Valerie had followed instructions and bolted the front door. Nevertheless, he placed his hand in his jacket pocket and took out his Glock. He followed close behind Valerie as she also stepped into the room and passed the wardrobe. Guy entered the room as Jenny turned into the main corridor.

"Just follow the passage to the stairs, Jenny" he instructed in a low voice.

The blow to the back of his head was sudden and vicious. Guy collapsed on the cold floor, unconscious, the Glock falling heavily by his side.

SEVENTY-THREE

Guy opened his eyes. It took a second or two, but he swiftly assessed his new situation. He was sitting on a hard, wooden kitchen chair, his wrists tied behind its arched, railed back. He tried moving his arms, but the fastenings were secure; the rope bit cruelly into his skin. Guy shook his head and blinked hard several times. His head throbbed and it took a few moments for his vision to sharpen. Looking round, he slowly absorbed his surroundings.

He was in an ornate, opulently furnished Victorian study. There was plenty of oak panelling and numerous bookshelves displaying leather-bound tomes of various vintages. Small landscape paintings were displayed around the walls, each with its own dedicated brass light. The heavy curtains were colourful and richly patterned, although somewhat shadowed by the lights. There were also two antique standard lamps and a smaller light that sat on the large pedestal desk dominating the floor in front of Guy.

"Welcome back," said a calm voice.

Guy realised a young man was reclining in a leather chair behind the desk, his feet stretched out on the surface, ankles crossed. He was so relaxed he was almost literally horizontal, chewing gum slowly and smirking at his captive.

Guy rolled his neck, seeking comfort, and looked at him. "Thanks for the chair."

The man manoeuvred himself into a more traditional seated position and placed his legs into the well of the desk. He leaned forward, resting his stubbly chin on his hands.

"So, Sir Guy Sterling, you've come after me then, have you? Impressive."

Guy studied the man's face – black hair, dark eyes, olive skin. This was surely the Egyptian assassin, Arman's lieutenant. Not how he'd intended to meet him.

"Mehrak."

Mehrak nodded, displaying a smug, self-important grin. "You've dared to enter the dragon's den in search of the damsel in distress. Very foolhardy, brave knight, very foolhardy indeed. And all on your own, without even a Lancelot for your Arthur? How heroic! And very, very foolish."

Guy said nothing, hearing his father's voice echo inside his throbbing head, "*Get the measure of the fight, boy - get the measure of the man.*"

"There was this, of course," Mehrak continued, standing up and walking slowly round the desk. Guy realised the man was holding his mobile, displaying it like a trophy of war. "But then you won't be needing it again, will you?" Mehrak dropped it on to the boarded floor, where it clattered and came to rest. He took a couple of paces towards it and stamped on the device hard, several times, with his heavy shoes. It offered little resistance, shattering under the force.

"Shame," Guy said quietly. "That's a good make."

"Not so much now, is it?"

"Have I you to thank for the knockout blow?"

Mehrak nodded, accepting the accusation as though it was an accolade. "Of course. Heard you talking down the passage. Behind that wardrobe was the perfect place to hide – I knew you had to walk past me in your pathetic attempt to leave."

"How long was I out?"

"Not long. Enough for me to get you safely tied to that chair – don't want you out of control again, do we?"

Guy looked at him. Behind his back he carefully flexed the muscles in his hand, which confirmed the ropes were tight. He persisted, slowly and rhythmically, willing the action to loosen the bindings. Without his hands he had no chance of survival, and he knew from what Tony had told him that Mehrak was a merciless killer – low on morals, the milk of human kindness long since spilled.

Mehrak walked to the desk and rested on its edge, arms crossed, facing Guy. Guy held his gaze with steely determination. Mehrak's eyes were malevolent, full of death and destruction; Guy saw no light shining from them, no soul or compassion. Still, he had the impression he was unnerving the man – he could see that in his eyes, too. He stared back for a few more seconds, the silence between them growing louder.

"Look down," Mehrak commanded.

Guy didn't.

Suddenly, Mehrak got up from his angled perch, stepped towards Guy and struck him hard in the face with his right hand. The blow jarred Guy's cheek, forcing him to look away. He shook his head, badly wishing he could rub his face, but his hands remained as securely tied as ever. He resumed gazing at Mehrak.

"Not one to take instructions, are you?" Mehrak

sneered. "I'll need to teach you."

"Where's Jenny?"

Mehrak stepped forward again and struck him again.

"Shut up," he spat. "It's nothing to do with you."

"It's everything to do with me."

Mehrak hit him once more, with his left hand this time. The blow was weaker, the connection not so true. *Okay, so he's right-handed.*

"Just shut the fuck up," Mehrak said, his face reddening and his eyes narrowing with clear hatred. "Every time you speak without permission, I'm going to land one on you. Got it?"

"Got it." Guy paused, looked at Mehrak, and said in a slow, innocent tone, "So, where's Jenny?"

Mehrak lashed out, even harder this time. The blow spun Guy's head to the right with considerable force. He shook his head, rolled his neck and attempted to massage the side of his face on the top of his left shoulder in a vain effort to ease the pain.

"I'll tell you where that brat is," Mehrak snarled. "She's back in her private, shitty room because the brave knight fucked up. And that's where she'll stay until I take her dead body out of there because, believe me, Arman and I will see the threat through. She'll die there with no food or water. But you won't be around to see that."

"What about her hand – didn't she have medical attention?" It suddenly dawned on Guy that during his desperate efforts to persuade Jenny to leave the room, he'd failed to pay any attention to the wound where her finger had been severed.

"Her hand's fine," Mehrak said. The self-satisfied smirk had returned to his face and he chewed his gum again ostentatiously.

"Fine?" Guy said incredulously, shocked at the Egyptian's levity. "How can you say it's fine when you've mutilated her as you have?"

"Her hand was cut, that's all. We just wanted her blood."

"Sorry?" Guy was confused.

"Her blood. That was my idea. That Casanova boyfriend of hers had real girlie hands, so effeminate. When he didn't need them anymore, I thought we could use one of his fingers for a little – what shall I say? – showtime. Jenny's blood, Sergio's finger – a winning combination." He chuckled cruelly.

"Why bother with all that charade? I'd have thought arseholes like you and Arman would have just sliced her real finger off…"

Mehrak stepped forward and hit Guy in the face again.

"You just don't get it, do you?" he said, leaning back on the desk and crossing his arms again. "I can do what the fuck I want to you, so you'd better start getting the hang of it – and don't forget it's payback time."

"Payback time?"

Another blow. Guy shook his head again.

"You'll speak when I tell you to – only when I tell you to," Mehrak hissed. "Yes, payback time. You killed Steve, didn't you? The two shots you mentioned? He and Tony had both gone to your place, apparently. Tony rang me when he was leaving – sounded like he was running through undergrowth, the lanky twat. He said he'd heard a couple of muffled shots and nothing further from Steve. Then you tell me he's dead. That can't go unpunished." He paused. "Anyway, where is Tony – he hasn't rung since?"

"He really is a Tony, then," Guy mused. "He's okay – well, sort of. Can you hear that singing?"

"What?" Mehrak looked puzzled.

"The singing," Guy continued. "That's your mate telling us all about what's going on."

"Tony wouldn't talk. You've killed him too, haven't you? I can't reach him on his phone."

"Tony's still in one piece – well, save for the ankle that got messed up when he tried to run away. Wasn't quite the tough guy after that, Mehrak. Told us quite a lot – like it was you and Steve who killed Sergio, for example."

"Bollocks – you're making it up," Mehrak said. "Tony wouldn't speak to you. He's loyal to me and Arman."

"If that's what you want to think, fine. But I can assure you that even now he'll be repeating the tale of his tragic life and all that you and Arman forced him to do to Detective Superintendent Grant of the West Midlands police force."

"Liar!" Mehrak's eyes burned with anger as he again struck Guy firmly in the face.

The pain was intense, but Guy just shook his head and defiantly stared Mehrak straight in the eyes.

"You're not going to leave that chair alive," Mehrak told him coldly, taking his Beretta out of his back pocket and caressing it fondly. "You're going to find out what real pain is. You'll be begging me to let you die."

Approaching Guy, he ran the end of the gun from the top of his head and down the side of his body until it rested on his right knee.

"Which knee do you want to lose first?" he asked, a sadistic smirk playing on his lips. He pressed the barrel of the gun firmly into the side of Guy's kneecap.

"Left or right? Or shall we make it a little bit more *personal* first?" He slid the barrel up the inside of Guy's thigh.

Guy tried to focus on his wrists, carefully trying to twist them, but there was no slack in the rope. He mustn't give up. He had to keep Mehrak talking, buy time through distraction. If the Egyptian shot him, he'd be completely disabled and at the man's mercy – or lack of it. Somehow, he needed to handle this and get free. He persisted in twisting his hands subtly behind the chair, flexing any muscle in his hands and wrists that he could control. There weren't many.

"That's brave," he said.

"What?" Mehrak looked puzzled again.

"That's brave, making threats when I'm tied up and unable to defend myself. Makes you quite the big man."

"Shut the fuck up."

"Your English is good. You've really got the hang of all the swear words."

Mehrak brought his sweating face close to Guy. He could smell the minted gum on his breath. "That's because I spent five bloody years in your country's lousy education system," he hissed.

Was it his imagination, or had Guy suddenly felt some give in the rope that bound his wrists? He carefully continued his efforts while staring at Mehrak.

"Your parents invested well. Look at you now – you can swear like a trooper and play with guns. They must be so proud of you."

Mehrak struck him again.

"And what about you, Sterling?" he sneered. "Look at you, my prisoner. Did you forget that? Someone has done something right in this situation, and I don't think it's you, yeah? My parents spent a lot of money on me and they *will* be proud."

Guy felt the rope give again. He needed to keep Mehrak talking.

"What, proud that you're running around shooting people at the beck and call of some lunatic? Bravely shooting an unarmed mother in front of her children from the safe distance that a sniper rifle gives you? That's real heroic stuff, Mehrak. Telling your parents that, are you?"

Mehrak was shaking, glaring at Guy with pure venom. He started to speak, but Guy interrupted as he felt more movement in the rope that confined him.

"I gather you and Arman have quite a passion for killing innocent people, Mehrak. All for just a few quid. Pathetic."

The rope eased, but something in his captor seemed to snap.

"I'm fed up with you staring at me and thinking you're so bloody clever, Sterling. You're just shit – pure fucking shit!" Mehrak's rage made him shake almost uncontrollably. Placing his Beretta on the corner of the desk, he took two swift strides towards Guy. He swung his right fist into the side of Guy's face, then his left fist, raining rapid blows one after the other. Guy tried to twist out of the way, but there was no sanctuary from the violence. Suddenly, Mehrak lowered his sights and struck Guy firmly in the stomach, winding him. The pain was intense but paled quickly as Mehrak leaned back and kicked with his right foot hard and fast into Guy's unprotected groin.

The shock forced him to try and double up, but the rope still restrained him. As Guy straightened up, Mehrak took a step back before leaping forward, right foot raised, landing a hard, long kick on his chest. Guy felt himself being pushed backwards as the chair's front legs lifted. He felt as though he was in a dentist's chair, held in a reclining position, before gravity took over. He craned his neck forwards, trying to protect the back of his head. Hitting the ground with force, his arms buffeted the floor and Guy felt pain scream from every part of his body as the chair slid slightly on the polished boards.

Mehrak suddenly appeared in his vision, looking down at him, and Guy realised his legs suddenly felt free. With as much speed and strength as he could muster, he lashed out with his right leg and struck Mehrak in the groin. The kick was firm and true, and Mehrak disappeared backwards. Guy rolled onto his right side, managing to free his right hand; after loosening the bindings as he'd sat there, the force of the fall had freed it entirely. His left hand, however, remained stubbornly secured.

Guy pushed himself up on to his legs, the chair

hanging behind him. Seeing Mehrak recovering from his pain and start towards him, he turned quickly and crashed the chair into the advancing figure. Turning back to face him, he swung his right fist into the side of Mehrak's face. The Egyptian was knocked backwards, then he tripped over a small coffee table and fell to the floor. Guy snatched the Beretta from the desk and ran at the wall, twisting at the last moment so the conjoined chair crashed against it. Pieces of wood fell away and suddenly his left hand was free. He shook the remnants of rope from his wrist and stepped over to Mehrak, who was starting to stand up. Guy kicked him solidly in the head and he fell back to the floor.

"That's enough, Mehrak," Guy said, pointing the Beretta at him. "Don't make me shoot you. It's over."

Mehrak looked at the gun, then at Guy, and his shoulders sagged. He said nothing.

"I'm going to call my Lancelot now," Guy said, walking to the desk, careful to keep the gun trained on Mehrak along with a watchful eye. There was an old-style black telephone on the desk, in keeping with the room's décor. Guy picked up the receiver and placed it on the desk, then began to dial the number with his left index finger. With two numbers still to dial, he suddenly heard a deep voice from across the room behind him.

"Put the phone and the gun down, Sterling, else you're dead."

Keeping his hands still, Guy looked slowly round. In the doorway, standing well in shadow, was the outline of an elderly, obese man. In front of him, pointing it straight at Guy, he held a Russian OTs-33 Pernach machine pistol. Guy knew immediately he was in the silver medal position; the man could fire twenty bullets into him in the time it would take him to lift the Beretta. He carefully did as instructed.

Guy watched Mehrak stand up, his face full of relief.

"Arman, great timing. I was expecting you."

"Shut it, Mehrak. He had you beaten. And I've told you before, in this house, in my home, you call me Mike.

SEVENTY-FOUR

Mike Burns advanced into the study as Guy turned his head to look at him. No black tie like the last time they'd met, at The Bull Club. He kept the machine pistol aimed at Guy's torso. Guy lifted his hands to head height, indicating surrender. He knew it was pointless to resist – in automatic mode, the gun was capable of firing over eight hundred rounds in a single minute. Inaccurate at over one hundred metres, ideal at fifty metres, it would be ruthless at the present distance of some five metres. He had to be patient; the right moment would surely present itself, as it had with Mehrak. He wondered how George was getting on.

Mike leaned forward and picked up the Beretta. Mehrak lifted his hand, clearly expecting Mike to pass it to him, but the businessman slipped it into his trouser pocket and backed away. Moving round the desk, he used the gun to gesture towards a Victorian chair.

"Sit," he ordered, as though Guy were a pet dog.

Guy took a few slow paces, sat down, crossed his legs and looked at Mike. He tried to keep his expression relaxed. "Well, this is quite a double life, Mike."

Mehrak started to speak. "Arman –"

"Shut it," Mike said, throwing him a warning glance.

Mehrak paused, then clearly decided obedience was the wisest course of action. He stayed standing.

"I guess it is a double life," Mike said, returning his attention to Guy. "You've met me as Mike and spoken to me as Arman. Arman loses the Brummie accent, doesn't he?"

"Well, hello Mike Burns – former business stalwart, self-made millionaire and ruthless extortioner and murderer." Guy was determined to keep calm, almost light-hearted on the outside. Inside, his mind was busy trying to put all the pieces together.

Mike smiled. "I haven't killed anyone, Sterling. Well, apart from once, when an idiot employee messed up."

"I think we're talking technicalities here, Mike. Paying someone to kill someone else still makes you a murderer in my book. I'd guess a jury will see it that way, too."

"That's something we'll never find out."

"I wouldn't count on it."

Mehrak started to speak again, causing Mike to throw him an irritated look. "Mehrak, do as I say, will you, and shut the fuck up? You're getting on my tits."

"Sorry, Mike," Mehrak said, meekly.

Guy noticed he looked genuinely fearful.

Mike mimicked him in a high, childish tone: "Sorry, Mike. Sorry, Mike."

Mehrak looked dejected, embarrassed. He thrust his hands into his pockets and rocked gently on his feet.

"Just get out of here," Mike snapped.

"Okay, I'm going. But before I do, I want my share of that money from Stewart. Perhaps even slightly more, seeing as I've landed Sterling for you."

"We've been through this before," Mike said. "A deal's a deal."

"Sure, but…"

"But what?"

"Nothing." Mehrak moved towards the doorway.

"Are you going to do as you're told, Mehrak?"

"Sure, Mike – of course."

"Good. Do you want your Beretta back?"

"Could be useful."

"It certainly could." Mike put his hand into his back pocket as Mehrak came back, arm outstretched. "In fact," he continued, "you can have it back a few pieces at a time."

Mehrak looked at him quizzically.

"Have these bits first," Mike said, firing three shots into Mehrak's chest without warning. His expression transforming into stunned surprise, Mehrak clutched his chest with both hands and collapsed backwards onto the floor. He lay there, twitching, struggling for breath.

Guy started to rise.

"Sit down, Sterling," Mike commanded, walking over to Mehrak and pointing the Beretta at his head. "Wondering why, huh? You're past your bloody sell-by date too, you Egyptian bastard. You've turned into a right greedy fucker and I've had enough." He fired a single shot into Mehrak's forehead.

Guy was finding the turn of events hard to handle. There'd been two madmen in the room with him, and two guns of which neither was at his command. Now he was down to one madman, in possession of both the guns, and it seemed the man responsible for Julie's death – and the deaths of many others – would not now confess to or face justice for his crimes. At least he had his hands free now, but he couldn't see any way of tackling and overpowering Arman – or rather Mike

Burns. And what was this alter-ego business all about?

"Now we can talk without interruption," Mike said, as though he'd just switched off the television. He settled himself in the desk chair, placing the Beretta next to his Pernach. "I need to talk to you, Sterling."

"Need to?"

Guy was trying to get his head around the current situation. Mike was talking calmly, rationally, as though they were discussing a business proposition or the previous night's football. He decided to test the water.

"How's Jenny?"

"Shut it, else I'll try this out on you." Mike waved the Pernach in the air. His tone was sharper, but not as aggressive as before he'd killed Mehrak. "Not used it before. Would be fun to see what it can do."

"You could have used it on your mate."

"He wasn't my mate – just another hired lackey."

"Like Steve and Tony?"

Mike looked surprised.

"I met them earlier today," Guy told him. "They came visiting my home looking to make trouble."

"Fucking idiots. And?"

"Well, Steve's a bit on the dead side."

"And the stick insect?"

"Singing canary-style - which doesn't actually amount to much, to be honest."

Mike nodded his head slowly. "No, it wouldn't. Steve's the one who could've told you more. For example, that all three of them hung Sergio in the woods. It was Mehrak's idea. Said he'd always wanted to do that to someone, and Steve knew the woods. He used to live round there or something, did some serious courting in them, finding all the quiet spots, as you would."

Guy was confused by Mike's relaxed tone, curious why they were now chatting like mates in a pub. But he said: "Frankly, I'm not interested in any of this, Mike. As I see it, you're playing some macabre game for your own amusement, but I don't give a toss. Save the story for your memoirs. I'm here for one reason and one reason only. Jenny. Is she back downstairs? And how come she's in your house? A bit of a different modus operandi."

Mike smiled. "I wanted to raise the stakes. I'd been thinking about this approach for a while. I had the cellar prepared, but the right visitor never came along."

"Until Jenny."

"Yep, until Jenny. Bit of luck there, I guess – teenage daughter of a multi-millionaire knocking about with a lowlife from my old neck of the woods. Crawled straight out from under a rock, he did. He did odd jobs here, was fucking useless, but I thought he might come in useful someday, and I was right. A few quid and he'd do anything. He brought her to one of my parties. I wasn't here myself, I'm not stupid."

"And she never left, did she? The CCTV was a set-up, your insurance for an inquisitive police officer, right? She was in the hallway, but she wasn't outside with Sergio, was she? She was being taken to the cellar by then, probably drugged. He was with a lookalike – most probably the girl I saw in his flat."

"Very good, Guy. Mehrak told Sergio that he

then had to claim he'd had some row with the bitch in his car and dumped her. I thought that as he was such a bloody scumbag it would be believable – you know, that he was capable of that."

"Except the police's ANPR system shows a girl sitting in the passenger seat as he returned to Birmingham."

A muscle twitched in Mike's cheek. "Sergio was a fucking prat. He was told to keep her low in the seat for just that reason."

"What the hell are you doing, Mike? It's not like you need the money. You have a respectable reputation. Why have you gone down this crazy route?"

"I could answer that," Mike said, standing up. He picked up the pistol and perched on the edge of the desk facing Guy. The mahogany creaked in protest at the sudden weight. "But I want you to answer me this first – how come you're involved? It's ironic."

"Ironic?"

Mike ignored the question. He relaxed the hand holding the Pernach in his lap.

"Why are you involved with Jenny – how come Stewart called you in? You're ex-army and live Shropshire how does he know you?"

"He doesn't. I found him. I was asked by David Richardson to help find the person who killed Simon's sister. I discovered the connection with Simon and made contact. When you kidnapped Jenny, Simon asked for my help." Put like that, it sounded simple and straightforward.

Mike looked at the Pernach for a moment, then got up and returned to his chair. He seemed restless.

"You might be interested to know," he said, "the deputy chief constable, Peter Wright, is an, um, professional friend of mine. He helps me when I need it. He's retiring soon, and evidently feels the police pension isn't that impressive, despite his years of apparently honourable service. Such rot. He's been exchanging information and favours for money with me for years. It didn't take much to get him to persuade David to put that overrated clown, Grant, on the case. No prospect of any progress with her in charge."

Guy smiled inwardly.

Burns continued, "Wright told me about David's plan to involve you. I had you followed. Had it confirmed you were staying where you told Peter."

"You bastard," Guy said, hatred dripping from the words as he sprang out of the chair. "So one of your guys ran Sophie down? You sick, sick bastard."

"Sit!" snapped Burns, unmoved. "Play with fire and you'll get burned, Sterling."

Guy sat back down. There was no other option. "Who did it? Tell me. Was it Mehrak?"

"Close. The greedy bastard has a younger brother called Haji. Touch more of a sadist than Mehrak – and has this thing for hurting women. He relished the job of running down your girlfriend and also did the job cutting Jenny. You can't stand in the way of guys like that, you just cut them some slack."

"Where is he?"

"I've no idea, actually. He fucked off a while ago and I've had nothing to do with him since. As Mehrak was the only communication channel, I guess that's a permanent goodbye."

"You'll need to watch your back, even in prison, Mike. A man like that won't take kindly to someone killing his brother."

Burns nodded. "I don't doubt you, but I'm not concerned about that."

Guy was silent as he tried to fill in the remaining gaps in his knowledge. "So, what's this all about, Mike? You don't need the money, surely?"

Mike leaned back in his chair. "As you say, Sterling, I was a very successful businessman. Made millions. More than I needed. But here's the rub. I had a daughter. I was in my mid-forties and never thought it would happen. She was illegitimate – a bastard in your class's speak, a beautiful daughter in mine. She had her mother's eyes, and her wonderful smile. She was just four years old when her mother died, and then she came to live here with me. It worked out well – we became very close. She did well at school and went to university. Clever, she was."

"Was?"

"Yeah. She caught that meningitis at eighteen. Died in my arms right here, upstairs. I won't ever forget that. With her gone, I felt I'd lost everything that was important to me. It changed my life – I felt everything was futile, boring. I started to sell my businesses – and then something happened." Mike paused.

Guy leaned forward. "What was that?"

"I met your parents."

It was like a slap in the face.

"My *parents?"*

"Yes. That's why I said it was ironic you're involved now. They were everything I wasn't. Sure, we both had money, stacks of it, but they had breeding, pedigree – I was just some self-made Brummie from the wrong side of town. They had three children – a successful soldier and two beautiful daughters. I was jealous, Sterling, fucking jealous. And it got me thinking. Why not hurt them, spoil it, do something exciting and different. Something that would make me feel alive again. I had the money and resources to achieve what I wanted to achieve. And so I became Arman – some random name I read in a book some place. It made sense at the time."

The conversation he'd had with David came flooding back to Guy. It had seemed fanciful at the time, certainly a second-best motivator to what Haji had done to Sophie. He stared at Mike. "Did you threaten my father?"

Mike smiled. "Of course I did – he was the top of my list. I asked for a million quid for the safety of his wife. He refused. Said he'd go to the police. Well in with David, the then-Shropshire chief constable. Your type always are."

Guy swallowed hard. The revelation was difficult to take in. He felt as though he was floating, observing the conversation from above.

"I had this bloke called John to help me," Mike explained. "Steve was about too, as I recall – he'd helped me with some minor irritations that would take the law too long – like debt collecting using means that were a touch unorthodox. I told John to wait outside the manor and follow your parents when they left. They drove out, but one of your sisters was in the car too. That wasn't in the plan. John followed. He overtook them in the road as I'd instructed him."

"To do what?"

"Just to frighten your father, no more. I told him to drive really slowly, and when your father overtook, he was to keep pace on the inside lane. If your father went faster, John should go faster. If your father slowed, John was to slow. It would force your father to stay on the wrong side of the road. If something came the other way, John was to move out the way at the last minute. It was just to scare him into paying up."

"But they were hit by a lorry and killed. All three of them." Guy said slowly, glaring at Mike with burning hatred.

"John fucked up. He told me there was a bend and that the lorry came round it, going shit fast. John left it too late to move and the lorry hit your parents' car head on. John drove off. He's the only bloke I've killed – I kneecapped and shot him by the Thames. His poor judgment ruined the game."

"The game!" Guy exclaimed. "*Game?* You sick bastard. That's not a game. Those were the lives of my family. You killed them." Guy made to stand up again.

"Sit down," Mike commanded, waving the Pernach at him. Guy did so. "You've done alright out of it."

Guy was struggling to think straight at this latest piece of news. "If you think –"

"Just shut the fuck up and listen. I'm almost through."

"Through? I'll see you hang, you bastard."

"But you'll need to get out of here first, won't you? Do you really think I'll allow you to leave

Murdoch Hall with what you know? Time's running out. I believe you about the police coming – I guess I've always known it would only be a matter of time. Something's changed, though."

"Changed? What do you mean?" Guy settled back in his chair with his hands on the arms. He felt like he was on some wild rollercoaster ride.

Mike continued, "Jenny's here, as you know. I saw her earlier today when I visited her. There was something about her situation that excited me, you know, sexually. She's an attractive girl. She begged me not to touch her and suddenly I wasn't looking at Jenny anymore. I was looking at Ellie."

"Ellie?"

"My daughter. Something struck me. I realised how far I'd fallen; how low I'd sunk from the person I used to be. Ellie would be ashamed of me. Jenny's eyes woke me up."

There was silence. In the stillness, Guy heard an owl hoot outside.

"There's time to put things right, Mike," Guy said quickly, starting to prepare himself.

"Like hell there is," Mike said. "It all finishes here. First you, then me. My sister will have to go into care – I've left provision for her."

"Your sister? Valerie?" Guy was still on the alert. "She's not your wife?"

Mike smiled, but without mirth or warmth. "Wife? No, I think not." He put the Pernach down on the desk, simultaneously picking up the Beretta. He studied it almost casually, then pointed it at Guy. "You know it all now, Sterling. So – you first, then me."

And then, just behind Mike, came a crash of glass. As he turned to look, Guy seized his opportunity. He threw himself at him, grabbing his wrist as they both crashed to the floor. The gun fired twice. Guy found himself stretched out across Mike, pinning him to the floor, his left hand holding Mike's right wrist preventing him from turning the gun on either of them. He could hear further noises from the window and then George was beside him, wrenching the gun from Mike's steely grip.

Guy stood up, reached for the Beretta, and pointed it at Mike. "Thanks, George," he said. "Long time since we've used that signal. I heard it loud and clear, though."

"No problem, sir. I got into the house and heard what was happening from the corridor." He pointed casually to the study door. "It seemed the only approach I could take without causing a lot of unpredictable shooting."

"Nice one." Guy turned back towards Mike who was still lying on the floor, nursing his right hand. "I should just shoot the bastard," he said, aiming the Beretta at Mike's head.

Mike stopped rubbing his hand and looked up. "Do it," he urged. "Do it now."

Guy hesitated. "It could have happened in the struggle," he suggested slowly. "Nobody would ever know."

George stretched over and laid a hand gently on the gun. *"We* would know," he said, softly.

Guy paused, nodded, and slowly lowered the weapon.

SEVENTY-FIVE

Leaving George to tie Mike's hands with the rope Mehrak had used, Guy moved towards the study door to go in search of Jenny. Noticing his Glock lying on a bookshelf, he pointed it out to George as extra enforcement. Almost running along the passageway, he found himself back in the hall by the front door where Valerie sat in a chair by one of the windows, knitting. She looked up as he entered.

"Are you alright, dear?" she asked, a concerned look on her face. "It sounded very noisy down there." She placed her knitting on her lap.

"I'm fine, thank you Valerie. Where's Jenny?"

"Who?" She looked genuinely puzzled.

"Jenny – the girl in the cellar."

"Oh, you mean Jane," she said, nodding her head slightly. "She's in her room of course. I've just taken her some supper as Mike said she was hungry again and asked me to give her some of my stew. I was worried when he'd said before that she wasn't hungry. Everyone should eat something."

Guy glanced at the door. The large bolt was in place; instructions were still being followed.

"Valerie," he said. "Mike wants you to unlock the door and then wait here. There are some visitors coming and you are to let them in. I'll go and collect Jane's tray for you."

"Of course, dear. That's kind of you. Remember to wear the cloth hood," she added as he turned to leave. Guy was reminded of a child being told to look both ways before crossing the road.

“I will,” he assured her, walking smartly out of the hall. He re-traced the route he’d taken with the elderly woman earlier that evening. Reopening the cellar door, he switched on the light and took the stairs two at a time, dipping his head to avoid the low roof. The first corridor was in darkness. He again focussed on what he needed to do. He found the light switch, flicked it, and moved quickly to the end door on the right. He turned the key, tugged it open and entered the room with the wardrobe. Feeling behind it, he released the hook, moved the wardrobe forward and entered the final corridor until, once again, he was outside Jenny’s door. He unlocked it, pulled it open and looked inside.

Jenny was on her bed. A tray with a cleared plate and an empty water jug lay next to her. She was looking at the door as he entered, clearly alerted by his footsteps, the grumbling key and the medieval hinges. A feeling of déjà vu washed over him, again.

“You okay, Jenny?” he asked with concern.

“Sure, *I* am – how about *you,* more to the point? What’s happening? You look a mess.”

Guy remembered the blows he’d received from the sadistic Mehrak and touched his face gently. It was sore now; the pain he’d felt earlier had been numbed while Mike was making his revelations in the study.

“I’m fine. And it really is over this time. No more bad guys. Come on.”

She needed no second invitation. Abandoning her shoes, which lay by the bed, she left the room without a second glance. Guy followed her through the corridors and up the stairs. As they entered the passageway, he heard voices. Jenny started to run, and he hurried after her. He entered the hallway just in time to see Jenny leap at Simon Stewart in a childlike embrace. The television star swung his daughter off the floor, holding her tight, before setting her down so she could hug her mother. The three of them clung together, crying with relief and happiness.

Noticing Guy standing to one side, Simon walked over with his hand outstretched. Guy took it, and the two men looked each other in the eye.

"I don't exactly know what happened here, Guy," Simon said, "but you found Jenny and that's all that matters to us. Thank you."

"It's a long story," Guy replied, trying to work out how they'd got here so promptly.

"You can tell me some day – looks like you've been through the mill for us. We owe you all the time in the world." Simon released Guy's hand.

"You can tell *me* now," came a brisk female voice from behind him.

Guy turned to see Grant walking towards him down the corridor, a man in his early thirties trotting behind her.

"This is Detective Sergeant Perry," Grant said, nodding at her companion. "And we want to know what the hell's been happening here. Some housekeeper let us in and showed us where 'all the noise' was coming from. I don't think she's quite all there, to be honest. She gone to wait in the sitting room with DC McMillan. Is that Mike Burns in there, trussed up like a turkey? Who's the dead guy? And the big guy, come to that?"

Guy smiled. "Yes, that's Mike Burns – otherwise known to us as 'Arman'. The dead guy's your sniper – some crazy Egyptian called Mehrak. The big hero in there is my handyman, George."

"Ah, *he's* the famous George – but 'handyman'?" Grant looked bemused.

"Oh yes, he's a very handy man." Guy grinned, then tried not to grimace as the action hurt his face. Those bruises would take time to heal. "We've also got two more idiots at Hofton Manor, although you'll find one of them isn't capable of conversation. Come to that, the other one's not that coherent either."

"So George informed us."

"He rang you, then?"

Grant nodded. 'I was with the Stewarts at the time, so not far away. Of course, they came with me when they heard the news. I've got some guys going over to Shropshire now, liaising with the local CID. I'll need a full statement from you. You should have involved me earlier, Guy," she rebuked him.

"And you'd have come running, would you? Dragged yourself away from your proper police work?"

Grant's face was impassive. "Sure I would. My judgment never lets me down."

And with that she brushed past him into the hall to talk to Simon, Sally and Jenny. There was the wail of an ambulance siren, growing louder as it neared the house. Guy went to find George in the study. "I can't thank you enough," he told him.

"Just doing my job, sir."

Guy smiled. "I'm going to leave you here. I need to go and tell Sophie all about it."

"This late? And like that, sir?"

"Like what?"

"With a beaten-up face, sir."

Guy touched his chin gently. "Mmm… Maybe I'd better hope she doesn't regain consciousness for a couple of days or so."

He patted George firmly on the back and left.

SEVENTY-SIX

It was shortly after 11pm when Guy reached the hospital, the lateness of the hour meaning plenty of free spaces in the car park. Guy was grateful that, as Sophie had her own room, he could visit at any time rather than during the official sessions. At that time of night, there'd be fewer people to see him with his post-fight injuries.

Making straight for the nearest toilet and inspecting himself in the mirror, he had to acknowledge that George was right. He was an alarming sight, with most of his face red and puffed up, early signs of bruising appearing around both eyes.

"Could have been worse," he muttered to himself, an image of Mike Burns pointing the Beretta at him flashing through his mind. "I live to fight another day." He smiled, then winced at the pain before heading back into the beige-painted corridor.

He knew where he was going by now, and a few minutes later he stood at the nurses' station. A young woman with Titian red hair appeared from a back office to greet him.

"Good evening, Sir Guy. Wow – looks like you've been in the wars. Are you okay?"

"I'm fine thanks, Imogen. It looks far worse than it is. No news?"

The nurse shook her head, sadly. "No, no change. We promised we'd let you know, Sir Guy, and we will, believe me."

"Sorry – I know you will, of course. I wasn't suggesting otherwise," he reassured her. "I'll just pop in for a few minutes and bring her up to date with my news." "You'll have to fight for her attention," smiled Imogen.

Guy looked at her. "Why's that?"

"Well, her brother-in-law arrived a few minutes ago – said he'd been on a late shift. He's with her now."

"Brother-in-law?" Guy exclaimed. "She doesn't *have* a brother–in-law!'

Turning quickly Guy ran down the corridor, almost colliding with a nurse who came out of a side door pushing a trolley. Reaching the end of the passage, he pushed open the door to Sophie's room. A dark-haired man, casually dressed, stood over her on the door-side of the bed. He held a pillow in one hand, the other reaching towards the oxygen mask covering her nose. As Guy crashed in, he turned to face him – causing Guy to do a double-take.

"Mehrak?" he said, recognising the dark eyes, olive skin and familiar features.

The man dropped the pillow onto Sophie's chest and bent to pull a small knife from a holster around his ankle. He pointed it at Guy and then, reaching behind him, held it to Sophie's exposed neck, sitting down on the edge of the bed as he did so. "Shut the door and stand still, Sterling, or I'll slit her throat," he hissed, in a strangely familiar voice.

"Haji." Guy closed the door. "Mehrak's brother. How come you're here?"

"Mehrak called me. Told me to finish the job. I travelled far, but I am here." His hand remained steady over Sophie.

Guy eased slightly nearer. "At least we know where you are now. Arman was quite concerned."

"What do you mean? Arman has no care for me."

"Oh, you'd be surprised. He cares a lot about you – he certainly felt strongly about your late brother, right up to the moment he shot him."

Haji stared. "You lie," he said, harshly.

"No, I'm afraid I don't," Guy said. "There's no easy way to break it to you, Haji, but it's true. I was there. Four shots from his own Beretta. I think the last words your dear brother heard as Arman shot him in the forehead was something like 'you're getting on my tits'. Sorry I can't remember it exactly, but then I wasn't expecting to have to deliver the eulogy."

"You lie," Haji repeated, but Guy could see a flicker of doubt cross his face.

"Now why would I do that?" he asked the Egyptian. "Do you really think Arman couldn't kill someone?"

Haji looked thoughtful for a moment, his hand with its knife still hovering near Sophie's neck as he remained looking at Guy. "He can kill, yes, but not Mehrak. He is the best, the very best."

"Well, he might have been touched to know you thought that, but he evidently wasn't the best this evening, Haji. He was definitely a loser."

"I don't believe you. I know you lie," Haji said. "Why would Arman kill Mehrak? It makes no sense."

Imperceptibly, Guy moved a little nearer. "I guess you had to be there to understand, Haji. I was. I was there when the police turned up, too. Steve's also dead, by the way, but that one is down to me – I don't go a bundle on trespassers. As for Tony and Arman, the police are having a nice little chat with them now. They'll be wanting to chat with you too, I guess, once those two have sought to save their souls."

Haji glanced doubtfully at the door.

"You don't think they're coming here? That they don't know you're here?" Guy asked.

"No, they don't."

"Perhaps not," Guy conceded. "But they know I am. They want a statement from me and are following soon. You see, I had to come here for one o'clock – that's when the doctors are doing it."

"Doing what?"

"Turning all this off." Guy waved his arm towards the machines and medical paraphernalia that was keeping Sophie alive. "We've made the decision to let her go."

"I will slit her throat!"

"You've killed her already, you arsehole. Do that now and I'll be on you before you can turn around."

Haji hesitated as he processed the logic. Then in one swift movement he brought his arm round and started to rise from the bed, the short knife now pointing at Guy, who was already moving to his right. Haji made the natural move to his own right, flashing the knife towards Guy in quick, darting strokes. Guy leaped back out of reach, his right leg connecting with the side of Sophie's bed. Haji now had his back to the door, a couple of metres away from Guy. His eyes moved wildly, wary of his opponent but with the confidence of knowing he had the weapon.

Guy snatched up the pillow Haji had dropped on Sophie's chest. Instead of a murder weapon, it would now be a shield. Folding it quickly in two, the ends clasped together in one hand, Guy prodded it rapidly towards Haji as they squared up to each other. Guy had the height and weight advantage, but he didn't underestimate his wiry and muscular adversary.

Haji held the small knife out in front of him, twisting and thrusting, stabbing and slashing in short, swift movements, not quite confident enough to make a decisive strike. Guy's eyes never left the blade. Whatever tricks Haji might try, knowing where the knife was would keep Guy in the game; lose sight of it, and the outcome could be disastrous. Guy hoped that by using the pillow as a shield, he would at some point be able to use the length and strength of his right arm to land a telling blow, disabling Haji enough to give him a few seconds to follow decisively through. There was also the possibility someone would open the door and cause a helpful distraction – Imogen at the nurses' station may well have reacted to Guy's sudden departure down the corridor, or the noise might have alerted someone. So far, though, the door remained steadfastly shut.

The two men stood a couple of metres apart in the centre of the room, dancing on their feet with shoulder-drops, random side steps and erratic feints. Guy sensed the endgame was close. Stepping back, Haji dropped his right arm until it was slightly bent, the knife at waist height still pointing towards Guy. Guy lowered his pillow to match. Haji moved quickly, his left hand swinging outwards in a distracting arc while his right wrist twisted into a coiled spring before flicking forwards with considerable force. The knife travelled towards the base of Guy's rib cage, where it could have done some serious damage had he not been focused on the blade. He raised the pillow but wasn't quite fast enough to match the speed and skill of Haji's throw; the flying knife was deflected upwards, slicing into the top of Guy's left bicep before it clattered to the floor and spun away.

Aware of the pain, Guy glanced down to see his own blood and staggered towards Sophie's bedside before he could regain his balance. Too late he realised Haji was bent low, sprinting to retrieve the knife from the other side of the room. All he could do was to push out a foot and hope; it was sufficient to trip Haji, the would-be assassin's momentum enough to send him pitching to the ground near the waiting knife.

Straightening up, Guy noticed a couple of used syringes nestling in a small metal bowl on a side shelf, protective plastic sheaths covering the needle. Snatching one up, he flicked off the cover as he moved towards Haji, who was scrambling in a commando crawl.

"I will kill you, I will kill you!" Haji shouted, reaching for his knife.

Guy threw himself down astride Haji's back, feeling the air being expelled from the Egyptian's lungs. Seizing a clump of hair, he yanked the man's head back and quickly stabbed the syringe into his throat, plunging it in and out repeatedly. A series of gurgles left Haji's mouth; his hand dropped the knife and he went limp. Tightening his grip on the black hair, Guy smashed his head forward twice onto the floor. When Haji was completely still, Guy tossed away the syringe and picked up the knife. He knew he hadn't killed him; he could feel signs of life, despite the amount of blood now pooling beneath the olive-skinned neck.

In days gone by, in the military, Guy knew he'd have slit the man's throat for good measure. The echo of a reverberating crack sounded in his memory. *That was for my country*. It had been necessary in that world, but it wasn't in this one. Or was it? He was sorely tempted – it would be justice, punishment for what Haji had done to Sophie rather than revenge. But justice was for the state to deliver; he knew that. It was a long-standing part of his personal creed.

And then he recalled his advice to Mike: *"You'll always need to watch your back, even in prison."* Would Haji recover and come looking for Sophie? He looked down at Haji's barely breathing body. He might not even survive, judging by the state of him. Death might be close anyway – but modern medical science could achieve miracles. Would Sophie ever be safe? It was now or never. He could suddenly hear George's voice in his head: *We would know.*

He looked across at Sophie, a sleeping princess, fighting for life while oblivious to Guy's recent battle for his – indeed, of his on-going moral dilemma. *Who am I when no one's looking?* He knelt beside the Egyptian, took his head in his hands, and broke his neck. "Sorry, George," he said quietly as he stood up. "*That was for my Sophie*."

Guy placed the knife on the bed and took a handkerchief from his trouser pocket, holding it tightly against the cut on his arm, pressing it firmly.

As he sat down on the edge of the bed, he heard footsteps race along the corridor outside. Two security guards in blue uniforms burst into the room, Imogen behind them.

"It's okay, fellas," Guy said, trying to raise his left hand while holding the bandage tight with his right. "All sorted – but thanks."

Imogen stepped into the room. "Are you all right, Sir Guy?" she asked in concern. "You're hurt."

Guy glanced at the bloodied handkerchief. "Just a scratch – it's nothing. Not sure about him, though." He nodded his head towards Haji. "He doesn't look too good. I fear the worst – it was a close thing, either him or me."

One of the guards was already kneeling at Haji's side, holding his wrist. "No pulse," he said. "Perhaps unsurprising, looking at him."

Imogen hurried out saying something about getting assistance. Guy stayed sitting on the bed. A few minutes later a doctor came who confirmed the Egyptian was dead. Eventually, Haji's body was taken away. At his own insistence, Guy was finally left alone with Sophie in the stillness of her room.

Lying down on the bed next to her, he kissed her pale cheek and gently stroked her hair.

"I love you, Soph," he said. "Please keep fighting and come back soon. We're all rooting for you." A tear ran down his cheek. "They say you can take as long as you need. I know you can do it – I believe in you; I believe in you so much. If you could hear me, don't believe what I told that Egyptian bastard. Just wake up when you can, as soon as you can. You're safe now, princess. And I've so much to tell you. We have so much life to live."

ACKNOWLEDGEMENTS

This novel has been in the writing stage for rather longer than planned. It rather got barged out of the way by my crime novel, *The Dreams that Make Us,* as well as by life in general. Apologies to Sir Guy for his later than expected arrival on the literary scene – it was only late by four years!

Early editorial input came from Amy Butcher at Amy Butcher Content in Montreal. I would like to acknowledge her patient and professional input which helped me craft the book towards the direction she suggested.

Latterly in the process, I would like to acknowledge the wonderful copywriting skills of Rebecca Parsley of Dolphin International Communications Ltd who tidied up my English and created the sentences I intended to write, and would have written had I paid better attention in my school English classes!

Thanks also go to my good friend Rob Whitney of Rob Whitney Graphic Design in Lincoln, UK for his technical and creative contribution, particularly for the whole cover design.

Finally, and actually most importantly, thanks to my terrific wife, Kim, for her encouragement and support. Writing is by nature a solitary activity and certainly not a spectator sport. Being able to spend time as a hermit is therefore much appreciated.

COMING SOON

What Lies Within

The second Guy Sterling thriller - 2020

The Christian church has received into its care an incredible and historic object, which has great religious importance. Unfortunately, it came to light in an Arabic dig on Temple Mount, and its global significance means its prospects of leaving Jerusalem are slim. The Archbishop of Canterbury turns to Sir Guy to assist in retrieving it and bringing it back to England in a less than traditional way.

However, the Church and Guy are not the only ones who know about the discovery. A violent organisation, fighting all religion and thought to be long defunct, is hell bent on destroying the find and, through treachery, have learnt about Guy's mission.

And the stakes are raised even higher when, through good fortune and courage, Guy discovers something further of massive religious and scientific meaning that makes even the original find of minor interest.

But the relative safety of England is far away, and even any successful return is still fraught with secretive and mortal danger to Guy and those he loves.

They Died Tomorrow

The third Guy Sterling thriller – 2021

Sir Guy leaves the comfort of Hofton Manor to assist in the investigation of an apparent murder.

However, the picture is bigger than he originally thought, leaving him to confront the very face of evil.

This third Guy Sterling thriller is in the early planning and writing stages.

More detail will be available on andrew argyle's website in due course: www.andrewargyle.com

ABOUT THE AUTHOR

andrew argyle was born in Tamworth, Staffordshire, one of four sons. He was educated at Thomas Barnes County Primary School, Hopwas; Yarlet Hall Prep School, Stafford; Shrewsbury School; the University of Birmingham; and the College of Law, Guildford (now the University of Law).

As a fifth-generation solicitor, he was in private practice with firms in Tamworth, Birmingham and Lincoln.

Now as a non-practising solicitor, he is involved in executive strategy and management.

andrew has four children and lives with his wife, Kim, in rural Lincolnshire with a multitude of animals including horses, Labradors, cats and chickens.

andrew is a man of faith and, aside from his writing, his passions are travel (especially cruising), film/theatre, watching football, rural living and socialising with friends.

For more information about andrew argyle, his books, and how to keep in contact with him, visit:

www.andrewargyle.com

Printed in Great Britain
by Amazon